*A family of pro[...]
scandal, sust[...]*

THE DA[...] TOBY, LEA & ADAM

A red-hot rancher, an illegitimate
daughter and a ruthless rival!

Three bestselling authors deliver three
more seriously sexy, sensational stories
in the Danforths dynasty saga.

We're proud to present
MILLS & BOON
Spotlight

a chance to buy collections of bestselling novels by favourite authors every month – they're back by popular demand!

March 2009
The Danforths: Toby, Lea & Adam

Featuring
Cowboy Crescendo by Cathleen Galitz
Steamy Savannah Nights by Sheri WhiteFeather
The Enemy's Daughter by Anne Marie Winston

Secrets and Desire

Featuring
Best-Kept Lies by Lisa Jackson
Miss Pruitt's Private Life by Barbara McCauley
Secrets, Lies and Passion by Linda Conrad

April 2009
The Danforths: Marc, Tanya & Abe

Featuring
The Laws of Passion by Linda Conrad
Terms of Surrender by Shirley Rogers
Shocking the Senator by Leanne Banks

The Chisholm Brothers: Friends, Lovers…Husbands?

by Janis Reamis Hudson

Featuring
The Daddy Survey
The Other Brother
The Cowboy on Her Trail

THE DANFORTHS: TOBY, LEA & ADAM

Cowboy Crescendo
CATHLEEN GALITZ

Steamy Savannah Nights
SHERI WHITEFEATHER

The Enemy's Daughter
ANNE MARIE WINSTON

DID YOU PURCHASE THIS BOOK WITHOUT A COVER?
If you did, you should be aware it is **stolen property** as it was reported *unsold and destroyed* by a retailer. Neither the author nor the publisher has received any payment for this book.

All the characters in this book have no existence outside the imagination of the author, and have no relation whatsoever to anyone bearing the same name or names. They are not even distantly inspired by any individual known or unknown to the author, and all the incidents are pure invention.

All Rights Reserved including the right of reproduction in whole or in part in any form. This edition is published by arrangement with Harlequin Enterprises II B.V./S.à.r.l. The text of this publication or any part thereof may not be reproduced or transmitted in any form or by any means, electronic or mechanical, including photocopying, recording, storage in an information retrieval system, or otherwise, without the written permission of the publisher.

This book is sold subject to the condition that it shall not, by way of trade or otherwise, be lent, resold, hired out or otherwise circulated without the prior consent of the publisher in any form of binding or cover other than that in which it is published and without a similar condition including this condition being imposed on the subsequent purchaser.

® and ™ are trademarks owned and used by the trademark owner and/or its licensee. Trademarks marked with ® are registered with the United Kingdom Patent Office and/or the Office for Harmonisation in the Internal Market and in other countries.

*This collection is first published in Great Britain 2009.
Harlequin Mills & Boon Limited,
Eton House, 18-24 Paradise Road, Richmond, Surrey TW9 1SR*

THE DANFORTHS: TOBY, LEA & ADAM
© Harlequin Books S.A. 2009.

The publisher acknowledges the copyright holders of the individual works, which have already been published in the UK in single, separate volumes, as follows:

Cowboy Crescendo © Harlequin Books S.A. 2004
Steamy Savannah Nights © Harlequin Books S.A. 2004
The Enemy's Daughter © Harlequin Books S.A. 2004

Special thanks and acknowledgement are given to Cathleen Galitz, Sheri WhiteFeather and Anne Marie Winston for their contributions to the DYNASTIES: THE DANFORTHS series.

ISBN: 978 0 263 87150 0

064-0309

Printed and bound in Spain
by Litografia Rosés S.A., Barcelona

Cowboy Crescendo

CATHLEEN GALITZ

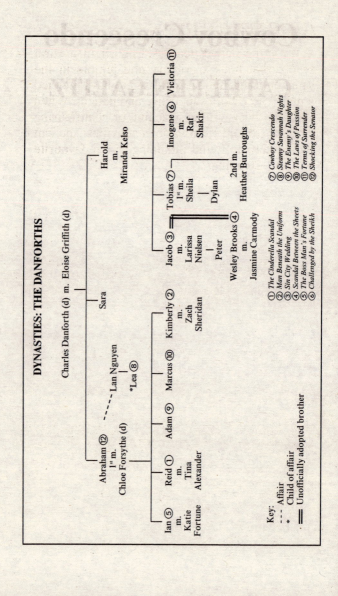

CATHLEEN GALITZ

a Wyoming native, teaches English in a rural school that houses primary and juniors in the same building. She feels blessed to have married a man who is both supportive and patient. When she's not busy writing, teaching or chauffeuring her sons to and from various activities, she can most likely be found indulging in her favourite pastime – reading.

One

Heather Burroughs stood in the doorway of her new employer's massive living room unable to believe what she was seeing.

Unable to stomach what she was hearing.

Since no one bothered answering her persistent attempts at making her presence at the front door known, she let herself in and followed the sound of a deep voice to the spot where she presently stood rooted in horror. Matching that voice to a particularly handsome face did little to allay Heather's fears that she had just been hired by a monster.

A monster who was presently taunting a child with a cookie.

"Say it, Dylan," the man coaxed, his voice straining with impatience.

He was so intent on imposing his will upon the toddler that he remained unaware of Heather's presence. A cherub of three reached out a chubby hand for the treat dangled in his face, only to have it snatched away the instant his fingers touched the sugary delight. Tears pooled in a pair of eyes the exact same color and shape as his tormenter's. It spilled down his ruddy cheeks and caused the monster to mumble a slight invective under his breath.

"Come on, Dylan. Just say it!"

Heather knew firsthand what it felt like to have a cookie dangled in front of one's face, and she wasn't about to stand idly by and watch her new employer play such mean-spirited games with his son—even if it did mean losing her job on the very first day of work.

Even if that job meant the difference between financial independence or possibly living on the streets.

"Give me that!"

Ignoring the man's startled look, Heather marched into the room and grabbed the cookie from his hands. She proceeded to bend down, wipe the tears from his little boy's face with the cuff of her sleeve and give him the cookie. Dylan accepted it with both hands and a look of pure gratitude, shoving as much of it into his mouth before his father could confiscate it. When he grinned up at Heather through a mouthful of gooey chocolate, it was all she could do to keep from sweeping him up in her arms and making a break for the front door.

"Just who do you think you are, lady, and what in the hell do you think you're doing?" Tobias Danforth demanded to know.

He glared at her from a squatting position on the floor. The denim of his jeans was stretched taut over thighs that strained as he rose to his full height of six feet. He towered over Heather, who barely weighed a hundred pounds soaking wet. In tennis shoes, she was almost a foot shorter than he was. She felt like David facing Goliath.

Without a slingshot.

Summoning her stage presence, Heather responded in a regal tone that belied the fact she was the underling and he, technically, her boss.

"I'm the nanny the employment agency hired, and what I'm doing is putting an end to you taunting this boy. In case you're unaware of it, Mr. Danforth, Dylan is a child, not an animal to be trained with doggie biscuits."

"How dare you—"

"I dare because I care," she countered, sticking her chin out as if daring him to take a shot at it.

Those icy-blue eyes of his pinned her to the spot like some hapless butterfly in a child's science fair project. Nonetheless, if this fellow thought he was going to label Heather Burroughs a mere cowardus interruptus, he had another thing coming. Having endured the training of some of the most sadistic music teachers on the planet, it was going to take a whole lot more than an imposing presence to make her back down.

"And you think I don't care?"

His voice was sardonic.

And as cutting as the eyes trained on her.

What she beheld glimmering in those arctic depths was a ferocity that would send a wild wolf scurrying for protection. Placing her hands on her hips, she held her ground. Albeit on shaky legs.

"I doubt if Protective Services would approve of your type of parenting any more than I do," she told him, suddenly glad for the schooling that kept her voice from quavering in times of duress.

"Get out of my home, lady."

Though spoken so softly that the child caught between the two of them didn't so much as flinch, the man's words tore through Heather like bullets.

Why after twenty-five years of compliance she had finally discovered her backbone was as much a mystery to her as it was to her parents. They had all but disowned her for turning her back on their dreams. A neophyte at standing up for her beliefs, Heather had yet to develop the skills needed to temper her newfound assertiveness with prudence. The truth of the matter was that she was in no position to sacrifice this job unless she was ready to humble herself and, as her father had so bluntly put it, "come crawling back" to him for his support.

Still, she had no desire whatsoever to work for a man who struck her as being so very like her stern, demanding father. A man determined to withhold his approval unless his child performed up to his level of satisfaction.

Stiffening her spine, Heather started toward the door. She reminded herself that throughout the ages, scores of renowned musicians testified that poverty was good for the soul.

A tentative, childish voice stopped her in her tracks.

"Gookie!"

Tobias Danforth's face might as well have been made of wax the way his son's sudden outburst rearranged his sharp, masculine features. Eyes that only a moment before had been as icy as a Wyoming lake in January thawed instantly. Dropping to his knees, he took the boy by both shoulders to peer into his eyes.

"What did you just say?"

Had his touch not been so overtly tender, Heather might well have jumped to the conclusion that he intended to shake a response out of the lad.

She wondered what kind of father couldn't understand his own child's adorable attempt at forming words. Because her throat had turned to dust, her own words sounded altogether too scratchy as she endeavored to enlighten the poor man.

"I believe he said *cookie*. For what it's worth, I think he'd like another one."

"For what it's worth, he can have the whole damn bag!" Tobias shouted in startling jubilation.

He grabbed Dylan up under the arms and swung him around in the air. The print of the boy's cowboy-themed shirt blurred into a brightly spinning top. The exuberant expression on his father's face caused Heather's pulse to skitter. It burst into a gallop before it came skidding to a dead stop. If it was possible that there might actually be a nice guy hiding behind the mask of a monster, she hoped he knew CPR.

Squealing with delight, Dylan repeated the feat that had earned him such an enthusiastic response.

"Gookie!"

That hard and judgmental something, lodged inside Heather's heart, softened to see unshed tears glistening in Tobias Danforth's eyes as he set his son down and ruffled his dark hair. The man was reputed to be worth millions and was looked upon by locals as somewhat of a reclusive mystery. Indeed, any outsider who could afford to treat ranching as a gentleman's hobby was generally regarded with suspicion among those born and bred of this unforgiving land. That such a man could actually be moved to tears by such an unremarkable accomplishment took Heather completely by surprise.

True to his word, Tobias grabbed the bag of cookies off a nearby ledge and handed it over to Dylan. Heather's dark suspicions about her former employer evaporated as the boy threw his arms around his daddy's neck and proceeded to cover his face with kisses. The scene was so unlike anything from her own childhood that Heather felt a pang of regret that her invitation to stick around long enough to get to know either of them better had been revoked.

As she turned to leave, she was halted by a Southern drawl as strong as a rope. And as tender as a prayer.

"And just where do you think you're going?"

Heather turned slowly around. The sight of her interrogator with chocolate-chip kisses smeared across his face did much to lessen the tension smoldering between them. The ghost of a smile made the angular planes of that face look far less formidable than the first impression Heather received of it.

"You just fired me," she reminded him gently.

Tobias took a clean white handkerchief out of his pocket and swiped at his face.

"Well, consider yourself un-fired."

Heather's heart banged against her chest. If there was any chance of salvaging this job, she had better put a smile on her face and a conciliatory tone in her voice. Aside from the fact that she didn't want to be reduced to begging her parents for money, it would be almost impossible to find a position better suited to her needs at the present time. Not to mention she felt such an immediate connection with the child who was to be her charge. She reached out and took the handkerchief from Tobias's hand.

"Here, let me help you with that," she offered, dabbing at a crumb hanging from his mustache.

What was meant as a friendly gesture turned suddenly intimate as Tobias's eyes bored into hers. A shiver starting at the base of Heather's neck raced through her and played with every nerve ending in her body. A telltale tremble caused the handkerchief in her hand to resemble a white flag of surrender. As a general rule, Heather liked clean-shaven men, but as her gaze lingered upon the curve of the mouth peeking out from beneath a well-groomed mustache, she didn't think it would take much persuasion to change her mind.

Have you gone completely crazy? Heather asked herself.

She refused to fall into the same self-destructive pattern that had ruined the last relationship she'd had with a man, who had professed himself to be her mentor. She struggled to find something to say that would put their relationship back on professional footing. Entertaining romantic notions about an employer, no matter how handsome or baffling to the senses, was risking emotional suicide.

"We'd better discuss the terms of my employment before I accept your conditions—especially if they include the kind of behavior modification I saw you using on your son."

Tobias reached out to take her hand into his. Heather gasped at the intensity of the voltage that coursed through her body at his touch. The sound caused him to immediately release his grip. The handkerchief fluttered to the ground between them, a symbolic victim of the war between the sexes.

"Let me assure you, Miss Burroughs, I have no intention of compromising your virtue while you're in my employment, if that's what you're worried about. I can also wipe my own face, and my own butt, as far as that goes. As frazzled as I might appear at the moment, I'm not looking for someone to take care of me. I'm perfectly capable of doing that for myself. What I desperately need is someone who will support my parenting efforts—and the exercises that Dylan's speech therapist prescribed for him, like the one you just so rudely interrupted."

It was Heather's turn to look nonplussed. It had never occurred to her that a three-year-old would be subjected to such treatment as part of a prearranged professional treatment. That in itself made her all the more aware of her shortcomings as Dylan's intended caregiver. If she ever hoped to obtain her teaching degree, she was going to have to stop jumping to conclusions and transferring her childhood trauma onto other people.

"I-I'm truly sorry," she stammered, wishing there were some way she could start all over again.

Tobias shoved the splayed fingers of one hand through a shock of dark hair that was anything but a quiet shade. Brown at the roots, the sun had frosted its ends with golden highlights. The fact that he was in need of a haircut didn't keep Heather from wanting to test its texture with her own fingers.

"Don't be. You just had more success with Dylan in the five minutes you've been here than I have since his mother left," Tobias admitted.

Bitterness laced his words and desperation creased his brow.

Heather wondered what had happened to Dylan's mother. Had she left simply because of the isolation of living on a ranch miles from the nearest neighbor? Or through some fault of her husband? Had she run away feeling as manipulated as a child reaching for a cookie that could only be earned by performing some trick?

Whatever the woman's reasons, Heather felt a surge of pity for any child forsaken by his mother. Having been sent away by her own parents under the guise of developing her artistic gift, she understood just how devastating it felt to be abandoned by those who professed to love you the most. And how desperately one would work to earn and to keep their approval.

Tobias's words drew Heather out of the past and into a present that was growing more and more complicated by the minute.

"In case the agency misrepresented this job, Miss Burroughs, Dylan is developmentally delayed."

The last two words seemed to stick in Tobias's throat. Although Heather was tempted to give him a reassuring pat to help him continue, she refrained from touching him again. As she saw it, the biggest drawback to this job was not working with a developmentally delayed child but rather living in such close quarters with a man who made her feel so keenly aware of her own sexuality. Falling for Josef had cost Heather her love of music. Falling for this man could well cost her what was left of her self-respect.

Tobias cleared his throat and continued. "You come highly recommended, and I was hoping that you and Dylan might find a common bond in your mutual talent."

He gestured to the grand piano against the far wall. Its black polish glistened beneath the natural sunlight spilling into the room. It evoked in Heather such a mixture of conflicting emotions that she had to reach for the back of a chair to steady herself. Part of her longed to run her fingers over those beautiful ivory keys. And part of her had already slammed the lid shut on that part of her life forever.

"Your resumé indicated that you are an accomplished musician. Dylan has some talent in that area. At the age of three with no formal training, he can already play melodies on the piano."

The buttons on the proud daddy's shirt swelled against a chest that was already broad enough to tempt a woman to run her hands across its width, and to see if she could lace her fingers together when her arms spanned its brawny circumference. Heather gave him a challenging look.

"I hope you aren't thinking of shipping him out to a specialized school like my parents did to me. While twice Dylan's age at the time, I wasn't nearly old enough to deal with the pressures of such a performance-driven institution."

Tobias's eyes widened in surprise. He shook his head emphatically. "I have no intention of shipping my boy off anywhere. His mother may have felt restrained by family life, but I most certainly don't. Whatever you think of my parenting methods, make no mistake about the fact that I love my son, and I'll do whatever it takes to help him find his voice again. Even bribing him with a cookie if that's what the speech therapist recommends."

Though Heather blushed at the implicit reprimand, she nevertheless wanted to make sure they were clear on what she perceived to be the differences in their respective teaching approaches.

"As long as you don't expect me to use those kind of techniques myself, I promise to do everything else in my power to support you. I'll be honest with you, Mr. Danforth. I'm not much of a behavior modification fan."

"Fair enough, Miss Burroughs," he said, matching her formality with a sardonic lift of an eyebrow. "All I'm really hoping for is that you can strike a common chord that will help bring my son out of his shell."

Recognizing that his words were deliberately chosen for their symbolic value, Heather selected hers with equal care. Well intended or not, she could never bring herself to force a child to perform as her parents had forced her, inadvertently turning the lovely gift God had given her into a curse.

"I would be more than happy to help Dylan with his musical gifts—as far as he wants to develop them."

Tobias looked relieved. Elated.

"Good, that's settled then. The rest of your job is secondary to attending to Dylan. While I expect you to cook and clean, I'm not particularly fussy about either of those duties, if that helps any to put your mind at ease."

Heather didn't think there was anything about working for a man as handsome as a movie star and as rich as Croesus that could possibly put her mind or her traitorous hormones at ease. Still, his words and accompanying smile did help reduce her stress level. Applying for a job was in itself a new experience for her. Groveling for the position was out of the question. However, since Heather was hardly in the position to be setting conditions for employment, she decided to withhold the fact that her cooking experience was almost as limited as her time spent actually working with children.

"It's way past time for introductions, but just so you know, I prefer being called Toby than either Mr. Danforth or Tobias," he said, offering her his hand.

Again the jolt of lightning at his touch struck Heather's heart. Tingling all over, she tried to focus on the fact that such an affluent man preferred the less formal moniker. She liked that almost as much as she liked the fact that hard work marked his hands with calluses. Josef's hands had been as smooth as a child's, and though they had played her like a concerto, she suffered terribly beneath their cruel ministrations.

"You've already met Dylan," Toby said, continuing introductions.

Hearing his name, the child abandoned his bag of cookies and stretched out his arms to Heather. She did not hesitate to take the sticky little urchin into her own arms. He smelled of chocolate and baby shampoo and unconditional love. Dylan wrapped his arms around her neck and squeezed hard. The kiss he placed upon her cheek left its mark upon her heart.

The smile that reached Toby's eyes held no hint of jealousy.

"It looks like love at first sight."

Heather flinched. Although she knew he was referring to her interaction with his son, her father had said the exact same thing when he had introduced her to Josef. That relationship ended disastrously, and she had no desire to let her personal history repeat itself. She reminded herself to guard her heart against getting too involved with either Dylan or his father. This job was nothing more than a way to make enough money to get her feet solidly under her so that she would never again be dependent upon any man. That included her father.

And her one and only past lover.

It was little wonder the two were so inexplicably intertwined in her memory. Indeed, when Josef turned his back on her, so had her parents. Having done everything but legally disinherit her, they were under the impression that withholding their financial support would work even better than withholding their approval had over the years. Heather's decision to abandon her musical career and pursue a teaching degree hinged on being able to make enough money in the coming year to put herself through school on her own. It was imperative that she separate her personal feelings from her better judgment.

For the first time in her life Heather was going to have to count every penny. Luckily, Toby Danforth was a generous man. Whether warning lights were going off in her head like some spectacular Fourth of July fireworks display was of little consequence in the greater scheme of things. Whatever her instincts were telling her, Heather simply could not afford to walk away from this job.

"When would you like me to start?" she asked with a determined smile fixed on her lips.

"As soon as you possibly can."

Toby gestured apologetically around him. Though messy, the room was not so dirty or cluttered as to be impassable.

"I don't know if the agency told you, but my

housekeeper retired two weeks ago due to serious health issues. To be quite honest, I'm in a real bind. A ranch doesn't run itself, and taking care of Dylan myself for the past couple of weeks has put me so far behind that I'm not sure I'll ever be able to catch up."

He looked so overwhelmed by his circumstances, so remarkably vulnerable and strong all at the same time, that Heather couldn't help but feel the stirrings of empathy. Not to mention the fact that she could no more turn her back on his cute little boy than she could walk away from a stranger bleeding on the street. She understood how difficult it must be for a proud man like Toby to ask for her help. The woman from the employment agency informed her in a conspiratorial whisper that the child refused to speak since his mother had walked away from them both. Heather wasn't sure if it was possible for three wounded hearts to be healed under the same roof, but she had little recourse but to trust in the infinite possibilities of tomorrow.

"My bags are in the trunk of my car. If you'd be so kind as to show me to my room, I'd like to get settled in and start right away."

The relief written upon Toby's face was so genuine that it made Heather grow prickly all over. She hoped in his exuberance that he didn't attempt to pick her up like he had Dylan and swing her around in the air. She was already feeling far too light-headed to think straight. Toby's next statement did nothing to lessen that feeling.

"If you don't have a couple of nice dresses packed, we can pick some up in town over the weekend. I'm planning on taking Dylan to a family reunion of sorts in the next couple of days, and I'd really like you to come along."

Heather shook her head as if to rid it of cobwebs. Not the typical slow-moving rancher who drove his pickup down the road at a leisurely pace, Toby Danforth moved fast. Goodness, it was hard to process everything happening at once. She had been fired, rehired and invited to a family gathering all in the course of fifteen minutes.

"That won't be necessary," she said, struggling to overcome her innate shyness around large groups of people she didn't know. "While somewhat limited, my wardrobe should be adequate for any occasion. I don't suppose it should be too hard to get myself and Dylan ready for a little family get-together."

As long as it's no farther than the next county... and it doesn't involve getting on a plane, she silently amended. Her fear of flying had been the bane of a childhood dependent upon traveling long distances to perform across the country. Whenever possible, Heather made alternate arrangements involving buses or trains.

The tension in Toby's face was replaced by a smile as wide as the boundaries of his ranch. It was the kind of smile that made Heather want to attribute the accompanying flutters in her stomach to nothing more than first-day-on-the-job jitters. Certainly not to a sharp sense of feminine awareness making her ache deep inside.

"I'm glad to hear it," Toby said. "I'd suggest you pack light clothes for the trip. My sister says the weather in Savannah is unseasonably warm for this time of year. Did I mention we'll be flying out this Monday?"

Heather's mouth fell open in surprise as Dylan clapped his hands in delight.

Two

There was something so regal in the way the new nanny carried herself, it made Toby feel as if he were working for her instead of the other way around. Of course, it went without saying that much in the way of a superior attitude was forgivable as long as she was kind to Dylan. Youth and inexperience, eyes as gray and unpredictable as gathering storm clouds, a luscious figure and even a pair of tempting lips drawn into a thin, disapproving line when she leaped to the conclusion that he was teasing Dylan with that blasted cookie were all imminently forgivable.

And lamentably unforgettable.

Dylan never took to strangers like he had to Heather. He had always been reticent—often even around his own mother. The fact that Heather happened to be the catalyst for Dylan to utter his very first words since Sheila left was more than enough reason for Toby to set aside any reservations he might have about her. Since dear old Mrs. Cremins recently suffered a heart attack, he was desperate to replace her with someone suitable—someone willing to live in what Sheila had dubbed one of the most desolate spots in the entire world. Based on his ex-wife's decision to abandon country life and her family altogether, Toby seriously doubted whether he could keep such a beautiful, young woman like Heather around for long. He hoped Dylan didn't get too attached to her before she, like his mother, found her wings and left them to pursue a more exciting life.

Personally, Toby loved the isolation and stark beauty of the Double D Ranch. It was, in fact, the culmination of a lifelong dream to break away from his politically connected and sometimes dysfunctional family to stake out a life for himself and his son. It was a dream based on the American ideal of pride in owning something built with one's own hands from the ground up. The Danforths had roots so deep in the soil of the Old South that Toby's decision to relocate to Wyoming had initially been perceived by some of his relatives as an affront to the glorious memory of the Confederacy itself. Indeed, Toby's choice to make something of himself in a way completely separate from his family's influence was the equivalent of the Emancipation Proclamation that set an entire nation free.

Nestled against the base of the magnificent Snowy Range, the Double D was Toby's idea of heaven on earth. It was his belief that a man could think clearly beneath clear, cloudless Wyoming skies that went on forever. Such country had a way of putting technology and politics in their proper place. They challenged a person to rely on his wits and the goodwill of neighbors who still put their stock in a hard day's work rather than a volatile marketplace run by crooks and thieves—who somehow managed to protect their mansions while their small, unsavvy stockholders were forced to declare bankruptcy.

It was hard to explain why Toby had felt so strangled by the gracious living of Southern gentry. It wasn't that he didn't love his family, but rather that he'd somehow felt like a changeling growing up in his own home. Ever since he'd fallen in love with his first cowboy movie as a little boy, Toby knew what kind of life he was cut out for. And it wasn't one that involved luxurious golf courses and hoity-toity social events requiring black ties invented to choke the life out of a man so some Southern belle could drag him around by the end of it wherever she had a mind to go.

As eager as Toby had been to leave Savannah four years ago, he nevertheless felt it important to keep his family ties strong—if only for Dylan's sake. Devoted to his own father, Toby would do anything that Harold Danforth asked of him—including returning home to show support for an uncle of whom he'd never been overly fond and enduring the kind of stuffy formal affair that he personally deplored. According to his father, Abraham Danforth was on the verge of making a political bid for the Senate. At Uncle Abe's behest, Toby's father had called his own children together for a Fourth of July extravaganza at Crofthaven, the family mansion overlooking Savannah's harbor. The mansion had been in the Danforth family for over a century, and though it held no special, warm memories for Toby or any of his cousins as far as he knew, it was the perfect spot for an impromptu family reunion. Not to mention a fabulous backdrop to launch the political campaign of a man, who in Toby's opinion was more devoted to promoting himself than raising his own family.

Toby felt no jealousy for the wealthier side of the family. When his wife died years earlier, Abraham Danforth had promptly rid himself of his children by sending them off to exclusive boarding schools. Busy making a name for himself, Abe farmed them out over school breaks as well. Consequently, Toby's cousins spent many of their holidays and summers at his own childhood home making happy memories, and eventually coming to regard Harold as a surrogate father in place of the one who had so little time for them.

Toby didn't mind sharing his father with the cousins who were like brothers and sisters to him. Kind and loving, Harold Danforth was the kind of man that little boys wanted to grow up to be like and little girls wanted to marry. It was just one of the reasons that Toby was so anxious to have his son get to know his grandfather better. He hoped exposing Dylan to his extended family would encourage the boy to express himself more openly.

Heaven knows, whenever the Danforths got together there was plenty of talking and laughing and debating everything from the latest in politics to varying points of view in recalling their youthful antics. Toby knew his family would do everything in their power to make Dylan feel at home and bring him out of his shell. Bringing Heather along would give the child an anchor—and unfortunately free Toby up for any number of his sister's ill-fated matchmaking attempts....

Despite his repeated protests that he had little interest in dating again, let alone getting remarried, there was no doubt in his mind that Imogene would have every available belle lined up for his perusal when he arrived in Savannah. As much as Toby appreciated the fact that she had his happiness in mind, he wished his family would accept his decision to raise his son as he saw fit—as a determined single father who didn't need the added pressure of belonging to one of the most influential families in Georgia.

As much as he hated to spring this trip on Heather so soon, Toby hoped the extravagant salary he was paying would help ease any misgivings she might have about accompanying him. Her dismayed reaction to his invitation made him wonder if she had an aversion to flying—or just to spending time with him. Using Sheila as a gauge, it would appear he had that effect upon women in general.

Heather Burroughs certainly wasn't the grandmotherly type with whom he had been hoping to replace Mrs. Cremins. Nor the mousy sort of shy musician that made her presence easy to overlook. A man could mentally forswear the opposite sex all he wanted, but unless his body cooperated, there was little chance he could convince himself, let alone someone as tenacious as his sister Genie.

Something jumped in his belly at the mere memory of Heather whirling into his living room like a tiny tornado. In a pair of tennis shoes and worn jeans, with her blond hair falling loosely about her shoulders, she'd looked more like a popular rock-and-roll diva intent on smashing a guitar over his head than the classical pianist he'd been led to believe was refined and aloof by nature. The fire he'd seen in those smoky-gray eyes left him wondering if the right man might be able to spark an even hotter blaze behind that wall of ice.

Toby didn't like the direction his thoughts were

taking. This sparsely populated region of the West was not known for its liberal attitude, and Toby didn't like the idea of compromising this pretty young woman by placing her in a situation that might cause loose tongues to wag. Living under the same roof with a single man in such a remote area couldn't be good for a lady's reputation. Nor for his own standing in a community he claimed by choice as his own.

Nor for a man's libido, for that matter.

Especially a man who was so lonesome at night that he preferred falling asleep rocking his son than facing the demons that tormented his own empty bedroom.

The immediate necessity of hiring somebody to replace Mrs. Cremins overshadowed Toby's apprehension. The possibility that Heather might get his son to speak again gave him a sense of hope that had been missing in his life since Sheila walked out. While it was probably just coincidental that Dylan chose to speak when Heather arrived, Toby couldn't overlook the possibility that she was in fact the catalyst for that momentous event. He was willing to cater to Heather's needs if she proved to be a miracle worker.

Only time and patience would tell.

"I'm pleased to make your acquaintance, Dylan."

Heather extended her hand to the little boy who was looking up at her with a skeptical expression on his face. His father had left them alone to take care of pressing ranch business. Clearly hesitant to leave Dylan with a stranger, Toby promised to be back in time for dinner, one Heather expected she would have to rustle up after getting herself settled. The sound of the front door closing behind him echoed through the house.

"You can call me Heather," she told the boy, "or anything else you'd like."

She took his dimpled hand into her own and gave it a grown-up shake. When the woman at the employment agency told her that Dylan was developmentally delayed, she had made it sound as if the child was mentally handicapped. After meeting Dylan herself, Heather was convinced that there was nothing at all wrong with his mind. Behind those bright-blue eyes, she could see the cogs of his brain spinning, sizing her up.

"What are you thinking?" she said, touching a finger to his forehead.

A clever little monkey, Dylan mimicked the gesture by tapping softly on Heather's brow.

"Me?" she said, supplying the words for him. "Oh, I'm thinking that since you and I are so very much alike, the two of us are going to get along famously."

Heather didn't let the serious expression on his face deter her from holding forth on the subject. Dylan's special needs had drawn her to this job, rather than deterred her from it. Having made the decision to put her musical training behind her and embark upon a new career in the field of education, she was eager to test herself in a real-life situation. That way, if her father and mother were right and she truly was making "the biggest mistake of her life," she wouldn't have wasted any time and money at the university. Heather certainly hoped no professor would ask her to subscribe to the kind of degrading motivational theory that Dylan's speech therapist sold his father. Heather believed that such techniques were as counterproductive as the blistering lectures her teachers gave their pupils for "their own good."

Threatening to drown her, memories of Heather's own difficult childhood came flooding back. A musically gifted youngster, her early years were filled with unbalanced adult expectations and a grueling practice schedule interspersed with high-stakes performances that inevitably left her feeling just short of ever being good enough. Valued more for the prestige and potential income she would someday generate for her own ambitious parents rather than as an individual with a will of her own, Heather was shuffled off to an exclusive music conservatory at the tender age of seven. Hundreds of miles away from home, she grew up under constant pressure with little consideration given to her emotional well-being. By the age of seventeen, she was a weary veteran of the recital circuit and talent shows....

"Again..." Mr. Marion demanded over a pair of

owlish glasses that intensified his disapproving scowl. "And don't bother sniffling like some urchin who stumbled in here off the street. Your parents are paying a hefty sum for me to discipline you. Let me assure you, tears are wasted on me. You will play that piece again until it is right. Until it is perfect…"

Heather preferred beginning her training with a challenging student who knew his own mind rather than a compliant one who accepted the scripts other people had written for him without so much as questioning their motives. Like she herself had done until so very recently. She had firsthand knowledge of just how much easier it was to beat the vitality out of a pup than to put it back in once its spirit was broken.

"Don't worry, Dylan. I won't try to make you talk if you don't want to," she said with a gentle smile, assuring him that it would be far easier learning the rudiments of housekeeping and cooking without a little chatterbox demanding all her attention.

"For what it's worth, I'm not much of a talker myself. That's one thing we have in common. You know, I wasn't much older than you when I was separated from my parents. Whenever I was lonely, I used to let music do my talking for me."

At that, Dylan cocked his head showing the first real sign of interest in what she had to say. He gestured toward the piano in the corner of the room.

"Would you like to play a song for me?" Heather asked.

He responded by bouncing a wooden block off the hardwood floor where he had halfheartedly stacked them. Heather bent down to pick it up and aimed it at the base of his crooked-looking chimney. Not even the tiniest hint of a smile toyed with Dylan's lips as the structure toppled and blocks scattered in all directions.

"So much for the Learning Tower of Pisa," she said, amusing herself with word play that was lost upon her charge.

Sighing, she rose to her feet and approached the grand piano with an air of confidence that belied her true feelings. Having come to associate music with her broken heart, it took an effort to lift the lid from the keys and drag a hand absently along the keyboard. Just as Dylan was drawn to that melodic sound in spite of himself, Heather couldn't help appreciating the quality of the instrument at her fingertips. She didn't know whether Tobias Danforth was a musician himself, but the man obviously placed a high value on providing his son with the best money could buy.

She played a couple of scales and was not at all surprised to discover the piano was perfectly in tune. With her back ramrod-straight and her hands poised over the ivory keys in the posture of a venerate pianist, she gave the impression that she was going to treat Dylan to some classic rendition intended to soothe the heart of the most savage beast.

"'Peter, Peter, pumpkin eater, had a wife and couldn't keep her.'"

The melody that she played on those polished keys was universally familiar. A voice more suited to compositions by the masters rose to meet the exposed log beams overhead.

"'Put her in a pumpkin shell and there he kept her very well.'"

Abandoning his blocks, Dylan hesitantly approached the piano and sidled next to Heather on the bench. There he proceeded to plunk out the final three notes of the silly little ditty.

Laughing, she noted, "It sounds very much like your blocks plinking on the floor, doesn't it?"

The twinkle in his answering blue eyes was the impetus for Heather's next selection.

"'Twinkle, twinkle, little star...'"

It had been so long since music held anything but pain for her that Heather was surprised to lose herself in the kind of happy nonsense songs that demanded nothing of a pupil but a willing spirit and an eager heart. She wondered if she might coax him into a duet with the all-time favorite "Chopsticks." Delighted to have made even such a tenuous connection with Dylan, she hoped his father wouldn't mind if their dinner consisted of grilled cheese sandwiches and tomato soup straight out of the can.

* * *

The sound of music stopped Toby short as he stepped through the front door. It had been so long since he had heard anything cheerful echoing off the walls of his home that he wondered if he had accidentally walked into the wrong house by mistake. As much as he missed the smell of Mrs. Cremin's fabulous homemade meals wafting through the house at the end of a long day's work, the joyous noise that greeted him was far sweeter and infinitely more filling.

He followed the sound to an impromptu recital in the living room.

With their backs to him, neither Heather nor Dylan was aware of his presence, providing him a perfect opportunity to observe the interaction between them unnoticed. Why someone with a voice as heavenly as Heather's would want to waste her life as a nanny was beyond him. Toby didn't give that question more than a minute of his time. If God wanted to send him an angel, who was he to question Divine Intervention?

While Dylan wasn't exactly talking up a storm, it was the most animated Toby could remember seeing him in a long time. In keeping with the pattern established earlier in the day Heather played the beginning notes of a simple melody, and his son completed it. Like the subtle fragrance that Heather dabbed on her pulse points, her very presence seemed to somehow change the molecular structure of the air itself. The oppressive aura that had dominated this house since well before Sheila took off felt suddenly energized with the possibility of healing.

The fact that the house was a mess and dinner not on the table, nor anywhere near the stove as far as he could tell, didn't damper the optimism rising in Toby's chest. An empty belly was nothing compared to the chronic worry that divorce had permanently damaged his little boy.

"Daddy's home," he announced in a voice made deliberately gruff to keep it from cracking with emotion.

At the announcement, Dylan flew off the piano bench and into his father's arms. Such wild enthusiasm was foreign to Heather who watched the reunion with something akin to amazement. The sight of this big man tossing his child in the air and catching him in a great, big bear hug made her heart beat against the barbed-wire barrier she had so painstakingly built around it. A similar greeting from her own father at that age would have likely sent her scurrying to her room in fear.

Heather's reserve was partly due to her embarrassment about jumping to the conclusion that this man could be a monster when it was obvious that his little boy adored him. It was also partly due to the fact that she had no desire to get any closer emotionally to her new boss than was necessary to maintain her present employment. Having just been dumped by someone she trusted first and foremost as a mentor and only subsequently as a lover, Heather was not about to risk her heart romantically again.

Just because at first glance Toby Danforth appeared to be Josef Sengele's exact opposite didn't mean there were no similarities between them. Past experience had taught Heather that men in general were not to be trusted. Strong-willed men like her father and Josef were adept at manipulating for their own purposes those they claimed to love. And Tobias Danforth struck her as one of the most determined creatures on the planet.

The only difference was that neither Josef nor her father showed the propensity for outward affection that Toby did. That was something to be counted in his favor. Assuming the silver-framed photograph displayed on top of the piano was of Dylan's mother, Heather was surprised that he hadn't done away with all evidence of his ex-wife. Undeniably beautiful, the woman in the silver frame spent the better part of the afternoon staring accusingly at Heather. As disconcerting as she had found that, Heather knew by the way that Dylan's gaze fell so often upon that lovely countenance that it was a comfort to him.

"I promise that I'll get around to the housekeeping tomorrow," she told her employer.

The apology in her voice was unnecessary.

"That's all right," Toby told her.

His smile was genuine and reassuring. That

Heather suddenly felt jealous of the toddler nestled so safely in those strong arms of his father came as a shock to her. Having given up romantic complications in her life, she could do little but let her emotions wash over her without outwardly acknowledging them.

"What you're doing with Dylan is far more important. What do you say I stick some frozen dinners in the microwave, and we can all relax in front of the television for the evening?"

Heather didn't know what to say. The invitation sounded tempting.

And dangerous.

The truth was she was ravenous. And for a lot more than the man was offering. There was no real explanation for why she felt like taking off running in the opposite direction other than the fact that something about this man put her into fight-or-flight mode. She didn't like what it said about her character that her body was inclined in the direction of the latter. Or that given the circumstances of her employment, avoiding Toby was going to be as impossible as controlling the chemical reaction that he set off in her every time he was around.

Heather's stomach answered for her, rumbling deep and loud in a manner that belied her dainty stature.

"That would be lovely," she said in a tone that gave away nothing of the conflicting emotions that left her feeling raw inside.

Three

"Fake it until you make it," Heather repeated to herself again and again as she stared out the tiny window of the airplane that was waiting for permission from radio control to take her straight into the heart of the South and Toby's family.

That same mantra helped her through innumerable recitals and contests over the years. Clutching a small purse in her lap with both hands, she did her best to pretend she wasn't frightened out of her mind. Considering what an admirable job she had been doing of hiding that very fact from her employer for the past few days, it should have been a piece of cake. That the plane in which she sat barely qualified as a puddle-jumper didn't do much to calm her nerves. When Toby told her that his uncle was sending his private jet to transport them to the family reunion, Heather had envisioned something far grander than the single-engine Cessna idling beneath her more like a motorcycle than an actual means of transportation designed to leave the ground behind.

"Are you all right?" Toby asked.

He reached across what only questionably passed as an aisle to peel one of her hands off her purse and take it into his own. He found her skin cold and clammy to the touch.

"Is there anything I can get you to calm your nerves?"

"I'm fine," Heather said grimly through gritted teeth.

Her stomach lurched as the propellers began spinning. She covered her mouth with her free hand. Used to dealing with preperformance jitters, Heather dreaded the thought of vomiting into a paper bag next to a man who was showing her such touching concern. At least before a concert, one always had the option of discreetly slipping away to the privacy of an isolated bathroom.

Toby's voice was as smooth as aged whiskey.

"Why in the world didn't you tell me you were afraid of flying?"

Why not indeed! For the same reason that she couldn't tell him she was afraid of the feelings that living with him had stirred in her. Standing on the edge of his close-knit family, she felt like a starving child with her nose pressed up against a candy store window without so much as a dime in her pocket. Unwilling to admit that, however, Heather forced an excuse through lips drawn in a thin line.

"I'll be fine. It's part of the job. I understood that when I accepted it."

Glancing over Toby's broad shoulder, she shot Dylan a brave smile. It was lost upon the child whose head was bent over the traveling musical keyboard his father brought along to entertain him. Even a three-year-old was more at ease with flying than Heather was. She felt like an idiot for letting Toby guess just how nervous she really was. Not that he had to do any more than look into her eyes to peer directly into her soul.

"I'll be right back," he told her.

Heather forced herself to let go of his hand as he rose to his feet. She was grateful that he hadn't tried placating her with some platitude about there being nothing to be afraid of. That was how her father tried dismissing her fear of the dark when she was little. As had Josef whenever she waited in the wings for her turn to perform before a house filled with critics.

And right before he took her virginity from her.

Lies.

She was doubly grateful when Toby returned a moment later as promised, not with some condescending statement about air travel being safer then driving her car, but rather with a stiff drink in one hand.

"I hope you like whiskey," he told her, passing her a tall tumbler. "You strike me more as the type who'd prefer an umbrella and a cherry bobbing in a fancy drink. But since I'm not much of a bartender, this is the best I could manage before the pilot announces it's time to fasten our seat belts."

Such instructions were unnecessary on her behalf. Heather had securely buckled her safety device across her lap the instant she sat down—and read every word of the informational materials provided in the back of the seat in front of her. Just in case an ocean happened to materialize between Wyoming and Georgia, she was prepared to use her seat cushion as a floatation device.

The ice cubes floating in her drink offered more immediate comfort. Heather took a tentative sip. As its dark amber color suggested, Toby made it plenty stiff.

"I hope your relatives don't mind if I'm not able to stand up once we get there," she murmured with a diminutive little cough.

His responding grin was enough to melt those ice cubes clinking against her glass. Heather wasn't sure whether the warmth spreading through her body was due to her hormones or the alcohol hitting her bloodstream.

"Don't worry," Toby told her. "As far as I know, my uncle isn't basing his campaign on any protemperance stance. Which is a good thing, considering his own past.''

Heather raised a slender eyebrow.

"My family isn't exactly without blemish," he warned.

"Whose is?"

She took another dainty sip of her drink to steady her nerves as they began the long roll down the runway. Not one to pry, Heather was nonetheless curious. Local gossip connected Toby to a glossy layout of some fabulous mansion touted in a magazine last summer. Much of what had been said regarding the article was mean-spirited and envious in nature. She supposed such a well-known family would have to expect to have every flaw magnified in the press. She wondered if that was part of the reason Toby deliberately put such distance between them.

Since her own family relished any media attention and rushed to put their daughter in the limelight every chance they could, it was a stance she could uniquely appreciate.

"What's your family like?" Toby asked.

Not sure whether he asked the question out of courtesy or as a way to distract her from their impending takeoff, she responded tersely.

"Quiet."

Squeezing her eyes shut as the engines growled and the airplane strained to lift off, she hoped Toby wasn't angry at her brusqueness. Her stomach leaped as they became airborne and hovered somewhere between her head and her heart. Tiny beads of sweat popped out above her lip.

"Take another swallow," Toby commanded, squeezing her hand. His voice was far more reassuring than the remedy he offered.

Unfortunately, his touch counteracted that effect. Warm and strong, it suggested an intimacy that was not at all appropriate between an employee and employer. Heather fought to remember that she was hired to look after Dylan, not to engage in foolish romantic fantasies that left one feeling used and forlorn in their aftermath.

No matter how much Heather wanted to let go of Toby's hand, she could no more have done so than she could slow her racing pulse. In so small an airplane, one felt every air pocket and bump right in the seat of the pants. Looking out the window only intensified the feeling of dizziness that swept over her. The landscape below, parched by drought, may well have been the surface of the moon for what little comfort its familiarity brought.

"Turn around," Toby told her.

"What?"

He touched her nape with his free hand. She flinched, and her already stiff shoulders bunched up around her ears as he began kneading the muscles on either side of her neck.

"Let me give you a massage. Trust me, it'll help you relax."

Although Heather started to protest, the sensation

of his masterful fingers stroking her skin was too heavenly to forgo, even for the sake of pride. Toby took his other hand from hers and began to massage her knotted muscles in earnest. Heather expelled a deep breath of air and felt every muscle in her body relax. Suddenly the sensation of floating high above the world didn't seem nearly so frightening. She arched against his touch and tried to keep from sliding out of her seat. Her eyelids fluttered shut.

"That *is* nice," she admitted.

The sound of giggling in the seat behind her so startled Heather that she almost spilled her drink into her lap. Dylan apparently did not share her aversion to air travel. His reaction to hitting an air pocket was to pretend he was on a roller coaster. Toby looked pleased. While his son had yet to speak again since that first day when Heather arrived, laughter was definitely a step in the right direction.

"I'm afraid the only quiet one you're likely to find in my family is Dylan," Toby told her. "And with your help, I think we might be well on the way to curing that."

Indeed he was right on that account. There was a small army waiting on the ground in Savannah to meet them. As delighted as Heather was to be back on earth in one piece, she found the rush of people surrounding them with hugs and squeals of welcome almost as oppressive as the humidity making the air heavy and redolent with expensive perfume. Her knees were wobbly beneath her, partly from the effect of the miraculous concoction Toby had mixed up for her on the plane—and partly from a sense that she was being suffocated.

Dylan threw his arms around one of her legs. Oblivious to that fact, Toby took her firmly by the elbow. Heather felt like a wishbone being pulled apart. Caught in a throng of some of the most beautiful people she had ever seen, she reached down and pulled Dylan up into her arms. He clutched her neck as if it were a life preserver.

"And this darling angel must be my nephew," cooed a Southern voice so balmy Heather thought it warranted a fan.

A stunning blonde stepped out from behind that voice to hold her arms out to Dylan. Her eyes immediately gave her away as Toby's sister. The exact same shape, they were as vivid green as his were blue—with equal shades of compassion glimmering in their depths. Heather held her breath when Dylan hesitated. Already protective of him, she didn't want anyone rushing him too soon.

When he leaned into his Aunt Imogene's arms, Heather heard Toby expel his breath at the exact same time that she did. The tightness in her shoulders returned with a vengeance. It wasn't that anyone went out of his or her way to make her feel unwelcome as much as the fact that there were so many Danforths to try to keep straight in her mind at once.

"I'd like you to meet my sister Imogene and my brother Jacob. His wife Larissa. My cousin Reid, his wife Tina."

Toby's sister gave him a scathing look and corrected him almost the instant her name rolled off his tongue. "The last time anyone in this family called me Imogene, it was followed by both my middle and last name. I believe it was a code signaling that I was in big trouble, more often than not because of something my ornery big brother instigated."

Toby's embrace may have encompassed both his son and his charming sister without putting any strain on those big arms of his, but his laugh pulled on Heather's heart. She imagined the sound of that robust laughter mingling with that of a host of other Danforths, raising the rafters of a fancy mansion profiled in magazines that touted the lifestyles of the rich and famous. Heather's first impression of this prestigious family was far less stuffy than what she had anticipated. And while that was a relief in some ways, it complicated her relationship as Dylan's nanny.

As far as she knew, servants weren't expected to like their superiors.

Although Toby's introduction accounted for all the adults present, a couple of children had tagged along to watch the planes land and take off as well as to welcome Toby home. He scooped each of them up in his arms, promising them a special present from his luggage as soon as he unpacked. After collecting their bags they proceeded to a waiting limousine where Heather took a deep, cleansing breath and embraced the sudden sound of silence.

"To Crofthaven," Toby told the driver.

No more directions were necessary than the name of the Danforth family estate where Toby promised "kith and kin galore." He either chose to ignore the look of panic that flitted across Heather's face at that pronouncement or simply missed it in the middle of fretting about Dylan.

"I was surprised he went to Genie so easily," he admitted.

"And that he wanted to stay with her at the airport," Heather added. A dear friend was flying in on a commercial flight arriving any minute, and Genie offered to bring Dylan back to Crofthaven in her personal car. "Your sister seems very nice."

"She is," Toby assured her with typical big brother pride. "Actually all my relatives are. The worst thing about living so far away is missing out on family functions—and," he added with a wry grin, "maybe the best thing, too."

When Heather gave him an odd look, he hastened to explain. "Don't get me wrong. I love my family. It's just that I'm not much for black-tie functions like the big party Uncle Abe is throwing on the Fourth to launch his political campaign. I wouldn't have agreed to come home if Dad hadn't specifically asked me to. That man's sense of family obligation doesn't stop at the state line. Nor Uncle Abe's—

hence the private jet that flew us here—although I suspect his motives are less pure than my father's."

Heather nodded her head in empathy. She had endured more than her share of the kind of black-tie events to which Toby referred, not to mention undue family influence about what she wanted to do with her own life.

"How were you able to strike out on your own without severing the family ties completely?" she asked.

Having done everything in her power to avoid being alone with Toby in his home for the three short days that she had been working for him, this was the first time they had actually been together without Dylan present. Given the state of her hormones whenever Toby was near, it was far less awkward than Heather would have imagined. Like the TV dinner they had shared in front of the television that first night of her employment, it was amazingly cozy. If she wasn't careful, Heather knew she might start feeling like a real part of Toby's family. She was both flattered and flummoxed that her boss treated her more like a friend than an employee.

"My family accepts me for who and what I am. Luckily, they don't feel the need to mold me into something that I'm not. They just reel me in once in a while and remind me that I'm one of their own."

"That must be nice," Heather said. Unable to come up with a better adjective, the wistful tone of her voice gave away the pain of her own family situation.

"It certainly makes me appreciate family all the more when I get the chance to come home. It's good for Dylan, too. A child needs to know that he's part of a tree with roots, not just some cottonseed blown across the continent."

Heather took the remark to heart. That was exactly how she felt. Like a seed tossed upon a hapless wind. She envied Toby the ability to do exactly what he wanted with his life without fear of being disowned for doing so. Dylan was a lucky little boy to be born into such a family.

She stared out the window. This was the first time she had ever been in Savannah. As the name itself suggested with its softly drawn syllables, it was a city of gracious living. The air was scented with magnolia blossoms as big as a man's open hand, dotting tree-lined streets that grew less and less modern the farther they traveled away from the airport.

The lush landscape of the South was a stark contrast to the wide-open spaces of Wyoming. They followed the Savannah River as it meandered through town. It reminded Heather of a grand old lady who was in no hurry to reach her destination but rather was intent on enjoying the journey itself. As the city gave way to the country, white-columned plantations evoked images of Scarlett O'Hara and a time lost to all but the blood of a civil war that soaked into the soil and permeated the very air itself. The voices of ghosts whispered through the Spanish moss hanging like tinsel from dignified oaks.

"What about your family?" Toby inquired, which pulled her gaze back into the vehicle and herself into the present moment.

Heather's voice was small.

"Not all parents are as understanding as yours."

Toby looked at her quizzically. "What do you mean?"

Naturally introverted, Heather wasn't inclined to speak of private issues, but for some reason she felt safe sharing a little bit of herself with a man whose eyes looked upon her so kindly. Perhaps a brief explanation might help him understand any perceived aloofness on her part when it came time for her to interact with the hordes of his siblings, cousins and aunts and uncles. She hoped he would approve a moment or two of the quiet contemplation that she needed to feel centered every day.

"As an only child, all the noise and confusion of a big family like yours is strange to me. Unlike your parents, mine pinned all their hopes on me fulfilling their dreams. I'm afraid I've disappointed them terribly."

"I can't imagine any parents not being proud of such a lovely, talented daughter," Toby said. "If they lost a child, they might well rethink their judgmental attitude."

His expression was so solemn, and his voice so

earnest, that it almost caused tears to spring to Heather's eyes. She wondered who in his family had lost a loved one tragically. All this talk of family only served to rip the stitches from fresh wounds. Just because this man had soothed her fear of flying on the plane didn't mean he had shoulders broad enough for more problems than his own. She tried to make light of her pain.

"It's understandable given the amount of money they spent on my training and…"

Heather's attention was momentarily diverted as the driver pulled into a driveway leading to what appeared to be a museum of sorts. A wrought-iron gate with a curlicued *D* announcing the Danforth estate swung open splitting the letter in two. She gasped in astonishment.

"This is where you grew up?"

"Thankfully, no." Toby's voice rustled in his throat. "The poor side of the family lives down the road."

The lack of bitterness in his voice led Heather to believe he was exaggerating his circumstances. The grounds surrounding Crofthaven underscored her initial impression of the prominent Danforths, portrayed in the media as a formidable and impenetrable dynasty. The estate itself was so huge and the gardens so elaborate that Heather surmised it would take an entire army of gardeners working full-time to tend the place. She wondered if the grounds ran all the way to the ocean, and made a mental note to walk the perimeter of the estate the first chance she got.

The main house, a large Georgian-style mansion, was listed as a historical landmark. Having been built over a hundred years ago, it showed no signs of neglect. Though it obviously had been modernized to include up-to-date electrical wiring and plumbing, great care had been taken to retain the original integrity of the property. Hollywood would be hard-pressed to find a better setting for an epic nineteenth-century saga.

"It's an amazing place," she said.

"It is," Toby agreed. "But not everything is as it appears on the surface. My cousins have far fonder memories of the time they spent at my parents' home than of their lives here. After their mother died, their childhood was marked by loneliness and some emotional neglect on the part of their father. Bricks and mortar don't make a home any more than money can necessarily buy character."

Heather couldn't argue that point. Out of the corner of her eye, she caught a slight movement that sent goose bumps crawling over her flesh. Beneath a massive oak tree, she saw the figure of a woman clad in ancient garb. She was too far away to make out much more than the dark color of her hair and her turn-of-the-century clothing, but there was no mistaking that the sorrowful-looking creature was wagging a finger directly at her!

In the blink of an eye, the apparition was gone.

Heather's fingers found Toby's arm.

"What's wrong?" he asked, covering her hand with his own.

She was grateful for the warmth of human flesh. Her own skin had gone deadly cold. Heather was on the verge of asking Toby if he, too, had seen the mysterious woman under the tree, but decided against it. She doubted he wanted to introduce her to the rest of his family as a loony.

Perhaps the woman was, in fact, part of a Civil War reenactment.

Perhaps a documentary was being filmed on site.

Perhaps Heather was overly tired from a long, arduous flight, and her mind was simply overcome by the aura of this incredible setting.

Or perhaps she was being warned from the grave to escape while there was still time....

Four

When the limousine came to a complete stop at Crofthaven's front door, their driver jumped out to open their doors. He was too late for Toby who was accustomed to opening his own doors and making his own way in the world without anyone's assistance.

"Thanks, anyway," he said, stuffing a generous tip into the man's hand. "And have a nice day."

As Heather stepped from the limousine, she tried to dismiss the eerie sense that some ghostly being was watching her. Surely it was only her imagination that chilled her skin and caused her to look over her shoulder. Letting the sounds of summer crickets and birds wash over her, she rubbed away her goose bumps and fixed a determined smile on her face. Dylan was eagerly waiting for them on the front steps along with half the population of Savannah, as far as Heather could tell.

They converged on Toby as if he were the proverbial prodigal son returning home. Contrary to her expectations, Heather wasn't shoved aside as much as swallowed up by the throng pushing them through the massive front doors. The Danforths were a jovial bunch who seemed more into bear hugs than the pretentious air kisses that her parents preferred on the rare occasions she was allowed to return home.

The apologetic glance that Toby cast in Heather's direction did not escape his sister Imogene's sharp green eyes.

Heather suspected little did.

At the moment, however, she was having trouble keeping up with all the names and faces crowded about. As if imploring a higher power, Heather cast her eyes to the high ceilings and ornamental fans so reminiscent of a Tennessee Williams production. Their gentle whirring stirred enough of a breeze to play a subtle tune on the chandelier sparkling overhead. As if sensing her discomfort, Toby put an arm around her shoulder.

She turned her face up to his as he bent down to whisper in her ear. "Thank you for being here for

Dylan and me. You don't know how much it means.''

His breath against her neck was cooler than the air that greeted her when she stepped off the plane but it melted her on the spot nonetheless. Need revealed itself in the shiver that raced down her collar and out the ends of her fingertips. That same sudden need made her shift even closer to him to take shelter in the crook of the arm draped protectively around her. It made Heather want a great many things that were not at all possible given her status among the rich and famous gathered together in such an incredible setting.

Heather was so accustomed to Josef abandoning her at social gatherings, while he curried favor among the patrons and attended to his own adoring fans, that Toby's attention to her well-being caught her unawares. Why was he being so nice to her? she wondered. Supposing she must look terribly overwhelmed to warrant such attention, Heather resigned herself to making the best of the short introductions to come, if only for the sake of common courtesy. She was glad she wore dress slacks and a sleeveless seersucker top rather than the shorts she had been tempted to don in expectation of the South's famous heat and humidity. Breathing a sigh of relief that she was neither over nor underdressed for the occasion, she smiled at the man who had brought her here as a servant but who was doing his best to make her feel like a guest.

The crowd separated to let a slender woman step forward. Heather was reminded of Moses parting the Red Sea. Like so many Southern ladies, she was of an indeterminate age. Her blond hair was swept up in a tidy, timeless style, and she wore a simple chiffon dress of pale lemon. Except for the warm blue eyes that were Toby's, she looked just like Imogene.

"Mom!"

Heather studied the joy reflected in Toby's face as he swept his mother into his arms. The love between them was so genuine that a ripple of jealousy washed through her. She could not remember a single time that her mother ever greeted her in such an uninhibited fashion. Nor when she felt truly accepted by the woman who brought her into the world. In the Burroughs family, color distinguished blood from water more than any particular thickening agent.

Toby's father was only half a step behind his wife.

"Son!"

How a single syllable could carry such implicit approval was beyond Heather, but it most certainly did. Whereas Miranda Danforth was effusive in her greeting, Toby's father stopped just short of a hug, reaching out instead to take his son's hand into his. The handshake they exchanged conveyed something so sacred and honorable that it caused Heather to feel the need to turn away.

"I really appreciate your coming home on such

short notice at my request, especially when I know how busy you've been," Harold Danforth said. His eyes held a shimmer of deeply felt emotion.

Toby reached out to embrace his father for a moment that transcended time altogether.

"I wouldn't miss a family reunion for the world—whatever the reason for it might be."

Uncomfortable with such an open display of affection in light of her own family's threat to disown her, Heather wondered if she might possibly slip away and do a little exploring—of the house itself as well as of the raw emotions that were twisting her guts up into knots.

"And who might this pretty young thing be?" inquired Harold, directing his attention her way and banishing any chance of imminent escape.

Kind blue eyes regarded her from beneath a pair of bushy, heavy eyebrows.

"This is Dylan's nanny," Genie volunteered before anyone else had a chance to speak. "Her name is Heather Burroughs. You might remember her from a concert performance at the Civic Center a few years ago."

Surprised that Toby's socialite sister cared enough to remember her name, let alone reference any background information about her, Heather gave Harold a timid smile. Unlike her own father, who was of slight build and sharp temperament, Harold Danforth was at least 230 pounds and had a contagious grin. Shorter than either of his sons, he was nonetheless a big man. Both in heart and stature Heather imagined, if her instincts were correct.

"I'm pleased to meet you," she offered, feeling an immediate kinship with the man.

"The honor is all mine."

Words that might sound stilted on the page warmed Heather from the inside out. The man appeared to be a true Southern gentleman through and through. For the life of her, she couldn't imagine why Toby would want to leave the affection of such a loving family to strike out on his own. Fearing she might even get attached to these people herself if she wasn't careful, Heather was glad that her job would likely occupy her time for the duration of her stay.

It was impossible to tell which of the children running about were related to one another and which were merely friends of the family. With an estate of this size, it certainly wouldn't be any trouble accommodating a full-scale nursery school. Heather would cheerfully volunteer to run it, if it meant she wouldn't be asked to put in a polite appearance at Abraham Danforth's big campaign party. She'd had enough of strained social functions in which she felt compelled to vie for the attention of wealthy patrons of the arts. It would be nice to fade into the woodwork for a change.

Her thoughts were interrupted by the sound of a child's squeals as he came ricocheting toward her from out of nowhere. Gathering her wits about her,

Heather spied a boy of about Dylan's age sliding down a fantastic spiral staircase by way of a banister polished by the seats of children for over a century. Startled, she jumped aside, fearing if she didn't move that she might well prove to be the boy's landing pad. Taking the opposite tack, Toby stepped forward to catch the boy in midflight.

"And just who do you think you are?" he asked, peering into a face that took him back into time. The child was the spitting image of his brother Jacob at that age. "Peter Pan perhaps?"

The boy giggled. "Not Peter Pan—just Peter!"

His father stepped forward to ruffle the boy's hair. "Toby, let me introduce you to your nephew."

The pride in his voice was as unmistakable as his affection for the child. Unaware that Jacob himself had only recently discovered the son he didn't know he had, Heather simply assumed that Toby hadn't had the privilege of meeting his impish nephew. She liked the way he connected with all children, not just his own. She supposed such a man would have more than enough love to accommodate more than one child. Dylan would surely love having brothers and sisters to fill the void that his mother had left behind.

Not that Heather was eager to marry Toby off or anything. Just the thought of it brought a blush to her cheeks.

"The boys will be good for each other," she overheard Jacob telling his brother. "A few months ago, Peter was as reserved as Dylan and almost as quiet. Living together as a family has really brought him out of his shell.''

Older than Dylan by only a year, Peter grabbed the younger boy by the hand and urged him, ''Come on. Let's go play.''

When Dylan looked hesitantly at Heather, she smiled at the pair of them and offered to accompany them.

Toby placed a restraining hand gently on her elbow.

''If you'd like to stick around, I'm sure I can locate somebody to baby-sit while the adults get settled in. You look exhausted.''

''I don't mind.''

The thought of going with the children and escaping the familial chaos definitely appealed to Heather. Hoping to maintain a low profile for the duration of her stay at Crofthaven, she was eager to begin exploring the grounds herself. The possibility of meeting up with that mysterious lady beneath the big oak tree held a weird fascination for her.

Besides, Heather asked herself, what good could possibly come of a mere peasant mixing with America's royalty? She imagined such behavior could earn her the label of a gold-digger among Toby's relatives. Having been coached how to ''work a room'' by her instructors, Heather was hoping never to need to put that particular skill to use again. No matter how likable they might be, why should one bother trying to forge ties with people she was likely never to see again?

Heather could think of only one good reason: it would undoubtedly help her to understand Dylan better—and his perplexing father. For the life of her, she couldn't understand why he was looking so displeased with her at the moment. The stubborn set of his jaw didn't bode well for any argument Heather might set forth.

"It'll do the boy good to make some friends his own age," Toby insisted.

"Oh, let her go," Genie chided her brother before turning her attention to Heather. "Why don't you familiarize yourself with the place while we catch up on old times? I'm sure you'd be bored with the exaggerated tales my brothers are sure to spring on my new husband in hopes of embarrassing me."

Heather shot Toby's sister a grateful look. She hadn't expected anyone so privileged to make it easy for her.

"But," she continued in a honeyed drawl, "I do expect you to accompany Toby to the festivities. If he shows up alone, he's sure to start a stampede of unattached Southern belles in his direction that will upset Uncle Abe by taking attention away from the big political announcement he's scheduled to make."

Toby's protests fell on deaf ears as she continued teasing him. Their playful banter diverted

Heather's attention from the matchmaking glint in Genie's eyes.

She attempted a feeble rebuttal. "But don't you think Dylan will—"

Genie cut her off with the same mulish set of her jaw as her big brother's. The delicate-looking lady was living, breathing proof that Southern women hadn't acquired the *steel magnolias* nickname for nothing. Her husband Sheikh Raf ibn Shakir preferred working with his Arabian horses to socializing with the jet set, but he promised his wife he would make an appearance at the family reunion later in the day. He was looking forward to comparing training techniques with his brother-in-law.

"Don't worry about Dylan. He'll be just fine. Uncle Abe's hired a score of qualified baby-sitters for all the children in attendance. There will be everything from clowns to magicians to giant inflatable toys to keep them happily occupied during the festivities."

Like a cool breeze, Miranda swept into the conversation with a soothing presence that had settled so many squabbles over the years. "Of course you'll want to stay close enough by to check on Dylan if he needs you for anything, my dear. That would put my mind at ease, as well, but we would consider it a privilege to get to know you better. After all, as Dylan's nanny, we consider you part of the family now. And as such, we would be honored to have you stay at our home. It's just down the road a ways.

With all the political hullabaloo going on here at Crofthaven, it will provide a calmer atmosphere for us to get better acquainted with our grandson.''

There was no way of sidestepping such a gracious invitation. It made Heather feel all the more keenly her desire for a mother who went out of her way to make a stranger feel at home. Even though she knew that Miranda Danforth was simply being cordial, her words put a lump in her throat. All she had ever known of family was outrageous demands and strict compliance to what others deemed in her best interest. Miranda's suggestion that people might actually want to get to know her as her own person was flattering in itself. Her invitation to consider herself part of the family when Heather's own had turned so viciously against her was salve upon an open wound.

"If you're sure I won't be in the way," Heather said, lowering her voice so as not to betray her feelings on the matter. "I would consider it a privilege to attend."

A chorus of responses assured her that she would not be in the way at all. In fact, if the conspiratorial look exchanged between mother and daughter was any indication, Heather was about to find herself the center of attention whether she wanted to be or not.

Five

Toby refrained from tugging on the tie he was convinced was invented to maintain a choke hold on mankind in general. Though no longer the same little boy who so vigorously resisted being forced to attend such stuffy affairs as this particular fundraiser in the heart of old Savannah, Toby still preferred the smell of horseflesh to the cloying perfumes wafting through the lobby of the elegant Twin Oaks Hotel. Nor had his palate ever evolved enough to appreciate the taste of caviar, which was heaped in crystal bowls strategically placed around ice sculptures. He'd still take fried chicken packed in a picnic basket any day over black fish eggs that looked better suited for bait than dinner. Not to mention how much better a beer quenched a man's thirst compared to the dry champagne in the flute he held.

His glass froze halfway to his lips as an enchanting creature swept into the room. His heart thumped hard once, twice, three times in a rapid staccato before skidding to a complete halt. Had a pair of misty-gray eyes not sought his out at that very moment and shocked his poor heart back to working order, he might have made a complete fool of himself by spilling that fancy champagne all over himself and his brother Jacob, who was attempting to have a conversation with him.

"Then she said..."

Toby feigned an interested expression and nodded as if he was actually listening. He did not, however, take his eyes off the vision in blue who was making her way across the crowded room. Even though he'd mostly seen her wearing casual jeans and baggy T-shirts, he would have to be blind not to have noticed how pretty his son's new nanny was. The gown she chose for tonight's gala affair was not nearly so unassuming. Its satin fabric hugged her figure and accentuated her womanly beauty in such a striking fashion that every eye in the room was drawn toward it. Or rather to the woman wearing it.

In such a gown, Heather looked no more like a nanny than Cinderella looked like someone destined to sweep hearths for the rest of her days. If anything, Heather reminded Toby of an ice princess as she coolly made her way toward him. The way her gown so lovingly caressed her curves made him believe it had been designed expressly for her. Classic in design, the garment was a shimmer of sequins and beads that glittered with each step she took.

The hemline was deliberately angled from below one knee to midthigh on the opposite side. At five foot two inches tall, Toby had no idea Heather's legs could look so long and shapely in a pair of strappy silver shoes designed to make a man want to hang himself with his necktie. Her legs went on forever. He tore his gaze away from the sight only long enough to glare at the other men whose gazes were transfixed on the heavenly apparition floating across the wide expanse of the lobby.

Jacob jabbed his brother in the side and asked, "Where the hell's that one been all your life?"

"Presumably checking on Dylan," Toby answered dryly.

He took inordinate pride in the fact that he managed a swallow of champagne without choking on it. He drained the flute and set it on a passing waiter's tray. Not wanting his brother to see that his hands were shaking, Toby shoved them deep into his pockets and leaned against a marble column for support. He struck a pose of accidental insolence.

"That's not what I meant and you know it," Jacob countered. "Not all women are like Sheila, you know."

"Don't tell me Genie's twisting your arm to get

you involved in one of her harebrained matchmaking schemes." His groan conveyed more than words alone ever could.

Though the smile that crossed Jacob's face might be considered sly, his manner was so sympathetic that it invited Toby to open up as he used to when they'd shared their deepest secrets from their bunk beds after the lights were turned off.

"I don't believe in pushing a man into something he doesn't want, but I've got to tell you, little brother, that after fighting it tooth and nail for way too long, marriage is the best thing that's ever happened to me. I'm not much for giving advice, but I'm going to tell you something that I hope you take to heart. Don't let one bad experience scare you away from happiness. It's one thing to carve a niche out for yourself in the wilds of Wyoming and quite another to hide from life completely."

Since those words came from his brother and because they were motivated by sincere concern, Toby chose not to hit him square in the mouth as he would any other man who would presume to chastise him. As it was, he simply stepped aside when his sister-in-law Larissa linked her arm through her husband's and drew him to the dance floor with an apology to Toby. The sight sent a tiny twinge of jealousy through him.

It was all well and good for Jacob—barely back from his honeymoon—to lecture him on the glory of wedded bliss, considering the fact that he had never been divorced. His marriage wasn't based on deceit. His wife hadn't lied about using birth control and deliberately gotten pregnant in hopes of "snagging" a good catch. Jacob had never had a hole punched through his heart. A hole so big that the wind whistled through it whenever he stepped outside. Never had a woman stolen his son's voice from him in her haste to move on with a more cosmopolitan life.

Or stolen his own faith in marriages like the one his parents shared for so many wonderful years. It was the kind of permanence he had taken for granted growing up. That his wife wasn't willing to work through their problems still stung. Toby didn't wish his brother ill. He just longed to find something as amazing as Jacob had. Fearing that was impossible, it was far easier to turn his back on love altogether than to risk being hurt again.

"Is anything wrong?" Heather asked, stepping beside him and studying the furrows lining Toby's brow.

She wore her hair loosely pinned at her nape and swept up in a style that was utterly feminine and flattering. A few loose tendrils framed a face that appeared unaware of its own beauty.

He shook his head as if to clear it of old cobwebs and resisted the urge to test the texture of a silken tendril between his fingers. "Nothing, except that you take my breath away. If you'll just be so kind as to stand beside me for the rest of the evening, your beauty should discourage all the single women my mother has lined up in hopes of fixing me up. Ever since the whirlwind romance that picked Genie up and deposited her in front of an altar with the man of her dreams, she's been wanting to duplicate the experience for me."

Heather crooked an eyebrow at him. "I take it you don't believe in whirlwind romances."

Who would have thought that a man who looked so at ease in saddle-worn blue jeans could look so fabulous in a tailor-made suit? Had he the inclination, Heather supposed Tobias Danforth could make a living as a model. Not one of those pretty-boy types who bounced a beach ball over a volleyball net, he would be better suited to sales that required a man of rough edges. Heather could picture him in an advertisement that juxtaposed a close-up of the character lines in his face against the backdrop of the Grand Tetons. Or playing blackjack in Monte Carlo wearing the same tuxedo he donned for tonight's festivities.

Or in a pair of underwear that left little to the imagination and shamelessly played on his sex appeal to sell their product...

A glass of champagne looked like a tempting way to wash away the dryness that had settled into her throat like a desert. Heather nonetheless politely refused the one offered her. She met Josef in a similar setting and, as she recalled, complimentary champagne had done nothing then but cloud her judgment regarding the man who came to be her mentor first—and later her tormentor.

She could sympathize all too well with Toby's cynicism.

"You'll have to forgive me if I'm a little sour on the subject of romance at the moment," he told her.

"There's no need to apologize." Certainly not to me, she added to herself.

Having no desire to pry into her boss's private life, Heather hoped to be accorded the same respect in regard to her personal affairs.

Affairs being the operative word, she thought bitterly to herself, wondering why she hadn't simply worn a hair shirt for the evening instead of something soft and feminine.

Sensing the change in her demeanor, Toby obliged by changing the subject. "How's Dylan doing?" he asked.

Heather smiled when she thought of Dylan and Peter chasing each other through an inflatable playground that had been set up in an adjoining courtyard.

"You were right. He's still not talking, but he and Peter are inseparable, and they seem to understand each other well enough without words."

"Who's to say that relationships don't function best that way? Words damned sure didn't keep Dylan's mother from turning her back on the two of us, and I guarantee there were plenty of words between us."

Heather could tell Toby regretted his words as soon as he'd said them. His angry outburst explained much and softened her heart toward him even more. The fact that he kept a photograph of Dylan's mother on the piano back home made her wonder if he wasn't still in love with her.

"You didn't have an amicable divorce?" she asked softly.

"That's an oxymoron if I've ever heard one," Toby replied.

"Sheila's decision to leave tore our family apart. It was especially hard on Dylan."

"Except for the day you arrived, he hasn't spoken a word since his mother left."

"I'm sorry."

Heather's heart went out to him. Not demonstrative by nature, she didn't stop to think about the ramifications of putting a hand gently to the side of his cheek. Just shaven, his jawline felt smooth and solid against her palm. A gesture born of compassion turned suddenly reckless, producing shock waves so intense in the pit of Heather's being that they nearly doubled her over. Every nerve ending in her body surged in response to skin touching skin.

Toby flinched and drew a hand from his pocket to encircle her wrist. Heather braced herself. There was no doubt the man could have snapped her wrist in two, had he wanted to, or simply have exerted enough pressure to let her know she had stepped over an invisible line between employer and employee. He applied only enough to let her know he would not release her until he was good and ready to. Heather was not so much frightened as exhilarated in some unfathomably and undeniably sexual way. The strength in his grasp was matched by the sudden flash of desire that turned his eyes the color of thunderclouds rolling across an expanse of blue skies.

"Don't," he warned.

The band ended a slow song and paused a moment before playing their next selection. Beneath his hand, Heather's pulse was beating out a much wilder number. Shuddering, she nevertheless kept her eyes level with his.

A lively Cajun tune started up complete with twin fiddles, a zydeco and an accordion. Like the man who held her captive, it was exciting and dangerous on many levels. Her teachers and parents had done their best to keep her from such "coarse and sensual" music, but alone at night with her radio turned down low, Heather allowed herself to dream her own dreams while her foot tapped out the rhythm of such common, joyful tunes. As far from her classical background as the rambunctious Danforths were from her dispassionate family, such music stirred the imagination. And her blood.

Heather watched his gaze drop to her lips. She refrained from darting a tongue out to moisten them, licking them in an act of nervousness left over from junior high school days.

"Don't," he warned again. "Don't go playing with fire in the midst of dry timber."

Heather opened her mouth to protest but discovered that her voice had abandoned her. A more aggressive woman might have attempted wrenching her hand free—or maybe even landing a slap upon the features that looked at her with such arrogance. Struck mute, Heather could only watch helplessly as he drew her hand to his mouth and rubbed his lips across the center of her palm. To a curious bystander, it might appear to be a gentlemanly gesture. Heather knew better as she struggled to keep her knees from buckling. His mustache tickled her skin and ignited the very fire which he warned her about.

Nothing but a torrential downpour could extinguish it. Since the day she'd brushed crumbs away from that mustache, Heather had been intrigued by it. Having never kissed a man with a mustache, she couldn't help wondering just what it might feel like.

Up until now, Heather believed it was impossible for a person to forget how to breathe. Her involuntary shallow gasp was so evident of her bewilderment that it caused a smile of masculine awareness to spread beneath that intriguing mustache of his. It was almost as if Toby knew she was considering the effect of such kisses were they to be scattered at random all over her naked body.

Somewhere between the cold shivers and hot flashes that put her body into a state of utter confusion, a sultry Southern voice rang out.

"Why, Tobias Danforth, you rambling, contrary man. I was under the impression that you had fallen completely off the face of the planet."

Heather snatched her hand away and hid it behind her back like a child. A cloud of sweet perfume and taffeta stepped between them. A pretty thing, the woman had the distinct advantage of feeling completely at ease among the Danforth clan. She exuded the perkiness of a cheerleader. Heather bet she was the team captain.

Toby fell into the same antiquated pattern of speech used to address him. "Well, I declare. If it isn't Marcie Mae Webster, all grown up into a sophisticated femme fatale."

Marcie Mae's laughter tinkled like wind chimes. Heather envied her the ability to blush on cue. She imagined the woman would be just as at home in a hoop skirt as the designer original that she wore.

"I dare say I've changed a good deal since the days we used to go skinny-dipping down in the old sinkhole."

Unable to endure another sugar-cured syllable, Heather excused herself with the kind of euphemism a woman like Marcie Mae was sure to appreciate.

"I think I'll go powder my nose, if you don't mind."

Clearly Marcie Mae didn't mind at all. Her smile stretched her lips over a set of perfectly straight, white teeth. Taking Toby by the arm, she led him toward a group of old friends she claimed were just dying to see him again.

Heather tried not to smirk as Toby tossed her a helpless glance over his shoulder. That his apparent misery gave Heather a measure of satisfaction made her feel small.

The feeling was only intensified by stepping into a huge bathroom that reflected the sumptuousness of the rest of the hotel. Potted plants and cut flowers decorated sinks gleaming with gold-plated fixtures. The bathroom boasted high ceilings, a chandelier and several white wicker chairs positioned welcomingly around the room. Staring into one of the many gilded mirrors, Heather recognized the same panic-stricken expression she used to wear before becoming sick to her stomach before a performance.

Heather had never felt completely comfortable performing before a live audience. Few people could appreciate the cutthroat nature of her training. Even though it merely underscored the training she had received at home from her parents, such constant pressure had wounded her sensitive spirit so deeply that she had forsaken her musical gifts altogether.

Turning the cold-water spigot, she ducked down to splash her face.

Heather suddenly realized she wasn't alone in the bathroom. There were two women in a darkened corner of the room, and one of them was sobbing so brokenheartedly, it made her stomach cramp in empathy. Not inclined to meddle in other people's affairs, Heather intended to make a quick exit without getting involved. She would have made it, too, had not the other woman, obviously trying to comfort her companion, cast a desperate glance in her direction and mouthed a request for a tissue.

Heather took one from a hand-painted porcelain container and walked it over to them. The woman who took it looked to be about her same age. Wearing a beautiful white satin gown that accentuated a petite figure, she looked like a guardian angel. The woman shrugged her shoulders and gestured to the slightly open tall door.

"I stumbled upon the poor thing crying like this," the lady in white explained. She spoke with a slight European accent of some sort. "I didn't feel right leaving her alone in such a state. You wouldn't by any chance be an acquaintance of hers?"

Shaking her head, Heather edged toward the door. Just then the injured party raised her head from where it had been hidden behind her hands to reveal twin rivulets of mascara streaming down a face that was too young and pretty to be so angst-ridden. Not old enough to qualify as a woman or young enough to warrant still being called a girl, she was caught in that terrible in-between stage in which one fluctuates miserably between maturity and juvenile behavior. Heather guessed her to be the traditional age when Southern girls had coming-out parties.

The teen's voice quavered pathetically as she offered two convenient strangers an unnecessary explanation. "It might seem funny to you, but nothing I do is ever good enough to satisfy my father. Absolutely nothing."

"It doesn't sound funny at all," Heather assured her in a gentle, understanding tone. "In fact, I can relate to that all too well myself."

"As can I," added the lady in white.

Surprised to discover a common thread holding them together, the women studied each other. In addition to being approximately the same age, the two older women were of similar height and build. And behind their initial wariness was an inability to abandon someone in need.

Rather than watering down the girl's drawl, her tears had the exact opposite effect. Heather strained to understand the words that slipped out between sobs.

"Can you believe that my daddy actually expects me to throw myself at some old man in the other room in hopes of landing some big business contract? Have you ever heard of anything so vulgar?"

Heather wondered if by "old" she was referring to someone in his midtwenties.

"It absolutely makes me feel like a whore!"

The young lady's choice of words required yet another tissue to stem the flow of tears that started all over again. Feeling like she was caught in some Victorian time warp, Heather wondered what kind of father would deliberately use a child as a sexual pawn to advance his own ambitions. The answer came to her in a flashback of the day her own parents hustled her across a crowded room to introduce her to Josef Sengele, the master pianist famous for grooming young prodigies for stardom.

"I know how you feel."

It was not Heather's voice but that of the beautiful woman standing next to her. She made note of the flicker of pain that creased the perfect beauty of that face. Her voice held a sad ring of resignation. Eyes as brilliant as the emeralds on her ears softened as she put a hand upon the young lady's shoulder.

"Sometimes you just have to do what has to be done. No matter how unpalatable it might be, business is business and family is family. Come what may, you only have one father in this lifetime."

The teenager's sniffles stopped as she paused to consider the free advice.

"I thought I'd stay just long enough to appease Daddy without having to actually compromise myself."

Having attended innumerable stuffy functions on behalf of her parents, often as the featured attraction of the evening, Heather could certainly understand the desire to please someone whose respect could never be earned. She could not remain quiet on this point.

"Or..." Heather put a hand on the girl's other shoulder and finished her thought. "Rather than putting off the inevitable for years to come, years that wear away your sense of worth, you could take a stand right now and claim your life for yourself. Trust me. It's better to risk being disowned by your family than to disown yourself."

Though her words were intended for the girl sitting between them, the woman in white turned as pale as her gown. She seemed genuinely moved. And oddly wounded by her words.

"You'll have to make up your own mind," the woman in white told the teenage girl. "Whatever you decide, just don't torture yourself with doubts afterward."

Heather nodded in agreement. Why she felt such a strong affinity to these two strangers was a mystery. She knew only that a delicate cord connected them for this brief moment.

When the bathroom door opened unexpectedly, admitting a pair of elegantly attired matrons, it jolted them all into remembering that they were not sharing confidences in the privacy of a home.

Sighing, the girl admitted, "I'm tempted to just run away and avoid making any decision at all."

Heather's life had been comprised of snapshots of so many fleeting encounters that she longed for a continued friendship, if only for this one strained evening.

"I really want to know how the evening works out for you," Heather told the distraught teen. "Maybe we could decide on a time to meet and find a good spot to watch the fireworks later."

The girl gave her head an apologetic shake, and

the lady in white choked on a dry, painful laugh as she reached first for her silver handbag and then for the doorknob.

"I doubt anyone will be able to miss them," she said cryptically before disappearing into the waiting throng outside.

Heather wished she had thought to ask for her name.

Six

Surrounded by a bevy of single women doused in warring fragrances, Toby studied his son's nanny from a distance. His worries that the shy little thing might not fit in at such an ostentatious gathering were proving completely needless. Heather looked so cool and sexy in that stunning dress that one might be inclined to think she was born to rule over these kinds of parties. The kinds of parties that his ex-wife had lived for. And ultimately left him for.

Toby washed away the bile that rose in his throat with a second glass of champagne. It lacked the bite of good, old-fashioned whiskey. But he doubted that even Johnnie Walker would make the sight of

Heather laughing at something one of his old classmates murmured in her ear go down any smoother. Freddie Prowell was from old money, and though his childhood acquaintance had always been a bit of a prig, Toby had never felt any kind of hatred toward him before tonight. The sight of Freddie leading Heather onto the dance floor caused his shoulders to bunch beneath his suit jacket.

Where had she gotten that dress? Toby wondered. It certainly didn't look like something one would pick up off the rack for a special occasion. As Freddie's hand dropped to the small of her back, Toby's fingers tightened on the stem of his champagne flute. He imagined it would be as easy to snap the other man's neck as the glassware in his hands.

Did Heather know that a backless gown could be even more intriguing to the male population than a plunging neckline. Toby's imagination kicked into overdrive at the sight of all that creamy skin and the realization that she wasn't wearing a bra. For all her aloofness toward him over the past few days, Heather didn't appear to mind a stranger groping her in public. Not that it was any business of his. As a free woman, she was welcome to dance the night away with any number of drooling idiots lined up to ask for the pleasure of her company.

For that matter, Heather could damn well return to Wyoming wearing another man's engagement ring if that was what she wanted to do—just so long as she didn't leave him...er...he meant Dylan, high and dry without any advance notice.

Toby swore softly under his breath. He didn't bother waiting for the song to end before breaking free of the circle of women holding court around him. He simply left them to speculate on his rudeness and the certain direction his steps took him.

He tapped too firmly on Freddie's shoulder to be ignored. "Mind if I cut in?"

Considering that he managed to step between the two of them and wrap an arm around Heather's waist in one fluid motion, the question was purely rhetorical. As such, it required no answer but for Freddie to step aside. He did so reluctantly.

"My, but don't you look lovely tonight," Toby said, drawing Heather close and breathing her in. Her fragrance was a subtle mixture of daisies and the devil herself.

Batting her eyes at him, Heather donned an exaggerated drawl that mimicked Marcie Mae's. "I do declare, Mr. Danforth, such flattery could turn a girl's head completely around."

A smile played with the corners of Toby's mouth. Was it possible she was as bored with this party as he?

"Sarcasm doesn't become you," he remarked dryly, moving her toward the French doors lest anyone dare try cutting in on him like he had Freddie.

Heather turned the conversation to a safer subject

as the music switched to a slow, dreamy waltz. "The band is amazing."

Unable to take her eyes off the handsome man who held her, she wasn't quite sure when they left the ballroom floor and began dancing beneath a canopy of stars. It was less crowded in the courtyard and far quieter than inside. Beneath a night sky redolent with magnolia blossoms, a tender melody was carried on a breeze that did absolutely nothing to cool Heather off. She was on fire in Toby's arms. Overhead a meteor flashed across the sky reminding her of what happened to stars that burned too hot.

As tempting as it was to think they were alone, Heather knew that eyes would always be upon the likes of Tobias Danforth. Whether he cared for it or not, no matter how far he roamed from his childhood home, family ties cast him in the light of celebrity. His sister, Genie, had already warned her about the paparazzi. Heather had little desire to be featured in some scandalous rag bent on pumping up its subscription with innuendo and compromising photos. For all she knew, the full moon might as well have been a spotlight cast upon them.

Nevertheless, Heather turned her face up to Toby, and for a blissful moment allowed herself the luxury of floating away in the arms of a strong man. Toby defined his own life his own way, yet he was wise enough to preserve ties with a family that obviously loved him. She wished he would share his secret with her. Instead of asking outright how he managed such a complicated feat, she merely ventured an observation.

"You prefer marching to the beat of your own drum, don't you?"

Sensuous lips twitched beneath his mustache. "I know it's been a while, but I hate to think my dancing is so bad that I make you feel like you're in the infantry."

Heather shook her head. He was a marvelous dancer, moving with a grace that defied time spent in the saddle. Her body fit nicely against his like a pair of nestled spoons. There was no need to think about her own feet as he swung her to the periphery of the concrete pad and steered her onto the grass. She supposed his mother had forced him into dance lessons at an early age and imagined he had resisted mightily any attempts to mold a would-be cowboy into a proper gentleman.

"You know what I mean."

"One could say the same for you," he replied, searching her face in the moonlight for an explanation of how someone who moved so easily in high society would want a position as a nanny in the backwoods of Wyoming.

He had no doubt that a woman like Heather would soon grow tired of the simple ranch life that he so loved. His ex-wife claimed the isolation made her crazy. Once Sheila realized that she would never be able to cajole or badger him into resuming his rightful place in society, she couldn't renounce her wedding vows fast enough. One of the nasty rumors going around tonight's little soiree was that she was off in Rio with some European playboy and the two of them were spending Toby's generous alimony as if it were an endlessly renewable resource.

When the music stopped, he paused to consider a tendril of Heather's hair. Holding it between his thumb and fingertips, he studied each strand as if they were filaments of pure gold.

When the back of his hand brushed against Heather's cheek, the spark that had been teasing her imagination all night long burst into full flame. Although every instinct told her to pull away, to run away and not bother to look back, she remained rooted to her spot on the dewy grass. She fought to draw air into lungs that had forgotten how to breathe.

The fact that she and Toby were no longer moving did not lessen the feeling that the world was spinning out of control. A deft twist of Toby's wrist loosened the pin from her hair and sent it spilling around her shoulders in a shimmer of light that caught and held the moonlight. She might have protested against the injury done to her sophisticated hairstyle had it not been for a Roman candle exploding overhead, signaling the beginning of what was to prove a spectacular fireworks display.

"Look!" she exclaimed.

Toby didn't bother looking heavenward. His attention was fixed on the slender curve of an outstretched neck and shoulders so white they might have been carved from marble.

"I am looking," he told her.

Heather lowered her eyes to meet a smoky gaze, a smoldering source of heat that rivaled the rapid-fire explosions overhead. Having wondered what it would be like to be kissed by this man, she was overcome by panic when it became obvious Toby was about to put her imagination to rest.

This is crazy, she wanted to say. *You're my boss, and I'm your son's nanny. It isn't proper. And it most certainly isn't smart.*

Still, those warnings didn't keep her from leaning into him as he curled his hand around her neck and crushed her mouth beneath his. She would have fought against such unexpected roughness had it not made her so weak in the knees and left her desperately wanting more. His lips were firm, and she discovered that she very much liked the texture of his mustache against her tender skin. It did not tickle at all as she had read in foolish books she had hidden from her parents when she was a girl. But it did make her feel soft and feminine in contrast. And it left her wondering how that mustache would feel brushed against every inch of her body.

Resounding booms were coming more and more quickly as the fireworks display drew the crowd out of the lobby and into the courtyard. Appreciative ooohs and ahhhs filled Heather's head. Sparkles trailing across the sky were a poor imitation of the tingles racing up and down her spine. Great explosions of color mirrored the quick succession of emotions bursting inside her. She had been kissed before, but never had she tasted a man and been rendered insatiable by it. Wanting him to feel the same sense of powerlessness that she did, Heather held nothing back and responded wantonly.

The lady might look as cool as a Grecian statue, but trembling in his arms she was all heat and wondrously giving. Emotions that sparked off one another the very first time they met now caught on fire. Fanned by passion, they spread like wildfire as need raged through them both. Though supple in his arms, Toby discovered that Heather was not as fragile as she looked. Having tasted the forbidden fruit of his secret desire, Toby wanted nothing more than to tumble her into the shadows and make her his own. Such thoughts in such a civilized setting were utterly inappropriate. It was an obsession, Toby was sure, born of a prolonged period of self-imposed celibacy.

That didn't stop him from kissing her deeply and plundering the sweet depths of her mouth. Heather met the thrust of his tongue with her own inquisitive exploration. Toby's hands roamed freely over the warm, smooth skin of her exposed back. Moving his mouth to her neck, he thrilled to the beat of her pulse beneath his lips and the mewling sound caught deep in her throat.

"I want you," he confessed in a voice made raspy with need. "Right now."

There was no telling what Heather's response might have been had not a flashbulb gone off in her face. Her startled gasp was lost in the shouts of a crowd mesmerized by the effects of Abraham Danforth's elaborately planned fireworks display. Heather and Toby had been so engrossed in each other they hadn't noticed people were laying blankets down on the ground about them as others gathered on the veranda to sip mint juleps and admire the show.

Horrified to have a moment of weakness immortalized on film, Heather tore herself away from Toby with a sob. If it wasn't enough to be made a fool of by Josef and be forced to endure whispering behind her back in her home state, now she would be whispered about in Savannah, too. If she knew the paparazzi, her shame was certain to be on display in magazines by the morning. She could write the caption herself: Most Masochistic Woman in the World Falls in Love with the Wrong Man All Over Again.

Tabloids were sure to fly off the shelves at the little country store where Toby bought his groceries. By the time Dylan reached preschool, she supposed everyone would believe that his nanny was sleeping with his daddy. Angry at herself for succumbing to the charms of yet another man in control of her future, Heather turned and ran, less from the reporter who violated their privacy than from her mental admission that she was falling in love with Toby.

Blinded by tears, she didn't wait to witness Toby chase the unwelcome photographer down the sidewalk.

The Twin Oaks Hotel was virtually abandoned. Most, if not all, of the guests were watching the fireworks outside, and Abraham Danforth's political machine was gearing up to pass the proverbial hat around to solicit contributions to the cause. Heather had yet to meet the would-be senator, dubbed by the press as Honest Abe II. She doubted he would appreciate being upstaged in tomorrow's newspaper by a picture of her in a compromising position with his nephew.

She slipped around to a back entrance of the old hotel. The door stuck initially, but Heather had enough adrenaline surging through her blood to force it open. Making her way down a dimly lit hallway, she searched for some secluded spot where she could pull herself together and put that soul-shattering kiss behind her. If she failed to locate an unoccupied bathroom, she'd settle for simply finding the wing of the hotel that had been reserved for the children. Just thinking of Dylan's heartfelt hugs had a calming effect upon her.

One hallway led to another and before she knew it, Heather was completely lost. The place seemed to go on forever. With each step, the halls grew darker. Antique wall sconces that had been modernized with electrical wiring glowed with flickering lights intended to replicate candlelight. It was a touch too real for Heather, who was on the verge of turning around and retracing her steps when she caught a glimpse of someone at the far end of the corridor gesturing to her.

She looked remarkably like the mysterious lady whom Heather had spied under the big oak tree back at Crofthaven on the day of their arrival. As this was a formal affair, Heather could have easily mistaken a modern floor-length gown for the period clothing she thought she'd seen the woman wearing that day. In the shadowy light, it was easy to imagine quite a lot of things, including the draft of cold air that raised goose bumps up and down the length of her arms.

Nevertheless, Heather was drawn down that dark hallway.

"Wait!" she called out as the woman disappeared around yet another corner.

Hoping she was winding her way closer to the lobby, Heather gave chase. As she rounded the next corner, a scream died in her throat.

In front of her appeared a young woman with dark hair, very pale skin and eyes rimmed with pain. The shadowy figure seemed to float in the air. A golden locket at her throat glinted in the flickering light. Having never seen a ghost before, Heather nonetheless recognized this apparition for what it was.

Stumbling against the wall, she felt a drip of hot wax fall upon her shoulder from the wall sconce. She winced.

As tempted as she was to run screaming back down that hallway, both Heather's voice and feet failed her at once. Her heart pounded out of control as the specter stared through her with sorrowful black eyes. Without moving her lips, she relayed a message to Heather.

"Don't fail his little boy like I failed my charges...."

The voice resonating in Heather's head lacked the Southern tone which she expected.

"I don't understand," she whispered.

"Don't fail the boy," the woman repeated, blowing a frightening puff of breath directly in her face. "Or your own heart."

With that, she vanished altogether, leaving Heather to wonder if she hadn't imagined the whole ghastly encounter.

Seven

By the time Heather found her way back to the hotel lobby, she was questioning her own sanity. What other explanation could there be for a delusional encounter with the other side? Considering that she had been nursing a glass of ginger ale for most of the night, it certainly couldn't be attributed to alcohol. Heather supposed it went without saying that a hotel as steeped in history as Twin Oaks was bound to evoke eerie feelings in its guests, especially one overwrought by the prospect of falling in love with her employer.

That the same sad-faced woman would appear to Heather both at Crofthaven and Twin Oaks seemed further proof that her imagination was playing games with her. All that nonsense about not failing her charge and her heart was probably just her subconscious sorting through her conflicted emotions. Between overloaded hormones and better judgment.

The only other explanation was one that chilled Heather's blood and left her visibly shaking as she accepted her first glass of alcohol all evening from a bored-looking waiter. She tossed it back like a seasoned drunk and set the empty glass back on the fellow's tray in one fluid motion. Scanning the premises, she hoped the fireworks display was coming to an end, marking the official end of a long evening. She, for one, was ready to call it a night.

A deep masculine voice intruded on her thoughts. "Most everybody's still outside in case you were wondering."

Heather wheeled around and bumped into a solid wall of masculine chest. Craning her neck, she peered into the eyes of a tall, well-built stranger. That his brown eyes beheld her with amusement left her feeling both disadvantaged and tongue-tied. She hoped he wasn't expecting a response from her.

"It won't be long," he continued, "before Abraham Danforth makes his speech. After that, the party should begin to wind down, except for the diehards, who are certain to be here until the sun comes up."

Heather hoped nobody expected her to stick around that long. She was even willing to use Dylan as an excuse if it would get her out of here any sooner. Ever since they had arrived in Savannah, family members had been so eager to spend time with him, and he had been so preoccupied with his cousin Peter, that her services had scarcely been needed. Nonetheless, all Heather wanted to do right now was head back to Harold and Miranda's house and fall into bed. With any luck, the entire night would seem like a bad dream by morning.

Her voice was as shaky as the hands she hid behind her back. "Will you be among them?" she ventured to ask. "The diehards, that is?"

"Yes, ma'am," the man said in a strong, slow drawl. "I expect I will."

He didn't strike Heather as someone inclined to excessive partying. Yet he had just admitted that he would remain at the fund-raiser with the last of the diehards. She couldn't help but wonder why he was there. Alert as he was in scanning the premises without drawing attention to the fact, the man's emotions appeared as tightly coiled as her own. Feeling an odd sense of kinship with him, she offered him her hand along with her name.

"Michael Whittaker," he rejoined, growing suddenly solemn. "Good Lord, your hand is as cold as ice. Are you all right? You look like you've just seen a ghost."

"Funny you should put it that way…"

Heather's bones suddenly turned gelatinous. Michael reached out to grab her by the elbow. Concern illuminated his dark eyes as he led her to the nearest love seat and positioned himself next to her.

"What happened?"

Heather shook her head. "You'll think I'm crazy."

"I doubt that."

The hard look that accompanied those terse words provided Heather a strange sense of comfort. Still, she hesitated to relay the vision that congealed her blood and left her babbling to herself. Thinking back to that dark, haunted hallway, she took necessary precautions before baring her soul.

"You aren't by any chance a reporter, are you?"

The smile that broke across the man's distinctive features assured her that he found the very idea preposterous.

"A security specialist. Who better to trust?"

Indeed. What harm could there be in sharing a ghost story with a stranger at this late hour? What difference would it make even if he thought her mad? In a few short days, she would be a thousand miles away from here, well on her way to ridiculing herself for being frightened by a figment of her imagination.

Heather let her breath out slowly and took a chance on a stranger's seemingly benevolent curiosity.

"As a matter of fact, I think I did just see a ghost—if that's what you'd call it."

Seeing no sign of derision in Michael's manner, she continued haltingly.

"She was a young woman. Dark but not particularly menacing. And she was intent on delivering a message to me."

Michael leaned forward. "What message?"

Bolstered by the intensity of his interest, Heather described the strange clothing the woman was wearing and relayed her message word for word.

"I can't exactly say that I saw her speak those words, but I distinctly heard each one conveyed loudly and clearly in my mind. It's the second time I've seen her," she admitted. "First from a distance standing beneath a huge tree on the outskirts of Crofthaven, and right here at Twin Oaks not ten minutes ago."

"Miss Carlisle," he declared without hesitation.

It was Heather's turn to look startled.

"You know her?"

"Not exactly," Michael assured her with a crooked smile. "But the woman you described sounds exactly like the same mysterious lady who accosted me a few days ago asking me for directions to Crofthaven. I was several miles away from there at the time. After pointing her in the right direction, I thought I heard her mutter the single word *father* before she simply faded away."

Since Heather discerned neither malice nor ridicule in his words, she asked him to elaborate. The circumstances and settings of the appearances were sharply different, but the details regarding the specter herself were chillingly similar—right down to the gold locket worn on a chain about the ghost's long, white neck.

Giving her a reassuring hug, Michael apologized for having pressing business that he had to attend to.

"Are you sure you'll be all right?" he asked before he excused himself.

Heather gave him a wobbly smile. "I'll be just fine as soon as I get some fresh air to clear my head."

Toby was sorry Heather had run off before he'd been able to catch up with the reporter who made the mistake of interrupting the most romantic moment of his life. Undoubtedly she would have enjoyed seeing him grab the man by the strap around his neck and rip the film from his camera.

"Get lost, you disgusting little parasite," Toby told him before giving the fellow a kick in the pants for good measure as he slunk away into the shadows muttering about inquiring minds having "the right to know."

By the time Toby turned around to assure Heather that she need not worry about appearing in print any time soon, she was long gone, leaving him to search the crowd, all the while cursing the notoriety of the Danforth name.

He was unprepared for the surge of jealousy that exploded in his heart and flowed like molten lava through his veins at the sight of Heather enveloped in another man's arms. That Michael Whittaker looked nothing like wimpy Freddie Prowell did little to dampen the urge to ram a fist right through the other man's dark, handsome face. Toby had heard rumors that the man was ruthless, but he hadn't thought that reputation extended to the opposite sex. Years of hard physical labor outside a fancy gym would more than make up for the difference in their size. Toby might not be as big as his uncle's bodyguard, but he damn sure was a match for anybody when his testosterone kicked in.

He was just about to take his tuxedo jacket off and roll up his shirtsleeves when Michael Whittaker saved him the trouble by abruptly leaving. Heather wandered off in the opposite direction. Toby was familiar enough with Twin Oaks to know that a secluded terrace lay outside the very door through which she left. Perhaps it had been an innocent embrace explainable by any number of simple circumstances, he thought.

He curbed his impulse to make a scene. If Heather had been so distraught by the thought of their kiss gracing the pages of some sleazy tabloid, he imagined photographs of him involved in fisticuffs over her wouldn't set well with her, either. Nor with the rest of the Danforth clan for that matter.

Toby had no desire to ruin Uncle Abe's big night any more than he wanted to probe the intense feelings that his son's nanny evoked in him. Having openly professed to be done with women forever, he couldn't understand his own volatile reaction to seeing Heather with someone else, especially considering what a short time he had known her. Envy wasn't something that often came calling on Toby. His ex-wife bitterly claimed he didn't have a jealous bone in his body. Sheila's outrageous attempts to goad him into a green-eyed fit, intended to affirm her desirability more often than not, left her looking foolish in public and incensed in private.

Even now, news of Sheila's involvement with an international playboy only made him thankful that he and Dylan had escaped her exploits relatively unscathed. Unscathed, that is, if one didn't count his little boy losing his speech and his heart.

As desperately as Toby wanted to believe that it was merely gratitude he felt for Heather for helping his son, the kiss they shared beneath the fireworks shattered that illusion once and for all.

What had he done by initiating such a kiss?

Toby no more wanted a long-term relationship with a woman than he wanted to be tied to a life of leisure in Savannah. And yet the likelihood of being able to ignore his feelings for Heather once they returned to Wyoming was slim to none. Going back to a look-but-don't-touch relationship would tax all his powers of self-control. Hell, he'd nearly taken both Freddie and Michael's heads off this evening for just having the audacity to talk to Heather, dance with her and hold her momentarily in their arms. Considering that he prided himself on being levelheaded and generally unruffled, it didn't bode well for his willpower.

He and Heather definitely needed to talk. The relative privacy of the terrace where she had retreated was as good as any place to initiate a conversation that was bound to be awkward at best—a conversation that could well pry the lid off Pandora's box. Toby wavered.

"There you are!"

Marcie Mae's voice rang out over the growing din in the room. Grabbing him by the arm, she tugged him in the opposite direction of the terrace demanding nothing less from him than his undivided attention.

"Thank you," Toby said.

"For what?" she wanted to know.

"For saving me from myself," was his enigmatic reply.

For the duration of their conversation, Toby kept an eye turned toward the dark doorway where Heather presumably sat in silence alone.

Taking up residence in a dimly lit corner, Heather did her best to work the ghost-induced chill from her bones. She wished she had thought to bring a shawl, but considering the time of year and the humid climate of the location, she hadn't dreamed one might be necessary. The ornate bench on which she sat was as cold to the touch as her encounter with the ghostly apparition. Heather had read that pockets of chilly air often announced that an unearthly creature was present, but never had she imagined the lingering effects of such an icy encounter upon her own human body. She longed to slip into a tub of steaming water and wash the whole experience down the drain before snuggling under the beautiful antique comforter on the bed that awaited her back at Harold and Miranda's home.

"I'm sorry. I didn't mean to be rude, but you bear a striking resemblance to someone I used to know."

The unexpected comment startled Heather from her reverie. Assuming the remark was directed at her, she looked to find the guest of honor himself, Abraham Danforth, had wandered upon her solitude. He was easily recognizable from the publicity posters scattered throughout the gala.

But he was not talking to her.

"Would her name happen to be Lan Nguyen?" asked a distinctly feminine voice.

The woman who stepped out of the shadows was diminutive in stature, no taller than five feet four inches in heels. Her dark hair glistened in the moonlight. Heather knew who Abraham was, but the woman was a complete stranger to her. Neither of them seemed to know Heather was there.

"Yes. Yes, it was," the older man responded. "How did you know?"

"Because I'm her daughter, Lea. *Your* daughter,

Mr. Danforth. The child you abandoned in Vietnam.''

Heather gasped silently. She hadn't intended to eavesdrop, and she wished there was some way to leave without interrupting. As it was, she hoped she wouldn't be called upon to administer the Heimlich maneuver upon poor Abraham. For once, the silver-tongued orator was at a loss for words.

Heather looked furtively around. She wondered if any reporters were within earshot. Or if one was perhaps setting Abraham Danforth up? Out of the corner of her eye, she caught a glimpse of Michael Whittaker slipping onto the terrace from a hidden door. She hoped she hadn't misplaced her trust in the man. When he motioned for her to remain quiet, she gladly deferred to his silent request.

Since Abraham hadn't bothered to dispute the claim, Heather wondered if the exotic beauty might not be speaking the truth. All this talk about fathers and their estranged children stirred up feelings in Heather that she was working hard to put behind her. Guests appeared to be conspiring with ghosts, breathing fire into Heather's ever present sense of guilt. As bitter as her relationship with her father had grown over the past couple of years, Heather couldn't imagine the courage it would take to walk up to a perfect stranger and introduce herself as his daughter. James Burroughs might have played the absentee patriarch for years and been a stern taskmaster, but Heather could nonetheless take comfort in knowing of whose flesh and blood she was conceived. She imagined life for abandoned Amerasian children must be incredibly difficult. How justifiably angry this young woman must be if she believed her accusations to be true.

Heather wondered how Abraham would ever explain to his grown children that they had a half sister. Or to the press, for that matter. Could his political aspirations survive such a shocking revelation?

When Abraham spoke again, his voice sounded like it was being dragged through broken glass. "Lan...survived? She survived the attack on her village? I thought she was dead. I—"

Lea didn't let him finish. "My mother is dead now."

Despite the defiant tone of her voice, she swayed on her feet. Michael Whittaker stepped out of seemingly nowhere to catch her when she fainted. Heather heard him mumble something softly in her ear before Abraham Danforth regained his composure and took control of the situation.

"Take her home, Michael," he said, sounding sincerely concerned. "Stay with her until I contact you. Until we can sort this out."

Heather couldn't imagine when that would be. Michael had mentioned that he was a security consultant. She hadn't guessed that he was actually Abraham Danforth's personal bodyguard. There was only one thing she knew for certain as the man of the hour visibly struggled to tamp down his emotions. By the time he was ready to return to the fundraiser, he was composed again. The woman who introduced herself only as Lea was in good hands for the moment.

Before leaving, Heather gave Michael her tacit promise to keep what she had witnessed to herself, as he handed over the care of his client to the rest of his security team. She saw no reason to drop such a bombshell on Toby. He had plenty to deal with already and would likely be suspicious of such a disclosure as nothing more than unwarranted gossip. Abraham Danforth was a big boy, and Heather assumed he could handle his personal life without any interference from his nephew's hired help. It certainly wasn't her place to make such an announcement.

Besides, blabbing about the incident she had inadvertently witnessed would likely only prolong their stay in Savannah. As opulent as Savannah was, Heather longed for the solitude of the Double D— and the opportunity to explore her feelings for Toby far, far away from prying eyes, nosy reporters and well-meaning but intrusive relatives.

Eight

The scene Heather witnessed between Abraham Danforth and the woman claiming to be his illegitimate daughter strengthened her resolve to never let herself be used by a man again. Just as Josef had manipulated her for his own selfish purposes, Toby's uncle had apparently left at least one brokenhearted lover behind with nothing but an innocent baby to remind her of their time together. Heather was sure that the young woman's mother had suffered public and private humiliation while Abraham Danforth had gone merrily about the business of rebuilding his life and his empire.

Studying Dylan curled up in his daddy's lap as

their chauffeur drove them to the private local airfield where Abraham Danforth's personal jet awaited their return trip home, Heather realized that wasn't entirely fair. Some women didn't accept responsibility any better than some men. It sounded as if Toby's ex-wife fit into that category. Not knowing the details of their divorce, she thought it wise to refrain from making any judgments on the matter.

Still, looking at Dylan's sweet little face, she couldn't help but harden her heart toward a woman who for all intents and purposes abandoned her own child—and a family that despite their notoriety had been nothing but kind and accepting of Heather herself. She hadn't heard anyone utter a solitary negative comment about Dylan's mother. As much as Heather had wanted to categorize the Danforths as superior snobs, she genuinely liked Toby's family.

The day after the fund-raiser, Toby's brother Jacob, his parents, his sister Imogene and Dylan's young cousin Peter had said a heartfelt goodbye back at his parents' house.

"Why do ya hafta leave so soon?" Peter had demanded.

Resting a reassuring hand upon the boy's soft hair, Heather waited to hear Toby's response as well.

"Even though I grew up here and I love my family very much, home for me is under the wide open Wyoming sky. Some people march to the beat of a different drum, Peter, and I just happen to be one of them. With any luck, you'll grow into the same kind of freethinker. And when the time comes, I hope your father will have enough integrity to let you go wherever your heart leads you—just like my parents did.''

Heather couldn't imagine what it would be like to have the kind of unconditional support that Toby took as his due. If she had been able to choose her own parents, she likely would have picked Harold and Miranda Danforth. True to her word, Toby's mother had never once made her feel a servant in their home. In fact, Heather felt more at ease in their presence than she ever had in her own home.

She swallowed against the obstruction in her throat.

Heather supposed all families had their problems. Looking at Harold and Miranda, one would never guess that tragedy marred what appeared to be their perfect life. In a private moment, Toby's sister, who insisted that Heather call her Genie like the rest of her friends, explained how their youngest sister Victoria had been kidnapped several years ago. Despite years of cold leads and discouraging statistical evidence to the contrary, the family never gave up hope that Victoria Danforth would someday return home. Given those heartbreaking circumstances, Heather didn't know how Toby's parents were able to let him out of their sight.

Thousands of miles out of sight.

A bump in the road and a flash of black alpaca

tore Heather from her present-day contemplations to the sight of a woman keening beneath the big oak tree. Heather's heartbeat slammed into a wall as their gazes collided. Time and distance dissolved as those black eyes bore into her. There was no mistaking the same specter that accosted her in the dark hallways of Twin Oaks. Nor could Heather ever forget the chilling edict she issued from the grave.

"You found your way back," she mused, recalling her conversation with Michael Whittaker.

"I like to think that I always will," Toby rejoined.

Heather didn't bother explaining that her comment hadn't been intended for him. She pointed out the window and, with an urgency that caught him off guard, said, "Tell me what you see over there."

He sighed before responding.

"My past."

The mysterious figure was gone.

With Dylan peacefully dozing, it seemed as good a time as any to ask Toby what he knew about the family ghost. He looked surprised when she broached the subject but did not disregard her inquiry out of hand.

"Stories have circulated for years about the spirit of a young woman hired as a governess to Hiram Danforth's children shortly after he built his mansion in the 1890s. All that's really known about her is that her name was Miss Carlisle and she was tragically killed on her way to Crofthaven when the carriage overturned in the dark just before she arrived."

Toby paused to gauge Heather's reaction before continuing. He reached out to take both her hands in his and found them to be the temperature of ice.

"She's supposedly buried beneath that big oak tree over there."

The blood drained from Heather's face. She didn't need to check any archives to know he was telling her the truth. It settled in her bones with a chill. She felt a connection between herself and the governess. Miss Carlisle had deliberately sought her out to offer advice as one caregiver to another. Whether one called herself a governess or a nanny made no difference.

"She spoke to me," Heather said in a small voice.

Toby offered her the warmth of his embrace, and she accepted it as eagerly as one shivering from the cold would wrap herself in a blanket. She was only vaguely aware of the fact that they had left the grounds of the Crofthaven estate.

"Do you think she might be trying to take possession of my body?"

Feeling her tremble, Toby gave her a comforting smile. His siblings and cousins used to scare the willies out of him with tales of the mysterious Miss Carlisle, and he didn't want to make light of the question. Nor did he want her to worry needlessly.

"From everything I've ever heard or read, she's

a benevolent spirit who never travels too far from Crofthaven.''

''Thank you for not thinking I'm crazy,'' Heather whispered in his ear before settling her head against his broad shoulder.

The rest of the trip to the airfield was uneventful. Savannah invited one to settle back and enjoy the verdant views. Heather couldn't help but contrast the lush vegetation to the drought conditions the West was experiencing. Here seeds needed only to be deposited by a gentle wind to take root and thrive in fertile soil. Back home, farmers had to work hard to scratch out a living from earth alternately baked, then frozen by elements that drove off all but the hardiest—and most persistent—individualists. Heather's father looked down his nose at those earning a living by the sweat of their brow, claiming that farming in the state of Wyoming was fundamentally a ceremonial occupation.

Toby reached across the seat to take Heather's hand into his own, sending an all-too-familiar frisson vibrating through her body. The goose bumps Miss Carlisle raised along her arms a moment ago disappeared as warmth washed over her in an equally disconcerting fashion. Heather took a moment to study the hand that enveloped hers. Strong yet gentle and marked by manual labor, Toby's hands did not look like those of a gentleman rancher whom her father might possibly approve. James Burroughs could probably forgive her daughter's employer his rough hands and individualistic mindset in exchange for a taste of Danforth name recognition and social prominence.

As much as Heather wanted children someday, she was grateful that Josef had not left her with a baby to raise alone—like Abraham Danforth apparently had done to some poor woman half a world away. Heather would have had little choice but to remain dependent upon her parents' charity to make ends meet. And such charity on their behalf would undoubtedly come with shackles, rather than strings attached.

She looked up into a pair of eyes as blue as the sky that was to carry them home. Unspoken promise glittered in the depth of those eyes. Her breath caught in her throat. Was it possible that not all men were like Josef or her father?

"We should talk," Toby said.

Heather wondered how he had read her mind. His voice was a caress. It may as well have been her heart and not her hand that Toby squeezed so reassuringly. The very tenderness of his demeanor was her undoing. She hadn't slept the night of the fundraiser, wondering if he would ask her to resign her position. Now, remembering how she had responded so wantonly to his advances, she wondered if he might propose a more carnal relationship that had nothing to do with her job at all.

Heather reminded herself to proceed with caution. Experience taught her that one's personal dignity is a precious commodity. As such, it shouldn't be gambled away recklessly. The repercussions were often more insidious than one might first imagine.

She was curious to see how Toby's uncle Abraham was going to handle the scandal to which she was privy. As with the question of where her relationship with Toby was headed, she knew it was only a matter of time before things came to a head.

"Talk?" she repeated dully. "About what?" Her voice sounded scratchy. Raw.

"About us."

As much as Heather appreciated Toby's candor, she was surprisingly grateful to see the airfield come into view. It was an unusual way to cure her fear of flying.

"Couldn't it wait until we're on board and Dylan's asleep?"

"I suppose that would be wise," Toby conceded with a sigh.

Heather couldn't know that he was thinking back to all the discussions that Sheila postponed, always promising that things would get better without ever really hashing through the tough issues. She heard only the resignation in Toby's voice and assumed that the conversation he wanted to broach was not going to be pleasant. If it would make things easier on him, she could always quit.

Even if it meant giving up a job and a family she was coming to love.

Farewells in Heather's family were brief and dispassionate. The contrast between what she was used to and the tearful goodbyes Toby's relatives exchanged before they were allowed to board Abraham Danforth's private jet were startling. Ever vigilant about not intruding upon Toby and Dylan's private lives, Heather hastened to board in advance lest she be in anyone's way.

"Where do you think you're going?" Miranda asked.

The hurt in her voice stunned Heather.

"I thought I'd give you some space to yourself," she explained. Her own tone was conciliatory.

"I thought you understood that we consider you part of the family now." That said, Miranda took Heather by the elbow and guided her into the circle of Danforths.

Genie piped up with characteristic optimism. "I hope my brother has enough sense to make it official before your next visit to Savannah."

Presuming that "it" referred to a most unlikely wedding, Heather blushed so furiously that she would not have been surprised had her blond hair turned the color of strawberry wine. She did not miss the killing glance that Toby leveled at his sister. Shrugging it off with typical aplomb, Genie whispered something confidential in his ear.

"Don't hold your breath, little sister," Toby muttered.

The smile on Heather's face faded. Although she could only imagine what transpired between them, she assumed herself to be the butt of an unflattering remark. Miranda patted her on the arm.

"Don't mind them, dear. No matter how many times their mother has told them that it's impolite to whisper in front of others, they persist in misbehaving. You can imagine how I earned all this gray hair raising such headstrong children."

Heather could see little gray in Miranda Danforth's hair. She was truly a beautiful woman. Both inside and out. Indeed, her own mother made her feel more an outsider in her own home than Miranda had a guest—and a servant at that.

"I'm sorry," Genie said, looking truly apologetic. But then she took a deep breath and said in a rush, "I know it's way too early to start foisting anyone as ornery as Toby on someone as sweet as you, and he seems to think you have better taste than to ever hook up with someone as ill mannered as he is. But as someone just recently married to a man who not so long ago referred to marriage as the worm that hides the hook, I feel I'm in a unique position to point out what a mistake my thickheaded brother would be making if he let you get away."

"Genie!"

Howard Danforth seemed to be the only one able to control his daughter, with nothing more than a firm parental look. Though she ceased her teasing immediately, her eyes still twinkled mischievously. Heather wasn't sure how to react to earning the Danforth Family Seal of Approval.

Again Howard stepped forward to intervene. "We are very grateful to you," he said, looking at Heather directly and making her wish that her own father approved of her half as much as this veritable stranger. "What you are doing for Dylan—as well as for my son—is beyond price. We will be forever in your debt. Please come back and visit us again soon."

Surprised how much the invitation meant to her, Heather was at a loss for words. Then a little voice said, "Bye-bye."

The Danforths all gasped and looked at Dylan, who'd wrapped his arms around his father's neck.

"What did you say?" Toby said, stunned.

Dylan responded with a giggle.

"He said 'bye-bye,'" Peter repeated, shaking his head in disbelief that all the adults gathered about had simultaneously gone deaf.

Since Peter appeared to be the only one not taken aback by Dylan's words, Heather wondered if it was possible that the two boys had been conversing behind their backs for the past few days. Intermittent tears of joy and laughter surrounded the little imp's accomplishment. Though Toby claimed it was all Heather's doing, she was more inclined to think a combination of solid parenting and the unconditional support of an extended family was what prompted the child to speak up. That and an apparent eagerness to put his relatives' mushy goodbyes behind him.

"I told you he'd talk when he was ready. And without having to be bribed with cookies, either," Heather told Toby a tad too smugly a short while later as she cinched the seat belt around her.

She prepared for takeoff by staring straight ahead and doing her best not to hyperventilate. Dylan was still enthusiastically waving out the window to his family as their plane began to taxi down the runway.

"Give me your hand," Toby commanded, peeling Heather's fingers off the armrest.

His touch was at once both reassuring and unsettling. She found that she already missed Toby's family. That she liked them was really no surprise. They were as charming and gregarious a clan as anyone could ever hope to meet. What really surprised Heather was that they seemed to genuinely like her back. So naturally shy that she was often mistaken as being aloof, Heather was touched that Genie would actually broach the subject of marriage to her brother.

Given the baggage that both she and Toby carried from past relationships, the odds were not good that either one would be making a commitment any time soon.

Yet the calluses on the hand that held Heather's comforted her during takeoff. Her own hands, once unused to traveling over nothing rougher than ivory keys, would have to adapt to soapy water and pulling weeds in rocky flowerbeds and kneading homemade bread. Such working hands longed for the touch of a good man at the end of a day's work.

"It's going to be all right."

She knew Toby was referring to many things—Dylan's speech, the flight to Wyoming and the fact that his family's teary goodbye had affected him. Tears had been shed the last time Heather had spoken to her own parents, but they were the hot, angry tears of deep disappointment.

"If you renounce your music, you can renounce your name as well. And any monetary help from us, too," James Burroughs shouted. *"You will be as good as dead to me."*

Recalling how her father predicted she would either come crawling back, ready to live her life on his terms, or wind up as trailer trash with a half-dozen rug rats to support on a waitress's income, Heather wished there was some way she could adopt Toby's parents. The thought prompted her to ask, "Why would anyone leave such a family?"

"It's not like I'm disowning them," Toby protested. "I'm just following my own dream. They respect that and wish me well."

He sounded so defensive that it made Heather wonder if he practiced that particular speech for the benefit of other family members or to convince himself. She wished she could somehow convey how lucky he was to have such a supportive family.

"I'm glad," she told him. "Not all parents are as understanding as yours. It would break my heart to see either you or Dylan estranged from such good people."

Toby gave her a long and searching look in response. He started to say something but seemed to think the better of it. Instead, he drew her attention to the fact that the plane had reached cruising altitude and suggested that she could relax now.

Heather was surprised that their conversation had so completely distracted her. Still, she was glad that Toby didn't let go of her hand as her fear abated. Looking out the window at the clouds, she pondered the fact that life in the South seemed to proceed at a more leisurely pace than what she was used to. The weather didn't necessitate that residents scurry from place to place in an attempt to escape the elements. That Toby deliberately chose to abandon the life of ease into which he'd been born mirrored Heather's own inclination to take a road less traveled. As beautiful as she found Georgia, the harsh climate of Wyoming suited her better. The weather there reflected her tendency to run alternately hot and cold on issues of the heart. Both extremes were potentially dangerous.

Only time would tell whether fire or ice would dominate.

Nine

Away from the glamour of Savannah and his family's resolve to marry him off, Toby Danforth was convinced he would be better able to resist Heather's allure. After all, few social events in Wyoming would require anything as glitzy as the dress she wore for his uncle's fund-raiser. Not that he would ever be able to get the vision of her in that slinky gown out of his head.

Or the memory of her lips upon his.

Toby was counting on the physical demands and grueling routine of ranch work to settle his libido so that he could do what was in the best interest of his son—and his pretty nanny. Namely, to leave her the hell alone. The last thing Heather needed interfering with Dylan's progress was him ogling her every time she turned around. The last thing Toby needed was for Heather to pack her bags in indignation and leave him in the lurch.

Deciding that his best course of action was to simply forget the impulsive kiss they shared beneath a shower of fireworks, he did not follow up on the conversation he'd initiated on the way to the airport. It was time for Toby to reestablish a professional working relationship with Heather and put aside any romantic notions once and for all.

The only trouble with that plan was that it might be easier to wipe the faces off Mount Rushmore than to erase the memory of their kiss. Despite his best efforts, Toby doubted whether things would ever be the same between them again.

Relieved that Toby hadn't decided to fire her, Heather did her best to cooperate with his unspoken plan. Back at the Double D, she went out of her way to avoid him as much as she could without being rude. First thing in the morning she fixed breakfast, which he wolfed down, and did not lay eyes on him again until the sun went down. Then he hurriedly ate the warmed-up leftovers from the dinner that she and Dylan had eaten at an earlier hour. Dylan hadn't spoken another word since his breakthrough at the airfield, but he made his feelings known by casting wounded glances in his daddy's direction whenever he stumbled in looking like he was single-handedly attempting to run a ten-thousand-acre ranch without the benefit of any of the hired hands on his payroll.

Secretly offended that Toby would go to such lengths to steer clear of her, Heather poured her energies into taking care of Dylan. Despite his continued reticence to speak, the boy was delightful to be around. His affinity for music matched Heather's own at his age and gave them a common bond on which to base a genuine friendship. Although his father's absence around the house left a void in Dylan's life that no nanny could fill, Heather used the time alone well. She worked with him on expressing himself the best way he knew how—through his music.

Watching his progress was gratifying. Reclusive by nature, Heather lost herself in the vast beauty of the Double D and in the sticky hands of a boy who she feared was coming to love her as a mother. She knew it was a slippery slope that she was treading but didn't know what to do about it. Heather could no more withhold her affection for the child than she could change the way her pulse skipped a beat whenever Toby was near. Just because they hadn't spoken about their feelings didn't make it any easier to deal with them.

In fact, it had the exact opposite effect.

Heather's determination to put her passion aside was becoming harder with each passing day. Having turned her back on her music and not having any close friends nearby, she didn't know how to deal with her complicated feelings. The joy Dylan derived from the melodies he produced on the keyboard took her back to a simpler time when she was able to express herself through her music. Unable to convey her own emotions, she did everything in her power to encourage Dylan to find his voice in his own way.

When she and Toby spoke, more often than not it was to argue over an adherence to the speech therapist's stringent behavior-modification plan to make Dylan talk. Heather had only met the woman once, but that was enough for her to know she didn't like her much. In her opinion, Miss Rillouso spent more of her time casting bedroom eyes in Toby's direction than in actually working with Dylan. As far as Heather could tell, the most the therapist had been able to coax from Dylan with her overly detailed plans was a grunt or two, and that was on the promise of some sugary treat to follow.

"If you earn at least twenty stickers on the chart I'm leaving with your baby-sitter, I'll bring you something special the next time I come back," Miss Rillouso promised Dylan.

Dylan couldn't have looked less bored with that proposition. Heather didn't take umbrage with the belittling term Miss Rillouso used to put her in her place. She merely tossed the chart in the garbage the minute she left the premises. Toby was furious to discover her treachery.

"If you're so sold on her stupid technique, you

do it,'' she challenged, handing him the sheet of stickers that went with the chart that Toby retrieved from the trash. "I refuse to waste my time bribing Dylan when it goes against everything I believe about raising healthy, well-adjusted children."

When Toby politely pointed out that he was paying her to do whatever he asked in regard to his son's treatment, Heather issued a dire warning of her own.

"If you're not careful, you'll create a monster out of that sweet little boy. A monster who won't take the trash out for anything less than a dollar or won't make good grades unless there's a reward attached to his report card."

Toby bristled. He'd seen too many children completely hooked on external incentives to disregard her counsel out of hand.

"Helen Rillouso is a professional who came highly recommended," he protested. If nothing else, the outrageous amount he paid her to drop by the ranch every other week to work with Dylan attested to that reputation.

"I beg you to let him find his own voice in his own way," Heather countered.

Toby couldn't argue that her gentle approach seemed far more effective with his son than anything he'd tried in the past. Dylan seemed happier with each passing day. Still, Toby was a man who could afford to couch his bets. Even though Dylan was making progress under Heather's tutelage, he saw no reason to discontinue the program that Helen Rillouso had so painstakingly set up.

"All I'm asking for is a little support," he countered. "If you can't get behind the program yourself, at least promise me you won't deliberately sabotage the groundwork that's already been laid."

Heather thought long and hard before nodding her head.

"Out of respect for you, I'll do my best not to undermine your authority. I just want you to know that I think forcing the issue of Dylan's talking is as bad as forcing a relationship before someone is ready for it."

Toby gave her a searching look. He supposed that was her subtle way of telling him to back off. Short of sleeping outside with the grizzly bears, he didn't know how he could give her any more distance without compromising his relationship with Dylan. He sorely missed spending time with his son in his attempt to avoid Heather. In all the time he'd been married to Sheila, he'd never had such difficulty controlling his thoughts or his sex drive.

Maybe that was because she pursued him so shamelessly, lying about being on birth control so that she could get pregnant and force him into a marriage that he wasn't sure he wanted in the first place.

Heather was not like that. Though she had only vaguely alluded to it, her natural introversion had obviously been intensified by a negative experience with the opposite sex. If anything were to come of the attraction between them, Toby would have to be the one to initiate it. A man used to having women fall all over themselves to gain his attention, he found Heather a challenge he couldn't resist.

The fact that he was feeling more and more inclined to make the first move had little to do with his gratitude for the fine job she was doing. Instead, it had everything to do with the realization that against his better judgment, he was falling in love with her.

Heather would have to be blind not to notice the scorching looks Toby gave her whenever he thought she wasn't watching. Those looks alone made her blood run hot, her muscles clench and her pulse skitter out of control. Such confusing messages caused her to stumble all over herself whenever Toby entered a room. That the man was a perfect gentleman, always offering to help in any way he could, didn't make her job any easier. In fact, Heather had never worked so hard in her whole life—to pretend her boss wasn't getting under her skin during the day and into her subconscious at night.

Falling into bed at the end of the day, Heather was exhausted from rebuilding the crumbling wall that defined their relationship into employer and employee. No matter how high or sturdy she constructed that barrier during the day, by nightfall it lay in pieces at her feet.

Heaven knew she was no saint. After her disastrous fling with Josef, she had given up even considering herself a "good girl." It was no aversion to sex that kept her from following up on the powerful chemistry pulling her ever closer to Toby. It was fear, pure and simple.

She worried that going to bed with Toby would destroy their relationship altogether. Her experience with Josef had certainly proved that. Heather had little desire to be used and discarded again—especially since she so desperately needed this job. She needed the position not only to provide a sense of security but also a sense of self-worth. If she were totally honest with herself, she knew there was more to it than that. She had come to value her friendship with the man who had hired her to look after his son's physical and emotional well-being. Aside from the fact that the lingering memory of Toby's lips upon hers was a constant reminder to Heather that she was in fact a desirable woman, every day he was proving himself a funny, kind and surprisingly insightful friend. When she drew away, he did not push himself upon her like Josef had, either emotionally or physically. Instead Toby stepped back and gave her room to make up her own mind on any given matter without outside pressure. This all but ensured that she move closer to him on her own volition.

Tired as Heather was at the end of every day, sleep eluded her. When she finally did manage to drift off, more often than not her dreams were haunted by Miss Carlise. In the dreams, Heather was Miss Carlisle wearing a dress of black alpaca, and she would finger the golden locket around her throat. Inside was a picture of a man she did not recognize. Instinctively, she understood that this man occupied a special place in the governess's heart. A heart that demanded that truths be revealed in the lives of this man's descendants, generations cursed by the sins of a father.

That night, Heather's dream changed. Horse hooves beat an eerie cadence upon the black drum of night. It drowned out the sound of her own fists pounding upon the carriage door and her pleas for the driver to slow down. Somehow she knew that a dangerous curve lay ahead. A curve destined to end her life over and over again for eternity—unless the past could somehow be rectified by the present.

By an unsuspecting and perhaps even sacrificial soul.

A blur of images and the echo of her own screams woke Heather. She sat up, bathed in sweat. Disoriented, she looked about in confusion to discover herself safe and sound in a bed torn apart by her own thrashing. That a cry for help was still reverberating in her ears caused her to doubt her own sanity. It took her a moment to realize the sound was not in her head but rather emanating from Dylan's room. Fear grabbed her heart with stone-cold hands.

Springing from bed, Heather rushed to the boy's

bedside. The poor thing was in the grips of a nightmare that appeared to rival her own. Dylan woke with a start to see her silhouetted in his darkened doorway. He called out in terror.

"Mommy!"

Heather was at his side in an instant, holding him against her and soothing him with calming words.

"It's all right, Dylan. I'm here. I'm here."

Punctuated with sobs, a voice rusty from lack of use implored, "Don't leave me."

Those words ripped Heather's chest. Dylan wrapped his arms about her neck, clinging to her with a desperation that belied his tender years.

"I won't, honey. I promise I'm not going anywhere."

"Don't say that unless you really mean it."

The voice that issued that directive came not from the darling boy in her arms but from someplace behind Heather. Sitting on the edge of the bed, she swung her head around to see Toby standing in the very spot in the doorway that she had just vacated. Wearing nothing but a pair of simple white briefs, he was a vision of sculpted perfection. Heather had spent hours imagining his body's contours, but her imagination had been sorely lacking. Such a body deserved to be carved out of marble and immortalized for posterity.

Laden with genuine concern, Toby's voice was a caress in the night.

It was Heather's ruination.

Her own voice was surprisingly steady in response.

"I do mean it."

Ten

In a simple white nightgown, Heather looked like an angel at his son's bedside. Moonlight streaming through the window outlined the curves of Heather's body, revealing the shape and size of a perfect pair of breasts. The dark areolas of her nipples blushed deep pink beneath the thin cotton material. Toby grew hard with wanting her. He had never seen a sexier piece of lingerie than the modest nightclothes Heather wore. Nor a more desirable woman than the one whose eyes widened when she felt his eyes upon her. The enchanted melody she was singing, to help

Dylan find his way back to peaceful dreams, died on her lips.

"There, there," Toby crooned, stepping into the room to offer a frightened child the solace of his presence. "It's all right. Daddy's here. You just had another bad dream, that's all."

As this was Dylan's first nightmare since Heather moved in, Toby was greatly disturbed. Despite his best efforts to be all things to the boy, Dylan obviously still missed his mother. Dylan opened his eyes, reluctantly let go of Heather's neck and allowed his daddy to coax him back under his covers. Toby's hand grazed Heather's as he smoothed back a lock of hair plastered by fear to his son's forehead.

Together they comforted the child with gentle words and touches. The lullaby that Heather continued to hum soothed the child. Toby's nerves were pulled taut by parental worry—and a growing awareness of Heather's effect on his son. He couldn't help but feel jealous of the position that his son took nestled in her lap.

Under such tender ministrations, Dylan fell easily back to sleep. Heather tugged the sheet under his chin as Toby tiptoed over to the door. He held it open for her and, when she took her leave, closed it with soft finality before bending to scoop her up into his arms.

Heather put up no protest as Toby turned in the direction of his bedroom. Nothing had ever felt more right in her whole life.

Lacing her fingers around his neck, Heather held on tight. His flesh was warm to the touch. She buried her head into the crook of his shoulder.

The scent of Toby's shower gel mingled with the clean smell of linen from the bed he'd just left and the faint but heady aroma of his own body's musk. Intrigued, she kissed the strong column of his neck and licked the trace of salt left upon her lips. A feral growl rumbled from somewhere deep in his throat. The sound caused Heather to tremble as they crossed the threshold of his bedroom where he proceeded to lay her upon the very bed that she made for him every day. The covers were in a state of disarray from being thrown back in haste, but they were still warm from the heat of his body.

Heather spread her hair upon the same pillow that she secretly pressed against her heart before smoothing it out each morning. It smelled just as she remembered—like essence of man untamed.

Toby turned on a lamp situated in a far corner and flooded the room with soft light before coming to the foot of his bed where he gazed upon Heather with unabashed lust. She squirmed beneath his scrutiny and prayed he did not find her lacking.

"Do you have any idea how incredibly beautiful you are?"

Eyelashes, self-consciously lowered, fluttered open in surprise. Having learned early on that her talent was her greatest strength, Heather had seldom paid attention to her physical appearance beyond what was necessary in making a pleasing stage presence. Toby's voice was too raw with emotion and she believed that his words were not mere flattery. Nothing could disguise his hunger for her.

She watched in rapt fascination as he peeled off his briefs and dropped them upon the floor. Her breath caught in her throat as he proceeded to remove a small silver wrapper from the top drawer of his bureau and sheathe an erection that was well defined and beautiful in the dim light. Glad he had the wherewithal to think of protection when her own mind had turned to mush, Heather bit her lip. She hoped her relative inexperience did not disappoint him. Toby lowered himself over her, taking painstaking care not to crush her in the process. His tenderness caused tears to spring to her eyes.

"Why are you crying?"

Because I'm not sure I'm ready for this. Because I'm afraid I won't be able to please you. And that you'll think less of me for surrendering my body to you and that you'll toss me aside the instant you get what you want.

"I'm not," Heather lied. She removed the moisture from her eyes with a quick wipe of her sleeve.

Toby's eyes caressed her. "I'm not in the habit of forcing myself on women who are crying in my bed—regardless of whether they are naked or not."

How he managed the proper combination of sincere concern and gentle humor under such circumstances was a wonder to Heather. She smiled at the absurdity of his words through a blur of tears before leaning up to kiss him soundly.

The sweetness and passion of that kiss dissolved all apprehension as the world ceased to exist beyond the sensation of skin against skin. For all her shyness outside the bedroom, Heather was an uninhibited lover. She took delight in teasing Toby unmercifully. She ran the tip of her tongue along the fringe of his mustache, and when Toby opened his mouth hungrily to gobble her up, she proceeded to trace its outline with bold strokes.

His tongue sought hers in an unchoreographed ballet of give-and-take that left him breathing hard. Toby touched the blond hair spread out on his pillow like a golden fan as if to reassure himself that he was not dreaming. Propped over her with his weight upon his elbows, he stared down upon an angelic face incapable of holding back her feelings. Heather didn't have to speak words of love to him. He could read them in her expression.

Fully aware that Heather was not the kind of woman who fell into a man's bed unless she loved him, he did not want to break her heart. Wanting and loving were not altogether the same thing in his mind, and Toby knew that Heather deserved better than someone unable to commit to her completely. He didn't think he was emotionally prepared to make any promises beyond the fleeting pleasures and demands of the flesh.

Yet Toby could no more turn away from what

Heather was so freely offering than he could forgo breathing. Never had he wanted a woman so badly in his life. No matter how hard he worked his body each day, his every thought was consumed with having her. Sleep provided no respite from dreams that twisted him in clammy sheets, woke him abruptly and left him frustrated. Lust might very well damn him to hell forever and a day, but Toby did not have the strength to resist his own weakness.

Work-roughened fingers had no patience with the dainty, faux pearl buttons running the length of Heather's demure nightgown. Grabbing both sides of a scooped collar, he gave a little tug. Buttons scattered in all directions. Heather's gasp failed to cover the faint sound they made hitting the bedcovers, the floor and the nearby wall. Hoping he hadn't scared her, Toby made a feeble apology for his lack of restraint.

She responded with a kiss and guided his hands to the hole in the fabric that he'd made.

"Don't stop," she implored, offering him the comfort of a body straining to please.

Toby needed no more encouragement than that. Since the first day this woman stepped inside his house and pointed her stubborn chin in his direction, he wondered what it would be like to have her beneath him. Since kissing her beneath a shower of fireworks in a sultry Savannah sky, he couldn't stop dreaming of what it would be like to be inside her.

He struggled for breath as she tested his manhood,

gently squeezing it in her hands. Heather gasped again. Pushed to the limits of human willpower, Toby could wait no longer.

Despite his heartfelt intention to be gentle, Toby felt himself lose control.

Heather couldn't tell whether the indistinguishable words upon his lips were an oath or a prayer as he plunged into her. She heard herself mimicking his language with soft, guttural sounds of her own—sounds that sprung from some dark, secret place inside her. There was no thought in their lovemaking, save a driving need to hold nothing back, as the passion that had been building inside both of them burst like a dam under unsustainable pressure. Raging, swollen waters swept them both away in a terrifying and oh-so-glorious ride.

Surrounding herself with him, Heather offered Toby not just her warm and willing flesh, but also feelings as real and enduring as the silver-rimmed mountains casting shadows through the open blinds. This acknowledgement came as a revelation. She dug her fingernails into the flesh of Toby's broad shoulders and discovered there was no way to keep from falling in love with the man who shuddered as he poured himself inside her with a moan that made her feel both small and powerful at the same time.

Heather squeezed her eyes shut and clung to the dream that he might someday love her back. That he continued to hold her and engage in tender afterplay was a new and wonderful experience. Still, she knew better than to proclaim her feelings in bed. Such declarations tended to be brushed aside in the harsh light of day.

Josef had been the kind of man to tell a woman he loved her, even if he didn't, just to advance his own needs. Heather suspected Toby might have trouble saying those words even if they came from the bottom of his heart. Between the two, she far preferred the latter. Coaxing sweet words from a man meant nothing if he said them only in an attempt to pacify a petulant lover or soothe his own conscience. Wrapping her arms around shoulders slick with sweat, she reveled in the comfort of a body made hard by honest labor. Spent, he was hers alone until the morning light climbed the peaks of the nearby mountains, and brought not only a new day but also a new chance at rebuilding her life.

Eleven

Dawn light spilled across the mangled sheets of Toby's bed, bidding him to open his eyes slowly and count his blessings as he did every morning. The woman curled against his body in a kittenish ball was first among those blessings today. Staring at his sleeping beauty, Toby had to wonder if he wasn't still dreaming. His body's involuntary response to her silky skin against his convinced him otherwise.

That he could awaken in such a thoroughly aroused state after a night of the most intense and satiating lovemaking of his life was as wondrous as the realization that Heather wanted him as much he wanted her. That she didn't seem inclined to demand more than he was capable of giving at the present added to the fact that she was already more than a mother to his son, and made their relationship as perfect as any he could imagine. He kissed her awake with the aching tenderness he had been incapable of giving her last night.

"Next time I promise to go slow," he whispered in her ear.

Stretching a body sore from a night of glorious lovemaking, Heather smiled up at him in a way that made his heart somersault inside his chest.

"I didn't find anything lacking in last night's performance, cowboy."

A sweet melody all on its own, her voice rivaled the meadowlarks and robins that were noisily competing for top billing outside. Never had a day seemed riper with opportunity. Had Toby not a ranch to run and a son to tend to, he would have been more than tempted to spend it in bed, leisurely showing Heather the many ways a truly dedicated man such as himself could please her. As it was, all that would have to wait until the sun set once again.

"We'd better get up and dressed before Dylan wakes up and stumbles on the two of us in bed," Heather said, stretching languidly and wondering when she would get around to explaining it to herself. "I don't think I'm up for that just yet."

"I suppose it could be traumatic," he murmured,

resisting the urge to tempt fate. "I'd hate to set his progress back any."

Though Heather nodded in understanding, her heart, which only a moment before was as light and spirited as a sparrow, fell like a stone to the ground. Reverting to her shy old self, she was out of bed in a trice. She grabbed her torn nightgown from the floor and pulled it around her, balling it in the fist of one hand. She may have been the one to initiate this particular topic of conversation, but it nonetheless hurt to think that her love could be considered disturbing at any level.

Was sex merely a prelude for all men to discard the women they conquered? The memory of Josef casting her aside for a new, improved and potentially more lucrative model came rushing back to haunt her. Determined to spill her tears in the privacy of her own room, Heather held her chin up high as she moved toward the door.

Toby reached out for her, pulling her onto his lap. "Not so fast," he said, pausing to nuzzle the back of her neck. "I said I intend to go slow with you, and I mean it. But that doesn't mean you need to rush out of here without giving me a kiss."

Heather worried that going slow only meant postponing the inevitable—a breakup that would cost her not only her job but also the last shreds of her dignity. God help her, she didn't think she could endure that.

Not when she was so completely in love with him.

There was no use in denying that fact any longer. Having already given Toby her heart, the only thing she knew for certain was that she would rather settle for a torrid affair with him than nothing at all. If it proved short-lived, as she suspected, she would cling to her memories to her dying day. The beautiful pictures in her head of their time together would always be her own to cherish and carry with her.

No one could take those from her.

In the time it took to turn around, Heather's jumbled thoughts sorted themselves out with the kind of clarity that eluded most people every step along life's predictable path. The kiss she gave Toby was sweet and full of promise.

It held no taste of the remorse clogging her throat.

There is a part of every woman that believes she can win a man's heart by completely satisfying his body. Heather was no exception to the rule. She opened her nightgown and let it fall to the floor in a puddle about her bare feet. Then she proceeded to push Toby back on the bed and straddle him. If they were to have only a short time together, she intended to leave a lasting impression upon him. One that would render him unfit for any other woman ever again.

Heather played him like a masterpiece. Lovingly. Her fingers ran over his most sensitive spots, evoking music from a place so deep inside, Toby was swept away with the profundity of it. His eyes widened to see this gentle, modest woman turn into a wild vixen.

His promise to go slow would have to wait to be fulfilled yet another time. Toby gave her all that she asked for and then some. His shaft was as demanding as the soft flesh that welcomed him home. He heard himself call out her name, filled his hands with breasts as soft as satin and suckled her until she came, again and again. Repeating his own name breathlessly over and over, Heather reveled in the glorious spasms rocking her body.

"I'm going to explode," Toby murmured through gritted teeth, as if regretting the fact that he could wait no longer to satisfy his own pleasure.

The crescendo carried him toward that explosion. Panting, he quivered in her arms, staring into a pair of eyes that mirrored his climax and accepted the warmth spilling into her with palpable satisfaction.

Holding her in his arms long afterward, the thrumming in his blood reminded Toby that he was a physical creature with needs, and that living life solely for one's children was always a mistake. Every man was entitled to seek happiness on his own terms. He believed that he, too, deserved to love and be loved for himself alone.

Love?

The word popped into his head, startling him. Could it be that Heather was looking for more than a physical relationship with him? Was it possible she wanted him without regard to what his name could do for her? That she might actually accept his dreams as her own? His arms tightened around her in the certain knowledge that one would have to be a fool to let such a woman go without a fight.

The days that followed were the happiest that Heather had ever known. Starting and ending her days in the arms of the man she loved was as close to heaven as she could imagine. In between, the time flew. She hummed while she worked and took enormous pleasure in the bouquets of wildflowers that Toby brought her every day. Dylan picked up on their happy mood and, though he still refused to speak, he smiled more readily, and the simple tunes he composed mirrored the joyfulness infusing a house that had only a month ago been filled with the sorrowful echoes of the past.

In helping Dylan express himself through his musical gifts, Heather was drawn back to the piano, as she had been when she was but a child herself. Now, however, rather than seeing the instrument as something that had once enslaved her, she began to rediscover her own love of music through the eyes and ears of a sensitive boy. Watching his little fingers move over the ivories, Heather came to understand that like love itself, when given of its own accord and accepted without strings, the talent they shared was truly a sacred gift.

Dylan smiled up at her instinctively. He nestled next to her on the piano bench and let the waves of that sweet melody wash over them and carry them both far away from troubles brewing in the distance.

Wiping his dirty hands on his work-worn jeans, Toby stood in the doorway of his house and admired the view in silent reverence. The curve of Heather's slender, white neck bent over the keyboard was enough to bring him to his knees. The softening light of the afternoon sun filtered into the room, casting a halo over her fair hair. The sight of his son snuggled up next to this miracle worker was something he wished he had the talent to capture on canvas for posterity.

Unfortunately, Toby was no artist. Nor did he share his son's musical gift. In fact, he once joked that he couldn't carry a tune in a 747 jet. His artistry and passion were reserved for the way he handled horses, a gift he had apparently been born with. He considered himself lucky to have parents who nurtured what others regarded as little more than a silly, boyish whim. That he was able to make a life around such a whim brought him great satisfaction—and the grudging respect of his neighbors. Toby had earned a name for himself among skeptical locals as well as breeders of national repute for the way he could gentle a horse without force. He didn't claim to be a horse whisperer. Still, anyone watching him could not help but be impressed with the way he communicated with even the most skittish of horses with a calming touch and softly murmured words into the animal's ear.

In all his years, never had he seen a more wary creature than the one presently coaxing music from his son's chubby little fingers. When the song ended, a metronome on the mantel continued to keep time to the blood throbbing in Toby's veins. He had faced divorce with the kind of stoic discipline that characterized his ideal of a strong man. Was it possible, he wondered, that he didn't have to face the rest of his life alone pretending to feel less deeply than he did? Would the words *I love you* ever come as easily to his lips as to his heart?

Where words failed both his son and himself, it seemed music had the power to heal. He had read somewhere that music could reach people with cognitive disabilities. Even stroke victims who are unable to speak could sometimes sing the lyrics to familiar songs. Feeling emotionally disabled, Toby worried he could very easily ruin everything by succumbing to the song of his own heart. Standing there as a silent observer, surrounded by a feeling of utter contentment unlike any he'd known before, he longed to ask Heather to marry him.

He wondered if she would think marriage was tantamount to tying a rock around her own dreams. Heather had confided little about her past to him, and Toby wasn't one to pry. Still, it didn't take a rocket scientist to see that she had been badly burned before and was leery of commitment in general. Toby had the feeling that she had one foot inside the threshold of his home and one firmly planted on a racing block outside. The last thing he wanted to do was scare her away.

Already devastated by his mother's abandonment, Dylan could ill afford losing the only other woman in his life he had come to trust and love. And Toby didn't think he could personally withstand losing the woman he had come to need as surely as a man needed air to breathe. He didn't know exactly when he had fallen in love with her, only that he had fallen hard. Just watching her now evoked such a fierce feeling of possessiveness that it would have scared a lesser man. He most certainly didn't want it to scare her.

Toby didn't know how Heather felt about taking on the responsibilities of instant motherhood. Or giving up her own dreams. Every time he thought about proposing marriage, he heard Sheila's mocking voice ringing in his ears.

What woman in her right mind would want to waste her life rotting away in the middle of such a godforsaken wasteland with a man who isn't smart enough to use his family influence to carve out a nice life for himself in the lap of luxury?

Sheila certainly had no compunctions about using her pregnancy to trap Toby into marriage. Nor walking away from that marriage once she discovered she would never be able to shape him into the gentleman of leisure that she wanted him to be. There was no doubt that marriage had left a bad taste in Toby's mouth. He supposed it was only a matter of time before Heather grew tired of the isolation that Sheila claimed would make any woman stir-crazy. And promiscuous if the rumors about his ex were correct.

In Toby's mind, it was far better to try out a relationship without a binding ceremony than to risk being so poorly used again.

So it was guilt, fear and bliss that competed for top billing as both Toby and Heather sorted through their feelings by day. At night the stars collapsed about them as they sought ecstasy in the warm, willing flesh given to two souls desperately seeking a permanent home in each other's arms. Come the following morning, they politely assured themselves that they were only interested in the moment.

Secretly they both wanted much, much more.

"Would you mind taking Dylan into town for his booster shot?" Toby asked Heather over breakfast one morning. "I'd do it myself, but I just got a call that Sun Dancer's arrival is going to be delayed. I really need to be here to sign the paperwork when he arrives."

Sun Dancer was the prize stud upon which Toby was betting a great deal of money to strengthen the bloodlines of his stock. Heather knew the paperwork was merely a front for the real reason he wanted to remain behind. Whatever place she held in Toby's heart, she suspected his first love would always be horses.

"Far be it from me to deny one stud the pleasure of welcoming another to his new home," she quipped. "Besides, it'll be a nice change to get away from the ranch for the day."

Reminded of Sheila's aversion to ranch life, Toby flinched. "Under any other circumstances, you know that I'd volunteer to go with you."

Heather didn't pick up on the concern in his voice. She was happy to do him the favor and thought nothing more of it. How could she know that any mention of leaving the ranch for a change of pace sent shivers of dread racing through the man she loved? Or that he feared the same pattern of boredom and desertion repeated itself in such an innocuous statement?

Toby reached in his pocket and pulled out a wad of bills. He peeled off a couple of hundreds off the top and shoved them along with a credit card across the table at her.

"Why don't you buy yourself something nice while you're in town?" he suggested. "Maybe something pretty to wear. Or a piece of jewelry. And don't forget to stop for ice cream on the way home. Dylan hates shots, and it'd be a treat for him that might help offset his fear of needles."

Heather protested his generosity. "There's nothing I need—and nowhere really to shop for that matter.''

Toby's eyes narrowed as he repeated Sheila's thumbnail description of the nearest town. "Just one cheap discount store and a couple of bars... I suppose it's not much of a place for a discriminating woman to make her mark on the world."

Heather laughed. Marathon shopping had never been her idea of having fun. "Good thing there's always the shopping channel on TV, then," she said, making light of his concerns.

An hour later, she was climbing into Toby's four-wheel-drive crew cab after securing Dylan in the child seat next to her. Toby put his hands around her waist and helped her up into the vehicle without having to strain himself any. Heather couldn't refrain from running her hands along the muscles of his arms and letting them rest there.

"You do look good in a cowboy hat," she said, ruffling the short hair curling at the base of his neck.

It amused her that he thought it too long if it reached the top of his collar. Because she thought he had a particularly kissable neck, she would never complain about its length. Toby returned the compliment by taking the hat off his head and placing it on hers. The hatband left a workingman's mark upon his hair that Heather smoothed out with loving care.

"You, too," he murmured and lowered his voice to add, "but you look even better in nothing at all."

They kissed. In the background a glorious backdrop of mountains shimmered in the rising heat, and any fears about the future dissipated like a dessert mirage. Heather had grown so used to his mustache that it no longer tickled—any part of her body. She cherished the warmth of his lips upon hers and wouldn't give up that feeling a second before she had to. Her entire world pivoted around this solid hunk of man. She clung to him as if fearing she might go spinning off into the cosmos if she ever let go.

In the distance a trailer kicked up a cloud of dust marking Sun Dancer's arrival. Toby's eyes lit up. Sighing, Heather glanced at her watch and put the vehicle in gear.

"I can't help feeling dwarfed by this monster truck," she admitted. "I should pack a stepladder so I can get in and out by myself."

"A sporty little car just doesn't have much place on a ranch," Toby apologized, leaning into the open window and trying to memorize the heavenly smell of the perfume she was wearing. "But if that's what you want, I'd buy one for you in a heartbeat."

Heather laughed and kissed him again before sneaking a peek at Dylan in the seat beside her. The boy didn't seem in the least traumatized by the affection between them. In fact, he wore a great big grin as he held out his arms and demanded a hug from his father, too. Heather made herself turn away from the poignant scene. It was dangerous to let herself feel like she was a part of a real family.

Bouncing down the gravel road a few minutes later, Heather reconsidered Toby's offer to buy her some new clothes. Perhaps that comment was just his way of letting her know he was tired of seeing her wearing the same few shirts and jeans that comprised the majority of her wardrobe. Feeling far from the glamorous picture of the ex-wife still gracing the top of the piano, she hoped Toby was not embarrassed by her simple attire.

Or by his relationship with her.

Ultimately it wasn't the size of the town that left Heather feeling small but rather the size of the minds that inhabited it. Dylan held up well under the practiced and blessedly quick shot that the doctor administered. Promising a brave boy a reward, she pulled into the dusty parking lot of the Whistle Stop Café a short while later and told Dylan that he could order whatever he liked once they were inside.

That the railroad had long ago bypassed the Whistle Stop didn't warrant a name change according to the string of owners who managed the landmark, through the subsequent booms and busts that pockmarked Wyoming's history. The latest proprietor boasted a bottomless cup of coffee and the best pie in the whole darn county. It also was the roosting spot for locals to catch up on gossip and bemoan the price of cattle on any given day. The noon rush consisted of a dozen or so customers.

As they took their seat at a well-worn booth, Heather had the oddest feeling that everyone in the place was looking at her. Brushing off the feeling as pure paranoia, she ordered coffee and an extra spoon for the brownie sundae Dylan ordered. Their waitress assured them it was twice as much as Dylan could dream of eating by himself. The woman, whose name tag announced her to the world as Nancy, was a big-boned blonde with nice features and a hairstyle popular in the previous decade.

"That her?" asked one of the fellows sitting on a revolving stool at the counter as Nancy refilled his coffee on her way to the refrigerator.

Despite the sizable wad of chew pinched between the man's lip and jaw, he spoke clearly and loud enough for Heather to hear.

"Shhh," the waitress told him returning with their order.

She discreetly closed the magazine that he had open on the counter. She then proceeded to put a huge scoop of vanilla ice cream on top of a saucer-size brownie, dripped hot fudge over it, gave it a noisy squirt of whipped cream from a can and topped off the caloric nightmare with a single maraschino cherry.

Nancy placed the gooey concoction before Dylan a moment later. His eyes grew wide in appreciation.

"Still not talking, huh?" the woman inquired. Concern creased her brow.

Heather allowed Dylan time enough to respond

should he have chosen to do so before supplying an answer for him. "I'm afraid not."

She assumed Nancy must know Dylan through a previous association with Toby and thought it nice of her to ask. A couple of bites of chocolate was enough to satisfy Heather's craving for something sweet. Setting down her spoon, she scanned a nearby rack of magazines and newspapers, hoping to find something to occupy her time while Dylan made a charming mess of himself. One publication in particular caught her eye—and by the looks of the prominently displayed, and nearly empty space, on that rack—everyone else's as well.

Exclusive Photos of Danforth Family Fourth of July Bash! was proudly proclaimed in bold print across its banner.

Heather snatched up the only remaining magazine and flipped it open without bothering to act nonchalant. While most of the coverage highlighted Abraham Danforth's political intentions, a number of interesting and potentially incriminating photographs were included as dirt on one of America's first families. Among them was a full-size picture of Heather wrapped in Toby's arms. Apparently he had been mistaken about destroying the only pictures of the kiss they had shared in Savannah. Another more surreptitious reporter had a captured a different angle from a spot he'd staked out earlier. An uncomfortable two-and-a-half-hour wait straddling a branch in a nearby tree ultimately earned the reporter a handsome commission from the tabloid. And Heather's undying disgust.

The caption proved as titillating as the picture. It insinuated that Toby Danforth hired a nanny to work with his "emotionally disturbed" son, more for physical attributes that were far more suitable for his bedroom than Dylan's nursery. Heather's face burned with shame. She glanced up to see every other patron in the establishment turn away in sudden preoccupation with their food or lack thereof.

Heather wished she didn't care a whit about what they thought. She knew she shouldn't.

Still, as a sensitive spirit, she was easily wounded. A wave of nausea washed over her as the coffee in her stomach soured. She gripped the edge of the table to keep her hands from shaking. Whether it was true or not, she had the definite feeling that everyone was laughing and pointing behind her back. The back of her neck grew hot and prickly.

When Josef humiliated her, she turned away from music to seek a new identity for herself. One that had given her a joyous beginning and faith in her own ability to shape her future. Unfortunately, she didn't know how to outrun the innuendo of a nationally syndicated publication, albeit one of dubious repute. Her parents, already disappointed in her, were sure to completely disown her now.

And what about Dylan? Heather knew how cruel children could be. There was no telling how his mother might react to such ugly publicity. Would she use it as ammunition in court to gain full custody of her son?

In her heart, Heather knew that falling in love with Toby had been a terrible, wonderful mistake. She simply hadn't counted on such a personal mistake being magnified and vilified in the press.

Dylan pushed his bowl away and swiped at the chocolate dribbling down his chin with the back of his arm, indicating he was ready to go.

Heather had to clear the lump from her throat before asking him, "Have you had enough?"

Nodding his head yes, the child looked perplexed by the tears shimmering in her eyes.

"Me, too," she said, meaning much more than he could possibly understand.

Heather paid their bill without saying another word and pretended not to hear the grizzled old man at the counter elbow his companion in the side.

"Think the little lady'd consider being my bed warmer—er, I mean nanny, Charlie?"

"Dunno, but I'd sure like a tonsillectomy like the one she gave her boss...."

Their words echoed in her ears as Heather stepped from the air-conditioned building into the bright light of day. The worst thing about falling in love with Toby was that her previous numbness had finally worn off, leaving her all the more vulnerable to the searing pain that engulfed her and left her feeling so all alone. If the highs with Toby were breathtaking, the lows were enough to suck the breath right out of her. Heather ached all over.

For once she was grateful for Dylan's silence. At least she didn't have to worry that he would tell his father about the many tears she'd shed on the long road home.

"I'm giving you my two weeks' notice."

Heather's words reverberated off the walls of the Double D and ricocheted inside Toby's brain like a bullet gone wild. Dylan was napping and the house was so still that every sound was amplified. The antique cuckoo clock in the kitchen alerted the house that it was three o'clock. The dishwasher clicked into its rinse cycle. And Toby felt the world shift beneath his feet.

He couldn't fathom what could have possibly occurred between the time he'd kissed Heather goodbye in the morning and now to make her say such a thing. A million thoughts raced through his head, most centering on what he could have possibly done to upset her. Picking one of the many excuses Sheila used to divorce him, he asked Heather if she simply found the town too rustic for her tastes. His attempt at flippancy fell as flat as his heart.

"No, too cosmopolitan actually," Heather replied, handing over the tabloid with shaking hands.

Toby scanned the article before hurling the magazine across the room in disgust.

"Is that what this is all about?" he demanded to

know. "I can't believe you'd let this piece of trash bother you."

"Maybe I didn't grow up with it the way you did. And maybe I'm more concerned about how this might affect you and Dylan than how it affects me personally."

"And maybe you're just looking for an excuse to run away."

Heather flinched, and he realized that he must have struck a nerve. He reached out a hand and brushed it against the side of her face. She took a deep breath and rested her cheek in the palm of his hand for a second. For eternity. With the pad of his thumb, Toby wiped away the tear that rolled down her face.

"What are you afraid of, sweetheart?"

"Of embarrassing you," Heather admitted. "Of compromising the progress Dylan's made for my own selfish desires."

Toby's laugh was almost a bark. "You could never embarrass me, and by the time Dylan will be able to read this, I'd like to think he'd have more discriminating tastes than to let something so base bother him. I certainly don't."

Heather pushed his hand away and swallowed against the tightening of her throat. "You can joke about it all you want, but the truth of the matter is it won't be long before Dylan will be old enough to question our relationship. A relationship stuck in neutral because neither one of us wants to commit to more than the physical. I can't see myself as your lover indefinitely, and I don't want to play the kind of games that require me to withhold love as a way to force you into marriage.''

She held up her hand to stop Toby from interrupting her.

"Look. I've studied this from every angle, and the only thing that makes sense is for me to go back to school this fall and work on my teaching certification. That way everyone can save face, and we can part as friends."

As she continued babbling on about her plans to obtain a student loan and register for classes early, Toby looked at her as if she were asking to be helped into a straitjacket. While it was true that he had become somewhat inured to unwelcome publicity very early on in his life, he couldn't believe that Heather would actually let something as inconsequential as the *National Tattler* come between them. He wondered if her hypersensitivity was rooted in a painful past, or if she was simply mortified thinking of her parents and friends seeing her in such a compromising photograph splashed across the page of such a scandalous rag.

Toby never claimed to understand the complexities of the female mind. His ex lived to see her picture in the press, all too often lamenting Toby's aversion to the kind of elite social events that attracted the media. She mistakenly assumed fame under any circumstance was a good thing. Knowing

Sheila, she'd be pea-green with envy at the very picture causing Heather such grief. As much as Toby preferred Heather's attitude toward tabloid journalism, given the circumstances, he wished she could see it for what it was worth—little more than the paper on which it was printed.

Toby experienced a terrible sense of déjà vu as he recalled the day that Sheila announced she was leaving him. He had been secretly relieved to end the charade of their marriage. When Heather said those same words, he was rendered completely incapacitated. It would be far easier to lose a limb than to lose the gentle soul who had infused his life with hope and love. Feeling sucker-punched, he knew he had to do something drastic to get her to stay. Somehow he had to fix things between them. He had to make her understand that tawdry words had no power to tarnish a love as rare as theirs. Heather was no more the gold-digging tramp the press made her out to be than he was the playboy that they wanted so desperately to portray him as.

The solution came to Toby so easily that he knew in an instant it was what he wanted all along—a reason to put aside old fears and make a forever commitment to their relationship. A way for Heather to save face. A way to keep his child's best interest at heart. A way to proclaim his love to the entire world. A way to make things right.

Without any further ado, he knelt down in front of Heather and took both her hands into his. He stared into her eyes as if searching the starry sky for answers to the universe. A universe he longed to share with her for eternity.

"Miss Heather Burroughs," he began, slipping into the distinctly lyrical pattern of speech with which he'd been raised. "Would you do me the honor of marrying me?"

Twelve

Heather looked at Toby in disbelief. Here he was on his knees asking her to marry him and he hadn't ever so much as told her that he loved her. She could think of only one reason for him to propose out of the clear blue like this. From his reaction to the article she had shown him, it had nothing to do with salvaging his family name. And everything to do with her decision to tender her resignation.

She should have known that concern for Dylan would supersede everything else in Toby's life. As much as she admired him for that, her heart would not let her accept the offer that her head told her only an idiot would refuse. Toby Danforth was handsome, rich and compassionate. He was a good friend, a great father and an even better lover. Nonetheless, Heather had come a long way in terms of demanding self-respect since the day she broke away from those who would manipulate her talents to their own ends. As much as she loved Dylan, she didn't believe that was reason enough to marry his father.

"I can't marry you just so you don't have to look for another nanny," she said softly.

Clenched inside the velvet gloves of her words were granite fists. Toby drew back as if he had actually been struck, then reached up to tenderly stroke her cheek with the back of one hand.

"Sweetheart, whatever gave you that idea?"

Heather's face tingled where he touched her. Still, she could hardly compromise her future for an endearment that could melt the polar ice cap. Weariness weighed down her reasoning.

"If nothing else, your timing."

A note of exasperation crept into Toby's voice. "I thought this was what you wanted. Why else would you throw that rag of a magazine in my face if not to make me feel obliged to make an honest woman of you and prove something to the rest of the world?"

Heather stiffened under the accusation. Ugly words hurt, but now that the truth was out in the open she had no choice but to deal with it. Clearly, Toby felt she was manipulating him in much the same way she felt he was willing to use her just to make his life easier. In the same way her parents and Josef used her to promote their own aspirations. She'd vowed never to let anyone claim her life for their personal goals again. She believed that she deserved to be loved as a woman first, and a mother second.

"Those aren't exactly the words a girl hopes to hear when a man proposes," she told him flatly.

"I never said I was any good with words."

Toby's voice climbed with his frustration. "And I imagine that even if I found the right ones now, they'd be suspect in your mind. Wouldn't they?"

Heather shook her head sadly. "Probably."

She was as taken aback by Toby's sudden anger as by the fact that, even under duress, he seemed unable to utter the three little words that were the foundation of all good marriages. She had to wonder if he even knew what they were. Having heard him profess his love openly to his son on numerous occasions, she was inclined to believe that was not the case. Toby simply wasn't in love with her.

Oh, she was good enough to be a mother to his son, good enough to warm his bed at night, good enough to marry out of convenience, but she did not lay claim to his heart—and suspected she never would. Heather supposed she should thank him for being honest with her rather than leading her on like Josef had, but at the moment it was everything she could do to keep her composure in front of him.

Inside she was falling apart.

"I'm sorry," she said plainly enough.

Her refusal stung. Pride kept Toby from begging. He was sorry that he ruined the moment with his inability to express what was in his heart. It wasn't exactly like he had a lot of experience in proposing. He'd never asked anyone to marry him before. Sheila had popped the question herself on the heels of announcing that she was pregnant with his child. Being of honorable character, he had simply gone along with her wishes and done the right thing. And although his brief marriage had brought him little happiness, because it had given him a wonderful son, he could not bring himself to regret it. He could not imagine what Heather's leaving would do to him, let alone Dylan.

Toby got off his knees and put his weight squarely back onto the same two feet that had carried him this far into life with his backbone, if not his heart, intact.

"I'm sorry, too. Sorry that I don't have the right words for you. It's obvious where my son gets his inability to communicate."

Heather held up her hands to stop him. She gestured toward the open doorway. "That doesn't affect his hearing any."

Dylan was standing there, clutching his favorite blanket and looking at them with a worried expression on his face. Though unable to verbalize his thoughts, he was clearly upset to hear the two most important people in his life raising their voices to one another. Heather rushed to his side and bent down to wipe away the single tear that rolled down his cheek.

Taking him in her arms, she hastened to assure him. "Everything's going to be fine."

"Don't lie to the boy," Toby barked. "His mother told him that just before she left for good. Until you showed up, the last word he ever said was goodbye."

He extended a hand to his son. Dylan looked to Heather. Unable to utter a single word herself, she simply nodded her approval and gave him over to his father without a fight. She didn't know what she could possibly say to make Toby stay and work out their problems, what she could possibly say to make him love her as much as she loved him.

"Come on, son. Let's get out of here before I say something I'll regret."

The door swung shut behind them with a bang that reverberated throughout the house. The immediate silence and a feeling of being completely alone again engulfed Heather. She put her head in her hands and sobbed without making a sound. How ironic, she thought, that she had come here to help Dylan find his voice and lost hers in the process.

An hour passed without any sign of the two men in her life. She imagined they had gone into town, leaving her to her own devices. Evening cast a long shadow over the gleaming piano in the center of the room. Having no other way to express herself without fear of further repercussions, Heather turned to the one friend who had never abandoned her—even in the dark days when she deliberately turned her back on it. Approaching the piano with a sense of trepidation, she hoped her hands remembered their training.

Nimble fingers gave voice to her angst. The song she played in the fading light was moving in the depth of emotion it conveyed. Echoing off the walls, the highs and lows of those notes resounded off mountain walls that sheltered them from the outside world. A world that did not understand the complexity of a woman's heart.

How good it felt to let the music speak for her. Heather was bent over the piano keys, immersed in a heartbreaking melody, attempting to loosen the pain deep inside of her, when Dylan appeared out of nowhere. Scratched and bloody, he tugged at her sleeve to get her attention and struggled to convey a message of grave importance.

"What's wrong?" she asked, jolted from her trancelike state by his appearance.

He opened his mouth, but no sound came out. Grabbing him by the shoulders, Heather implored, "Please, Dylan, tell me what's happened."

Tears pooled in eyes the exact shade as his father's. Squeezing them shut, he concentrated hard and opened his mouth again.

"D-d-d...D-d-daddy...hurt..."

Fear swallowed Heather whole. She was off the piano bench in an instant and racing toward the front door. Her feet never hit the floor. Dylan was right behind her. Not knowing which way to go, Heather stopped only long enough to scoop the frightened toddler into her arms.

"Where's Daddy?"

Dylan pointed with a dirty finger. Heather spied a tractor in the back pasture. Her heart stopped beating. All too often, ranch accidents proved fatal. Praying she didn't twist an ankle, Heather sprinted across freshly tilled soil with Dylan on her hip. The roar in her ears drummed out all other sounds, even the screaming of her own voice as she called Toby's name again and again.

As she closed in upon the scene, Heather saw that the tractor was overturned. She might have known Toby would take his frustrations out on big machinery, trying to score a drought-hardened earth he found softer than her own hard heart! What she would give to replay the incident that drove him to fate's destructive path.

Looking like a fallen dinosaur, the tractor was still running on its side. Going nowhere, one wheel spun uselessly in the air. Even if Toby were able to respond to her frantic calls, Heather knew it would be impossible to discern his voice over the roar of machinery. Setting Dylan on the ground, she prayed the man she loved was not pinned beneath the immovable mountain of metal. When the tractor had toppled and Toby realized there was nothing he could do to prevent it, she imagined his first thoughts were for his son. In her mind's eye, Heather could see him throwing Dylan clear before giving thought to his own safety.

Thunder boomed in the distance.

Heather circled the tractor and found Toby's lifeless form next to it. His blood stained the long prairie grass and seeped into the parched earth. One arm was bent beneath his twisted body. He had fallen on the side of the field that he had just plowed, somewhat cushioning his fall. Dropping to her knees beside him, she sobbed and pressed her head to his heart. The faint sound of its beating kindled hope in her breast.

Checking his pulse, she imagined minuscule pressure in return when she squeezed his hand. Her lips upon his caused his eyelids to flutter open briefly. She bathed his bloody face with her tears.

Dialing 911 was of little use in this situation. By the time an ambulance arrived, Toby could well bleed to death. Heather looked to the gathering storm clouds and tore back across the open field. Promising to be back in a minute, she told Dylan to stay put. Their only hope was to get Toby to the emergency room as quickly as possible.

Out of breath by the time she reached his pickup, she silently thanked him for always leaving his keys in the ignition. Snakebites, grizzly maulings and unforeseen accidents were far more likely than theft in such a remote region. The only crime that concerned Heather at the moment was the possibility of Toby dying without her ever telling him she loved him.

A few scattered raindrops splattered against the windshield as Heather started up the one-ton pickup. Any other day she would be grateful for the moisture. Today she could scarcely afford to run the risk of getting mired in the mud. Swearing, she turned the vehicle toward the scene of the accident and lurched forward, mindless of nothing but getting to Toby as quickly as possible. She threw the vehicle into four-wheel drive and fastened her seat belt on the fly. Had she not, it was likely she would have knocked herself out by hitting her head on the roof as she raced across the rough plowed field.

Dylan was crying next to his father when Heather pulled up beside them. She parked the pickup as close as she possibly could without endangering either of them. She didn't have enough adrenaline to lift an entire tractor off a man, but there was enough of that life preserver flowing in her bloodstream to manage to hoist a 175-pound man into the cab of a pickup. It wasn't until she tried getting Toby to his feet that she realized how grotesquely disfigured his arm was. Try as she might to be gentle, it was all she could do to fold him into the front seat. He groaned before slipping back into unconsciousness, his arm flopping uselessly at his side.

Heather tossed Dylan into the truck beside her and

told him to hold his father's head in his lap. It seldom rained in Wyoming, but when it did it usually arrived in a torrent, flooding gullies and washing away precious topsoil. If she could make it out of the field before it turned to clay, Heather figured there was a good chance they wouldn't get stuck.

Her wheels spun. Every minute counted, but she didn't want to bury the pickup by gunning it in her haste. She pressed down on the accelerator slowly and eased her way toward the gravel road. The only thing separating her from that road was a nasty-looking barbed wire fence. It stood no chance against her will and seven thousand pounds of Ford-tough truck hurtling toward it in the rain.

Like the pop of a starting gun, the twang of barbed wire signaled Heather's hope of making it to the hospital in record time. Gravel churned in all directions as they hit the county road. Just about that time, the hail started. The size of marbles, the hailstones plinked off the roof and the hood of Toby's new vehicle, rippling it with dents. Considering the new barb wire bra across the front of the truck, Heather doubted the insurance company would quarrel over the cost of such mundane repairs.

Once they reached the main highway, she placed that 911 call on the cell phone that was considered standard equipment on most Wyoming trucks, and alerted the hospital to expect them shortly. She flipped on her emergency flashers. The road was slick, and she took care not to hydroplane at high speeds. The last thing she wanted to do was cause yet another accident in her haste to save a life. All the way into town, Dylan petted his father's head and cooed reassuringly into his ear.

Without taking her eyes off the road, Heather told him, "You're a real hero."

In light of his own traumatic experience on that tractor, Dylan's speaking in order to save his father was nothing short of a miracle. Heather always believed that the boy would talk when he was ready. She just hadn't counted on a life-and-death situation proving her right. Nor had she realized just how important it was to speak from the heart while there was still time for those precious words to be heard. If God would but spare Toby's life, Heather vowed to never again let pride get in the way of love's true course.

"I love you. I love you. I love you," she repeated over and over to the rhythm of the hail and the swish of windshield wipers.

"Looks pretty bad. We may have to amputate."

The emergency room nurse was not aware that Toby was conscious when she uttered that dire prediction. Even if she was, she would have sworn that the shot she administered immediately thereafter would make him forget anything he heard while she was prepping him anyway. She was wrong.

Because his son needed him and because he was a fighter, Toby Danforth hung on to those words through a fog of pain as he clung to life itself. Tenaciously.

When he came to, hours later, he was surprised to see Heather asleep in the chair next to his bed. Her neck was bent at an uncomfortable angle causing her hair to spill over her shoulder in a waterfall of gold. Dark circles rimmed her closed eyes. Toby longed to reach out and touch this delicate creature just once more, but his strength failed him. It hurt to think that any chance they may have had for a future together was as shattered as the arm he heard crack just before he passed out.

Wrapped tightly in blankets and as yet unable to move, he couldn't tell whether that arm was still attached to his body beneath his hospital garb. The nurse's remark about amputation echoed in his ears. If Heather hadn't wanted him when he proposed to her before the accident, he couldn't imagine asking her to accept him as less than a whole man—without two strong arms to hold and protect her.

As if the incredible woman who rescued him needed his protection. Thinking it unfair to ask her to marry him given the reclusive nature of his life and his son's special needs, he wouldn't expect Heather to sign away her youth and vitality to a cripple. The sight of her stirring in a shaft of light filtering in through the window touched all of his senses at once. Her eyelids opened to reveal a pair of dove-gray eyes that softened the instant she saw him.

"God, but you're beautiful," he mumbled.

Toby wasn't sure why that would cause her to burst into tears, but she did. Smothering him with kisses, she told him just how happy she was that he was alive. He wasn't so sure about that. Once Heather left for good, his life wouldn't be worth much to anyone—except to a sensitive little boy who needed him to be both his mother and father. And the parents who would likely expect Toby to move home so they could treat him like an invalid for the rest of his life.

Heather tucked a strand of hair behind one ear and stepped back to stare at him earnestly. Having an epiphany on the long, perilous ride to town, she was ready to bare her soul.

"If it's okay with you, I'd like to reconsider that proposal you made earlier today."

The jump in Toby's heart rate registered on the monitor next to his bed.

"You think you could do a better job, I suppose," he said. His voice, though weak, reflected an amusement that his eyes did not share.

Giving him a lopsided smile, Heather knelt beside his bed in a classic proposal position. "I love you."

As much as Toby needed to stop her from making a fool of them both, those words filled him with such a sense of joy that he wanted more than anything else in this world to believe his ears.

"Ssshhh…" he whispered. "You don't have to—"

"Don't shush me. God and I had a nice, long talk on the way to getting you here, and we decided that you need me. Not just Dylan, big boy, but you. It seems I need you, too. I'm willing to work at marriage on whatever terms you think fair. If you'll just give me a chance, I think I can make you learn to love me."

Toby choked on the fist that was stuck in his throat. "Learn—to love you?" he stammered. For a woman who said she wanted romance in a marriage proposal, she certainly made hers sound more like a business proposition than a matter of the heart. A man who believed in proving himself not by words but by actions, he couldn't fathom that she didn't know how out-of-his-mind crazy in love with her he was.

Was it possible she truly believed he proposed to her simply because she was good with Dylan? Was she really so thick that she believed he would make a lifetime commitment based on anything other than his feelings for her? Didn't she know that the kind of earth-moving passion they shared was something so special that poets couldn't find words to describe it adequately?

He was such an idiot! When she rejected his proposal out of hand, he had reacted like some hot-headed kid, rushing off without getting to the heart of the matter. Attempting to assuage his wounded pride by getting behind the wheel of a monstrous tractor and running it into the ground wasn't the smartest move he'd ever made, either. Luckily for him, Heather was made of sterner stuff. If not for her cool head, he could well have died within walking distance of his house.

He berated himself for not staying to work things out when she first called his motives into question. Now it was much too late for mending fences or limbs.

"My arm—" he began.

"What about it?"

That she looked so genuinely surprised he would mention it made Toby ache for opportunities lost.

"I can't expect you to marry half a man."

"Tobias Danforth!" Heather exclaimed. "I can't believe you think I'm so shallow that I care more about how you look than what's inside you."

She, too, had heard the hospital buzz that his arm might be amputated, but refused to believe it until she heard it straight from the doctor's mouth. Even then, Toby's parents, who she called immediately after admitting him, assured her that they wanted a specialist to look at their son before any such drastic measure be taken. Having booked a private jet, Harold and Miranda were due to arrive any moment to lend their support and help their son and grandson any way they could. Heather envied Toby their limitless love—and longed to share it with him.

"Whether you have one arm or three makes no difference to me. I love you. Not your arm or your pocketbook or your family name or some stupid, strong-and-silent cowboy stereotype that you'd let ruin your life if it weren't for me. Understand this—nothing is going to change my feelings for you. Nothing. I love you, and I love your son. It's that simple. Let's not make it any more difficult than that."

"I love you, too."

Seeing the tears spill down her cheeks at the admission, Toby rebuked himself for not saying those words long ago. They had the power to make him feel whole.

Even though he wasn't.

No matter what he wanted for himself, Toby could not in good conscience let such a young, vibrant woman throw her life away without giving serious consideration to what it would be like to be married to a man who would need help simply getting dressed every morning. On more than one occasion, Heather had told him his disposition was less than sweet on his good days. He imagined he would be a bear to live with as he learned to function without an appendage. It wouldn't be right to hold her to a declaration of love made under the duress of such a terrible accident. He didn't want her to make a commitment to him out of a sense of pity.

Again Toby tried to explain. "I love you and I'd ask you to marry me again, but my arm—"

"Is full of pins, and you won't be doing any manual labor for a while. But don't worry. A little mending and a lot therapy and you should regain full use of it in time for the fall stock show."

The doctor who stepped into the room was young and cocky. The fact that he happened to be wearing cowboy boots and was the bearer of tremendous news excused his high-flying bedside manner. Toby closed his eyes and exhaled the accumulated fear from his lungs as the surgeon continued with his prognosis.

"You also have a bad concussion, which must explain why I thought I heard you talking about marriage when I walked in the room. The Toby Danforth I know vowed he would never get married again, and made me promise to knock some sense into his head if he ever so much as mentioned it."

Toby's smile lit up the entire hospital wing. "That won't be necessary. I knocked some sense into my own head the hard way."

He turned his attention away from the doctor and focused his entire being on Heather. "Like I was saying, I love you. And I want to marry you. For all the right reasons."

The glow on Heather's face erased all doubts Toby might have had. She wasn't the kind of woman who needed roses and exotic settings and romantic music in the background to accept a man's heartfelt proposal. She just needed to hear the right words. He thanked God that he had found them in time to turn his life around. A future brimming with promise need not be overshadowed by the mistakes of the past.

"I'd be honored to be your wife."

There was no false fluttering of eyelashes or Southern belle pretense in Heather's words. Just joyful acceptance. And a shimmer of passion glowing in her eyes.

Doc Cameron cleared his throat. Truth be told, he was jealous as could be. And a little uncomfortable being present at such a private moment. "I'd shake your hand if it weren't busted all to hell. What d'ya say I leave you two lovebirds alone to set a date?"

"If it were up to me, I'd have the minister who arrived to give me last rites marry us before he leaves the building. Barring that, you can expect an invitation any day," Toby informed him.

"I wouldn't miss it for the world," the doctor said. With that, he took his leave, promising to return momentarily with Dylan.

Toby felt his heart swell as he looked at his lovely wife-to-be. Moved by her courage and beauty, he couldn't help but ask, "Are you sure you're not the one with the concussion?"

"As positive as I am that I intend to take advantage of you all wrapped up tight in your blanket, helpless to resist my advances."

"Good thing I didn't crush that part of my anatomy," Toby whispered, glancing down at the prominent protrusion beneath his hospital covers.

Heather simultaneously blushed, laughed and

agreed with him as he proceeded to let her know he was already well on the road to recuperation. Despite his weakened state, Toby managed to free his good arm from under the covers. He wrapped that arm around her waist and dragged her close. Leaning over his bed, Heather kissed him tenderly, as if afraid of hurting him further. Toby would have none of it. He parted her lips with his tongue and intensified that kiss. When Heather made a move to draw away, he nuzzled the swell of her breasts straining against the buttons of her shirt and refused to let her go. She could scarcely breathe for the tightness surrounding her heart. Her knees grew so weak that she had to support herself by leaning a hand against his thigh.

"I do believe there's just enough room in this narrow little bed for two people if they were of a mind to consummate their upcoming wedding vows," Toby told her with glint in his eyes.

"Behave yourself," Heather warned as Dylan skipped into the room, clutching the hand of a cute high school candy striper who dropped him off at the door.

She had to restrain the boy from climbing up on the bed and accidentally injuring his father in his haste to give him a hug. He stood next to the bed as proud as could be and asked, "I did good, huh, Dad?"

Toby's eyes widened. The expression on his face said it all. He looked to Heather for confirmation that he wasn't imagining things. Running a hand through Dylan's unruly hair, she nodded her head.

"Your son saved your life. He was the one who came and got me. He *told* me you were hurt and led me to your side."

"He *told* you?" Toby repeated in disbelief. Was it possible God was so generous that He would grant a man more than one miracle a day?

"And, according to the nurses, he's been bragging to everyone in the hospital about what a big hero he is."

It took a moment for her words to sink into Toby's fractured skull. When they finally did, he almost jumped out of bed, forgetting that he wasn't up to a doing a jig just yet. Heather accommodated him by lifting Dylan up and setting him on the edge of the bed so they could share a group hug. That joyful embrace marked the beginning of their life as a family together.

A life that gave voice to all of their dreams.

* * * * *

Steamy Savannah Nights

SHERI WHITEFEATHER

SHERI WHITEFEATHER

lives in Southern California and enjoys ethnic dining, attending powwows and visiting art galleries and vintage clothing stores near the beach. Since her one true passion is writing, she is thrilled to be a part of the Mills & Boon® Desire™ line. When she isn't writing, she often reads until the wee hours of the morning.

Sheri's husband, a member of the Muscogee Creek Nation, inspires many of her stories. They have a son, a daughter and a trio of cats – domestic and wild. She loves to hear from her readers. You may write to her at: PO Box 17146, Anaheim, California 92817, USA. Visit her website at www.SheriWhiteFeather.com.

To the eHarlequin.com community members
on my *Thief Of Hearts* and *Savannah Secrets*
threads. Thank you, all of you, for making
those stories so much fun.

Prologue

July 4th
Savannah, Georgia

Security consultant Michael Whittaker remained on hawk-eyed alert. The fund-raiser was in full swing, and he'd been hired to protect Abraham Danforth, the man of the hour, the fifty-five-year-old widower running for state senator.

Michael, once a kid from the wrong side of the tracks, had earned his way to the top. His high-profile clients trusted and respected him.

In turn, he put his ass on the line to save theirs. But he didn't mind. That was his life's work, his chosen profession.

Along with hand-selected members of his security team, Michael had been acting as Danforth's personal bodyguard for months, after a female stalker, an unknown assailant Michael was still pursuing, had threatened the older man.

Assessing the activity in the Twin Oaks Hotel ballroom, he stood fairly close to Danforth. A small group of guests interacted with his client, while others mingled throughout the expansive setting, chatting amicably.

Michael shifted his attention to the petite brunette near the bar. She'd arrived late, keeping to herself. As far as he could tell, she hadn't spoken to another living soul.

Why? What was her agenda? Her expression proved difficult to discern, and that unnerved Michael. Normally he could read people. He possessed a sixth sense, a gut instinct that enabled him to see beyond the obvious, to get past the surface.

But everything about her mystified him: the creamy shade of her skin, the sleek dark hair fashioned in a ladylike twist at the nape of her neck, her exotic-shaped eyes.

Even her attire, a silky blue dress that flowed to her ankles, baffled him. The color was bold, as vibrant as a cobalt sky, yet she carried herself with understated elegance, with a soft, reserved nature.

She turned and caught his gaze, and for a moment, for one breathless instant, they looked at each other from across the room.

And that was when he saw the emotion she'd been masking, the flash of pain. She glanced away quickly, but the damage was already done. Suddenly Michael wanted to protect her, to hold her, to...

What? Kiss her? Cover her mouth with his?

Hell and damnation.

He cursed his hormones, the unwelcome blast of testosterone warming his blood. This wasn't the time to form an attraction, to get knocked off his feet.

The only female who should be occupying his mind was Danforth's stalker, and the lady in blue, that delicate little brunette, didn't fit the stalker's description.

As Danforth excused himself from the small circle of partygoers he'd been talking to, he glanced at Michael and motioned to a nearby terrace.

Apparently Danforth needed a short break. Michael shadowed his client, and together they stepped outside.

The terrace was empty, aside from a blonde seated on an ornate bench. Although she'd taken up residence in a dimly lit corner, Michael recognized Heather Burroughs—a polite, rather shy girl who worked for Toby Danforth, one of the politician's handsome young nephews, a single father who'd hired her as a nanny.

Michael knew Heather wasn't a threat to the Danforth clan. He'd checked out everyone employed by the family, including the new nanny. He'd even chatted with Heather earlier that night.

Respecting her privacy, he turned away and focused on his surroundings instead. The summer air was warm, the evening sky sprinkled with budding stars.

Just a short while ago, a fireworks display had lit up the night, cracking like thunder. The massive lawn and adjoining terraces, including this one, had been besieged with people. But things were quiet now.

As Danforth leaned against a columned wall, Michael stood near an empty doorway. And then he looked up and saw her. The brunette he wanted to kiss. The mysterious lady in blue.

Was it him or the man he'd been hired to protect that drew her near? That motivated her to follow them outside?

Danforth righted his posture, and Michael realized the brunette and his client were staring at each other. Did Danforth know her? Was she someone Michael should have been briefed about? Or did she have that mind-numbing effect on every man who locked gazes with her?

The politician snapped out of his trance. "I'm sorry," he said to her. "I didn't mean to be rude, but you bear a striking resemblance to someone I used to know."

The brunette blinked, and Michael suspected that Danforth's admission wasn't what she had expected to hear.

What the hell was going on?

"Was her name Lan Nguyen?" she finally asked.

"Yes. Yes, it was," the older man responded, a perplexed line creasing his brow. "How did you know?"

"Because I'm her daughter, Lea. *Your* daughter, Mr. Danforth, the child you abandoned in Vietnam."

Good God.

The father in question, the former Navy SEAL, couldn't seem to find his voice.

Concerned about a security leak, Michael moved forward and glanced in Heather's direction, motioning for her to keep quiet. She met his gaze and nodded, letting him know she hadn't intended to eavesdrop.

He acknowledged her compliance, then called his second-in-command, alerting his team to keep anyone else from coming onto the terrace.

Most likely, Heather could be trusted, but the last thing Danforth needed was a gossip-bound partygoer walking headfirst into this conversation. Or, heaven forbid, a reporter.

The Vietnam veteran hadn't denied the possibility that this mixed-blood beauty could be his daughter. Which meant what? That her claim could be true?

"Lan...survived?" The older man cleared his throat, the roughness breaking his voice. "She survived the attack on her village? I thought she was dead. I—"

"My mother is dead now," Lea interrupted, then teetered, swaying on her feet.

Worried she might faint, Michael reached for her shoulders, steadying her. He could feel her limbs vibrating, feel her weaving in his arms. "Hold on. Don't pass out."

"Take her home, Michael. Please, take her home." The request came from Danforth, who seemed genuinely concerned. "Stay with her until I contact you. Until we can sort this out."

Then to Lea, he said, "You can trust him. He won't hurt you."

She didn't argue, and neither did Michael. Much to his credit, Danforth did a damn good job of steeling his emotions. He returned to the fund-raiser under the careful watch of the security team, while Michael kept a trembling Lea by his side. He stopped briefly to speak with Heather, who made a solemn vow she would keep quiet. He thanked her, then escorted Lea to an inconspicuous exit.

Once they were in the limo, her tears began to fall. Without thinking, he covered her hand with his, promising everything would be okay.

But by the time he secured her address and got her home, he wasn't quite sure how to make everything okay. They entered her apartment, and she nearly collapsed, crying in earnest.

He reached for her, hugging her in the folds of his jacket, holding her against his heart.

"I thought it would be different," she whispered against his shirt, staining the starched white cotton with streaks of mascara. "I thought telling my father..." Her sentence trailed, drifting into nothingness.

She seemed so small, so fragile. Michael didn't know much about the post-war children who grew up as Amerasians in Vietnam, but he'd been called a half-breed for most of his life. And the derogatory connotation still twisted his gut.

She stopped crying, but he didn't let go. For nearly an hour, he rocked her, offering comfort.

Then something changed, and they became aware of each other's bodies, of his fly pressing her stomach, of being strangers locked in an intimate embrace.

She lifted her head and looked into his eyes. "I noticed you," she said.

He knew she was referring to the fund-raiser, to that instant in time, to the moment she'd revealed the ache in her soul.

He dried the moisture on her cheeks, tempted to taste the saltiness, to absorb her pain, to turn it into pleasure. "I noticed you, too."

"The way you're noticing me now?"

"Yes." He'd wanted to kiss her then, and he wanted to kiss her now. Desperately, he thought. More than words could describe.

One

On Saturday afternoon, Lea answered her door, then stared at the man on the other side.

Michael never visited her at this hour. He never arrived at her apartment during the day, yet the Savannah sun blazed bright and hot, framing him in a warm glow.

He looked incredible, with his dark hair and dark eyes, his square-cut jaw and stunning cheekbones. His shirtsleeves, she noticed, were rolled up to his elbows, but his trousers were pressed to perfection. Michael Whittaker, the CEO of Whittaker and Associates, possessed a conflicting charm: rough yet polished, right down to the slow, Southern drawl.

A voice that sent naked shivers down her spine.

Nervous, she smoothed her blouse and wondered

what had prompted him to stop by. Did he want sex? Would he sweep her into the bedroom? Run those skilled lover's hands all over her body?

"Afternoon," he said.

"Hello." She looked past him and saw a shiny black Mercedes parked on the street. Was that his car?

Lea had been sleeping with Michael for the past month, yet she didn't know what kind of vehicle he drove. Somehow that made her feel cheap, like a bar girl in Vietnam.

Would he discard her after their secret liaison ended? Forget she existed?

She shifted her gaze from the car to the man and then considered touching him, wanting to smooth the lock of hair that slipped onto his forehead. The midday light cast a slight auburn sheen to the dark-brown strands, something she hadn't been aware of before.

But why would she? This was the first time she'd seen him standing in the sun.

"Aren't you going to invite me in?" he asked.

She blinked and nodded. He wasn't a vampire, although up until now, that was how she thought of him: her midnight fantasy, her forbidden lover, the tall, dark shadow who took her breath away.

On the night of the fund-raiser, she and Michael had ended up in bed, touching and kissing and making emotion-drenched love. Much to her surprise, he'd returned the following evening for more, until a month of hot, lust-driven nights went by.

And now, here he was in broad daylight—

"Lea?"

"What? Oh, yes." She stepped back, realizing she'd been blocking his entrance.

He strode to the center of her living room, his hands tucked in his pockets. She couldn't read his body language. Michael wasn't the sort of man a woman could predict.

Should she offer him a drink? Lea honestly didn't know what to do, how to react to his presence. When he arrived at night, the scenario played out like a naughty dream. She would open the door, and he would take control. Without words, without false pretenses, he would start the fantasy, thrilling her with his imagination.

Sometimes he led her to the bedroom. And sometimes he stripped her where she stood and dropped to his knees.

"Lea?" He said her name again, and her face went hot.

Was she blushing?

"Are you all right?" he asked in that spine-tingling drawl.

"Yes, I'm fine."

"I saw the paternity test results."

He met her gaze, and her heartbeat staggered. She shouldn't be having an affair with her father's bodyguard, with the security consultant hired to protect him. "Then you know for certain that Abraham Danforth is my father."

He cocked his head. "Yes."

"Is that why you're here? To convince me to speak with him?" After the fund-raiser, she'd agreed to take the paternity test Danforth's attorneys insisted upon. But even so, she refused to form an alliance with the former Navy SEAL who'd sired her. Of course, she couldn't explain why, especially to Michael.

"I'm not here on Danforth's behalf." He reached for the oversize seashell on her glass-topped coffee table, studied it and set it back down. Next, he assessed the drawings she collected, the sketches from sidewalk artists on River Street. She kept her bungalow-style apartment furnished with items that reflected the local culture, with no reminders of home, no painful memories of Vietnam.

"Will you stay with me, Lea?"

Her pulse jumped. "Stay with you?"

"For a few weeks. At my house."

"Why?" was all she could think to say. "Why are you inviting me to your home?"

"So we can get to know each other better." He moved a little closer, but he didn't touch her. "So we can spend more time together."

It was a compelling offer. Mystifying. Exciting. But Lea knew she should refuse.

She toyed with the barrette confining her hair. "I have to work. I'm not on a holiday."

"Neither am I. But that doesn't mean we can't have an adventure. Visit some clubs, go out to dinner, walk along the shore. Get to be friends."

Her reserve wavered. She wanted Michael's respect, his friendship. But did she deserve it?

"Well?" he asked, a smile playing on his lips and crinkling the corners of his eyes.

"Yes," she finally said, anxious to be near him. "I'll stay with you for a few weeks."

"Good." He smiled again, then gave her directions to his house and told her to meet him there at five o'clock.

When he turned and headed for the door, he left her in a daze.

She watched him walk to the shiny black Mercedes, flick the electronic lock, get behind the wheel and drive away.

At least she knew what kind of car he drove, she told herself, as she rummaged through her clothes and fretted about what to pack.

Michael left Lea's house and proceeded to Crofthaven, the impressive mansion and estate her father owned.

He took the paved drive to the gate, the path flanked by magnificent moss-draped trees. Southern beauty at its finest, he thought, cursing to himself.

He was deceiving Lea, and now he was about to deceive Danforth, as well.

But what choice did he have?

Michael arrived at the columned mansion, a historical landmark built over a century before. Crofthaven boasted prestige and charm, as well as its own tragic ghost.

A member of the household staff ushered him into the sprawling entryway, where he opted to wait for his high-profile client.

Moments later, Abraham Danforth descended a spiral staircase. He was new to politics, but he had the kind of charisma that bolstered his squeaky-clean image. So much so, the media had dubbed him Honest Abe II.

Danforth decided to conduct their meeting in the garden, a location that provided plenty of privacy. They took up residence on a marble bench, summer blooms flourishing around them. Beyond the garden, a peach orchard scented the air. But the peaceful surroundings didn't pacify Michael's nerves, didn't make this meeting any less stressful.

"What's on your mind?" Danforth asked. In spite of the temperature, he looked cool and composed in pale gray trousers and a short-sleeve designer pullover.

Michael wasn't faring quite so well. A line of sweat trailed down his back. The hot August day would develop into a hot August night. And heated nights had become his obsession. As well as his downfall.

Because of Lea.

"There's something I have to explain." Feeling like a traitor, he met the older man's gaze. No matter how he tried to justify his behavior, bedding Danforth's daughter wasn't a gentlemanly thing to do. "Lea and I are—"

"Are what?" the politician prodded.

"Involved."

One eyebrow lifted. "How involved?"

"We're lovers," he responded, as honestly as he could. "And she's going to stay with me for a few weeks. So I'll be working a light schedule. My security team will continue to provide protection for you, but I probably won't be available."

Danforth squinted in the sun. "When did all of this occur?"

Michael knew he meant the affair. "It started that first night. I didn't intend to be with her, not like that. But we were attracted to each other, and..." He let his words trail. He wasn't about to admit that sex was all he and Lea had in common.

For the past month, they barely talked, barely communicated beyond a primal level, beyond late-night hours of passion.

"That first night?" Danforth stared him down. "I asked you to take her home and you slept with her? I entrusted you with her safety."

"I know. I'm sorry." He paused, keeping his emotions in check, the tightness in his stomach, the confusion Lea stirred. "But she needed me. And I needed her. Sometimes these things just happen."

"Yes, I suppose they do," Danforth responded, his tone quiet.

Michael nodded, realizing the other man wasn't going to press the issue any further. But why would he? The widower was burdened with his own brand of guilt. He'd been married when he'd made love with Lea's mother. An affair that resulted from a war-related injury and a bout of amnesia, but an affair just the same.

Although the media hadn't caught wind of it, Danforth wanted to come clean, to schedule a press conference and introduce Lea to the world, but she refused to have anything to do with him.

"I wish things would have turned out differently," Danforth said. "I never meant to leave Lan behind."

"I know." But Lea's mother was dead now, Michael thought. It was too late for Danforth to apologize to her.

Honest Abe's honesty only took him so far.

As the politician lapsed into silence, Michael pondered his recent suspicion, his belief that Lea might be the stalker he'd been tracking.

Yes, Lea. The woman he seduced almost every night.

She didn't fit the stalker's description, but she could have altered her appearance. And she was a computer analyst, more than capable of sending threatening e-mails and writing the virus that had crashed her father's computer several months before.

But he wasn't about to reveal his suspicions to Danforth. Not until he knew the truth.

The older man shifted his weight. "Why won't Lea give me a chance?"

"I don't know. She's still hurting, I guess." Michael couldn't speak for Lea, which was exactly why he'd invited her to his home. He needed to spend some time with her, to get to know her on a deeper level. To prove, he hoped, that he wasn't sleeping with the enemy.

Michael lived on a private street. A brick wall and an electronic gate encompassed the perimeter of his property.

Lea stopped at the intercom and announced her arrival. Once she was permitted onto the grounds, she followed a tree-lined driveway to an impressive two-story home.

She parked her car and Michael came out of the house wearing jeans and a T-shirt, his hair combed casually away from his face. His feet were bare and instantly she was reminded of her childhood, of the place she'd left behind.

"Is your luggage in the trunk?" he asked.

She looked up at him. He stood nearly a foot taller than her, with broad shoulders and long, lean muscles. "Yes, it is."

"Will you flip the lock?"

"Of course." She met his gaze, but she couldn't decipher the emotion in his eyes. But she never could, not even when they were in bed.

He removed her suitcase. He was a passionate man, an erotic lover, but he was complicated, too. Sometimes he smiled and sometimes he seemed stern. She suspected that he kept his true heart hidden. But she did that, too.

They approached the door and she stalled.

"What's wrong?" he asked.

"Nothing." She glanced down, debating what do about her shoes. He watched her, making her self-conscious. She decided to leave things be. She'd worked hard to shed her Vietnamese habits, to become an American woman. And women in the states didn't remove their shoes before entering a home. Instead, she took extra care to wipe her feet on the Welcome mat.

They entered the great room, where expansive windows offered a tidal marsh view. "Your home is exquisite," she said. The architectural detail included oak cabinetry, stucco walls and a massive skylight.

"Thank you. It's totally secure, with a state-of-the art security system. The exterior is equipped with intrusion sensors. It was designed with my clients in mind." He gestured broadly. "Sometimes they stay here when they're avoiding the media. Or taking refuge from personal threats."

"You created a fortress."

"Whittaker and Associates protects high-profile clients."

"Like my father."

He nodded, and they both fell silent.

She glanced at the fireplace and noticed the stonework was inlayed with chunks of coral. The furnishings were white, with turquoise-colored accents. He'd spared no expense to make his home into a showplace. "Has my father ever stayed here?"

"No. He's well protected at Crofthaven."

She knew the name of Danforth's mansion, the place where his other children were raised. Lea could never be like her half siblings. They were blue bloods, born into a prestigious American family. She was *my lai,* an Amerasian born on the fringes of Vietnamese society.

"Let me show you to your room." Michael reached for her suitcase. "It's upstairs, just down the hall from the master bedroom."

They ascended an oak staircase and she followed him into an elegant suite, with wood floors and a four-poster bed. Glass doors led to a balcony overlooking a private dock.

"This is beautiful." The walk-in closet was far too big for her simple belongings and an adjoining bathroom provided a sunken tub and a separate shower. Lights framed a vanity mirror. "I'm humbled."

"It's the most feminine suite in the house."

"It's more than I imagined. Thank you." Would he visit her later? Slip into her room? Stay the night? Although they were lovers, they'd never awakened in each other's arms. Michael always left her apartment before the sun came up. Lea longed to cuddle with him, to bask in the afterglow of their lovemaking, but she wasn't brave enough to tell him that.

He placed her suitcase on a luggage stand. "Come on. I'll show you the rest of the house."

He led her down the hall, and his room left her speechless. She wandered around the suite, taking in every piece of furniture, every carefully thought-out detail. Even the bathroom was gorgeous, providing his and her sinks and a cedarwood sauna designed for a couple.

"Do you plan to get married someday?" she asked.

"Yes, but I'm not searching for a wife." He shifted his stance. "I'm hoping the right woman will come along."

She tried to picture his future bride. A tall, slim blonde, she decided. A lady who wore fashionable clothes and hosted Southern parties, making use of his extraordinary home. "Do you want children?"

He nodded. "Do you?"

She glanced away, wishing she hadn't started this conversation.

"Lea?" He pressed.

She adjusted her purse strap, pushing it farther down her shoulder, keeping it from rubbing against her neck like a hangman's noose. She was having an affair with Michael because she needed the closeness his body provided, the comfort of his touch. Dreaming beyond that was dangerous. But she dreamed just the same. "Yes, I want children. And a husband who loves me." A husband who wouldn't judge her, a husband she could tell her secrets to.

"I want that, too. With a wife, I mean. I want the kind of marriage my parents didn't have."

"They were unhappy?"

The muscles in his face tightened. "All they did was fight. Scream and curse at each other."

"I'm sorry." She'd assumed he'd been reared in a respectable environment. "Children should be nurtured. They shouldn't be subjected to anger."

"Or pain," he said, smoothing a lock of her hair, leaving a lump in her throat.

After an awkward beat of silence, he escorted her from his room. They went downstairs and he gave her a tour of the ground floor. An eight-hundred-square-foot gym led to a landscaped yard and a gazebo-framed hot tub. The game room was equipped with a pool table, air hockey and a jukebox. A wet bar offered sodas and spirits.

"You live well," she said.

"It keeps my clients entertained."

What about his lovers? she wondered. How many other women had he invited to his home?

"What's in here?" she asked, as they passed a closed door.

"Surveillance monitors. It's a security office."

She nodded and moved on, not wanting to steer the conversation in that direction.

Michael offered her a casual meal, and they spent the rest of the evening eating sandwiches and talking about inconsequential things. At bedtime, he walked her to her room.

They stood in the doorway, gazing at each other. She couldn't think of anything to say. She could smell the faded scent of his cologne, a woodsy fragrance that made the moment even more intimate.

He touched her cheek, and her knees went weak. She tried to keep her breathing steady. She didn't want him to know how nervous she was.

He caressed her face with the back of his hand, and her heart pounded much too hard. He didn't kiss her, but she didn't expect him to. He would come back later, she thought. When her room was dark, when moonlight dappled the bed.

He dropped his hand, but his eyes were still locked onto hers. "Good night, Lea."

"Good night, Michael."

Tall, dark Michael. She watched him head toward the master bedroom. He still wore jeans and a T-shirt, and his feet were still bare.

She closed her door and suddenly she panicked. She didn't want to need him this badly. She didn't want to lie in bed and wait for him. But by the time she bathed and climbed into bed, the sheets enveloped her in anticipation.

Had Michael bathed, too? Would his hair be freshly washed? Would the damp strands trail water over her breasts? She could almost feel him leaning over her, lowering his mouth.

Lea glanced at the clock, anxious for her lover.

But as the night wore on, as the moon slipped behind the trees and disappeared into a void of darkness, she found herself alone, waiting for a man who never came.

Two

Lea entered the kitchen the following morning, trying to keep her emotions under control. Michael was at the stove, scrambling eggs. He looked up from the pan, and she couldn't seem to find her voice to greet him in a casual way.

He spoke first. "I gave my housekeeper a few weeks off. I thought it would be easier for us to be alone."

Why? she wondered. Why did it matter if they were alone? If he didn't intend to be with her, to treat her like a lover, there was no reason to hide their relationship.

"Did you get a good night's rest?" he asked.

Lea merely stared at him. She hadn't fallen asleep until dawn, and the sun was too bright on the window shades, too cheerful for a woman whose vampire never appeared. "I was restless."

"Me, too. Maybe we'll sleep better tonight." He turned off the flame and steered the conversation in another direction. "I hope you can stand my cooking. Madeline usually fixes meals for my guests."

Lea couldn't help but wonder why he hadn't slept well. "Madeline is your housekeeper?"

"Yes. She and her family live nearby. She's been a trusted employee for years."

"I don't mind cooking. I took culinary classes in college." And she knew how to make all sorts of American dishes.

"Good." He reached into a cabinet and removed two plates. "I'll hold you to that. But for now, we'll have to survive on my efforts."

She moved forward to take the china. She assumed they would eat breakfast in the morning room, a cozy enclave located off the kitchen.

His hand touched hers in the exchange. "You look pretty, Lea."

"Do I?" She'd brushed her hair until it shone, allowing it to fall freely to her waist. Her flower-printed dress was made of summer cotton, with thin straps and a simple bodice. She'd chosen sandals for her feet.

"You always look pretty." Although his expression gave nothing away, his words remained kind. "Sometimes I think about the fund-raiser. About how easy it was to notice you."

She clutched the plates to her chest. She could almost hear her heart pounding against them, making a clanking sound. "I noticed you, too."

"Of course you did. I was your father's bodyguard."

"You still are."

"Not for these next few weeks. I told him I was working a light schedule. That my staff would be providing protection for him."

"Why? So you could spend more time with me?"

He snared her gaze. "Yes. That's exactly why."

She wished she could admit that she'd waited for him last night, but she wouldn't dare. She wasn't about to embarrass herself.

Five minutes later, they sat across from each other at a wrought-iron table, the sun filtering through the blinds. Besides the eggs, he'd fried a platter of ham and toasted wheat bread. The coffee was bitter and dark, but Lea preferred tea.

"I forgot the orange juice." Michael went back into the kitchen and returned with a plastic carton. He poured the juice into Lea's glass. "I can tell you don't like the coffee."

She looked up. "I'm sorry. I don't drink much coffee."

He smiled a little. "I'll have to make a note of that in your file." He moved his fingers in the air, typing on an imaginary keyboard. "Lea doesn't drink much coffee."

He didn't really have a file on her, did he? She glanced at his mouth, at the slight tilt of his lips. He must be teasing her. "You sound like a cop."

"I was an MP." He scooped a second helping of

eggs onto his plate. He'd scrambled enough to feed an army. "Military police."

"I assumed that's what you meant."

"I've always been a law-and-order type of guy." He leaned forward, his smile gone, his gaze much too intense. "Being a security specialist suits me."

She tasted the ham, chewing carefully, trying to appear more relaxed than she felt. Whenever his features turned hard, whenever his eyes went dark, he seemed ruthless. Maybe he did keep a file on her, notes about the anxious woman who'd waited for him last night.

"I'm an investigator, too," he said. "I'm investigating a case for your father."

Lea's pulse skyrocketed, hammering horribly at her throat, throbbing at her temples. Had Michael been hired to find the woman who'd threatened Abraham Danforth? To bring her to justice? "I don't want to talk about my father."

"Why not?"

She gripped her fork a little harder, hoping her hand didn't tremble. "He abandoned me and my mother."

Michael's voice gentled. "He didn't mean to. He thought Lan was dead."

"I know. He told me that on the night of the fund-raiser."

"Then why won't you give him a chance?"

Because her guilt wouldn't permit it, she thought. Because it was safer to stay away from Abraham and his family.

She looked across the table at Michael. Did he

suspect her? Had he invited her to his home to keep an eye on her?

No, she thought. No. She'd been cautious, covering her tracks. The evidence wasn't supposed to lead in her direction.

"You have no right to do this," she said.

"Do what? Convince you that your dad is a decent guy?"

Lea didn't respond, so she and Michael finished their breakfast without finishing their conversation. She helped him clear the table and load the dishwasher. When he glanced at her, his expression grim, she struggled with her conscience. At one time, she'd believed that her vengeance was just, that she had a right to hate her father. But now she wasn't so sure.

"I have to unpack," she said, finding an excuse to retreat to her room, to hide from the shame of threatening Abraham Danforth, of deceiving his bodyguard, of wishing that Michael would wrap her in his arms and wash her sins away.

Michael checked his watch. How many hours was Lea going to avoid him? It was noon and she still hadn't emerged.

He sat in his home office, sorting through his notes about Lady Savannah, the woman who'd been threatening Danforth.

Troubled, he leaned back in his chair. Did Lea fit Lady Savannah's profile?

Yes, he thought. She did. But he couldn't condemn her without proof. What if he was wrong? What if Lea wasn't the stalker? What if she hadn't sent those cryptic e-mails? Or crashed her dad's computer? Or given herself the name Lady Savannah?

He put the file away and went upstairs to knock on her door. She answered, seeming lost, vulnerable—much too fragile, with her delicate bone structure and slim curves. He wanted to hold her, but touching her would only complicate his dilemma, making it worse.

The four-poster bed caught his attention, and he frowned at the mahogany posts and peach-colored duvet cover. He'd had every intention of stealing into her room last night, of making love to her, but he'd paced his quarters instead, fighting the urge.

How could he continue to sleep with her? With a woman he suspected of a crime? How could he use her for his own pleasure, then cast her aside if she were Lady Savannah?

"I'm sorry I upset you at breakfast," he said, moving farther into her room.

"I'm sorry, too." She sat on the edge of the bed and smoothed the front of her dress. The feminine fabric fit her graceful style and so did the backdrop of pillows, the romantic display of ribbon and lace. "I overreacted. I blamed you for being loyal to my father. But that isn't fair. You wouldn't work for a man you didn't trust."

"No, I wouldn't. But that doesn't mean Danforth is a saint. From what I understand, he was an absent father to the rest of his children, too. After his wife died, he pawned them off on other people. Relatives, nannies, au pairs, whoever was available. And then there were the boarding schools."

She seemed surprised. "I assumed he was close to his other children."

"I think he's trying to make amends with them now that they're grown."

"He's running for state senator. Maybe he's worried about his image." Thoughtful, she paused. "Maybe that's why he's taken an interest in his family. Why he's willing to accept me."

"That's possible, I suppose. But I think it's more than that."

"How can you be sure?"

"I've got a knack for figuring people out." But not Lea, he thought. She baffled him. When she bent her head, the gesture made her seem younger than her twenty-seven years.

Finally, she looked up and their eyes met. She had beautiful eyes, exotically shaped, with a sweep of thick, dark lashes. He wanted to cup her face, to kiss her, to forget that she was a suspect. But he knew he couldn't.

"Do you really have a file on me, Michael?"

"Yes, but I was just kidding about the coffee earlier." He sat next to her. "The day after the fundraiser, I started a background check on you." Something he refused to apologize for. "I had to. It's part of my job."

"Because you slept with me?"

"Because you claimed to be Danforth's daughter, and he's my client." He'd given Danforth information about her, facts he'd uncovered. Of course, Michael hadn't suspected her of being Lady Savannah then. Now he analyzed those facts in a different light. "Your file is mostly government documents. Your immigration papers, things like that. I'll show it to you if you'd like." But he wouldn't show her Lady Savannah's file. Not yet.

"Is there a copy of the paternity test in my file?"

"Yes. But Danforth gave it to me. It was sent to him, just as it was mailed to you."

For a long, drawn-out moment, they didn't say anything else, making his investigation seem like a sham. But deep down, he knew it wasn't. His suspicions were valid.

"Tell me about your childhood," he said. "About growing up in Vietnam."

"What good will that do?"

"How else am I going to get to know you?" He tried to picture her, a little girl living in a war-ravaged country. "To understand what you've been through?"

She reached for a pillow and hugged it. "My past isn't important."

"You were born after the fall of Saigon, after the U.S. withdrew." He rose from the bed, putting a physical distance between them, stopping himself from touching her, from feeling too much. Already he wanted to hold her, to give comfort. "You were a child of the enemy. That couldn't have been easy."

"Some of the women who had babies like me threw them away." She cradled the pillow as though it were an infant. "But my mother tried to protect me."

"She loved you."

"And I loved her. But it wasn't enough."

He thought about his family, about the shame of being gossiped about, of watching neighbors turn away in disgust. "Were people cruel to you?"

She went still, the ceiling fan above her head stirring her hair, feathering the long, loose strands around her face.

He remained near the window, watching her, studying her features, the ethnicity she couldn't deny.

"Other children used to throw rocks at me," she finally said. "Taunting me with an ugly *my lai* rhyme. But their parents didn't care. No one reprimanded them. It was like that from the beginning, from my earliest memory." She paused to take an audible breath. "My mother was treated badly, too. Like a whore. I was glad to leave Vietnam."

"And now you're in the land of the free." But was she any happier? Had she moved on with her life? Or was she still trapped within her grief, blaming Danforth for her pain?

Michael knew Lea had come to America through the Amerasian Homecoming Act, an act that allowed Vietnamese Amerasians and specified members of their families to enter the U.S. as immigrants. "I obtained copies of your records from the Philippine Refugee Processing Center." The refugee camp where she'd lived, he thought. Where the government had sent her before she'd come to America.

She cradled the pillow again. "It would have been easier if I wasn't alone. If my mother had been with me."

Michael nodded. Lan had died soon after Lea's

eighteenth birthday, the year her application had been processed.

"I worked hard in the PRPC classes," she said. "I wanted to learn English, to speak like an American."

"And you do."

"Like someone who was born here?"

"Yes. Very much so." And that had been her intention, he realized. Once she'd arrived in the States, she must have spent years perfecting the language the PRPC had taught her, losing the Asian inflection in her voice, listening to Americans, mimicking their gestures and casual phrases.

She looked up at him. "I wish I could talk like you."

He couldn't help but smile. "You lived in California. I was born and bred in Georgia."

"I could practice." She imitated his drawl and made him laugh.

"I don't sound like that." He trapped her gaze, teasing her, exaggerating his accent. "Do I?"

She shook her head and the moment turned gentle, warm and inviting. Too warm, he thought, as his heart stirred. Too inviting.

He blew out a rough breath, breaking the spell. "I told Danforth about our affair."

Her skin paled. "You told my father? Why?"

"I work for him. I wanted him to know the truth."

The ceiling fan whirred, the blades cutting through the air like knives, feathering her hair again. "Are you really interested in being my friend?"

If she were innocent, he thought. If his investigation cleared her name. "Of course I am. In fact, I think we should go out tonight."

"Where?"

"To an art show."

Her eyes lit up. "At the new gallery downtown? I've heard about it."

Michael jammed his hands in his pockets. He didn't want Lea to be the stalker. He didn't want to look into those beautiful eyes and see the vicious things Lady Savannah had done. "My assistant told me about it. Cindy always knows what's going on."

"I don't socialize very much." Distracted, she glanced at a crystal trinket box on the nightstand. "But it took me a while to find a job and get used to this area. I was nervous about moving here, about approaching my father. I've only been in Savannah for eight months." She sighed. "But you must know that already."

Yes, he knew. But he also knew that Lady Savannah had begun to threaten Danforth in February, a month after Lea, his prime suspect, settled in Savannah.

The gallery was located in a three-story historic building, each floor presenting a theme. The garden level was just that, a garden of artistic expression that led to outdoor sculptures and carefully tended foliage.

Lea walked beside Michael, awed by the moment, by the floral fragrance and haunting displays. They stopped in front of a ghostlike statue, a chalk-white female figure with gems in her eyes.

"She looks like she's watching us," Michael said. "But it's just an illusion."

Lea turned to face her companion, wondering if their affair was an illusion. If he would ever return to her bed.

They proceeded to the next sculpture, a male angel with his arms raised to the sky. He was strong and powerful, his armor painted an iridescent shade of blue.

"He's a warring angel." Michael gestured to the slain demons at the celestial being's feet.

"Good versus evil." Lea noticed a row of white flowers circling the display. "Good triumphs."

"So it seems." He tilted his head. "Sometimes it's hard to tell who's good and who's evil."

A lump formed in her throat. Maybe he did suspect her. Maybe he was playing a game of cat and mouse. "Good people are capable of doing bad things."

"Is that a confession?"

"For what?" she asked, testing him, waiting for him to accuse her.

He touched her cheek instead. He looked familiar in the moonlight, her dark-skinned vampire come to life.

"You're so warm," he said.

"The air is warm." She wanted to kiss him, but that would only allow him to taste her anxiety, the fear that he might be investigating her.

"We should go inside." He escorted her to the main entrance on the parlor floor. They took a set of concrete stairs, chipped and faded from wear.

Then suddenly the tone of the gallery changed. Other patrons gathered in the reception area, around a buffet table laden with catered appetizers and multicolored napkins. The lights were bright, the wood floors polished to a high sheen. A cut-glass chandelier cast a glow over a temporary bar, where plastic cups beckoned for tips.

"There's Cindy," Michael said. "My assistant."

Lea watched a tall, stunning blonde approach them. With her strappy heels and trim white suit, she received a slew of admiring glances, turning heads along the way. Her throat was bare, Lea noticed, except for a hint of lace beneath her jacket.

"Michael." The blonde leaned forward to give him a quick peck on the cheek. "You brought a companion."

He introduced the women, and Cindy extended her hand. She was Lea's idea of Savannah chic, with a gilded voice and a blooming smile. Somehow she managed to blend Southern grace with an uptown attitude, a lady who always kept her cell phone charged.

"Well, now." Cindy measured Lea's petite frame and waist-length hair. "Where has my boss been keeping you?"

"In my dungeon," Michael interjected.

"I'll bet. She's beautiful."

Next to Cindy, Lea didn't feel beautiful. She felt small and insignificant in her two-piece silk garment. A *my lai* who'd been pelted with rocks.

"I hope you're both enjoying the show." The blonde clutched a jeweled handbag. On her wrist, she wore a diamond tennis bracelet.

"It's lovely." Lea managed to speak up, wishing she'd chosen an outfit that didn't resemble *Ao Dai*. She tried so hard to be an American, yet here she was, dressed in mock-Vietnamese attire, a long flowing smock and baggy trousers, created by a crafty U.S. designer.

Cindy chatted with Michael, then excused herself, gesturing with her diamond-draped arm. "I'm going to mingle for a while." She turned to Lea. "It was nice meeting you." That said, she departed, leaving Michael and Lea alone.

Silent, they remained near the buffet table, their gazes locked. Cindy's perfume, an orchid mist, still lingered.

"Would you like a drink?" he asked.

"No, thank you." Lea waited a beat. She was curious about Cindy, but she hated to bombard him with questions so quickly. "Are you going to have one?"

"Maybe later."

She thought about the angel in the garden, about good and evil. "How long has Cindy worked for you?"

"About three years."

"Is she your personal assistant?"

"She's my administrative assistant." He smoothed the front of his hair. It was straight and dark, but the auburn highlights had emerged, a reflection from a nearby lamp. "Cindy's very efficient."

"She's stunning."

"Yes, she is." He moved closer. "But she wears too much perfume."

"Is that your only complaint?"

"I'm not a complainer." He moved even closer, his loafers tapping the wood floor. One, two three...and he was there, just inches from her. "I like being around beautiful women."

Lea's heartbeat staggered. She wanted to latch on to his shoulders, to absorb the power of his body, but she wanted to push him away, too. "Have you ever been lovers?"

"Who? Me and Cindy?" His expression turned hard, making his face more angular, his cheekbones more prominent. "That's a hell of a question. But no, we've never been together. She isn't my type."

Liar, she thought. Cindy was nearly every man's type. "Does she have someone in her life?"

"She did. They split up a few months ago. It was his choice. She didn't take it well."

Suddenly Lea felt bad for the other woman. "She loved him?"

Michael shrugged. "I suppose, but she's getting over him now. She has her sights set on someone else."

"Who?"

"I don't know. She hasn't told me his name. But I have a feeling he's a colleague of mine. She's been asking me for advice. Asking me how to get this mystery man to notice her." He laughed at that. "Women can be so dramatic."

"It wouldn't take much to notice her. He must be preoccupied." She glanced around, looking for Cindy, but the blonde had vanished. "I wonder who he is."

"Someone with money, I'll bet. Her last boyfriend was loaded."

Lea recalled the wealthy man she'd dated in Little Saigon, the man who'd destroyed her innocence. "Sometimes rich men use women."

"Cindy's too shrewd to get used."

But I'm not, she thought, as Michael's gaze swept over her. I'm not.

Three

Michael and Lea wandered around the gallery and Lea stopped at an unusual display.

"This is my favorite artist." She moved closer to the three-dimensional wall hanging, a larger-than-life piece comprised of discarded objects. "They say he turns trash into treasure. He finds things in junkyards and Dumpsters and makes something important out of them."

Michael didn't respond. He just looked at Lea, at her long, flowing hair and delicate profile. He wanted to tell her that she wasn't an unwanted object. That she was strong and beautiful.

But then he thought about Lady Savannah and the tenderness in his heart twisted like vines, leaving him in a state of confusion.

Stalking was a serious crime, a dangerous crime. Michael had spent countless hours holed up in his office, poring over Danforth's case, trying to piece together the puzzle. And the clues kept leading to Lea.

To the woman he wanted to hold at night.

"I'm ready for that drink," he said, anxious to dull his senses. "What about you?"

"No, thank you. I'd like to stay here."

With the trash that had been turned into treasure, he thought. With old rakes and paintbrushes and books with torn covers. With greeting cards not good enough to save, with letters someone had thrown away.

"Why don't I bring you a drink?" he said. She couldn't seem to take her eyes off the display and he imagined her disappearing into it, slipping into scenery that made her feel safe.

"Maybe some cranberry juice." She remained where she was, her gaze fixed on the wall hanging. "With a little ice."

He went downstairs, wondering if he should have offered her a plate of food, too. The parlor floor was still busy, still bustling with art patrons enjoying the festivities.

He ordered a beer for himself and juice for Lea. He spotted Cindy with a group of Savannah socialites, but luckily she didn't see him. He didn't want her accompanying him upstairs and intruding on Lea's solitude. It didn't take a genius to figure out that Cindy intimidated Lea, that the dark-haired beauty didn't feel comfortable around the statuesque blonde.

He returned to Lea, only to find her in the same

frame of mind, lost in a world of throwaway art. He handed her the cranberry juice.

"Thank you."

"You're welcome." He had the notion to run his hand along her cheek, but his fingers were cold from carrying the drinks.

Did she know how much alike they were? he wondered. That somewhere deep down, they were connected?

"How do you say half-breed in your language?" he asked.

Her skin paled. "Why?"

"Because I want to know."

She didn't answer.

"Tell me, Lea. Tell me what it is."

She took a step back, moving away from him, making him feel like a monster. He couldn't imagine how he was going to feel if she were guilty, if he had to turn her over to the authorities.

"Just say it," he persisted, pushing her for a response.

"Con lai," she snapped.

"Did people call you that?"

"Yes." Her pretty features distorted, signifying her pain.

Michael reached out to skim her cheek, giving in to the need to touch her. "People used to call me a half-breed when I was growing up."

"Because you're part American Indian?"

He nodded and took his hand away, knowing he'd left her chilled. His hands were still cold. "Even my dad called me that. He was white. My mother was from the Seminole Nation."

Her voice quavered. "Your father was cruel to you?"

"Not with his fists, but with his words." He glanced at the artwork consuming the gallery wall. "Every time he put me down, I was determined to make something of myself. To prove that I was better than him."

"And what about your mother? What kind of relationship did you have with her?"

"It was strained. She was obsessed with my dad, with the affairs he was having. Whenever she suspected him of cheating, she went ballistic, clawing and scratching at him, screaming so everyone in the neighborhood knew what was going on."

"He had no right to cheat on her." Lea clutched her cup, holding it to her chest. "She was his wife. She deserved better."

"I know. But the way she carried on just made things worse. Sometimes she used to throw his clothes onto the lawn, right in front of our apartment building." Michael could still recall the shame, the embarrassment that overwhelmed him. "People thought she was crazy. That screwy Seminole, they used to say. That schizoid squaw." He paused, took a breath. "I hated people calling her that."

"Schizoid?"

"Squaw."

"Is that a dirty word?"

"Some say it translates to the totality of being female, which is a good thing. But others think it's slanderous and offensive. That it refers to a woman's private parts."

"Your neighbors didn't mean it in a good way when they said it about your mother."

"No, they didn't." He turned, looking for an escape route. "I need some air. Do you want to join me?"

She nodded and they proceeded outside, where a third-story balcony overlooked a collection of historic buildings.

The summer air proved muggy, but Michael was grateful for the Southern sky. He leaned against the wrought-iron rail and drank his beer.

Lea stood beside him. She'd barely touched her drink, the ice in her cup melting into the bloodred liquid, thinning the contents.

"My dad had a thing for blondes," he said. "I have no idea why he married a Seminole."

"He cheated with women like Cindy?"

"I never said anything about Cindy. You can't lump all blondes together."

Her chin shot up. "I wasn't."

"Weren't you?" he accused. "Cindy isn't a bad person. She's just tough. She grew up the way I did. Poor, determined to climb her way to the top."

"She doesn't seem sincere."

"Do I?" he asked.

Lea didn't respond. She sipped her watered-down juice instead.

"I don't, do I?" Because he wasn't, he thought. Because he suspected her of a crime. "I like you, Lea. I swear, that's the truth. I feel something for you."

Her eyes locked onto his. "Something?"

He set his cup on a nearby ledge. "Kinship. Lust. Confusion. I'm not sure if I can explain what I feel."

"You just did." She gave him a shaky smile. "I feel those things, too."

"Why haven't we ever talked before now?" He dragged his hand through his hair. "We slept together for a month and we barely communicated. I've never been that callous with a woman before."

"Are you apologizing to me, Michael?"

"Yes." God help him, he was. But that wouldn't stop him from investigating her.

"I'm not very good at relationships." She tilted her head and moonlight framed her face, casting a silvery glow over her skin. "There was a man in California, in Little Saigon. I thought I loved him. I thought he loved me."

"What happened?"

"I slept with him." She sipped her drink, the ice still melting. "I wanted to wait until we were married, but he said I didn't need to remain a virgin."

Michael studied her posture, the tension in her shoulders. "He took advantage of you."

"I was young. Only nineteen. He was older than me, close to thirty. A wealthy Vietnamese businessman, very traditional. I should have known better. He had no intention of marrying me. It didn't matter if we were in America. I was still *con lai* to him." She set her cup next to Michael's. "He bought me pretty things, but I didn't know I was his whore. Not until he told me he was marrying someone else, a girl his family approved of."

"And what did you do, Lea?"

"I worked hard to better myself, to get a college education, to stop being *con lai*."

"There's nothing wrong with being a half-breed. It's who we are. It makes us special."

"It doesn't make me feel special."

"I know. I've been fighting that feeling all my life." He looked into her eyes and saw a reflection of himself. "Are you ashamed of your mother's culture? Of the things she taught you?"

"Sometimes. But I don't want to be."

"Then share some of it with me."

"How?" She seemed lost, like the child she'd once been, a little girl who'd never found her place in society.

"You can teach me how to make a Vietnamese meal. Tomorrow, after we both get home from work."

"It's been so long since I've—"

He placed his finger over her lips. "Don't make excuses. Just say yes."

When he took his hand away, she didn't say yes. But she didn't say no, either. She simply watched him, and he wondered what she was thinking.

"Are you going to share your mother's culture with me?" she asked.

Michael realized he didn't have a choice. He couldn't expect something from her that he wasn't willing to give. "I'll do the best I can."

She assessed his response. "The best you can?"

"There are a lot of things I was never taught. My mother gave up her traditions to marry my father, to live his way." He reached for his beer and finished it, combating the dryness in his throat. "Her family was from the Big Cypress Reservation in Florida, but she moved to Atlanta to be with my dad. That's where I was raised."

"I thought you were from Savannah."

"No. I moved here later. After I got out of the service, after my mother died."

"Is your father gone, too?"

He shrugged. "I have no idea. He split when I was still in high school. He left my mom and me with nothing." Nothing but a roach-infested apartment and a welfare check, he thought. "She cried for him almost every night. She waited for him to come back."

Lea moved closer. "Why did she love him so much?"

"It wasn't love. Not in a healthy sense of the word." Michael glanced up the sky, at the stars lighting up the night. "She was fixated on him, on everything he did, and he knew how to charm her, especially after an argument."

"But he didn't charm you."

"I'm not a woman. He had a way with women."

Her voice turned soft. "So do you."

"Not like him." Michael had the urge to kiss her, to drag her against his body and release the tightness in his chest, the ache of needing her. But he wasn't about to play his father's game.

He was already guilty of keeping the spark between them alive, of inviting her to his home, of toying with both of their emotions in a dark and dangerous way.

The following evening, after Lea's workday ended, she arrived at Michael's house using the security code he'd given her to open the electronic gate. With her arms full of groceries, she tackled the keyless-entry front door and headed straight for the kitchen. After placing the bags on the counter, she spotted a hand-written note from Michael.

Don't start the meal without me.

Fine, she thought. But where was he? And how long would he be gone?

Unsure of what else to do, she unpacked the groceries and then went upstairs to change, to remove her summer suit, panty hose and heels. Lea worked for CCS Enterprises, a networking and consulting firm that specialized in corporate computer solutions, and her position required professional attire.

Eager to relax, she slipped on a pair of jeans and a T-shirt, then banded her hair into a ponytail. But by the time she descended the stairs, she got an ominous feeling.

A feeling that she was being watched.

Did Michael have surveillance cameras hidden throughout his home? Had he left her alone purposely? Was she being filmed?

She looked around the great room, telling herself to quit being so paranoid. Of course Michael had surveillance cameras in his home, but he probably only used them when he was protecting a client, when he and his security team were inspecting the premises for intruders.

He wouldn't film a lover.

Would he?

The front door opened, and she froze, like a proverbial deer caught in the headlights.

"Evening." Michael filled the doorway, with his broad shoulders and tall, muscular frame. He wore a black suit, a white shirt and a gray-and-black tie. His hair caught a ray of the setting sun and his jacket was slung over his arm.

"Hi." She managed a casual greeting, even if her heart was pounding at warp speed. After a moment of awkward silence, her anxiety returned. "Where were you?"

He closed the door. "At the office."

"But you left me a note."

"I wrote that this morning, before I went to work. You were already gone and I didn't get a chance to talk to you."

"I had an early meeting." She dusted some imaginary lint from her T-shirt. "Are you hungry?"

"You bet. I need to change, then we can get started on the meal."

He headed toward the staircase, but she stopped him. "I thought you were working a light schedule."

"I am. This is light for me. I'm not usually home for dinner." He loosened his tie. "Do I have time for a shower?"

Lea's mouth went dry. How was she supposed to stay here for the next two weeks, missing him, wishing they were still lovers?

"Of course you have time for a shower." She proceeded to the kitchen to get a glass of water, to focus on the food, to keep her mind occupied.

He returned fifteen minutes later, wearing drawstring sweatpants and a tank top. When he moved closer to inspect the ingredients on the counter, she noticed the ends of his hair were damp and he smelled like her favorite soap.

"So what are we making?" he asked.

"Chicken with lemongrass and a rice-noodle salad." Recipes she'd chosen just for him. "They're both fairly simple to make."

"Good." He sent her a boyish grin. "You know I'm not a very creative cook." He picked up a glass bottle. "What's this?"

"*Nuoc mam.* Fish sauce. It's used as a condiment and a flavoring. The way soy sauce is used in Chinese cooking." She took the chicken out of the refrigerator. "I found the *nuoc mam* at an international market. I bought chopsticks, too."

"Really?" He gave her another heart-stirring grin. "I'm glad you agreed to do this."

"So am I." Lea tried to think of something else to say, but she couldn't seem to find her voice. She hadn't expected Michael's interest in her culture to make her want him even more. Still silent, she unwrapped the chopsticks.

"What are you thinking about?" he asked.

You, she wanted to say. The nights they used to make love, the sensation of his mouth against her skin, the bedroom murmurs he'd whispered in her ear.

She glanced down, avoiding his gaze. "I'm thinking about the chopsticks."

"What about them?"

"They became a popular eating utensil because they could replace knives at the dinner table."

"And why was that important?"

She looked up, meeting the curiosity in his eyes, the electricity between them. "Knives were associated with war and death, but chopsticks were used in pairs, so they represented harmony, prospect and peace."

"That's nice. Really nice." He reached out to smooth a strand of her hair away from her face. Already pieces were coming loose from her ponytail. "You're going to have to show me the proper way to use them."

"I will." She just stood there, letting him touch her, letting him make her weak-kneed and girlish. Submissive. "I feel like *Miss Saigon*." A feeling that troubled her.

He stepped back. "What do you mean?"

"Nothing." Uncomfortable, she cut the chicken into small pieces, keeping her hands busy. "You can chop the cabbage for the salad."

They worked side by side, with Lea instructing him from time to time. While she fried garlic and onions, he leaned against the counter, watching her.

"Tell me about the man you dated in California."

She sprinkled ground chilies and minced lemongrass into the pan. "I already told you about him."

"What was his name?"

"Thao."

"I'm sorry he hurt you."

"I was naive." She added the chicken, stirring it with a wooden spoon. "I thought living in America would make a difference. But Thao was too traditional to want a wife like me."

Michael boiled the noodles for the salad. "Did you date anyone in Vietnam?"

"No. Never."

"There weren't any Amerasian boys who asked you out?"

She shook her head. "I was the only *my lai* in the village where I lived. Besides, couples in Vietnam don't date the way they do in America. A boy must introduce himself to a girl's family and seek their approval before he can take her out. And even then, it's very proper. They don't kiss or touch or hold hands in public."

"Are girls supposed to remain virgins until they get married?"

"Yes. But it doesn't matter that I slept with Thao. It was a long time ago, and I can't keep dwelling on the past."

"You're an incredible lover, Lea."

She nearly dropped the spoon. She could feel Michael's body heat, feel his gaze sweeping over her. "Thao was my only lover. Besides you."

"Then I'm honored." He touched her hair again, tucking a strand behind her ear. "But it isn't right for us to sleep together anymore."

"Why?" she asked, her voice barely audible, her pulse leaping to her throat.

"Because I don't want to use you."

She found the courage to question him further, to say what she was thinking. "What if I decide to use you?"

He raised his brows at her, shifted his feet, frowned and then ended up with a half-cocked smile on his face. "Do I look like a helpless male to you? A guy who could get used?"

"No. But men like sex." She lifted her chin. "You like sex. And that gives me power."

"Spoken like a true woman." He came up behind her, bringing her closer to the stove, crowding her, making her much too aware of him. "Don't burn the chicken."

"I'm not." Flustered, she pushed him back, nudging his chest with her shoulder. He'd taken the power away from her. He'd made her weak-kneed again.

And Lea tried so hard to be strong, to fight the chains, the emotional turmoil, that bound her.

Four

Michael and Lea decided to eat on the patio, at a glass-topped table, decorated with citronella candles. The dancing flames and fragrant smoke presented a compelling atmosphere. And so did a distant view of the marsh.

It almost seemed like a date. Almost, Michael thought. But not quite. His relationship with Lea grew more complicated by the minute. He missed their affair, the midnight rendezvous and secret passion.

"It's beautiful here." She sipped her tea. "I like being outside."

"Me, too." He studied the teapot and the tiny cups she'd purchased at the international market. They looked so domestic, so feminine. Just like her.

No wonder she turned him on. Lea was everything

he'd always wanted, everything he used to hope for. She was strong yet gentle. Understated yet elegant. When he climbed into bed at night, he longed to feel her body next to his.

"Sometimes I wonder if I'm fooling myself," he said.

"About what?"

"The white-picket-fence thing. A wife, kids, a friendly pooch in the yard."

"Why? Because your life is more of an electronic-gate, guard-dog-type thing?"

"Exactly." His career took precedence over everything, especially the relationships in his life. "You're an observant lady, Lea."

"I try."

No, he thought. She did more than try. She made decisions with her heart and analyzed them with her head. And she was too smart not to worry about her situation, to not wonder if he considered her a suspect.

He adjusted his chopsticks, handling them fairly well for a beginner. But Michael did everything fairly well. He took pride in being competent. "Tell me about your job."

"What's to tell? You already know what I do. You have a file on me."

"That isn't the same as hearing you talk about yourself. I want to get to know the real you." The woman who might be Lady Savannah, he thought.

She tasted her chicken, utilizing her chopsticks as easily as she wielded a fork. "I'm a computer systems analyst. I improve existing computer systems, as well as develop new systems."

"So you write programs?"

"Sometimes. CSS, the company I work for, specializes in corporate solutions. We tailor computer systems to fit our customers' needs."

"What about viruses?"

She stopped breathing. "What about them?"

"I was just wondering if you've had any significant experience in that realm. If you've ever designed security software."

"No, I haven't. But isn't my job history tucked away in that file?" She blew out the breath she'd been holding. "I don't understand why you're asking me about things you already know."

He sat back in his chair, luring her into his trap, loving his job, hating it, wishing he didn't have feelings for her. "You're getting defensive."

She reached for her tea, cradling the cup, grasping the tiny blue flowers painted on the porcelain. "That file bothers me."

He remained where he was, his posture easy, his mind sharp. "As it should. I wouldn't want someone investigating me just because I was a politician's illegitimate daughter."

"You're not anyone's daughter, Michael. You're a man." That said, she resumed eating, putting him in his place.

Just as she lifted a glob of rice to her mouth, he came forward in his chair. "I think you should help me with my case."

The rice nearly fell onto her plate. "What case?"

"The one I'm working on for your dad. I could really use a woman's perspective."

"I'm not a detective."

"But you harbor resentment toward your father. And so does the suspect in my case. You might be able to help me figure her out."

She jammed the rice into her mouth, but she didn't go after another bite. The chopsticks landed on the table, untouched. So much for harmony, prospect and peace, he thought.

"Figure whom out?" she finally asked. "Who is she?"

"A woman who's been stalking your dad."

She froze. She literally didn't move, and he realized his words had stunned her. If she were Lady Savannah, she hadn't thought of herself as "a stalker." But most stalkers didn't. They justified their behavior on their own terms.

"We can get into the specifics later," he said. "When we have time to go over my notes. Maybe Saturday."

"That's five days away."

"There's no hurry." He wanted her to fret about it, to wake up every morning and wonder what he had up his sleeve.

"I'd rather discuss it now."

"I'd prefer to wait. I don't want to spoil this beautiful evening talking about another woman." He scooped up some of the salad, looked directly in her eyes. "Not while I'm dining with you."

Lea turned on the bedside lamp, flooding her room with light. She couldn't sleep; all she could think about was the case Michael had mentioned.

Was he being sincere in asking for her help? Or was this his way of trapping her?

Much too warm, she pushed away the covers. After she went into the bathroom to rinse her face, to wash away the anxiety, shame coiled in her belly like a snake.

He'd called her a stalker. For some naive reason, Lea had never associated that word with the things she'd done. But apparently that was what Michael had termed Lady Savannah. That was her criminal calling card.

She leaned against the sink, holding her stomach, trying to keep the snake from striking, even though she knew she deserved to get bitten.

When her mouth turned dry, she crept downstairs for a glass of ice water, for something to temper the discomfort.

An amber night-light cast a ghostly glow in the kitchen, creating odd-shaped shadows on the walls. On silent feet, she opened a cabinet, grateful the hinges didn't creak. As she placed her glass beneath the ice dispenser, the frozen cubes made a crashing sound, jarring the stillness, making her heart jump out of her chest.

Feeling foolish, she added the water and took a sip, cooling her fears, quenching her thirst. And then Michael's voice came out of nowhere.

"Are you all right?"

She spun around to see him standing in the doorway, wearing a pair of loose-fitting shorts and little else. His chest was bare and his straight dark hair was tousled, falling across his forehead rebelliously.

She glanced at his stomach and noticed how low his shorts rode on his hips. What would he do if she seduced him? If she whispered something erotic in his ear? Lea wanted to make love with him again, to pretend their relationship was real. "I'm fine."

"You don't look fine. You look pale."

"Do I?" He looked like a bronzed statue, strong and solid, with chiseled features. He moved closer and she wondered if his skin was cool to the touch. "I couldn't sleep. I was hot."

"I can turn up the air conditioner."

"That's okay. There's a fan above my bed."

"You just said you were hot."

"I am. I was." She sipped her water again. "I'm better now."

He came over to her, pressing his hand against her forehead. Her bones almost melted, and she cursed his proximity.

"You don't feel feverish."

"Because I'm not. I told you I'm fine."

He trapped her gaze. "Do you ever sleep?"

His eyes were magnetic, his irises flecked with light. Suddenly she feared he would hypnotize her, trick her into admitting her crimes.

"Do you?" she asked.

"Do I what?"

"Ever sleep?"

"Not much. Not lately." He dropped his hand and stepped back. "What did you mean earlier when you said you felt like *Miss Saigon?*"

Her pulse pounded at her neck. "I didn't mean anything."

"You wouldn't have said it if meant nothing."

"*Miss Saigon* is a play," she told him.

"I know. I've heard of it." He shifted his weight. "What's it about?"

"The heroine has an affair with an American soldier. And after he leaves, she gives birth to his son." She paused. "A child like me."

Michael frowned, and Lea feared she might be falling in love with him. That somewhere deep down, she was losing her soul. Why else would she want to sleep him with him again? Crave to be in his arms?

"That sounds more like Lan's story than yours," he said.

She nodded, her emotions too close to the surface. "My mother waited for my father to come back for her. To bring us to America." Tears burned her eyes, but she wouldn't let them fall. "She always said good things about him. She believed in his honor."

"Then maybe you should, too."

"I did when I was a little girl. I waited right along with my mother, thinking he would save us from our persecution." The glass began sweating in her hand. "But he was here, in Savannah, with his wife and other children."

"He needs you to forgive him."

And what about what I need? she thought. What about her feelings for Michael? "I don't want to discuss my father with you. Not now."

He sighed, and they both turned quiet. Shadows still haunted the walls and the microwave clock displayed an after-midnight hour.

"I still don't understand why you felt like *Miss Saigon*," he said, breaking the silence.

"Sometimes you make me weak," she admitted. "Submissive. Not like an American girl."

"You think American women don't stumble into affairs? Don't get mixed up with the wrong men?"

Her chest constricted. "Are you the wrong man?"

"You know damn well I am."

"Because you're my father's bodyguard?"

"Yes," he said solemnly.

"Then why did you keep coming back to my apartment? Why didn't you just leave it as a one-night stand?"

He thrust his hand through his hair, pushing the errant strands away from his forehead. "I couldn't stay away. I wanted you too much."

"But you don't want me now?" she challenged.

His gaze roamed over her, and she realized how she must look, her nightgown clinging to her body, floating around her ankles like mist.

"I don't want to use you, Lea. I already told you that."

"And I already told you that I should have the right to use you." She set her glass on the counter and then turned to face him again, letting him see the woman she was. "Why should you call all the shots? Why should you make all the decisions?"

"You want to talk about decisions?" He cursed and grabbed her wrist, slamming her palm against his chest, forcing her to hit him. "About calling the shots?"

Lea tried to pull way, but he kept her there, his heart pounding wildly beneath her fingers. "Michael—"

"This is what you do to me. This is my weakness." His heart thumped even harder. So hard, he fought his next breath. "Do you think it's easy for me to give you up? To keep my hands off you?" He cursed again, a crude word, a sexual word, the act he wanted to commit. "I'm going crazy."

Lea pulled free of his grasp. "Now you know how I felt, waiting for you night after night. Wondering how long our affair would last."

"I was wrong. Damn it. I was wrong. But getting too close to you scared me."

And now they were arguing, she thought. Battling their feelings for each other. "Go back to bed, Michael."

"What for? I won't be able to sleep."

Neither would she, but what else were they supposed to do?

He reached out to graze her cheek, to touch her as gently as he could, but Lea backed away, her heart lodged in her throat, her emotions spinning out of control.

Getting close to him scared her, too. Yet she needed him, more than she'd ever needed anyone.

Michael awakened in a fog and glanced at the window, trying to make sense of his drifting-on-a-dream state. It was still dark out; the sheers were shrouded in moonlight.

He rolled over, his eyelids heavy. But a moment later, a creaking sound caught his attention and he shifted his gaze to the door, where the night-darkened image of a woman stood.

He blinked, certain he must have conjured her up in his mind. That she was an illusion. That his eyes and his ears were playing tricks on him.

The illusion moved forward, just a little, like a fragment in time, an all-too-real dream.

No, not a dream. He was awake. "Lea?"

"Yes." She responded to him, her voice as smoky as her image.

He didn't turn on the lamp, afraid she would disappear with the light, afraid he would lose her for good. "Why are you here?"

"To touch you. To take what I need."

Heat flooded his body, like wax melting over his skin, seeping into his pores.

She stepped farther into the room and he knew he should send her away, stop her from seducing him. But he was already aroused, already ignoring the danger of getting caught in her web.

Deep down, he knew she was Lady Savannah. With each day that passed, the clues got stronger, the truth hovering in the air. But tonight he didn't care. Tonight he wanted her.

He waited, watching. She paused at the foot of the bed and slipped off her nightgown. He squinted to see her clearer, to force his eyes to adjust, to combat the darkness.

She was wearing panties; that much he could tell. He could see them, an iridescent swatch of cotton between her legs. When she removed them, anticipation pounded at every pulse point in his body, making him ache.

"You shouldn't be doing this," he said.

She crawled onto the bed and leaned over him, her unbound hair falling like silk, her lotion-scented skin grazing his. "This is my power, Michael. It's the only advantage I have over you."

He thought about the commitment he'd made to find Lady Savannah, to bring her to justice. "I can't make any promises. I can't give you a future."

"I'm not asking you to." She rubbed her mouth across his. "I'm doing this for me."

She kissed him, soft and slow and sweet. She was naked, clinging to his shoulders, making his heart skip erratic beats. She moved down his body, and he sensed her purpose, the erotic act she intended to perform.

She licked his navel, tracing a path with her tongue, tugging at his shorts, removing them. Michael lifted his hips, eager to surrender, to give her everything she'd come to take.

Everything and more.

He threaded his hands through her hair and the dark mass caressed his thighs. The ultimate seduction, he thought. It thrilled him, shamed him, made him curse the ache between his legs. And then she touched him there, a featherlight kiss, a promise of pleasure.

Michael thought he might die.

"You're so warm. So hard." She wrapped her hand around him, preparing for her next move.

"I want to turn on the light. I want to watch." He reached for the lamp, and she took him into her mouth, barely giving him time to think, to react, to do anything but pray for relief. A golden light flooded her image, giving him a dream-enhanced view.

He opened his legs, accommodating her, allowing her to set a smooth, sensual rhythm. He moved with her, making love to her mouth, caressing her face, losing part of his soul.

"Lea." He said her name and she looked up at him. Their eyes met and held, creating even more intimacy.

She took him deeper, so deep he hit the back of her throat. He shivered, wondering if he'd ever been this aroused, this desperate for a woman.

Before it ended, before he lost control, he pulled her up and ran his hands all over her body, making her sigh.

"Let me do it to you," he said.

She smoothed a strand of his hair. "You used to do it all the time."

"That's right, I did." He skimmed her cheek. "And I know just how you like it."

She smiled, and he kissed her. Tonight they would do everything, he thought. Every erotic thing they could think of, every position that gave them pleasure.

Anxious, he lifted her legs onto his shoulders, and she arched against his mouth.

She was warm and wet, sweet and musky. He filled himself with her flavor, teasing her with his tongue, arousing her the way she'd aroused him.

She touched herself, heightening the sensation, the need to be naughty, to make the feeling last. He licked between her fingers, and she made throaty little sounds.

As she fisted his hair, he looked up at her. Everything about her turned him on: the shape of her eyes, the color of her skin, the subtle curve of her hips. She rocked against his mouth, urging him to kiss her in that special place, to make her come.

And when it happened, he tasted her release, the pleasure convulsing her body.

Beautiful, dangerous Lea. He should have resisted

her, but her magic was too strong. Michael lifted his head, and she smiled at him, drugged from her orgasm.

"I don't want tonight to end," she said.

"It's not over yet." He reached into the nightstand drawer and fished around for a condom, securing the foil packet.

They caressed each other, rolling over the bed, tangling the sheets. Her hair fanned across the pillow and over her breasts, making her look even more exotic. He loved her hair, the long flowing length, the silky texture.

Sensation slid over sensation, the rhythm sleek and inviting. He rode her; she climbed on top of him; he straddled her. They kept switching places, driving each other half mad.

He withdrew, then entered her again, intensifying the feeling. Their gazes locked and their fingers entwined, completing the symmetry. They were good together, he thought. So damn good. Yet he knew it was wrong.

She wrapped her legs around him, holding him close, dragging his mouth to hers, kissing him. And then she climaxed in his arms, all warm and soft and beautiful.

Michael closed his eyes and let himself fall, spilling into her, lost in the feeling of being her lover.

Five

Dawn streamed through the window sheers, awakening Lea in a morning-after haze. She rolled over and landed against warm, solid flesh.

Michael.

She'd stayed in his room; she'd slept in his bed. Rising onto her elbows, she leaned over him, peering down at his face.

His eyes were closed, his hair mussed, his jaw peppered with beard stubble. He looked gloriously rumpled, a man who'd made hot, hard-driving love last night.

Lea glanced lower, at his chest and stomach. The sheet was draped low on his hips, exposing the shadow of hair that led to his—

"What are you looking at?"

She jumped back. "I thought you were asleep."

"You were checking out my—"

"I was not." Her cheeks flamed. She could feel them turning a thousand shades of pink. He was half-aroused. She could see the masculine shape through the sheet, tenting the fabric between his legs.

He mocked her with his brows, raising them in smart-aleck amusement, and she realized she was naked too, completely exposed to his high-and-mighty gaze. Self-conscious, she searched around for her nightgown and found it at the foot of the bed, along with her discarded panties.

"You're not so brave in the daylight," he said.

She put on her clothes, then reached for her pillow and smacked him with it. She hated the way he made her feel. The nervousness he never failed to evoke.

Stunned, he merely stared at her. "What the hell was that for?"

"You're supposed to cuddle with me, not complain about being seduced."

"You want to cuddle?" He lunged, grabbed her, pinned her to the bed. And then he tickled her, his hands rough yet gentle. Big and strong and boyish.

She laughed; she squirmed; she melted like a pat of honey-flavored butter. She'd never interacted this way with anyone before. Her life had been filled with serious issues.

"You have no shame." She tried to swat his bare butt, but he kept eluding her. "You're getting turned on by this."

He secured her wrists, holding them above her head. "I knew you were looking down there."

"I can feel it, Michael."

"'Cause it's so big."

She bit her lip to keep from laughing. He was poking her stomach, trying to make his overinflated, male ego point. "It's not that big."

"Says the woman who can't wait to touch it again."

"That's not what I meant by cuddling." She broke free, and they grinned like a couple of foolhardy kids. But when he moved a strand of hair away from her cheek, tucking it gently behind her ear, they stopped smiling and gazed at each other, silent in the morning light.

"We shouldn't be getting this close," he said.

"I know." But how was she supposed to stop herself from falling in love with him? How was she supposed to pretend it wasn't happening? "I'll only be here for two weeks. We're not talking about an eternity."

He was still poised above her, his naked body brushing her nightgown, leaving shivers along her skin.

"I wish it could be different, Lea."

"Me, too." But deep down she knew he was suspicious of her. He hadn't come right out and accused her of stalking Abraham Danforth, but she could see it in his eyes, drifting between them like a bad dream.

She skimmed his jaw, wishing she wasn't the woman he was investigating, the lady who'd plotted her childhood revenge, who'd destroyed the only chance she'd ever had at happiness.

"Do you want to get ready in here?" he asked.

She nodded. She had to get dressed for work and so, she assumed, did he. "I need to get my toiletries first."

"That's fine." He waited for her in the master bathroom, the place designed for a married couple, with his and her sinks.

When she returned, he was in the process of shaving. She went about her daily routine, as well.

After she removed her nightgown in front of a mirrored wall beside the tub, he came up behind her, slipping his arms around her waist.

"Do you want to take a bath with me?" she asked.

"Not yet." He slid his hand down the front of her panties, rubbing her, making her wet.

"Michael." She whispered his name, the sound soft and sensual, even to her own ears.

He met her gaze in the mirror, and she knew he wanted her to watch. So she did. She watched everything he did.

After he pushed her panties halfway down her legs, he thumbed her nipples, leaving her warm and wanton. Lea took a deep breath, letting him seduce her, letting him make her heart beat much too fast.

"Lean forward," he said.

She pressed her hands against the glass, her heart pounding even harder. "Like this?"

"Yes." He rubbed the front of his body against the back of hers, sending a trail of heat along her spine.

He was going to make love to her in this position, she thought. He was already hard, already nuzzling her neck.

When he showed her the condom in his hand, she

marveled at how effortlessly he'd acquired the foil packet from a bathroom drawer. "Do you keep those everywhere?"

"A guy needs to be prepared." He sheathed himself, then angled her hips to accept his penetration.

He entered her slowly, sensuously, intensifying the moment. Lea focused on the mirror, not wanting to miss their naked reflections, the image of their joining.

He kept moving inside her, taking what he wanted. The motion was warm and compelling, a rhythm that flowed through her veins, making her dizzy. She could feel him thrusting deeper, stroking her womb.

She twisted her head to kiss him, to slip her tongue into his mouth. He tasted like spearmint, like the flavor of spring. She inhaled his aftershave, an icy-blue sensation filling her senses.

He pressed against her, pushing her forward, flattening her breasts against the mirror. The glass was smooth and cool, but her nipples were hard, stimulated from the pressure.

"Lea." He bit the back of her neck, like a stallion, a feral animal on the verge of climaxing.

She closed her eyes and let it happen to her, the rough, carnal feeling sweeping her away.

A few hours later, Michael sat across from Clayton Crawford in the other man's office. Clay owned Steam, a trendy club and restaurant downtown. Michael had provided the initial security for Steam, and within no time, their association had developed into a strong and loyal friendship. They were both Indian mixed bloods who'd battled their way to success. Clay had grown up poor, too. Not poverty-stricken like Michael, but poor enough to be considered from the wrong side of the tracks.

"So you think she's the stalker," Clay said, pondering their conversation.

Michael nodded. He'd confided in his friend about Lea. At this point, he needed to talk to someone and Clay was the logical choice. Michael wasn't ready to go to Danforth to spill his suspicions.

"And you're sleeping with her?" the other man asked.

"Best damn sex I've ever had."

That got a smile out of Clay. "Then screw the stalking thing. Who the hell cares?"

They looked at each other and laughed. There was no way Michael could ignore the stalking issue, but Clay's twisted humor helped him relax. "I feel like such a bastard. Like I'm using her."

"Reality check, buddy. She came to your room last night."

"And I kept going to her apartment before that."

"You didn't suspect her then."

"Well, I do now."

Clay picked up a paperweight from his desk. The glass object was shaped like a dolphin, reminding Michael of Danforth's seaside mansion. "Her father is going to be furious."

"That you're banging her?"

"That she's the one who threatened him. He already knows we're sleeping together." He gave Clay a harsh look. "And I'm not *banging* her. It's more than that."

The club owner raised his brows. "Good God, Mike, listen to yourself. You're falling for her. You're getting emotionally attached."

"And you're less than three weeks away from the altar." He shifted uncomfortably in his chair. "I don't see where that gives you room to talk."

"I'm not in love with a stalker."

"Did I say I was in love? It's just an affair."

"But not a banging-her-type affair." Clay put down the paperweight. "Makes me wonder what kind of affair it is."

"One that's driving me nuts."

"So what are you going to do?"

"I don't know." He finished his coffee, pushing the cup away. He'd already juiced his veins with caffeine earlier. Pretty soon he'd be bouncing off the walls. "Got any suggestions?"

Clay leaned back, looking like the lord of the hot-spot manor. His club reigned over Savannah society, giving him the respect he'd always craved.

"Well?" Michael said, prodding him for a response.

"Do you think she feels bad about what she did?" his friend asked.

"I don't know. I hope so."

"Maybe you should bank on that for a while."

"You mean try to guilt-trip her into a confession? I already asked her to help me with the investigation."

"Then keep going in that direction. Immerse her in the stalking thing."

"And wait for her to come clean?" Michael blew a rough breath. "It's a dangerous game."

"Yes, it is. But at least you're giving her a chance."

Michael nodded, and Clay drummed his fingers on his desk. The window in his office sent a stream of light across his face. His features were hard and angular, reflecting his heritage. Michael supposed he bore a similar look. "Lea had a difficult life. In her country, she was a half-breed, like us."

"Technically I'm a quarter-breed, and having a difficult life is no excuse for what she did."

"I know. And that's the part that's twisting my gut. How am I supposed to forgive her? Hell, I don't even know if I'm part of her scheme, if she's playing me for a fool. Her vulnerability could be a ruse."

"Great sex messes with a guy's brain."

"That it does." Yet he couldn't wait to make love with Lea again, to taste all that warm scented skin, to kiss her, to hold her. "I could get addicted to being with her."

Clay frowned. "I think you already are."

"Maybe she isn't the stalker. Maybe—"

"Maybe what?"

"Nothing. I know she's Lady Savannah." He cursed his hunger for her, the obsession weaving its way into his bloodstream. "I can feel it."

"Yeah, but you don't have enough evidence to rat on her."

"Rat on her? It's my job. It's what I do."

"Sorry. Poor choice of words."

Michael shrugged. "I'm already bending the law. I shouldn't be sleeping with her."

"You're a private investigator. It's not as risky for you to bend the law, not like a cop. But when push comes to shove, you'll do the right thing."

"I'll turn her in," Michael said.

"Yes," Clay agreed. "You will."

At noon, Michael decided to stop by Lea's job, to pay her an unexpected visit.

CSS Enterprises was located in the financial district, with offices that consisted of gray cubicles and an array of employees, each assigned to his or her mousetrap-type space. Michael had always pitied people who worked in crowded, colorless environments, probably because it reminded him of being poor—an unimportant speck on the wall of society. Of course, Lea made a fairly decent wage, with medical benefits stirred into the mix. CSS wasn't a sweatshop.

He asked for directions to her cubicle and found her hunched over her keyboard, typing at a rapid speed. She didn't notice him, so he took a moment to study her.

She wore a lavender-colored blouse and a matching skirt, but he'd seen her get dressed this morning. He shifted his stance, recalling what she had going on under her clothes. Her front-closure bra was beige and her panties were the thong variety, with a hint of ladylike lace.

She glanced up and saw him. "Michael? What are you doing here?"

He stepped into her cubicle. "I was thinking about your underwear."

"What?" She looked around for eavesdroppers. "Is this a joke?"

"No. I came by to ask if you could get away for lunch, but then I started thinking about your panties and bra."

Lea dragged him farther into the confined space, offering him a chair that was crammed against a makeshift wall. He sat, tempted to pull her onto his lap, to shock the nerdiness out of her computer-geek co-workers.

She leaned against her desk, too pretty for her own good. "I read somewhere that men think about sex every six seconds."

"That's got to be an exaggeration. I've only thought about it twice today." He grinned at her. "After we did it."

She returned his smile, and he wished that he could trust her, that she wasn't Lady Savannah.

"So can you take time off for lunch?" he asked.

"It's a little early, but I suppose I could."

He motioned to her computer. "What were you working on?"

"I'm writing a manual for a system I designed."

"You don't look like a computer nerd."

She rolled her eyes. "That's such a cliché, Michael."

Oh, yeah? he thought. What about the Poindexter types he'd seen boxed up in their cubbyholes?

"There's a sandwich shop nearby. Is that okay with you?"

"Sure." She reached for her purse and slipped the strap over her shoulder. "I go there all the time."

Once they were outside, the sun glinted off Lea's hair. She'd styled it long and loose, but Michael hadn't given her much time to fuss with it this morning. His sexual appetite had gotten in the way.

They walked to the eatery and ordered chicken salad sandwiches and two tall plastic cups of lemonade. The young man working the counter gave Lea a special smile, and Michael felt a pang of possessiveness.

Not a good sign, he told himself.

They sat across from each other at a small white table. The sandwich shop offered a floor-to-ceiling view of Johnson Square, where financial advisers and bankers spent their workday.

Lea opened her potato chips and when she offered him one, feeding it to him, he started thinking about sex again, wondering if every six seconds wasn't too far off the mark.

The guy behind the counter looked disappointed, realizing, it seemed, that Lea and Michael were a couple, not co-workers.

Tough luck, Michael thought.

She sipped her lemonade and started in on her sandwich. He ate, too, considering she only had thirty minutes for lunch. He knew her daily schedule. He'd investigated every aspect of her professional life.

"This is good," she said. "I was hungrier than I thought."

"We missed breakfast."

"Yes, we did." She moistened her lips. "We were too busy to eat."

The every-six-seconds curse returned. "You're driving me crazy, Lea. Being with you is all I think about."

"Me, too."

Their gazes locked, and he knew he was in trouble. He'd never been this attracted to anyone before. Most of his relationships were over before they even started. Yet here he was, losing his common sense, getting sidetracked by a female who'd committed a psychological crime.

She smiled at him. "I'm glad you invited me to lunch. It was a nice surprise. Sort of romantic."

His heart clenched. He hadn't asked her to lunch to romance her. This was part of his job. "Actually, I was wondering if you'd like to help me with my case tonight." He paused, steeling the emotions she kept tying into knots. "There's no reason for us to wait until Saturday."

She broke eye contact. "Are you sure you need me to do this? I don't think I'm going to be much help."

"Sure you will," he said, hating this twisted game. "I already told you, I could really use a woman's perspective."

The beautiful, seductive woman who'd become his obsession, he thought. The lady leading him straight to hell.

Six

Lea hadn't expected Michael to make their stalker investigation session so cozy. He'd placed a platter of fruit and cheese on the coffee table and encouraged her to have a glass of wine with him. So she sipped chardonnay and nibbled on apples and Brie, pretending she wasn't a nervous wreck.

"I guess I better start at the beginning." Michael plucked a grape and popped it into his mouth. "The first e-mail your father received was in February. It said, 'I've been watching you.' The second one that arrived said, 'You will suffer' and the third said, 'I'm still watching you.' All three were signed Lady Savannah."

When he searched her gaze, she forced herself to

remain calm, to keep her hands steady. "Did anything happen after that?"

Michael nodded. "In March, Lady Savannah sent him a virus that crashed his computer."

"How did you know it was from the same person? Was there a message attached?" she asked, hoping her questions sounded believable.

"Yes." He moved a little closer. They sat side by side on his sofa, the skylight above their heads reflecting a star-speckled evening. "The note said, 'Expect the unexpected. This isn't over.' That was her most cryptic message. Coupled with the virus, we knew she was serious." He paused. "What do you think 'This isn't over,' means, Lea?"

"I don't know." The wine hit her stomach like liquid fire. Could he tell she was lying? Was he assessing her body language? The way she shifted on the couch? "What do you think it means?"

"That she had something significant in store for Danforth, something that hasn't come to fruition yet."

She took another burning sip of the chardonnay. "Like what?"

"I haven't figured that out yet. But it's rather puzzling why so much time has passed without her contacting Danforth again." He ate another grape, contemplating the case. "It's got to be one of two things. She's waiting for the perfect opportunity to make her next move, or she changed her mind for some reason."

Yes, Lea thought. She changed her mind; she couldn't go through with it. "What do you know about Lady Savannah? What sort of details do you have?"

"I've worked out a profile on her." He reached for a file he'd left on the end table. "First of all, there are three types of stalkers. Low-threat, medium-threat and high-threat." He opened the folder and shuffled through the papers. "Lady Savannah is a medium-threat stalker. This type of stalker usually knows the principal, the person they're stalking."

"How well do they know them?"

"More often than not, the stalker has a disgruntled association with them, like an ex-lover, a former friend, an ex-business partner."

Or an abandoned child, she thought. A *my lai* who'd been left in Vietnam. "Are medium-threat stalkers dangerous?"

"They can be. The biggest danger is that they usually know a lot about the principal. They're not like a low-threat stalker who's just trying to get close to the principal, hoping to attract his attention, like an adoring fan. Medium-threat stalkers have a stronger agenda and are more suspect in their motives."

Guilty, Lea took a deep breath. She'd threatened her father to get back at him, to make him pay for her pain. "What about high-threat stalkers?"

"They're severely dangerous, but Lady Savannah doesn't fit that profile. High-threat stalkers are delusional, men and women living in a fantasy world. They usually have a history of mental illness and are obsessed with the principal. They don't have any regard for the law, and they don't care about the consequences."

"But Lady Savannah does?"

"Yes." He tasted the Brie. "She was cautious in her approach. I think she lives and works in the mainstream world and doesn't want her life ruined by a police inquiry or a restraining order. She cares if she gets caught."

"Are the police involved in this investigation?" she asked, her heart pounding against her breast.

"Damn straight they are. Danforth is running for state senator. He isn't leaving anything to chance, which is why he brought me in on the stalking case."

Lea fell silent, wondering what Michael would say if she told him the truth, if she admitted why she'd sent the virus and what "This isn't over" meant. Would he forgive her? Or would he look upon her with disdain?

Anxious, she glanced up to find him watching her. "Do the police have a description of Lady Savannah? Has anyone seen her?"

"Yes." He broke eye contact and paged through the file again. "Her e-mail messages were traced to public computers. First a local library, then two different copy centers and finally an Internet café, where the virus was sent."

"And the employees at these places remember her?"

"The manager at the Internet café does." He handed Lea a sketch of Lady Savannah. "It's a crude likeness, but it's all we have."

She studied the drawing, grateful it didn't resemble her. "Mid- to late-twenties, with auburn hair and tinted glasses."

"Exactly. But I've come to the conclusion that

her hair was a wig, and that the glasses played a bigger part in her disguise than the police realized."

Lea wasn't about to ask him to expound on why Lady Savannah needed to mask her eyes.

"I think her height was altered, too," he went on to say. "That she was wearing platform shoes, but the hem of her pants was too long for the manager to notice. He said she was tall and slim, like a model, but I don't think that's correct."

"You think she's short and plump?"

He raised his eyebrows at that. "I think the shoes gave her the illusion of being model-like. She's obviously lean enough to be considered slim and the extra height made her look even thinner."

Lea recalled the manager at the Internet café, recalling the way he'd checked her out. "Do you think he likes tall, thin girls? Do you think that's why he remembers her?"

"Yes, that's exactly what I think. He gave us a better description of her body than her face."

"So she could be anyone? Anyone who's had an association with my father?"

"Anyone with cause to threaten him," Michael corrected.

"Yes, of course." She returned the sketch, wanting him to bury it in the file, to hide it from view.

But he didn't. He kept the drawing in his hand. "I think she's computer savvy. That she wrote the virus herself."

"If she's so computer savvy, why did she use public computers?"

"Because she wanted the e-mails to get traced.

And she wanted to be seen. She was trying to create a false description of Lady Savannah."

Her palms began to sweat. "Maybe you're wrong, Michael. Maybe she really is a tall, slim redhead."

He shook his head. "It was just a clever disguise."

Maybe so, Lea thought. But Lady Savannah was a coward, unable to admit the truth, to let her lover turn her over to the police.

"I've investigated every angle of this case," he said. "In the beginning, I even suspected John Van Gelder, your father's opponent. I thought maybe Van Gelder hired the stalker as a ruse to scare Danforth into withdrawing from the race." He glanced at the sketch. "But this isn't about dirty politics."

She didn't respond. Because, like Michael, she knew John Van Gelder didn't have anything to do with her father's stalker. Lea Nguyen was Lady Savannah.

John Van Gelder gazed out the window, peering at the moonlit walkway and grassy perimeter of the yard. The boxy little house belonged to Hayden Murphy, a member of his advisory team.

Hayden was a kid, as far as John was concerned. Twenty-three, the same age as John's daughter.

Releasing an exhausted sigh, he turned away from the window and found Hayden watching him. The kid was on a low rung on the political ladder, but he wasn't as opinionated as the seasoned members of the team. He did as he was told.

"You look troubled," Hayden said.

"Gee, I wonder why."

"I'm digging as deep as I can, sir."

"Well, dig deeper. Find some dirt on Danforth." John intended to win the senatorial race, even if it meant slinging a crap-load of mud. "Find something to tarnish that Honest Abe image of his. Something tabloid-worthy."

"I will. I promise I will."

John squinted at Hayden. With his blond hair and fraternity-boy features, he looked more like a university student than an adviser, reminding John that his daughter had completed her European college studies this year.

John was a widower, and Selene was his only child. Would he be so damn driven to win this race if he'd had a son?

Not a son like Hayden, he thought. So far, the ambitious young yes-man hadn't uncovered one shred of scandalous information. John really needed something to discredit his opponent. He'd spent most of his life believing that he was the second choice to Abraham Danforth and he wasn't about to come in second this time.

Frustrated, he turned his attention back to Hayden. "Maybe you're not ready for a job of this caliber."

The younger man squared his shoulders. "That isn't true. I'll get what you're looking for."

"You better," John threatened. "Because if you don't, I'll find someone who will."

Lea cleared the half-eaten fruit and cheese platter and Michael gathered the empty wine glasses. They went into the kitchen together, but their conversation was stilted, the Lady Savannah session leaving them tense.

He set their glasses in the sink, and she studied apple slices that had already begun to brown. The grapes were salvageable, but that was the least of Michael's concerns. Lea certainly seemed preoccupied with the task, making more of her kitchen duty than necessary.

"Don't worry about that," he said.

She looked up. "I don't believe in wasting food."

Because she knew what it was like to go hungry, he thought. "Fine. Whatever. Save it all if you want to." He'd been hoping for a confession from her, yet here she was, fussing over their wilted snack, giving a few measly apple slices her undivided attention.

He glanced at the clock, noting it was bedtime. "You seem uptight."

She bagged the fruit, her movements a bit too jittery. "It's been a long day. Maybe I just need to relax." She opened the fridge and ducked her head. "Maybe I just need you to hold me."

To alleviate her guilt? he wondered. Or to work up the courage to tell him the truth? "You should move into my room."

"Are you sure?" She closed the fridge and turned to face him, her eyes full of hope. "If you'd rather keep your privacy."

"It doesn't make sense for us to have separate rooms." And being affectionate with her would help his cause, wouldn't it? "We're already involved."

She gave him a shaky smile. "Yes, we are."

He helped her transfer her clothes into his closet,

and he realized this was the first time he'd come close to having a live-in lover. Two weeks wasn't much, but considering the circumstances, it felt like a monumental commitment.

Side by side, they got ready for bed, brushing their teeth and changing into sleeping attire. He chose a pair of drawstring shorts, and she put on a virginal-looking nightgown.

They climbed into bed, and he turned out the light. The room wasn't overly dark. A low-hung moon cast a romantic glow over the sheets.

Lea moved closer, and he slipped his arms around her. She rested her head on his shoulder, her hair tickling his chin.

"Thank you, Michael."

"For what?"

"For holding me."

"Sure." He told himself he didn't have a choice. Being near her was his only option. She sighed, and he knew she wasn't going to confess her sin, at least not tonight.

"Tell me about being Seminole," she said. "You haven't taught me about your heritage yet."

He considered what to say. He wanted to tell her something pretty, something that made the pain from his childhood more bearable. "According to Seminole legend, the Creator, the grandfather of all things, created the Earth and everything on it. He made sure that certain animals and plants possessed healing powers. But he chose Panther to walk the Earth first."

"Really? Why?"

"Panther was his favorite. He said Panther was majestic and beautiful, with patience and strength."

Michael paused, his memories drifting back to his youth. "My mother told me about that because we're from the Panther clan."

Lea seemed intrigued. "I always thought of panthers as fierce."

"My mom was fierce when she got angry at my father." He sighed. "Infidelity isn't common among the Seminole. She never even considered that her husband would cheat on her."

She adjusted the sheet draped around their hips. "I feel sad for her."

He shrugged, even though his emotions had turned tight. "It's over. She's gone now."

"But she's still part of who you are, Michael."

That much he couldn't deny. He was his mother's son, but he hadn't been able to save her, to shake his two-timing father from her blood.

When he fell silent, Lea snuggled closer to him. "Did your mother ever cook Seminole meals for you?"

"Sometimes she made pumpkin soup. It was my favorite."

She snuggled closer. "Do you think you could duplicate the recipe? Maybe teach me how to make it?"

Could he? He used to sit at the kitchen table and watch while it was being prepared. "I can try. From what I recall, my mother used to add extra nutmeg and sugar to it."

She smiled. "No wonder it was your favorite."

He linked his fingers through hers and brought their joined hands to his lips, brushing her knuckles with a soft kiss. "I do have a bit of a sweet tooth."

She shifted in his arms, and when she put her head against his chest, he knew she was listening to the rhythm of his heart. Like rain falling on a metal roof, he thought. "I've never been to the reservation where my mom grew up. That's crazy, isn't it? I've never seen my mother's homeland."

"Then you should go there someday."

"I should. But my mom had a falling out with her family. It would probably be awkward." He glanced up at the ceiling and saw shadows above his head. "The Seminole are a matriarchal society, but my father didn't respect that."

"Yet your mother married him."

"I think she wanted him because he was forbidden to her. Her parents didn't want their daughter to make eye contact with Stan Whittaker, let alone marry him."

"Stan? That was his name?"

He nodded. "My mom's name was Peggy Ann Tiger."

"Is Tiger a common family name?"

"You mean among my mother's people? It seems to be."

"In Vietnam, her name would be Tiger Ann Peggy," Lea said. "A family name comes first, then a middle name, then the first. But that doesn't mean you refer to someone by his or her last name. You use their given name."

He pondered their conversation for a moment. "Do given names have special meaning?"

"Most do. Lan means orchid. Sometimes I buy orchids at the flower shop to remember my mother."

"Do you have a picture of her?" he asked.

"Just one. Taken with my father. Nearly everything in her village was destroyed, but she found that picture among the rubble." Lea's voice turned sad. "It was all she had left."

He stroked the length of her hair, comforting her, comforting himself. "I have a few pictures of my parents. But I don't know why I saved the ones of my dad."

"For the same reason I saved the photo my father is in. You knew it would've mattered to your mother."

He wanted to point out that Abraham Danforth was a better man than Stan Whittaker, but he doubted Lea would agree. She'd threatened her father, something Michael would have never done.

Then again, maybe he...

He what? Should have stalked his old man? Made the bastard fear for his life? He blew out a rough breath, knowing his mind was taking him down a dangerous path, trying to find ways to condone Lea's crime.

"Are you all right?" She reached up to skim his cheek, and suddenly the room turned dark, moonlight fading from the bed.

Emotional déjà vu, he thought, as his heart thundered in his chest. "I'm fine," he managed. "Just fine," he added, as she rolled over to kiss him, making everything but the sweet, warm taste of her disappear.

Seven

Whittaker and Associates was encased in a single-level, freestanding structure, with parking lot access and double-glass doors.

Lea told herself to relax, but her guilt kept getting in the way. She should be arriving at Michael's office to turn herself in instead of bringing him a sugary snack.

She let out the breath she was holding and entered the building. The lobby was vast, with a black-and-white tiled floor and a marble reception desk. Leather couches and brass accent tables offered a modern seating arrangement, and original works of art added splashes of bold, bright color.

Anxious, Lea approached the reception desk, but

the middle-aged woman manning the attractive workstation was already aware of her.

"Good afternoon." The woman gave her a pleasant smile. She wore wire-rimmed glasses and her ash-brown hair was cut in a sleek, professional style. "May I help you?"

"I'm looking for Michael Whittaker."

"Mr. Whittaker isn't in. Would you like to schedule an appointment to see him for another time?"

Lea hadn't considered the possibly that Michael wouldn't be in his office at this hour. "No, thank you."

Just then, the door beside the reception desk opened and Cindy emerged, wearing a stunning black suit, her golden-blond hair coiled into a soft chignon. Her skirt rode above her knees, showcasing long, shapely legs. When she moved forward, her shoes hit the floor like a round of well-aimed bullets, ringing in Lea's ears.

Cindy answered that ring with a wide-eyed expression. "Well, hello, Lea. How nice to see you."

"It's nice to see you, too." She noticed the receptionist had gone back to work, giving them the illusion of a private conversation. "I stopped by to visit Michael, but he isn't in." She shifted the pastry box in her hand. "I'll catch him later."

"No, no. Don't rush off. He should be back shortly." Cindy gestured to the door from which she'd emerged. "Have some coffee with me. I'm due for a break."

Lea thought it would be rude to refuse, so she followed the blonde to her office, which was just as chic as the lobby, with the same leather-and-chrome decor.

"How about decaffeinated cappuccino?" Cindy asked, without bothering to wait for an answer. She went about making the gourmet brew, filling the room with the hiss of frothing milk.

Lea took a chair, unable to admit that she rarely drank coffee.

"There. Now isn't this divine?" Cindy placed an oversize mug in front of her. "Don't you just love cappuccino? It's too late in the day for caffeine, though. Don't you agree?"

"Yes, I suppose it is." She lifted the pastry box from her lap. "I brought a snack for Michael, but there's plenty if you'd like one."

"Oh, let's see." The blonde peered inside. "That's quite a selection."

"Michael told me he had a sweet tooth."

Cindy looked up with a slow, Southern smile. "I'll just bet he does." She declined a pastry and drank her coffee instead.

Lea wasn't sure what to make of the sexual innuendo. She was still getting accustomed to women like Cindy. There weren't any brazen blondes in Vietnam, at least not within the sphere of her *my lai* existence.

"I know who you are," Cindy said.

"Excuse me?"

"I know you're Abraham Danforth's daughter. But I'm the only person at Whittaker and Associates who knows. Besides Michael, of course."

"He must trust you."

"I'm in charge of making sure your story doesn't hit the tabloids." Cindy sat back in her chair. "What puzzles me is why you won't allow Mr. Danforth to call a press conference. If it's handled correctly, it won't end up on the front page of some tacky gossip rag."

"I'm not ready to face the media. And I'm not sure I ever will be."

"Your father is a fascinating man. Wildly handsome, too. I can't imagine turning away from him. I think you're a fortunate young woman."

Lea didn't know what to say, so she drank her cappuccino and kept quiet.

"Have you ever seen Crofthaven?" the blonde asked. "Who wouldn't want to be associated with a seaside mansion like that? I simply love old money." She laughed a little. "I love new money, too."

"That doesn't matter to me." Lea supposed she couldn't fault Cindy for being honest, but she still wasn't comfortable around Michael's gorgeous assistant.

"Are you familiar with The Landings?" the other woman asked.

"The gated community on Skidaway Island?"

"Exactly. Golf courses, tennis courts, a fitness club. I used to live there with my boyfriend until he kicked me out." Cindy tossed her head and sent the diamond-studded hoops in her ears dancing. "But it doesn't matter because I'm interested in someone else now."

Who? Lea wondered. Abraham Danforth? Was it possible that Cindy had set her sights on Lea's father?

"Speaking of someone else..." The blonde released a sensual sigh. "That boss of mine is certainly a working girl's dream." She leaned in close. "How lucky are you?"

The coffee burned Lea's stomach like acid. "Michael told you about us?"

"That you're sharing his bed?" The earrings spun again. "He didn't have to. I saw you two at the gallery, remember? And I've been around him long enough to sense these things."

Lea fought the urge to frown, to make her displeasure known. Why should Cindy care whom her boss was sleeping with? And why did she feel compelled to mention it?

"My, my." The other woman glanced at the door and smiled. "Speak of the devil. Look who just popped his head in."

Lea spun around to see Michael. He met her gaze, and her coffee-riddled stomach unleashed a horde of decaffeinated butterflies.

"Speak of the devil," he mimicked. "Were you ladies talking about me?"

Cindy rose from her chair and made an elegant sweep across the room. "You mean you didn't hear us?"

"No, I can't say that I did."

"Well, then, we're not going to tell you what we said. Are we, Lea?"

Instead of indulging Cindy's game, Lea walked toward Michael, offering him a lover's smile. "I got off work early, so I stopped by to see you. To bring you some pastries."

He smiled at her. "That sounds good. I'm about ready to call it a day."

Lea turned to Cindy. "Thank you for the cappuccino."

"Don't mention it." The blonde watched them depart without another word.

Lea and Michael left in separate cars and by the time they arrived at his house, he was just curious enough to question her. But she expected as much.

"So what were you and Cindy talking about?"

"This and that." She went into the kitchen and removed two dessert plates from the cupboard. "Which one would you like?" She opened the pastry box and extended it to him.

He chose a chocolate éclair. "Come on. What'd you talk about?"

She handed him a fork. "Cindy told me that she knew I was Abraham's daughter. But I guess you had to tell her."

"That's right, I did. Cindy always handles media control."

Lea reached for an apple fritter, wishing she trusted Michael's administrative assistant as much as he did. "Is she working on the stalking investigation, too?"

"No." A frown furrowed his brow. "That's my area of expertise."

"So you haven't discussed Lady Savannah with her?"

"No," he said again. "I haven't."

Silence stretched between them, a reminder that their relationship was based on a lie. But even so, Lea knew Michael didn't have any evidence on her. If he did, he would have confronted her by now.

She glanced at her plate, knowing she owed him the truth. But in this case, the truth wouldn't set her free. She would lose the man she loved.

"What are you thinking about?" he asked.

You, she wanted to say. And how sorry she was to keep deceiving him. But how could she look him in the eye and admit that she was a stalker? Just the term alone shamed her.

"Lea?" he pressed.

"I'm not thinking about anything."

"Then tell me what else you and Cindy discussed."

She wasn't about to repeat the blonde's flattering remarks about him. The other woman's flamboyant manner was already rubbing her the wrong way. "I think Cindy's interested in my father."

He started. "You mean romantically?"

"It fits, doesn't it? He's rich and powerful and handsome. And you said you thought her mystery man might be one of your colleagues. So why not a client?"

"I suppose it's possible." He finally cut into the éclair. "But I doubt it will do her any good. I think Danforth has feelings for his campaign manager."

This time Lea started. She hadn't expected her father to have a woman in his life. "What's her name?"

"Nicola Granville. But I'm not positive about this. I just get a vibe whenever I see them together." He stopped eating to look at her. "But some people have that tangible kind of chemistry."

"Almost as if you can touch it?"

He moved closer. "Yes."

"Like us?"

"Yes," he said again, leaning in to kiss her, to slide his hands through her hair.

She melted against him, and he unbuttoned the

front of her blouse. His hands were warm and strong and possessive. When he unzipped her skirt, she wondered if he could sense that she loved him, if he had any idea that he'd captured her soul.

He ended the kiss, and they stared at each other. She was partially undressed, and his breathing was hard and labored.

"You taste like chocolate," she said.

"And you taste like everything I shouldn't have." He pushed her skirt down. "Everything I want." He snapped the elastic on her panty hose. "Take those damn things off."

She leveled her gaze. "You're demanding."

"And you're messing with my brain." He pinned her against the counter. "Just take them off."

"Why should I?" she challenged, even though her knees had gone as weak as her heart.

"Because it's what I want."

She tilted her chin. "Then do it yourself."

That was all it took. He grabbed her nylons and literally tore them from her body, but Lea didn't care. She needed to feel his passion, the desperation that drew him to her.

Struggling for balance, she closed her eyes, and he dropped to the floor, kneeling in front of her. When he yanked her panties down, her pulse pounded like a rawhide drum.

"Do you know where it is, Lea?"

She opened her eyes. "What?"

"The hidden camera."

Properly stunned, she froze. "Michael—"

He seized her hips and pulled her against his mouth.

Heat slammed through her system and she pitched forward, gasping for her next breath. Was the camera running? Was he filming her surrender? The idea shocked her. But it aroused her, too.

He tasted her, deep and slow, and she couldn't stop the pleasure—the forbidden wetness, the sweet, spiraling sensation.

Lea moved against his mouth, wanting to remember this feeling forever. She'd never imagined that being in love could be so erotic. He did wicked things to her, and she traced his features, memorizing him in her mind, using the tips of her fingers.

"Do you want more?" he asked.

"Yes." So much more. Need rushed through her veins, spilling like a luminous fountain. Colors blurred, then separated, streaking across her heart.

Giving her what she wanted, he heightened each kiss. She lost the battle and shuddered against him, yielding to her emotions, to an orgasm as slick and moist as the pressure between her legs.

He came to his feet and she fell into his arms, her body still quaking, colors still spinning.

"Lea?"

"Hmm?"

"The camera isn't on."

She blinked through the kaleidoscope behind her eyes. "I wouldn't have cared if it was."

He gave her a masculine smile. "I know."

She held on to his shoulders, regaining her senses. "You're cocky, Michael."

"Am I?" He took her hand and rubbed it against his fly.

"Yes, you most certainly are." She unzipped his

trousers and suddenly their flirtation turned to frustration, to something neither of them could deny.

He was angry at himself for needing her so badly, she thought, as he pushed his tongue into her mouth, devouring her in one fell swoop, making her head spin.

He removed a condom from his wallet and fought to open the package, anxious to thrust into her, to take what he wished he didn't want. Lea had no intention of stopping him. She let him curse in her ear, knowing it wouldn't change the passion that was about to erupt.

He bit the side of her neck, becoming her vampire once again. She yanked off his clothes, and they made love like maniacal bloodsuckers, until they ended up on the kitchen floor, nearly bruising each other's skin.

She wrapped her legs and around him and he braced his arms above her, kissing her hard and fast. She could taste herself on his lips, a flavor that only added to the frenzy.

Their worlds were colliding, crashing like shattered glass. But that didn't seem to matter. Not now, not while they were naked, not while he was moving inside her.

"This is going to happen fast," he said.

"I don't care." She scraped her nails down his back and felt his spine shiver.

"Neither do I." He pumped even harder, filling her as deeply and desperately as he could.

They climaxed at the same time, at the very same instant, gasping into each other mouths, their hearts beating wildly.

When it was over, when Lea could see through the blinding haze, she knew their words were a lie. They both cared, far too much.

On Saturday morning, Michael paced Clay's office. The other man sat on the edge of his desk in a T-shirt, frayed jeans and sleep-tousled hair. Michael had awakened him with a cell phone call, and the club owner was still feeling the effects of his late-night work hours.

"I'm sorry," Michael said. "I shouldn't have bothered you."

"What are friends for?" Clay scrubbed his hand across his jaw. "Besides, it's no big deal for me to meet you here."

"No, I suppose not." Michael stopped pacing to face his friend. Clay had a loft-style apartment above the club. He lived and worked at Steam. "Is your fiancée still asleep?"

"No. The phone woke her up, too."

"She must think I'm a pain in the ass. Calling you at this hour."

"Naw. She just thinks you're in love."

Michael scowled. "I suppose that's what you think, too?"

The other man walked over to a wet bar and removed a carton of orange juice, pouring two glasses. He spiked Michael's with vodka and handed it to him. "You know damn well I do."

"Well, you're wrong." He accepted the screwdriver and took a long, hard swallow, knowing he needed it.

"If you say so." Clay settled in with his orange juice, resuming a spot on his mahogany desk.

Michael refused to entertain thoughts of love, to let his mind take him in that direction. Yet he couldn't keep going on the way he was, holding Lea each night, wanting her, waiting for his heart to explode. "I came up with a plan to trap her."

"Is that what brought you here at this ungodly hour?"

"Yes, but I feel like I'm betraying her."

"Makes a person wonder why."

"Knock off the love crap. I'm guilty because I'm sleeping with her." And cuddling with her, he thought. And having sex on the kitchen floor.

Clay shook his head. "I wish you hadn't gotten involved with her."

Beyond frustrated, Michael poured himself another drink, adding an extra shot of vodka, not giving a damn that he was having alcohol for breakfast. "What if my plan to trap her only makes things worse?"

"How much worse can it be? You're already an emotional mess. She's already getting to you."

"I'm going to lose her. Once I turn her in, it's going to be over." Michael blew out a ragged breath, squinting in the dim light. The blinds on the windows were drawn, shutting out the sun, matching his mood. "There's a part of me that wishes I could forget about what she did. Pretend it never happened. Tell Danforth the case is getting cold and probably won't be solved."

"I'm not going to comment on that. Whatever you decide is up to you."

"I'm going through with my plan." Because he needed to hear Lea's confession. He needed her to take responsibility for her actions. "I can't obstruct justice."

"When is this going to happen, Mike?"

His chest turned tight. "Today. This afternoon. I've already got everything ready to go."

"Then I'm not going to ask you what the plan is."

"No, there's no point. I didn't come here to discuss the specifics. I just needed to get it off my chest. To say it out loud." To convince himself to go through with it, he thought. To trap Lea into telling him the truth.

Eight

"Why won't you tell me where we're going?" Lea asked.

Michael checked his rearview mirror. He wasn't sure if he was being a conscientious driver or avoiding his lover's gaze. "You'll see when we get there."

"You're being so secretive, Michael."

He merely nodded. Giving her information ahead of time wouldn't work in his favor.

Silent, he continued driving. Their final destination was located in the vicinity of Savannah State University, and he knew Lea would recognize the side streets once they got closer. But would she say anything? Or would she pretend the area was unfamiliar?

They stopped at a red light and he could feel her

watching him. Wondering, he assumed, what the hell he was up to. He turned toward her and, for a moment, they simply stared at each other. He wanted to reach out, to skim her cheek, but touching her would only make him ache.

"The light's green."

"What?"

"The light."

"Oh, of course." He engaged the gas pedal and sped across the intersection. He was still a bit hungover from earlier, from drinking screwdrivers at seven in the morning.

"I wish you'd tell me where we're going," she said.

"You'll find out soon enough." He'd never expected a woman to affect him so badly, to make such a mess out of his neat and orderly life.

By the time they arrived at the Internet café, tension brimmed like steam in a pressure cooker. He suspected Lea had begun to sweat.

"What are we doing here?" she asked.

He parked the car. "I'm going to interview the manager about Lady Savannah."

She gazed out the windshield, refusing to look at him, refusing to unbuckle her seat belt. "But you've already done that. He already gave you a description of her."

"I want to talk to him again."

She remained motionless. "Then I'll wait here."

Michael prepared to exit the vehicle, knowing he was doing the right thing and hating himself for it. "You can't. I need your help."

"That doesn't make sense."

"Sure it does." He flipped the automatic lock on the trunk and got out of the car. "Come on. I'll show you what I mean."

Lea finally budged and followed him to the back of the Mercedes. He removed a handled shopping bag and presented it to her.

She peered inside and saw the auburn-colored wig. Instantly, her skin paled.

"It's almost identical to the one Lady Savannah wore," he said. "There's a pair of platform shoes in there, too. Oh, and tinted glasses." He reached into the bag and removed the plastic-rimmed specs. "I bought these at an optometrist downtown. They're the same shape as the glasses she had on."

"You're going to show all of this to the manager?" she asked, her voice barely audible.

"No." He kept his gaze locked onto hers, pinning her in place. "You're going to dress up as Lady Savannah for me."

She didn't respond; she didn't utter one quavering word. Silence stretched between them, like a motionless gap in time. When she attempted to return the bag to him, he refused take it. Instead he waited for her to speak, the midafternoon sun beating brutally on his back. But Lea fared much worse. She looked as though she were wilting, fading right before his eyes.

"I can't do this, Michael."

He blinked, losing sight of her for a second, wishing he didn't feel like a ruthless bastard, wishing she hadn't put him in this position. "Why not?"

"I just can't."

"Why not?" he asked again, his tone harsher this time.

Her body swayed. "You know why."

"Do I?"

"Yes." She dropped the bag and it hit the ground with a clunk, landing on its side, spilling the lid to the shoebox. The wig fell out, too. For an instant, it looked like dried blood on the pavement. "I'm her, Michael. I'm Lady Savannah."

His heart picked up speed. He'd been waiting to hear her say those words out loud, waiting for the truth. "You sent the virus?" He gestured to the Internet café. "It was you the manager saw that day?"

"Yes." She glanced at the fallen articles. "I wore a wig like that. And platform shoes and glasses. But I bought everything in California. Before I came to Savannah."

She teetered on her feet, the way she'd done on the night of the fund-raiser. Michael feared she might faint. The weather was unbearably hot, the air much too sticky.

"Get back in the car," he told her.

She didn't argue, but he shadowed her just the same, preparing to catch her if she passed out. When she was secure in her seat, he picked up the fallen bag and climbed behind the wheel. She glanced over at him, and he started the engine, running the air conditioner to cool her off.

Her hair blew gently around her face, making her look soft and vulnerable. Michael cursed his attraction to her.

"You're not going to make me go into the café?" she asked.

He shook his head.

She blew out a shaky breath. "You don't need the manager to identify me?"

He let the car idle, choosing to remain where they were. He wasn't ready to pull into traffic yet. "You already confessed."

"Will you take me home?" She leaned her head against the seat rest. Her skin was still pale and her hair still fluttered around her face. Even her blouse gave her a lost quality. It was made of crinkled cotton, sheer enough to expose the outline of her bra.

"I'll take you to my house." He put the car into gear. "You have a lot of explaining to do, Lea."

"Are you going to turn me in?"

Michael exited the parking lot. He didn't want to discuss his actions with her. Hell, he didn't even want to look at her. He didn't want to see the fear in her eyes.

Those beautiful Amerasian eyes, he thought.

He couldn't allow himself to think of her as a wounded mixed blood. A half-breed. *Con lai*. He had to think of her as Lady Savannah, the woman who'd threatened Abraham Danforth, the stalker Michael had been tracking.

Michael drove Lea to his house, and she went straight to the refrigerator and poured a glass of orange juice, hoping to stabilize her blood sugar. She hadn't expected him to trap her into a confession, to leave her weak-limbed and shaky.

"You okay?" he asked.

She sipped the juice and nodded. He was being attentive, but not in a warm, caring way. The man watching her was cool and cautious. But she could hardly blame him. Why should he trust her?

"Can we go to the game room?" she asked.

He raised his eyebrows. "Why? Do you want to challenge me to a game of pool? Wager on whether or not I'll turn you in?"

Her chest constricted. "No. I want to play some music on the jukebox." Something to calm her nerves, something soft and familiar.

"Be my guest." He gestured, indicating for her to lead the way.

Once they were in the game room, she scanned the jukebox, making her selections, choosing classic love songs.

Michael didn't comment. He got himself a bottled soda and settled onto a bar stool. He looked tired, she thought. Hard-edged and exhausted.

"I never meant to hurt you," she said. To drag him into her sordid existence.

"But you meant to hurt your dad." He removed the cap on his cola and tossed it into a trash can beside the bar. "You meant to threaten him."

"Yes, but it took years for my hatred to build, years of hoping and praying that he would return to Vietnam someday, that he hadn't forgotten about my mother." She sat on a futon couch near the window. The room was decorated with casual furnishings, offering seating arrangements around the pool table and air hockey game table. "When I was in the refugee camp in the Philippines, I struggled with my hatred. The camp was filled with other Amerasians and most of them still had hope of finding their fathers and being accepted into their lives. And deep down, I wanted to feel that way, too."

"So when did you start hating Danforth enough to threaten him?"

"After I came to America and discovered that he'd been married when he slept with my mother, that he had other children." She sipped her juice, combating the dryness in her mouth. "My mother told me that he was injured when they'd met, that he was struggling with his memory. But she never entertained the possibility that he could have been married."

Michael leaned forward. "Why not?"

"Because she said he wasn't the kind of man who would forget that he had a wife. No matter how injured he was."

"Amnesia doesn't work that way."

"It can. Some people have selective amnesia. Besides, he told my mother his first name." She glanced out the window, tears fogging her eyes. "That much Abraham knew about himself."

"Maybe so, but he didn't remember that he was married. It wasn't his fault."

"It felt like his fault to me. He seemed like a liar and a cheat."

Michael turned quiet, and Lea took a ragged breath. When another song began to play, the lyrics drifted like childhood ghosts, floating between them, making her eyes water even more. But even so, she knew there was nothing left to say in her defense. Threatening her father was wrong.

"What did the note with the virus mean?" Michael asked.

Shame coiled around her heart. "Expect the unexpected? This isn't over?"

"Exactly. Explain that to me."

"It meant what you assumed it did. That Lady Savannah had something specific in mind for Abraham Danforth."

"Which was?"

"Destroying his political career at a public event, announcing to the world that Honest Abe had cheated on his wife, that he'd abandoned a child in Vietnam."

Michael frowned. "And that public event turned out to be the July Fourth fund-raiser?"

"Yes. I attended the fund-raiser with a synchronized plan. First, I would confront Abraham and tell him who I was. Then, while his head was still reeling from the news, I would make the same announcement at the podium, letting everyone know that he was a liar and a cheat."

"But you never approached the podium." He glanced up and snared her gaze. "You started shaking instead."

"Because Abraham didn't react the way I'd expected. He didn't deny that I could be his daughter. He didn't even try to defend himself. And I could tell he wasn't lying when he said that he thought my mother had died when her village was destroyed." Lea held Michael's gaze, even though it was difficult to look at him, to know he was judging her. "At that point, it was all I could do to remain standing, to stop myself from falling apart."

He closed his eyes, and she sensed he was thinking about the way she'd cried in his arms that night, the way they'd touched and kissed and made sweet, desperate love.

"Are you sorry for what you did?" he asked.

"For threatening my father?" She crossed her arms, hugging herself, wishing Michael would hold her instead. "I'm extremely sorry. If I could take it back, I would."

He shifted in his seat. "Did you honestly think that you'd get away with it? That someone wouldn't connect Lady Savannah to you?"

"I didn't leave any evidence, so what proof would there be? I thought I was safe."

"And you were." He paused to finish his drink, to push away the bottle, to leave streaks across the lacquered bar top. "Until you started sleeping with me."

Yes, she thought. She'd gotten too close to her father's bodyguard, too close to the man investigating the case. "I don't regret being with you."

"Even now? After I trapped you?"

"That doesn't change how I feel." She couldn't make herself stop loving him. She couldn't turn off her emotions. "This is part of your job."

"And now here we are. The stalker and the detective." When the music stopped, he glanced at the jukebox. "We never really got the chance to enjoy each other's company. Not the way a regular couple would."

She understood what he meant, but they couldn't change the nature of their relationship, not after what she'd done. "Are you going to turn me in?"

"Yes," he responded. "But not to the police. I've decided to leave that up to your father."

She reached for a decorative pillow and held it against her heart, against the thundering beats. "Do you think he'll press charges?"

"I have no idea."

"What are you going to say to him?"

"I'm going to tell him the truth."

"When?" she asked, her heart still pounding.

"Today. Right now." Michael rose from his chair. "And you're coming with me."

Lea changed her clothes four times, which made no sense. It was too late to make an impression on her father, yet she was determined to look nice.

Michael probably thought she was crazy.

And what would Abraham Danforth think? she wondered. What would he think once he learned the truth? That Lea Nguyen was Lady Savannah?

"I don't want to do this," she said, wishing she could bolt, but knowing there was nowhere to run, nowhere to hide. "I don't want to face him."

"You don't have a choice." Michael steered the car toward Crofthaven, a magnificent Georgian-style mansion just outside Savannah. Along the way, oaks festooned with Spanish moss made a glorious presentation.

When the white-columned house came into view, Lea's anxiety worsened. She didn't want to feel like a frightened little girl with rock welts on her body, but how could she feel strong and secure? Worthy of being Abraham Danforth's daughter after what she'd done?

"*Bui doi,*" she said.

Michael turned to look at her. "What?"

"*Bui doi.* It means dust of life. The poorest of the poor."

His expression softened. "Is that what you were in Vietnam?"

"No. But many *my lai* children were. They lived on the streets. They committed crimes. They took drugs. They became prostitutes. They were the underbelly of society." She smoothed her skirt, fidgeting with the carefully ironed fabric. "My mother did everything she could to stop that from happening to me."

"Lan must have been an exceptional woman."

"Yes. But now I've shamed her. I've dishonored her memory."

He parked in an exquisite driveway. "Because you committed a crime?"

Lea nodded. "Against my father, no less."

He frowned at her. "That doesn't make you the dust of life."

"Then what does it make me?" she asked, gazing into his eyes and watching the afternoon light shift in their depths.

When he didn't respond, her heart turned sad. She wasn't the poorest of the poor, living in the bowels of society, yet she'd behaved as though she were.

"Let's go," he said. "I called ahead. Danforth is expecting us."

She stood on the massive porch with Michael, the mansion looming over her. "Did you warn him what this meeting was about?"

"No. I just said it was important."

She took a deep breath. Flowers bloomed, scenting the air with sweet, sunlit fragrances.

A housekeeper opened the front door and a few minutes later, Lea and Michael waited in a sitting room rife with antiques, two glasses of freshly squeezed lemonade at their disposal.

To Lea, Abraham's home was a Southern castle, with crystal and china and a collection of what she assumed were real Fabergé eggs displayed on a glass shelf.

As a child, she'd assumed all Americans were rich, but her young *my lai* view of rich couldn't compare to the trappings of a place like Crofthaven.

"How are you holding up?" Michael asked.

"Fine," she lied. She'd never been this nervous before, not even on the day she'd arrived in the States.

When Abraham Danforth entered the room, Michael stepped forward to greet him. The men shook hands, and Lea noticed that Michael, at six-two, stood several inches taller than her father, but Abraham's wide shoulders made him seem equally strong.

He turned to look at her, and her heart crawled straight to her throat, nearly blocking her windpipe. Abraham was a charismatic man, with dark brown hair and stunning blue eyes.

"Lea." He said her name and smiled. "I'm pleased to see you."

"You won't be," she managed, as she came to her feet. "Not after Michael tells you why we're here."

The politician made a perplexed face and addressed his bodyguard. "What's going on?"

"Your daughter is Lady Savannah," Michael said.

The air in Abraham's lungs whooshed out, and Lea flinched, wishing she could die a thousand sword-tipped deaths. Abraham's capable shoulders turned rigid and anger blazed in his eyes. He spun around to stare at her and she felt horribly sick inside.

"You sent those notes? That virus?"

"Yes."

"Why? Why would you do that me? To my family?"

"I wanted to hurt you. To destroy your political career."

"I never suspected you." He shook his head. "I never even considered the possibility. Do you hate me that much, Lea?"

"I did. But I don't anymore." Because she was afraid her legs wouldn't hold her, she sat on an ornate settee and looked up at him. "I thought you used my mother."

He didn't move. He simply stood before her, the light from several windows bathing him in a soft, summer glow. But even so, he remained big and powerful. "Is that what Lan thought, too?"

"No. My mother trusted you."

"I was on a clandestine mission to rescue POWs," he said. "I never intended to have an affair. But after I was injured, Lan sheltered me. She gave me food and medical care. And I—" His voice broke a little. "I didn't remember that I had a wife and children in America."

"My mother believed with all her heart that you were single."

"And so did I." He glanced at the windows, at the landscaped view of Crofthaven. "But I'm not sure why a married man would feel that way. Even a man with amnesia."

He frowned, and Lea wondered if he'd told his wife about his Vietnamese lover or if he'd kept his guilt bottled up inside. Either way, his marriage had suffered. Of that much, she was sure.

When Abraham sat next to her, Lea struggled to breathe. He was so close, she could see the tiny lines around eyes. She wanted to touch his face, to imagine him forgiving her, but she didn't dare.

"I cared very deeply for Lan," he said.

"Did you?" she asked, clasping her hands on her lap.

"Yes, very deeply. But after I was rescued and taken to a U.S. Naval hospital in Hawaii, I was told that Lan's village and all of its inhabitants were destroyed. Because of me," he added. "Because of the aid they'd given a U.S. soldier."

"My mother didn't die." Lea looked around for Michael and noticed that he remained standing, like a sentry, at the opposite end of the room. He caught her gaze and gave her a small nod of encouragement, letting her draw from his strength. "She lived for many years after that."

Her father sighed. "I wish I had known."

"Why?" she asked honestly. "What would you have done? Brought her to America once diplomatic relations with Vietnam were restored? Presented her to your wife and children?"

Abraham's response was troubled, as painful as

his solution. "I wouldn't have left her there. I wouldn't have betrayed her. Lan and her family risked their lives to keep me safe, to hide me from the Viet Cong."

"Yes, she told me that. She said her uncle was involved in the secret mission you were on. That he brought you to their village because you were badly injured and separated from your unit."

"He was injured, too. But he didn't survive his wounds." Although Abraham cleared his throat, he wasn't able to clear the discomfort from his voice. "Did Lan wait for me? Did she hope that I would come back for her someday?"

"Yes. And I hoped and prayed you would, too."

"Until you started hating me?"

Her stomach clenched. This was the man her mother had loved, the man who'd fueled Lea's childhood dreams, the flesh-and-blood hero she'd lost. "I'm so sorry I threatened you. I had no right to make you fearful. To force you to worry about your family."

"It's so hard to believe it was you."

She wanted to curl up and cry, but she knew it wouldn't lessen her crime. "You can contact the police. I'll understand if you turn me in."

Abraham sat quietly for a moment, contemplating her words; he glanced at Michael, then back at her. "I could never do that."

"Why not?" she asked.

"Because you're my daughter."

"But I lashed out at you. I didn't treat you like a father."

"You were hurting." He handed her the lemonade she'd yet to drink. "You're still hurting."

"And so are you." She could see how deeply Lady Savannah had affected him. "I don't deserve your compassion."

"But I want you to accept it. For yourself and your mother."

She sipped her drink, clutching the glass like a lifeline. Somewhere deep down, he was still angry with her, she thought. Still disappointed in Lan's child. But he was trying to do the right thing. "Thank you for your kindness."

He gave her a small smile. "Maybe you and I should get to know each other. Maybe we could spend some time together this week."

"I'd like that." She tried to keep her hands from trembling, her heart from spilling over with tears. "I'd like that very much."

Nine

After Michael and Lea left Crofthaven, they went back to Michael's house. But they couldn't seem to think of anything to say. Neither of them had anticipated her father's forgiveness. Lea's encounter with Danforth had turned out differently than they'd assumed it would. Better, but far more emotional than either of them could endure.

Lea's eyes, he noticed, were damp with unshed tears. Happy tears, sad tears, tears of shame. Michael wasn't sure how to comfort her.

"I should pack," she said.

"Pack?" he parroted. They stood in the great room, beneath the skylight, just looking at each other.

"To go home. Back to my apartment."

"But you've only been here a week. I invited you to stay for two weeks."

"You brought me here because you were investigating me. And the investigation is over."

He couldn't deny her claim. He'd suggested that they become friends, but his offer was based on solving Lady Savannah's case. "I did what I had to do." But he didn't like feeling this distant, this disconnected from her. "It was part of my job."

"I know." She glanced up at the skylight. "I think my father accepted me so readily because of his guilt."

"Because he cheated on his wife? Because Lan's village was destroyed? Because she raised his child on her own?" Michael blew out a rough breath. "He has a lot to contend with."

"I shouldn't have threatened him." She turned toward the stairs. "I only made things more difficult."

"It's over now. And you're both trying to make amends." He followed her upstairs, but he didn't stop her from packing, from making the choice to leave.

She removed her suitcase from the closet and placed it on her side of the bed. He sat on the opposite end, watching her, thinking how fragile she looked.

"Do you think my father will introduce me to his other children?" she asked.

"I imagine he will. Maybe not right away, but eventually."

She began folding her clothes, stacking them neatly in the suitcase. "Once the pain lessens?"

"Yes." A strand of her hair fell forward and Michael imagined tucking it behind her ear, touching the side of her face, absorbing the warmth of her skin. "I have no idea how your brothers and sister will feel. Some of them are probably still struggling with their relationship with their dad."

She held a ruffled blouse against her chest, clinging to the feminine fabric. "What if I cause more trouble than I'm worth?"

"You won't." He resisted the urge to hold her, to wrap her in his arms, to ask her to stay. But he knew they needed some time away from each other, time to sort out their feelings, to cope with the lies and betrayal.

She placed the ruffled blouse in her suitcase, smoothing the lapels. "I couldn't bear to hurt my father again." She stopped packing, her voice laced with shame. "Do you how I located him to begin with?"

Michael studied her weary expression. "No. How?"

"By chance." She smoothed her errant hair. "When I first came to America, I was young and poor and naive. I had no idea how vast this country was or how difficult it would be to locate someone."

"So what did you do?"

"Not much, not when I first got here. I showed his picture around, but that got me nowhere." She made a sad sound. "Do you know how many Amerasians were doing that? Carting around old photographs of their fathers?"

"But you found your dad."

"Only because he was running for state senator. By that time, I was conducting Internet searches, using *Abraham* and *Vietnam veteran* as key words. And one day, an article about Abraham Danforth popped up. There was a picture of him when he was in his twenties, when he fought in the war." She stopped packing. "I recognized him instantly. I knew it was the same man."

Michael thought about the snapshot she'd been carrying around. "I don't understand why Danforth agreed to have his picture taken with your mother, especially after the fall of Saigon."

"He didn't agree to it. He didn't know he was being photographed."

"Who took the picture?"

"Trung, my mother's younger brother. He was an amateur photographer."

Which meant he'd developed it himself, Michael thought. "Why was Trung sneaking around? Taking risky pictures?"

"Because my mother asked him to. She wanted a tangible connection to my father, something to hold on to if he was captured or killed."

Michael shook his head. "That picture could have gotten *her* captured or killed."

"I know. But she promised her brother that she would keep it well hidden. That she wouldn't let the Viet Cong find it." Lea paused. "But her promise hardly mattered because everyone in her family died, including Trung. She was the only person in her village who managed to escape."

Michael pictured Lan running for her life, dodging bullets, grenades and mortar blasts, hiding in a makeshift shelter, alone and afraid. "Will you show me the photograph Trung took? I want to see what your mother looked like."

"It's at my apartment." Lea resumed packing, folding her clothes, gathering her toiletries, keeping her hands much too busy. "You can stop by sometime to see it." She glanced up, and suddenly their gazes locked, trapping him in a timeless moment.

If he stopped by to see the photograph, would he end up in her bed? Would he become her midnight lover again?

"It wouldn't be right," he said.

She blinked. "What?"

"Nothing. I was just thinking out loud." And wishing their relationship wasn't so forbidden, that his feelings for Lea weren't tied up in knots, that he wasn't missing her already.

Lea told herself she enjoyed living alone, but on Monday, after her workday ended, she wandered around her apartment as restless as a caged cat.

She changed into a halter dress, dusted her furniture, turned on the TV and switched channels a dozen times.

When the doorbell rang, she leaped off the couch, hoping it was Michael. She missed him terribly.

Anxious, she answered the summons and found Cindy on the other side. The blonde was dressed in a mint-colored suit, looking as cool and fresh as the icy green fabric. Somehow, the sweltering August weather didn't seem to have an effect on her.

"I hope you don't mind that I stopped by," Cindy said. "I got your address from your file at the office."

"Of course I don't mind." Lea wasn't sure what to make of this visit, but she invited the other woman inside.

"What a lovely apartment." Cindy looked around with unabashed curiosity. "Smart and tidy."

"Thank you. Would you like some iced tea? I always keep a fresh pitcher on hand."

"That sounds good." The blonde followed Lea to the kitchen, making herself at home. She sat at the glass-topped table near the window and crossed her legs.

Lea poured their drinks and joined her. "Did you come here directly from the office?"

"Yes. As a matter of fact, that's why I decided to stop by. Michael drove me crazy today." Cindy accepted the tea and took a small sip. "He was so moody." She leaned forward. "I assume you two are having some problems."

Lea didn't know what to say. She certainly couldn't tell Cindy that Michael had been investigating her. "I have a lot going on in my personal life."

"With what? Your father?"

"Yes. We're going to try to get to know each other."

"So you're ready to let him announce to the world that you're his daughter?"

"No. I mean...I think it's still too soon for that. I'd prefer to keep our relationship private for a while."

Cindy tilted her head. "I wonder if he'll include you in his will."

Taken aback, Lea could only stare. She hadn't expected the other woman to pry into Abraham's financial affairs, at least not in such a blatant manner. "I'm not interested in my father's money."

"Then what is it you want from him?"

"Acceptance." And forgiveness, she thought. Absolution. Redemption.

The blonde fluffed her hair, tossing loose waves over her shoulders. "I'd rather have his money. Let's face it, that man owes you. There you were, abandoned in Vietnam and struggling to get by while his other children were attending fancy boarding schools."

At this point, Lea wasn't sure if Cindy was friend or foe, enemy or ally. "I used to think that he owed me something, but I don't feel that way any more."

The other woman's tennis bracelet glinted in the light. "I didn't mean to speak ill of your father. Abraham Danforth is a fascinating man. A bit too old for my taste, but charming nonetheless."

Too old? Did that mean Cindy wasn't keeping a romantic eye on him?

"Now Michael is perfect, don't you think?"

Lea stumbled. "P-perfect? For what?"

"Someone our age." The bracelet caught another ray of light. "I'm twenty-seven. Just like you."

"I never considered Michael's age as a factor in our relationship."

"Didn't you? Well, think about it. A successful man in his midthirties is just what a career-oriented woman in her late-twenties needs."

When Lea didn't respond, they sat quietly, drinking sugar-spiked tea and listening to the background noise of the television, a talk show offering marital advice.

"I'll bet he's going to show up here," Cindy said.

"Who?"

"Michael."

"Why would he?"

"Because he was thinking about you all day. He didn't tell me he was, but he didn't have to. I know him better than anyone. I can read his moods." The other woman sighed. "I wish someone like Michael would brood over me."

Someone *like* Michael? Lea wondered. Or Michael himself? With Cindy, it was impossible to tell. The blonde never quite made her intentions clear.

Cindy leaned back in her chair. "It's a sexual obsession."

Lea's pulse jumped. "What?"

"The way Michael feels about you. I'll bet he'll ask you to move in with him. Just to have you next to him every night."

"He won't—"

"Yes, he will. That's what my old boyfriend did with me. And once the excitement wore off, he got rid of me." Cindy rose, leaving her half-empty glass on the table. "I should go. I have some errands to run."

Dazed, Lea could only stare.

With the grace of a Savannah socialite, Cindy reached out to give Lea a hug, confusing her even more. And by the time the blonde swept out the door in her mint-green attire and diamond trinkets, Lea's head was spinning.

Fifteen minutes later the doorbell sounded, but Lea wasn't surprised to find Michael waiting on her stoop. Cindy claimed that he would stop by, and she was right.

Michael gave Lea a cautious smile, and her heart melted. God, how she loved him.

"Should I have called first?" he asked.

"No. I'm glad you're here."

He entered the apartment, and they stood quietly for a moment, just looking at each other. He was dressed in a white shirt, black trousers and a silk tie, with his hair combed away from his forehead. She wanted to kiss him, to lead him to her room, but she couldn't bring herself to do that, not after what Cindy had said.

He lifted the grocery bag in his hand. "I got the ingredients for the pumpkin soup. I found a Seminole recipe online that's similar to what my mom used to make."

"Then come into the kitchen and we'll cook."

"Okay." He smiled at her again, leaving her breathless.

Lea cleared the iced-tea glasses from the table, and Michael set the groceries on the counter. When she turned to face him, he was removing his tie and rolling up his shirtsleeves.

She moved closer to unpack the ingredients, and he roamed his gaze over her.

"Is that a new dress?" he asked.

She nodded. "I bought it yesterday."

"It's backless." He tossed his tie over the back of a kitchen chair. "Braless."

Her nipples went hard. Guilty for wanting him, she fussed with her hair, bringing it forward, covering her breasts. "It's been so hot lately."

He jammed his hands into his pockets. "Do you think it's too hot to make soup?"

"In Vietnam, we used to have soup for breakfast. I can eat it anytime. In any kind of weather."

"Me, too." He unpacked the grocery bag. "The recipe calls for two cups of chicken stock, so I bought bouillon cubes. Is that okay?"

She still wanted to touch him, to lead him to her room, to hold him as close as she could. "Sure. That's fine."

"I got canned pumpkin. I didn't see any fresh pumpkins at the market." He handed her the recipe he'd printed from the Internet. "But supposedly either one works."

She glanced at the paper. "I'm sure it will be good."

"I hope so." He stepped forward, closing the gap between them. "I've missed you so much, Lea. It's only been two days, but I can hardly stand it."

When she looked up at him, the room nearly tilted. "I feel exactly the same way."

"I kept hoping you did." He brought her against his body, stroking a hand down her naked back, creating a blanket of warmth over her skin.

She put her head on his shoulder and inhaled the familiar scent of his cologne. He was everything she wanted, everything that mattered.

"We need to start over," he said. "A clean slate. No lies, no false pretenses. No Lady Savannah."

"I'm not her anymore." Lea lifted her head. "I swear, I'm not."

"I know. I trust you." He cupped her face. "We'll have a real relationship this time. Deeper than before."

Their conversation swirled around her like a soul-shrouding mist. Michael stood before her asking her to become a significant part of his life. Yet somewhere deep down, it didn't feel right.

Because of Cindy, she thought. Because the seed of doubt had already been planted. "It scares me."

He took his hand away. "Why?"

"It seems too good to be true."

"There's nothing that can spoil it this time. Move in with me, Lea. Share my house."

Her knees nearly buckled, Cindy's prediction reverberating in her ears. "Maybe we should date for a while first."

"Why? What's wrong with living together?"

"If it doesn't work out, I don't think I could survive. We've been through so much already." And she couldn't bear to think that his feelings for her were based on sex, on an obsession he couldn't control. "We shouldn't rush into this."

"Okay. Fine." He scooped her into his arms. "Then I'll court you. I'll wine and dine you. I'll do all those romantic things women want." He dragged her heart against his. "I'll make you swoon."

Her insides turned to mush. "You already have."

"Then I'm just going to keep doing it." He kissed her, deep and rich and slow.

He tasted like a forbidden dream, like the mysterious vampire from her past. His lips were smooth and moist, his chin bristling with a five o'clock shadow. She liked the raspy feeling, the slight roughness against her cheek.

By the time the kiss ended, her heart was reeling. She wondered if it would always be this way or if Michael would lose interest in her someday.

He touched a lock of her hair. "Can I see that picture of your parents?"

"Of course." She wanted to share it with him. She wanted him to know every part of her. "I'll get it."

She went into her bedroom and removed an envelope from her jewelry box. After she returned to the kitchen, she handed Michael a photograph ravaged by time and the remnants of war.

He studied it carefully. "Lan was beautiful. You look a lot like her."

"Thank you. My father was handsome, too." Abraham was young and tall and lean, a secret soldier recovering from his injuries.

"Have you heard from him?"

She nodded. "He called me at work today. He invited me to Crofthaven."

"When?"

"Tomorrow, before it gets dark. He wants to walk on the beach."

Michael returned the photograph. "That sounds nice. There's a private cove. I'm sure you'll enjoy it."

She tucked the picture into the envelope, closing the flap, preserving the only image she had of her mother. "I'm nervous about it."

"You'll be fine."

He reached out to hug her, to press a gentle kiss on her forehead, and she let herself fall deeper in love, no matter how dangerous it was.

A moment later, she told herself to take a cleansing breath, to live one day at a time, to cook the soup with Michael and fill her kitchen with the aroma of pumpkin, parsley, sugar and thyme.

Ten

Seagulls flocked along the shore, and the sky reflected a prism of summer hues.

"This is beautiful," Lea said.

Her father guided her along the secluded beach, the sun-warmed sand glistening at their feet. "It's peaceful. A good place to be alone."

Lea nodded, then turned to look at him. His hair blew in the breeze, stirring lightly in the air. She wanted to apologize again, but she feared talking about Lady Savannah would break the spell.

Self-conscious, she smoothed her wind-ravaged T-shirt. She'd fussed over her appearance, worried that she would never be as pretty as his other daughter. Abraham had five legitimate children, four boys and a girl. Lea had seen newspaper pictures of them.

They were adults, like her, but as far as she knew, they'd never done anything as cold-hearted as threaten their father.

"Have you told your other children about me?" she asked.

"Yes, I have. I told them after I received the results from the paternity test."

"Were they upset?"

He stopped walking. "They were upset that I'd slept with another woman while I was married to their mother. But I think they're coming to terms with the amnesia."

She studied his frown. "Are you?"

"My marriage wasn't as strong as it should have been."

Because of his guilt? she wondered. Or because he wasn't a good husband to begin with?

"Do you want to meet your brothers and your sister?" he asked.

Lea took a deep breath. "Yes, very much." She looked into her father's eyes, hoping his other children were interested in her.

Abraham held her gaze. "Then I'll let them know and they can contact you when they're ready. I don't want to arrange a family dinner. I think it would be better to let everyone handle this in his or her own way."

"I understand. I think I'd prefer that, too. I'd be too nervous at a family dinner."

"It will get easier with time." He gave her a reassuring smile. "We're already making progress."

She returned his smile, knowing her mother

would be pleased. "I have something to show you." She reached into her backpack and removed the faded photograph, handing it to him.

He gazed at the black-and-white image of himself with Lan. "I didn't know someone took a picture of us." He handled the glossy paper carefully, his voice edged with emotion. "It must have been Trung."

"It was. But at my mother's request. She wanted a picture with you." Lea thought about the years her mother struggled to survive, the days she'd cried for her American lover. "She missed you."

"I'm sorry, Lea." He watched her hair blow across her face. "I'm so sorry."

"So am I." She stepped forward to take a chance, to embrace him. "For everything I've done."

He returned her hug, holding her tentatively at first, then stronger, smoothing her long, billowing hair. She closed her eyes for a moment, realizing her mother's picture was between them.

When they separated, her eyes turned misty.

"I'm still willing to call a press conference," he said. "To let the public know about you. To claim you as my daughter."

"That means the world to me, but I'm not ready to talk to reporters, to have them coming to my door. I'd prefer to remain in the background for a while."

"That's fine. I just wanted you to know the offer still stands."

He returned the photograph, and Lea decided her mother was right. Abraham Danforth was an honorable man.

* * *

John Van Gelder accepted a snifter of brandy from Hayden, giving his young adviser a wary look. At this point, John didn't know whom to trust. Honest Abe was leading in the polls, fooling the public into believing he was the candidate of choice. "This better be good."

"The brandy?"

"Your news."

"It is." Hayden leaned against the desk in his study, a bit too confident, too sure of himself.

He reminded John of a peacock fanning its feathers, but that wasn't enough to convince him that the boy had done his job. "What do you have? What did you find out?"

"Abraham Danforth took a paternity test last month."

John didn't react, not at first. "How accurate is this information?"

"My source is extremely reliable. The person I spoke with is absolutely certain that Danforth fathered an illegitimate child."

"Well, I'll be damned." A smile spread across John's face. "That is good news." He finished the brandy, savoring the feeling, the sudden flavor of success. He knew it wouldn't take long for Danforth's reputation to crumble, not once this juicy little tidbit was leaked to the press. "I believe we just caught Honest Abe with his pants down."

"Yes, sir," Hayden said, refilling John's glass. "I believe we did."

* * *

After Lea returned from the beach, she got ready for a date with Michael. He'd offered to take her to a popular nightspot, keeping his promise to wine and dine her. So she put on a short black dress and piled her hair loosely on top of her head, hoping to look chic and stylish.

At 9:00 p.m. they arrived at Steam, a trendy club and posh restaurant located downtown. Less than five minutes later, they were seated at one of the best tables in the house.

Intrigued, Lea glanced around. The dining room was located on the second floor, directly above the club. From her vantage point, she could see the stage below. Both the restaurant and club were decorated in red velvet, with touches of mahogany and marble.

"Clayton Crawford owns this place," Michael said. "He's a good friend of mine."

She reached for her menu. "No wonder we're getting the royal treatment."

"I told Clay about you. He knows about Lady Savannah, the whole bit. I had to confide in someone."

"He must think I'm awful."

"I let him know you were working things out with your dad."

She relaxed a little. The lamp on the table glowed, and their glasses were already filled with wine. "I assume I'll get to meet Clay tonight?"

"And his fiancée, too." He looked over the balcony. "They're down there somewhere. We can hook up with them later."

When their server came by, Lea and Michael ordered the same meal: a steak and seafood platter, with sautéed vegetables and Cajun spices.

"This is nice," she said.

He met her gaze. "It is, isn't it?"

"You know how to treat a woman right."

"You're the most important person in the world to me." His voice turned rough, laced with trepidation, with tenderness, with a jumble of emotions. "Am I that important to you?"

Her heart nearly quit beating, but that didn't stop her from reaching across the table for his hand, from admitting the truth. "I love you, Michael."

"Really?" Although he gripped her fingers like a vise, his voice still sounded rough, still edged with anxiety. "Then why won't you move in with me?"

"Because you're still struggling with your feelings."

He didn't dispute her claim. "Clay thinks I love you. He thinks I've got it bad."

And Cindy thinks it's about sex, Lea thought. So who was right?

When the server brought their bread, they separated, taking their hands back, leaving the table free.

"How do you know that you love me?" he asked suddenly.

"I just do." She wasn't sure how to explain her feelings, not to a man who was watching her with fear in his eyes. "It's okay if it scares you."

He picked up his wine. "All I ever think about is touching you. Putting my hands all over you." He leaned forward. "Is that what love is supposed to be like?"

"I don't know what it's like for men."

He frowned a little. "Neither do I." He finished his drink, then poured another glass. "Maybe we should stop talking about it."

Lea agreed, so they sat quietly, sipping chardonnay and buttering warm bread. When their meal arrived, they ate filet mignon and grilled shrimp, catching anxiety-ridden glimpses of each other between bites.

Halfway through their food, Michael started another conversation. "I'm going to be the best man at Clay's wedding."

She tasted her vegetables. "When is it?"

"Near the end of the month. Do you want to go with me?"

"Yes. I'd like that very much."

"Good." He smiled at her. "I want this to work, Lea. I want us to make it."

"Me, too." She looked into his eyes and saw her own dreams, the wishes of a *con lai* girl who'd fallen in love with a half-breed boy.

After dinner, they took a gated elevator to the lower level, and once they were in the club, he introduced her to Clay Crawford and his fiancée, a stunning redhead named Kat.

Lea couldn't help but admire them, the soul-stirring way they looked at each other, the tender yet subtle way they touched.

Clay seemed to be watching her and Michael, too, analyzing them, judging their relationship. But Lea didn't mind. If the other man thought that Michael loved her, then she was more than willing to consider him an ally.

Within a few minutes, Clay and Kat excused themselves, insisting they had work to do. But Lea wasn't buying their excuse. She suspected that they wanted to give her and Michael some romantic time alone.

Once his friends were gone, Michael gazed at her. She looked back at him, wishing she could lock him inside her heart.

"Do you want to dance?" he asked.

She nodded and reached for his hand. Together, they walked onto the dance floor, finding a cozy spot among the other couples.

The music was deep and sensual, as rhythmic as the motion of their bodies. He lowered his head to kiss her, and she tasted the wine he'd drunk with dinner, the flavor of intoxication on his lips. Lea had never danced like this before. She'd never moved so erotically, not with her clothes on.

He nuzzled her neck, breathing softly against her skin, and when he loosened the pins in her hair, she wondered if he knew he was seducing her.

"Will you stay with me tonight?" she asked, not wanting to be alone, to be without him.

"You know I will." He kissed her again, and at that desperate moment, Lea told herself it didn't matter if Michael knew the difference between lust and love. All that mattered was his hands and his mouth and the slow, sensual way he caressed her.

Yes, she thought. All that mattered was the beauty of making love with him, the comfort of his touch, the sweet, summer-bound safety of sleeping in his arms.

* * *

Michael awakened in Lea's bed, in a room with lavender sheets and whitewashed furniture.

Feeling out of place in the feminine surroundings, he tried to acclimate his emotions, the fear of falling in love, of being overwhelmed by it, of not knowing which way to turn or what to do.

Confused, he breathed against her neck, inhaling the familiar scent of her skin. She was still asleep, still wrapped in his arms.

He disengaged their bodies and rose on his elbow, leaning over her. She squinted and opened her eyes, fluttering her lashes, fighting grogginess.

"What are you doing?" she asked.

He managed a smile. They'd made sweet, syrupy love last night, touching and kissing for hours, making every breathless minute count. "I'm looking at you."

"Why?"

"Because you're so pretty." And because when he was with her, when she was by his side, his life made sense. And when she wasn't, he went crazy. "I wish you'd move in with me."

She reached out to graze his cheek. "We agreed to take our time about that."

Michael frowned. In some ways, he understood her reluctance. And in other ways, it made him ache. "You think I'm being impulsive."

"You are." She traced the troubled lines in his forehead. "But I'm still in love with you."

He lowered his head to kiss her, wishing he had more control over what was happening. The only time their relationship seemed stable was when he was inside her, when their bodies were joined, when they got lost in each other's arms.

She slid her hands through his hair, pulling him closer. They were still naked, still warm and sticky from the night before.

"I don't have any more condoms with me," he said.

"It's okay. We don't have to be together."

"But I want to make you feel good." Unable to resist, he rubbed his thumbs over her nipples, making them peak, drawing one into his mouth.

Lea arched and sighed, and he took comfort in the closeness, in the intimacy that never failed to arouse her. Anxious to please her, he roamed her body, molding her, taking possession.

She gave him a glazed look, and he knew she'd slipped into a state of carnal consciousness, that his soul was seeping into her pores.

"I can't concentrate when you touch me," she said. "I can't think clearly."

"Good." He didn't want her to behave rationally. He wanted her to come unglued, to surrender to him. "Do you like this?" He licked his way to her navel. "And this?" He nipped her skin, moving lower, making her moan.

When she opened her legs, inviting him to taste her, he kissed between her thighs, using his tongue, giving her what she wanted, what they both needed.

Heat, he thought. Primal sensations. Sleek, seductive shivers.

She made a throaty sound, and sunlight spilled

into the room, bathing her in ever-changing hues, in colors his mind had conjured.

Lea wasn't shy. She lifted her hips and rubbed against his mouth, showing him how much she liked what he was doing.

He liked it, too. For Michael, oral sex was more than foreplay, more than a teasing game. To him, it was the ultimate act of submission, of trusting your partner.

When she climaxed, he tasted her release, sipping her deep and slow. She fell onto the bed, her stomach muscles quivering, her limbs shaking.

He'd never seen a more beautiful woman.

"You're spoiling me," she said.

He kissed his way back up her body, brushing her lips with his. "That's the idea."

She rolled over. "Maybe I should spoil you."

His pulse pounded. Everywhere. "You don't have to."

"What if I want to?" She crawled between his thighs, making his breath catch. He was already hard, already turned on.

Michael shifted his legs, giving her full access to his body, letting her have as much as she wanted, as much as she was willing to take.

She took all of him, with her hands and her mouth, increasing the tempo, setting a strong, fluid rhythm.

Mesmerized, he toyed with her hair, twining it around his fingers, making the moment even more erotic. Falling deeper under her spell, he yielded to the pressure in his loins, to the warmth and the wetness.

He knew he should warn her that he was getting close, that he was on the verge of losing control, but he couldn't summon the strength to give up the pleasure, to lessen the mind-blowing gratification. So he watched her instead, getting more and more turned on.

Time passed, seconds, minutes. He didn't care. He couldn't think beyond the sucking motion, beyond the way she made him feel.

She gave him everything—every raw, ravenous sensation a man could imagine, every hot wicked thing he could fantasize about.

Michael cupped her face, knowing he was going to spill into her, knowing she was going to let him.

After it was over, they stared at each other, stunned, confused, strangely aroused. He wasn't sure if he should apologize or drag her against his body and kiss her senseless.

He did neither. He simply accepted their newfound intimacy, curious when she ran her tongue across her lips.

"Salty?" he asked.

She nodded, then reached for the bottled water beside her bed and took a sip. "I've never gone that far before."

His skin turned warm. "Me, neither." He'd always pulled back before he climaxed, never expecting any of his lovers to do what Lea had just done. "What an incredible way to start the day."

"For you," she said, making a face.

He laughed, and she splashed him, spraying his chest. He grabbed her, and they tumbled over the sheets, wresting with the plastic bottle and dumping the rest of the water onto the bed.

And at that silly, lighthearted moment, he prayed that he would never lose her, that she was his to keep.

His cell phone rang, interrupting their horseplay, jarring his tender thoughts. Cursing his job, he answered it, sensing it was a business call.

"Michael?" Cindy's frantic voice came on the line. "Have you seen the paper this morning?"

"No. I'm at Lea's. What's going on?"

"It made the front page."

"What did?" he asked, although he was already gathering his clothes, already preparing to get dressed. Cindy wasn't the type to overreact.

"The paternity test. Someone leaked it to the press."

He glanced at his lover, cursing out loud this time. "Does the article mention Lea?"

"No. It's speculation, mostly. But it doesn't look good for Mr. Danforth."

He yanked up his pants. "Lea and I will meet you at the office. Send the rest of the team to Crofthaven."

"I already did."

"Good. We'll see you soon." He hung up and told Lea to get ready, knowing all hell was about to break loose.

Eleven

Lea sat at a long wooden table in a meeting room at Whittaker and Associates, with the newspaper strewn in front of her. She'd barely had time to catch her breath and now her stomach was burning from drinking the coffee Cindy had poured into her cup. She still hadn't told the other woman she preferred tea, and Michael was too preoccupied to notice.

"I feel so responsible," Cindy said. She walked around to the other side of the table, moving closer to Michael. "It was my job to make sure this didn't happen." She took the chair next to him. "Maybe it was someone at the lab."

"Or someone who works for Danforth's attorneys." He smoothed his sleep-tousled hair. "There are only a handful of people who knew about the test. And this is only going to get worse."

Cindy agreed. "The tabloids are going to have a field day. They'll probably link Mr. Danforth with every socialite in Savannah. Married, single. Anyone with a young child."

Silent, Lea glanced at the article about her father. The press didn't know he'd fathered a grown daughter. And being omitted from the scandal made her feel like a cheat, like she'd skimmed by purposely, allowing her dad to take the fall.

Michael blew out a frustrated breath. "Being a political figure isn't easy. The press plays a dirty game."

"They sure do," the blonde said.

Once again, guilt clawed at Lea's conscience. Hoping to settle her stomach, she reached for a croissant and took a small bite. Cindy had provided a variety of baked goods, something, Lea assumed, the blonde did for her boss every morning.

He decided to eat, too, spreading cream cheese onto a bagel. He didn't look like a man who'd spent the last hour engaging in erotic acts with his lover. He was all business now, except for his wrinkled clothes, the same shirt and trousers he'd worn to the club the night before.

Lea wasn't faring much better. She'd grabbed a T-shirt and jeans, barely having time to wash her face and brush her teeth. Cindy, of course, looked as polished as a new penny. Everything about her shimmered, including the copper-colored buttons on her designer suit.

"How's it going at Crofthaven?" Michael asked his assistant.

"Our team is keeping the media circus away," she responded.

Lea finally spoke up. "I'm the one who's responsible for this mess. If I had agreed to a press conference with my father, none of this would have happened." She reached for the paper. "Is it too late to do it now?"

Michael glanced up at her, ignoring his half-eaten bagel. She caught Cindy's attention, as well.

"It's not too late," he said. "But it won't be easy on you. The press will want to delve into every aspect of your life."

She put on a brave face. "I owe this to my father."

Cindy chimed in. "I think it's the perfect solution, Michael. If Mr. Danforth and his Amerasian daughter show a united front, it will create a positive image for both of them." She turned to Lea. "And there's nothing in your past that won't endear you to the public."

Except Lady Savannah, she thought. And that was a private matter, between her and her father.

"Are you sure you're ready to do this?" Michael asked.

"Yes, I'm sure." What choice did she have? She couldn't let her dad suffer. She couldn't allow the media to make up stories about him, pairing him with half the women in Savannah, gossiping, speculating about who had given birth to his child.

Michael leaned forward. "I'll call your father and

let him discuss this with his campaign manager. They can arrange the press conference." He snared her gaze. "It would probably be better if you moved in with me, at least for a while. My house is secure. The paparazzi can't bother you there."

"I'll be okay." She didn't want to use this as an excuse to live with him. She wanted to be sure he loved her first, that he wasn't confused about his feelings.

"Fine. I'll make that call from my office." He stood, taking his coffee with him. "I'll be back in a few minutes."

After he left the room, Cindy picked up a blueberry muffin. "You wounded his pride."

"I know." And now she feared she might lose him. "But what else could I do?"

"Nothing. You made the right decision."

"Did I?" She gazed at the other woman, a sudden chill icing her spine. A warning, she thought. But hadn't there been warning signs all along? "Who's the man you're interested in?"

Cindy lifted her chin. "Who do you think he is?"

"Michael," she said, her pulse pounding in her ears.

His assistant remained calm, poised as ever. "That's crazy." She picked at her muffin, taking delicate bites. "If I didn't know better, I'd think you were a suspicious shrew."

Lea narrowed her eyes. "Oh, really?"

"Yes, but you're not. You're just insecure."

"Why? Because you've convinced me not to move in with the man I love?"

"Living with Michael won't make him feel the same way about you. It will only give him what he wants." Cindy dusted the crumbs from her fingers. "A bedmate, someone to satisfy his needs. And you'll end up getting hurt."

Lea pushed away her croissant. She was already hurting, already fighting her fears.

A moment later, Michael came back, ready to resume their meeting. Both women turned to look at him, but neither of them breathed a word of the conversation they'd just had.

The press conference was being held at the Twin Oaks Hotel, the same location as the July Fourth fund-raiser where Lea had first confronted her father. For now, she waited in a hospitality suite, where Nicola Granville, Abraham's campaign manager and image consultant, had been giving her one last briefing, one last boost of encouragement.

Nicola was outgoing and confident, as well as smart and pretty. Lea had no idea if the other woman was involved with her father, but she recalled Michael's observation, his gut instinct that Abraham and Nicola were attracted to each other.

Nicola glanced at her watch. "I'm going to head over to the conference room to check on some details. Just relax, Lea. And I'll come back for you when it's time."

"Is my father here yet?"

"No, but he should be arriving shortly."

"Okay. Thanks." She reached for the root beer she'd been nursing. Michael was already at the conference room, but he'd stationed a bodyguard outside the hospitality suite in case anyone bothered Lea.

Nicola exited the room, leaving her alone with her thoughts. She had no idea where Cindy was today, but she was glad the deceptive blonde wasn't hovering nearby, making her more nervous than she already was. Although she intended to talk to Michael about his assistant, she wanted to wait until the press conference was over, until she could think clearly.

The bodyguard knocked on the door, then poked his head inside. "Two of your brothers are here to see you, Miss Nguyen."

"My brothers?" Lea hopped up from the couch, nearly spilling her drink. "Are you sure?"

"Yes, ma'am. I verified their identification. Adam and Marcus Danforth."

"Then send them in." She smoothed her dress, praying that she met with their approval.

A second later, when her brothers entered the room, Lea forgot to breathe. They looked more handsome in person than they did in the photographs she'd seen. Taller, broader, chiseled and strong.

"I'm Adam." The older of the two stepped forward. She knew his age—twenty-nine—because she'd memorized details about her siblings, things she'd read in newspaper and magazine clippings.

"I'm Lea." She smiled, and the greeting turned warm. Adam gave her a quick brotherly hug, and she sensed that was his way of welcoming her into the family.

"I don't suppose this is much fun," he said. "The press conference and all that."

"I'm nervous," she admitted, studying the hazel-gold color of his eyes. She'd come across some old tabloid articles about Adam, claiming that he'd been involved in a love triangle. Were the allegations true? She had no idea. But either way, he seemed to empathize with her situation.

Finally, her other brother moved forward. His eyes caught hers, and they gazed at each other. She knew he was a Harvard-educated lawyer, an attorney for Danforth and Company.

"You're Marcus," she said.

"Call me Marc."

Once again, they simply looked at each other. She couldn't explain the instant bond, the feeling that she trusted him already.

"I'm sorry about your mother, Lea. That you lost her before you came to America."

"Thank you." She hadn't expected any of Abraham's children to mention his Vietnamese lover. She'd assumed Lan would be a taboo subject, someone they would prefer to sweep under the rug if they could. "I'm sorry you lost your mother, too."

"It was a long time ago," he said. "I was just a kid."

But it hadn't been easy on him, she thought. "I'm so glad you and Adam stopped by. This means so much to me."

"You're our new sister." Marc glanced at his brother. "We've always been loyal. To each other," he added, indicating that their father hadn't always garnered their loyalty, that his absence, the years he'd spent on his military career, had created a void in their lives. "Ian, Reid and Kim couldn't make it today. But I'm sure you'll be hearing from them before long."

Overwhelmed, she blinked back tears. "I'm looking forward to meeting my other brothers, and of course my sister, too." She paused to take a much-needed breath. "I was worried about how she would feel about me."

Adam spoke up. "Kim should enjoy having another female around." He laughed a little. "Not that she didn't learn to hold her own around all of us."

Lea smiled, then realized she'd forgotten her manners. "Would either of you like a drink?" She gestured to the wet bar. "Nicola said it was stocked."

Her brothers declined the offer, admitting that they would prefer to skip out before their dad arrived. "It'll be easier if it's just the two of you at the press conference," Marc said, sounding like the attorney he was. "And Adam would just as soon avoid the limelight. Wouldn't you, bro?"

"You got that right." Adam reached for Lea's hand to say goodbye, wishing her luck. Marc said goodbye, too, giving her a hug this time, making her feel warm and protected.

After they left, she resumed her spot on the couch and waited for her father, for the man who'd given her a family.

When the press conference ended, Michael invited Lea to his house for dinner. After a day filled with public scrutiny, he wanted her to enjoy a quiet evening in a secluded location.

He turned to look at her. She seemed preoccupied, as though her thoughts kept drifting. While he mashed potatoes, she panfried pork chops and made gravy, but they hadn't talked about anything other than the meal.

"Are these too lumpy?" he asked.

She came over to him and checked the potatoes. "It depends on how you like them."

"It doesn't matter."

"Then go ahead and add a little milk."

"How much is a little?"

"This much." She poured the milk for him, and he took the opportunity to move closer to her.

"It went well today," he said, watching her, pretending to be focused on the potatoes.

"Yes, it did, considering the circumstances. It wasn't easy for my father to admit to the press that he'd committed adultery, even if his amnesia was to blame."

"He's been willing to do that since he met you."

"I know, but I still think it took a lot of courage on his part."

Michael took back the bowl, even though she'd finished mashing the potatoes for him. "The reporters are going to verify his story. They're going to research his medical records to make sure it's true."

"It doesn't matter." She turned down the flame on the stove, then covered the pork chops. "He doesn't have anything to hide. Not like me."

"The press isn't going to find out about Lady Savannah, Lea. That's not going to make the papers."

"No, but our affair probably will."

"I don't care if they figure out that we're sleeping together." He tried to search her gaze, wishing she would look at him. "Do you?"

"No." She fussed with the salad, adding a layer of grated cheese on top. "We don't have anything to be ashamed of."

Then why was she behaving so awkwardly? Perplexed, he leaned against the counter. "Are you okay? You seem sort of distant."

She finally glanced up. "I do have something on my mind."

"What?"

"Arranging some vacation time at work. I don't think I can handle being in the public eye right now."

"That's understandable." His heart began to pound, reminding him of the effect she had on him, of his need to be close to her. "Did you change your mind about staying here, too?"

"Yes, but just for a few days, just until the media attention dies down." She set the salad aside. Behind her, the pork chops sizzled, sending a mouthwatering aroma into the air. "You don't mind, do you?"

"Of course not. I offered to let you stay here." He moved to stand beside her, to brush her shoulder with his. "I'll take some time off, too. We can lounge around together."

She sent him a gracious smile. "Thank you. I really need your support right now."

He sensed that she had more on her mind. That she hadn't told him everything. But he decided to drop the subject until she had a chance to relax.

"I'm investigating the paternity test leak," he said, letting her know he intended to find out who'd created this mess.

"Really? Do you have any leads?"

"Not yet. But there are only a couple of avenues to follow. Only a few sources who knew about the test."

She stirred the gravy. "I'm sure you'll find out."

"I hope so." He liked the way she looked in his kitchen, creating a domestic atmosphere, making him feel warm and homey. "I'm certainly going to do my best."

A short while later, they dined by candlelight, with music playing on the stereo. Over dinner, she talked about her brothers and how happy she was that they'd made an effort to see her. Michael smiled, pleased Adam and Marc had endeared themselves to her.

After their meal ended, he suggested dessert on the patio. She agreed, and they sat outside, listening to the sounds of summer and eating chocolate ice cream.

The air was mild, the sky dotted with stars. In the distance, he could see his private dock and a boat he sometimes used on security detail.

Silent, he turned to study Lea. She still had on the

same clothes she'd worn to the press conference, and her hair was loose, falling to her waist like rain.

"Tell me what's going on," he said. "Besides your concern about being in the public eye."

She took an audible breath. "I'm having some problems with Cindy."

Concerned, he leaned forward in his chair. "What kind of problems?"

Lea stirred her ice cream. "I think she's trying to come between us."

Stunned, Michael could only stare. "Why would she do that?"

Her eyes locked onto his. "Because she's interested in you. You're the mystery man she's been pursuing."

"Did she tell you that?"

"No. She denied it, but I can tell it's true."

He shook his head, wondering what the hell was going on. He'd never expected a conversation like this to evolve, not with Lea. "Give me the facts, support your claim."

Her voice quavered a little. "She keeps telling me that your attraction to me is purely sexual. That it will never be anything more than that." Her eyes were still magnetized to his. "She says I'll end up getting hurt."

"And this is coming from a woman who's supposedly interested in me?" He set his bowl on the patio table. His appetite was gone, his stomach muscles tense. "Come on, Lea. Why would she want me if she thinks I'm such a dog?"

"Maybe she thinks you'd develop a deeper relationship with her. Or maybe she doesn't care, as long as you're rich. But either way, she's trying to drive us apart."

"You must have misunderstood her intentions. Cindy has been my assistant for nearly three years, and she's never come on to me. There's never been anything between us. It just isn't there."

"You hired her because of the way she looks. You even admitted that you like being around beautiful women." She lifted her chin. "You said that when we were at the gallery downtown, the first time I met her."

"I remember where we were and what I said." He struggled to hold his temper, to keep this discussion grounded. "But you're taking my statement out of context. I hired Cindy because she's competent. Her appearance was secondary."

Lea shoved her ice cream bowl next to his. "That's like saying men buy *Playboy* for the articles."

"What the hell is that supposed to mean? That's she's only pretending to be competent, and I'm too busy drooling over her to notice?" He resisted the urge to kick the rail of an empty chair. Already he was reliving the arguments his parents used to have. This was too damn close to the accusations his mom used to make, even when his dad wasn't screwing around. "There's nothing going on but your overactive imagination."

She heaved a labored breath, and his heart twisted in his chest. Didn't Lea realize how much she meant to him? Didn't she know how often he'd suffered because of her? How much he ached? How confused he was?

"My feelings for you aren't based on sex," he said, defending his jumbled emotions.

"Maybe not." She wrapped her arms around her middle. "But your feelings aren't based on trust, either."

He didn't respond. He couldn't think of an appropriate answer, not while his parents' screaming matches were spinning in his head. The anger. The jealousy. The infidelity. He'd sworn that he'd never let anything like that taint his life.

Lea came to her feet. She did her best to remain strong, to keep her legs steady, but he could see that she was starting to shake.

"You're playing right into Cindy's hands," she said. "And before long, she'll console you right into her bed."

"I'm not interested in my assistant. And she's not interested in me. Why can't you see that?" He stood, too. He towered over her by nearly a foot, and he wished she didn't look so delicate, so soft and pretty. "Cindy has been a model employee. As loyal as they come. Granted, she's shrewd. Tough, a little ruthless. But that's her business side."

"It's her personal side, too."

"I know she intimidates you, Lea. I noticed it from the beginning."

"And so did she. That's how she managed to get away with this. She probably wants us to argue about her, hoping you'll defend her."

"I can't condemn her, not without proof."

"I should be your proof. My instincts should be

enough. A woman knows when another woman is after her man."

"What about my instincts?" he snapped. "I'm the detective." And he knew jealousy could get out of hand, whether or not it was warranted.

Lea didn't respond. She turned and walked into the house, leaving him alone.

He cursed under his breath and followed her. "What are you doing?" he asked as she retrieved her purse.

She spun around to face him. "Did you expect me to stay here now?"

He struggled with his feelings, with letting her go, with losing her. "There's probably paparazzi camped outside your apartment."

She ignored his comment and moved toward the front door. "I'd fight for you if I could, if it would do any good. But how can I wage a war with Cindy when you're taking her side?" She looked into his eyes. "How can I have a future with a man who doesn't trust me?"

When she was gone, he realized she was right. He hadn't given her a chance. And that scared him as much as falling in love with her.

Nearly two hours later, Michael checked his watch. Anxious, he studied the Swiss timepiece, watching the second hand make another gut-wrenching sweep. He hadn't been able to get in touch with Lea. He'd been calling her house, but the answering machine kept picking up. How many messages could he leave?

He reached for the cordless phone again, only this time he dialed Abraham Danforth's private number.

The older man answered on the fourth ring. "Hello?"

"Evening, sir, it's Michael."

For a moment, silence met him on the other line. Then, "Are you calling for Lea?"

His pulse spiked. "Is she there?"

"Yes, but I can't promise that she'll speak with you. You hurt her, Michael."

"I know. I'm sorry. Things are just so messed up." He pulled a hand through his hair. "I'm messed up."

"You've been drinking?"

He glanced at the bottle on the end table. "Yes. I mean, no, not really. I've had a couple beers. Will you ask Lea if she'll talk to me?"

"Hold on, and I'll check."

"Thank you." Michael grabbed the beer and took it into the kitchen, pouring the rest of it down the sink. He wouldn't mind getting drunk, blurring his senses with a desperate buzz, but he knew it wouldn't help his cause.

Whatever the hell his cause was.

Danforth finally returned, jarring his thoughts, making him take a quick, choppy breath.

"I'll transfer your call to Lea's room," the former Navy SEAL commander said. "But if you upset her again, you'll be answering to me."

"I understand." Michael wasn't about to get cocky with her father. He'd created enough trouble for one night.

While he waited for Lea, he walked outside for

some air. The dessert bowls were still on the patio table, left over from their meal.

"Michael?" She came on the line. "My father said you wanted to talk to me."

He sat at the table. "I just wanted to know if you were okay. I've been leaving messages at your apartment."

"I went by there, but I saw some reporters, so I drove to Crofthaven instead."

"And your dad invited you to stay at the mansion?"

"Yes. I'm in one of the guest rooms."

He pictured her among the finery, sitting on a Chippendale bed, with a satin quilt and gold-tasseled pillows. "I'm glad you're with your family."

"Me, too."

He stared at the bowl in front of him, then recalled the way his mom used to break their dime-store dishes, smashing them after her husband had stormed out the door. "This reminds me of my parents."

"What does?"

"You, me. This thing with Cindy."

She sighed into the receiver. "Then you should understand how I feel."

"My dad couldn't even talk to a woman without my mom getting jealous."

"I'm not jealous of Cindy."

"You don't trust her." And that made him feel as though Lea didn't trust him, either.

Her voice turned sharp. "She did all of this on purpose, and you don't believe me."

He held his temper, knowing it wouldn't do any good to rehash the same argument. "If Cindy is as devious as you claim she is, then I've been tricked by two women. First by Lady Savannah and now my assistant."

"Lady Savannah only foiled you for a little while. Then you trapped her. You caught her at her own game."

Meaning what? That he was supposed to trap Cindy, too? What if he couldn't uncover any proof? What if there was nothing concrete, nothing but Lea's word against Cindy's? "I'm not going to the office for a few days. I don't want to deal with this until I've had some time off." He squeezed his eyes shut. "My nerves are shot. They're ripped to the bone."

"So are mine."

He opened his eyes. "I never meant to hurt you."

"But you did."

Yes, he'd hurt her. But he wasn't convinced that she hadn't just misunderstood Cindy, that she wasn't blowing everything out of proportion. "I need some time to think this through."

"I'm not stopping you, Michael."

"I know." He adjusted the phone, cradling it closer to his ear. She sounded distant, like she was fading from his life already. "Do you believe what I said earlier?"

She released an audible breath. "About what?"

"Our relationship. That my feelings for you aren't based on sex."

"I don't know. I'm not sure. It started off being about sex. We slept together on the first night we met."

"It's more than that now."

"Is it?"

"Yes." It was about what they'd confided in each other, the hours they'd spent talking, the moments they'd laughed, the comfort of holding her in his arms, of watching her sleep. "It's our friendship. The closeness we share."

"But we're losing that. It's going away."

Because the trust they'd built was shattering, he thought. Because another woman had come between them.

"I should go," she told him, her tone still distant, still faraway. "It's been a long day, and I'm tired."

He glanced up at the sky, at the shallow light from a three-quarter moon. "I guess it is getting late." And they'd run out of things to say, their conversation dissolving into the night.

Twelve

The following week, Michael stared at the wall in front of him, wishing he could bang his head against it. He'd screwed up and now he was faced with the consequences.

Seated at the desk in his office, he dialed Cindy's extension. His assistant picked up, and her voice scraped his spine like tree-sharpened talons, like claws gouging his skin.

"I need to talk to you," he said.

"Just give me a second, and I'll be right there."

He tensed his jaw, hating himself for what he'd done. He'd broken Lea's heart and destroyed his own. He'd ruined what they had together, and now he missed her so much, he could barely breathe.

Cindy entered his office with a concerned expression. "Is there a problem?"

He gestured for her to sit. She took the leather chair in front of his desk and crossed her legs. Her skirt rode a little higher than usual, revealing too much thigh.

"I wonder what Lea would think of your outfit," he said.

She tilted her head. "We're not going to discuss that business with her again, are we?"

He raised his eyebrows. Three days ago, he'd confronted Cindy about Lea's accusations and she'd adamantly denied any wrongdoing. She'd even phoned Lea to apologize, but Lea had refused to take the call. "So you're sticking by your story?"

"It's not a story. I already explained why I said those things to your girlfriend."

He kept his gaze fixed on hers. "Because you were only trying to be her friend? Hoping to stop her from getting hurt?"

"That's right, but she twisted my good intentions." Cindy made a sympathetic sound. "Have you seen her? Spoken with her?"

"Not since she spurned your apology. And quite frankly, I don't blame her."

"I see." She shifted her legs, drawing her skirt up a little farther. "Are you angry that I told her that I thought you were using her? I'm sorry, Michael. But Lea is terribly insecure, and you're incredibly aggressive. Too powerful for her."

"Aggressive? Powerful? You mean ruthless, don't you?"

"Yes, I suppose so. But I'm the same way. You and I are cut from the same cloth."

"Which means what?" He reached for a loose paper clip on his desk. "That you and I would make a good team?"

She tucked her hair behind her ear, where a diamond hoop sparkled. "We already make a good team. We work well together."

He twisted the paper clip, bending its perfect shape. "That's what I used to think."

She tilted her head. "Used to? What's going on? Why are you treating me this way?"

"Cut the crap, Cindy. I'm not falling for your innocent routine this time." And it shamed him that he'd taken her word over Lea's, that he'd believed his backstabbing assistant and all of her carefully conceived lies. "I've been investigating the paternity test leak, and guess where all of the clues lead?"

She didn't respond. She simply waited for him to continue, her legs still crossed, her head still tilted.

"To this office," he said. "To you."

She barely flinched, barely batted an eyelash. "Do you have proof beyond a reasonable doubt?"

"I'm still working on the proof, but there's no reasonable doubt in my mind. You had the opportunity and the motive."

"What motive?" She squared her shoulders, giving him a cool, calculated look, showing him how ruthless she really was. "That squinty-eyed lover of yours?"

He pressed his palms on the desk, leaning forward, fighting the urge to clench his fists. "If you were a man, I'd deck you. I'd beat the living crap out of you."

"But I'm not a man, am I?" She came to her feet, smoothing her blouse, refusing to let him ruffle her feathers. "And there's no way you'll ever prove it was me who leaked that information. All you have is a few measly clues."

She was right. His chances of securing physical evidence were slim to none. But her poison-tipped reaction was enough. It was all he needed to end her sick game. "I want you out of here. Today. Now."

"That's fine by me. I'll find a better job." She fluffed her hair. "Even without a recommendation from you."

"Go clear your desk."

She shrugged, telling him in no uncertain terms that she would take as much time as she needed to gather her belongings.

When she walked out of his office, he picked up the phone, praying that Lea would forgive him.

Lea arrived at Whittaker and Associates. Filled with trepidation, she entered the building, preparing herself for another bout of pain.

And then she saw Michael.

He leaned against the reception desk, wearing a black suit, a white shirt and a narrow tie. A strand of his hair fell across his forehead, but it was the only thing out of place. He looked tall and strong and composed.

She glanced around the room, catching glimpses of leather and chrome. The building seemed vacant, almost hollow. Or maybe it was her emotions, the emptiness inside her. "Are you the only person here?"

He shook his head. "Cindy is in her office."

She steeled her gaze. "Then why did you ask me to come here?"

"So you could watch her walk out the door. She's packing, Lea. I fired her."

To keep herself from reacting too strongly, she headed over to the sofa and sat down, waiting to hear what else he had to say. He raked his hand through his hair, messing it up a bit more, and she realized he wasn't as collected as he appeared.

"Was it difficult for you to fire her?"

"Not in the least." He sat on the sofa, too. "But this is difficult. Looking at you, knowing you probably hate me."

"I never said I hated you."

He nearly ransacked her gaze, his eyes much too intense. "Does that mean you still love me?"

She took a deep breath, trying to stabilize her pulse, the jittery sensation in her veins. "I never stopped loving you, Michael."

He managed to smile. "I kept hoping you'd say that." His smile fell. "I'm so sorry that I didn't believe what you said about Cindy."

Lea glanced at the door that led to the offices. It was closed, tight and secure. "Did she do something to make you change your mind? Did she come on to you?"

"Yes, she did something." He removed his jacket, placing it on the arm of the sofa. "She didn't come on to me, but I discovered that she leaked the paternity test."

Weary, Lea clasped her hands on her lap. "So you fired her for a security breach?"

"It's not as simple as that."

"Why? Because she managed to break us up? Because you didn't see through her?"

"Yes." Sunlight spilled into the room, mocking his features, intensifying the discomfort he couldn't hide. "All the signs were there, but I wasn't thinking straight. Cindy started asking me for advice about this mystery man around the time I met you. But I was too absorbed in our affair to realize that she was talking about me. You were all I thought about. You were all that mattered." He paused, his voice rough. "You were on my mind before I opened my eyes in the morning, while I was at work, after I came home, when I went to sleep at night. You were always there."

"Me and Lady Savannah."

He reached for her hair, letting the dark strands slip through his fingers. "I thought about you more than Lady Savannah. Until I suspected the truth. Then both of you became my obsession."

She wanted to touch him, too. But she didn't dare, not now, not while her heart was pounding anxiously against her breast. "Why did you trust Cindy so much?"

"Because she never gave me any reason to doubt her in the past. She seemed tough and intuitive, like me. And I thought those qualities made her a good assistant."

Her stomach clenched, recalling how many times

the other woman had predicted what Michael would do. "She said she knew you better than anyone."

"That isn't true." Although he stopped touching her hair, his gaze was still strong and magnetic, still locked on to hers. "She has no idea what's going on inside of me."

And neither do I, Lea thought. She was never sure what was he thinking, what he was feeling.

He fell silent, and she glanced at the floor, studying the black-and-white tiles. The building still seemed empty, in spite of Cindy being holed up in her office.

"What did she say when you confronted her about leaking the results of the paternity test?" Lea finally asked, resuming their conversation, trying to break the awkward lull.

Michael made a disgusted sound. "She didn't admit it, but she didn't deny it, either. She insulted you, then challenged my evidence, insisting I couldn't prove it."

"Can you?"

"Probably not, but I'm still going to try."

Troubled, Lea sighed. "Have you figured out Cindy's motive?"

"For leaking the information?" He blew out a windy breath. "I think she was trying to push you toward your father and away from me. She wanted you to arrange the press conference, to get closer to your dad. That way you'd go to him when our relationship faltered." He shifted in his seat. "But I don't have any family left. So where would I go?"

She frowned. "To your faithful assistant?"

"Or so she hoped." He reached for her hand. "Do you forgive me, Lea?"

"I already told you that I still love you."

"I know, but that isn't the same as forgiveness." Once again, his gaze locked on to hers. "Is it?"

She wanted to pull away from him, to punish him for her pain, but she couldn't. She could see the truth in his eyes, the remorse, the shame. "We both made mistakes."

"Does that mean you forgive me?"

She kept his hand in hers, wishing his touch didn't leave her aching for more. "Yes."

"Are you sure?"

"Yes," she repeated her answer, moving closer, angling her legs toward his, nearly bumping his knee. He meant everything to her, and he always would. "I won't hold this against you."

"Cindy was a fool to think she could take me away from you." His breath rushed out. "Nobody can replace you. Not in my heart."

Every nerve ending in her body came alive, sizzling beneath her skin, filling her with electricity, with anticipation. "What exactly does that mean?"

"That I finally figured out what love feels like." He grabbed the front of his shirt, as though his heart were racing, pounding rapidly beneath it. "I think deep down I always knew, but I was too afraid to admit it. There was so much turmoil between us. And as soon as Lady Savannah went away, the problem with Cindy started."

Lea's mind started to spin. "You love me?"

He nodded. "Desperately, madly. I've been going

crazy this week without you. But that's how it's been all along. When you're not with me, I can't function." He leaned forward. "But I didn't know that was love. Not until I screwed up. Not until I realized that I'd made all the wrong choices."

"I can't function without you, either." And now she understood why he hadn't been able to clarify his emotions, why being in love confused him.

"Can we start over?" Michael asked.

"Of course we can." She noticed he was still clutching the front of his shirt. "Do you still want me to live with you?"

"More than anything."

"Me, too." Her eyes misted, and he kissed her, brushing her lips with his, giving her the tenderness she craved. She held on to his shoulders, to the strength of his body.

When they separated, they gazed at each other, still caught up in the emotion, in the need to be together.

"It's over," Lea said. "Cindy is out of our lives."

"I can't believe I fell for her ploy. I should have listened to you from the start."

Just then, the door to the offices opened and the blonde strode into the reception area, carrying a small box with her belongings. She looked cool and crisp and a bit too showy, her clothes designed to get her noticed.

"I see you two are talking about me," she said.

"You think?" Michael shot back.

"Jerk," she retorted, her heels sounding on the floor, her skirt hugging her rear.

When she stopped to look at Lea, they glared at

each other. Lea wanted to scratch the other woman eyes out, but only for a second.

By the time Michael's former assistant swept out of the building, she hardly cared.

"Good riddance," he said.

"I'm not as angry as I thought I'd be," Lea admitted.

"How can you say that after what she did to us?"

"Because I'd rather forget that she ever existed."

"So would I." Michael glanced at the door. "But first we have to agree that she's a first-rate bitch."

Lea couldn't help but laugh. "I never said she wasn't a bitch."

He laughed, too. And then he hugged her, holding her close, making the moment last, the incredible feeling of trusting each other, of starting over, of being in love.

John Van Gelder walked among the live oaks at Forsyth Park. He'd spoken to a few people along the way, folks who recognized him and promised him a vote. But that didn't put his mind at ease.

His opponent was still leading in the polls.

Who knew that Abraham's illegitimate child would turn out to be a beautiful Amerasian woman singing her father's praises?

John lifted his shoulders and kept walking, doing his damnedest to appear confident, hoping to make an impression on anyone who saw him.

Didn't it just figure? Only Abraham could engage in an illicit affair and come out of it twenty-eight years later still looking like a war hero.

The son of a bitch had been stricken with amnesia when he'd cheated on his wife. But even so, he'd taken full responsibility, giving the interview of a lifetime.

Once again, Honest Abe had lived up to his name.

Sunlight dappled the walkway and scattered through the trees, making John wish the historic setting would calm his nerves. He loved Savannah. This was his home.

When he looked up, he saw Hayden cut across the path and head toward him. He frowned, wondering why the kid had tracked him down. They hadn't arranged a meeting today.

"Sir?" Hayden approached him, a bit too breathless. The young man looked as though he'd seen a blood-soaked ghost. His skin was pale, his eyes ringed with shadows. "We have a problem."

What now? John thought. How much worse could it get? "I'm listening."

"The woman who helped me was fired from her job. She worked for a security company and the information about the paternity test had come from their files." Hayden's voice vibrated. "Her boss is investigating her."

"That's not our problem."

"What if her boss finds out I was involved?"

John slowed his pace, keeping a safe distance from potential eavesdroppers. "The newspaper isn't going to reveal their source. Her boss isn't going to be able to prove a thing."

"That's what she said." Hayden wouldn't let it go. He shoved his hands in his pockets and exhaled a loud breath. "But it doesn't matter. I can't take this anymore."

"Take what?"

"Digging up dirt on your opponent. I'm turning in my resignation, sir."

John stopped walking, still surrounded by the grandeur of live oaks, still keeping his shoulders back. "Do you think I care? The information you uncovered wasn't worth a plugged nickel. Why didn't that woman tell you the whole story?"

"Maybe she didn't know all the details."

"And maybe she had her own agenda. Maybe you weren't smart enough to see through her."

The kid ignored the insult. "I'm leaving town. I'm going back to Boston. I never liked the South anyway." He rubbed his arm as though a gnat had just bitten him. "I've had enough."

"Then go." John didn't want the little weasel working for him anyway. Anyone who didn't relish Savannah didn't deserve to be part of his campaign. "I'll win this race without you."

Sooner or later, he would come up with another plan to knock Honest Abe off his high-and-mighty pedestal. Because there was no way John was going to settle for less than a seat in the United States Senate.

The wedding was spectacular, the social event of the season. Dusk colored the sky in shades of mauve and blue, and tea lights floated in a lily pond.

The ceremony took place at a Savannah estate, a Greek Revival mansion owned by the bride's family and boasting of old money.

Lea sat with the other guests, watching the procession. Flowers from the formal garden lined the way, making a breathtaking path.

Michael was at the pergola, a limestone structure custom-built for the ceremony. He stood next to the groom, both men wearing black tuxedos.

Clayton Crawford seemed anxious, eager to marry Katrina Beaumont, the woman he called Kat. When the *Bridal March* began, the traditional wedding song seemed to stir his heart. He turned to watch his lady, his expression filled with wonder.

Lea's eyes started to water. Michael watched the bride, too. She captured everyone's attention, with her jeweled gown and cathedral-length veil. She looked like a feminine mystery, the train on her dress trailing gloriously behind her. Her father held her arm, offering her to Clay with a proud nod.

After the vows were spoken and rings exchanged, a pair of white doves were released, followed by a shower of rose petals.

Lea could only imagine how Kat felt, marrying the man she loved, knowing she would spend the rest of her life with him.

An hour later, Lea and Michael sat at the head table at the reception, where she'd been invited to dine with the wedding party since she was Michael's date. She assumed Clay and Kat had made those arrangements, wanting her and Michael to be together.

The ballroom in the mansion was exquisite, with ornate ceilings, stained-glass windows and beveled-glass doors. Trellised balconies offered an expansive view.

A local chef had prepared the meal, and Lea thought the food looked almost too pretty to eat.

Michael reached for his wine. "This is quite an affair, isn't it?"

She nodded and glanced at the bride, wondering if Kat felt like a princess. "A storybook wedding in a Southern castle."

Michael leaned into her. "Is it true that most little girls dream about their weddings? Did you do that when you were young?"

She shook her head. "I tried not to dream too much, but weddings in Vietnam are as important as they are here."

"Tell me what they're like."

His curiosity didn't surprise her. Although she was living with him now, he still asked questions about her culture, wanting her to share bits and pieces of her homeland with him. "The couple who will be married can't see each other on the day before their wedding," she said. "Seeing each other on that day can bring bad luck. Some families don't observe this tradition anymore, but my mother believed in it."

"What else did she believe?" he asked, the flame from a nearby candle reflected in his eyes.

Lea tasted her meal, thinking how handsome he looked in his traditional tuxedo. "She believed the bride's mother should comb her daughter's hair the night before the ceremony."

"Why? Does it mean something special?"

"Yes, especially the third comb. It brings luck and happiness."

He cut into his meat, but he didn't take a bite. He simply held his fork and gazed at her. "I love your hair. It's so pretty, so silky."

She nearly caught her breath. There were hundreds of people all around them, yet somehow it seemed as if they were alone. "In ancient times, a girl's hair was valued, praised in literature, poetry and art. She didn't dare cut it."

"I'm glad you wear yours long." His gaze was still riveted to hers, as though he were memorizing this moment and every word they spoke. "Tell me more about a Vietnamese wedding. What does the bride wear?"

"A traditional bride would wear a dress called *Ao Dai,* and the most appropriate color is red. It represents love and passion."

"What color does the groom wear?"

"Black, with a red flower." She glanced at her plate, at the baked lobster and prime rib, at the seafood-stuffed mushrooms and artfully prepared vegetables. "The food is important, too. There's at least twenty dishes at a Vietnamese wedding, and the egg rolls should come in pairs, so they are like the couple."

"That's nice. Romantic." He smiled at her. "In the old days, when a Seminole girl wanted to find a husband, she draped herself in extra beads and silver ornaments."

"I like that." She returned his smile. "Women adorning themselves for love."

When they both fell silent, one of the bridesmaids engaged them in another conversation and they socialized with everyone at their table, chatting amicably with the wedding party.

The festivities continued, with champagne and cake and a toast from the best man, from Michael. He raised his glass and honored Clay and Kat with humor and warmth, with words that tugged at Lea's heart. Each day that she spent with him, she fell deeper in love, deeper under his spell.

Everyone watched the bride and groom dance, and a bit later Michael and Lea danced, as well. She could smell the woodsy scent of his cologne and the boutonniere pinned to his jacket was the color of fire. Love and passion, she thought.

"I have something for you," he said.

"You do?"

He nodded and led her to the nearest balcony, where they stood in the night air, gazing at the garden below. He reached into his pocket and removed a white gold necklace. "It's a panther."

Awed, she studied the diamond-studded, ruby-eyed cat. "Because you're from the Panther clan?"

"I wanted to give you something that was unique, something special between us."

"It's beautiful." More stunning than anything she'd ever hoped to own.

He moved closer. "It's an engagement gift."

Stunned, Lea lifted her gaze. He was looking at her the way Clay had looked at Kat when he'd watched her walk down the aisle. "Are you asking me to marry you?"

"Yes."

"Oh, my God." She clutched the panther against her heart. "I didn't expect this. Not now, not this soon."

Fear flashed across his face. "Is it too soon?"

"No, not at all." Her eyes misted with tears. "I'd marry you tonight, tomorrow, the next day. I'd become your wife in an instant."

"I don't want to wait, either. We'll do it as quickly as we can." He took her in his arms and stroked a hand down her hair, holding her close. "You're the woman I love, the woman I want to exchange vows with." He stepped back, searching her gaze. "Will you wear a red dress at our wedding?"

"Yes, and I'll wear this, too." She held up the necklace, the jeweled cat shimmering against her skin.

"Let me help you put it on." He moved to stand behind her, then fastened the clasp and brushed his lips against her neck.

She felt her knees go weak, knowing he would have that effect on her for the rest of her life. "I love you, Michael."

"I love you, too." When she faced him again, he touched the panther, then slid his hand a little lower. A simple touch, an erotic touch. Finally he leaned in to kiss her.

He tasted like Cristal, like the French champagne they'd drunk, like the flavor of a fine yet complex bouquet, creating a sensation of creaminess, of white-fleshed fruits and spine-tingling fullness.

"I want to make love," she said.

He smiled against her lips. "Here?"

She smiled, too. "When we get home."

"Then we'll go home soon."

He kissed her again, and she knew she had everything she could want, including the spark that first drew her and Michael together, the beauty of passion, of steamy Savannah nights, of a world only they could create.

* * * * *

The Enemy's Daughter

ANNE MARIE WINSTON

ANNE MARIE WINSTON

RITA® Award finalist and bestselling author Anne Marie Winston loves babies she can give back when they cry, animals in all shapes and sizes and just about anything that blooms. When she's not writing, she's managing a house full of animals and teenagers, reading anything she can find and trying *not* to eat chocolate. She will dance at the slightest provocation and weeds her gardens when she can't see the sun for the weeds any more. You can learn more about Anne Marie's novels by visiting her website at www.annemariewinston.com.

For Laurie
It's good to see you glow,
And for Bert
Welcome to the tribe!

One

The coffee shop was surprisingly busy for the middle of a Wednesday afternoon.

Selene Van Gelder paused just inside the door of D&D's, an upscale coffeehouse located on a bluff above the river's edge in the historic district of Savannah, Georgia. The air conditioning felt wonderful, since the heat was still oppressive in early September. She took several deep breaths, feeling the jittery unease in her stomach increase. This was foolhardy. She shouldn't be here.

She had told herself she needed to go shopping today, but when she'd found herself standing outside the wood-and-brass doors of D&D's with their frosted window panes, it was time to admit to herself that after two months she finally couldn't resist the urge to find out more about Adam Danforth.

So this was his business. At least, partly his, she thought, recalling that he'd said his cousin and his oldest brother were his partners. Breathing deeply of the rich blend of coffee aromas, she looked curiously around the interior.

It was as elegant as she'd expected, but the atmosphere was one of warmth and invitation. Rich dark-paneled wood set off gleaming brass, and café curtains spanned the wide windows on which the Danforth & Co.'s stylized logo, intertwined *D*'s with a lavish ampersand, appeared in gilt letters. Along one wall was an enormous fireplace, though she wondered how often they actually got to use the thing, with a climate as mild as Savannah's.

Strangely, the sight of the fireplace calmed her nerves. It reminded her of her youth growing up in European boarding schools. Roaring fires were more a necessity than a luxury during the chilly northern winters on the Continent. And though one didn't normally think of boarding school as a great place to be, for Selene school had meant comfort and security.

But you're not in Europe anymore, Selene, she reminded herself. No, she was home—if she could really call Savannah home. She supposed it was as familiar as any other place stateside, and at least she had some connection to Savannah, however tenuous it felt. She'd been born here in the heat of a summer evening. And her mother's grave was here, beneath the live oaks in one of the stately old cemeteries where the city's first families routinely were interred.

Her mother. She sighed, wishing she'd known the woman who had given her life. But Elisabetta Horne

Van Gelder had died mere hours after the birth of her only child, breathing just long enough to give Selene her name and bid farewell to the husband who had loved her so dearly. How different, she wondered, might her life be today had her mother lived?

Pulling herself from introspection that she knew from experience would prove painful, she crossed to the counter and ordered a tall cup of D&D's special Brazilian mocha blend to go. She looked around the room at the waiters and the staff working the sophisticated machinery, but she didn't see Adam.

A wave of disappointment swept through her, and she told herself not to be ridiculous. The co-owner of the business, particularly an entrepreneur as wealthy and successful as Adam Danforth was reported to be, would hardly be working behind the counter.

Besides, the last thing either of them needed was a public meeting that could be witnessed by someone who might identify them. Wouldn't that make a nice tidbit for the gossip columns?

It was time to go. She was half regretting the impulse that had brought her here. Hadn't she been telling herself since July that she couldn't get involved with Adam?

Not to mention that it was terribly arrogant of her to assume he would still be interested if she did look him up. After all, she hadn't heard a word from him since she'd received a lovely bouquet of roses and lilies the morning after the dinner-dance where they'd met.

As she turned with her drink in hand, she nearly bumped into a blonde in a trim navy suit behind her. With a quick sidestep, she murmured, "Sorry."

The other woman barely acknowledged her. "Honey," she was saying to her companion, a brunette who looked to be a member of the downtown business community as well, "he is the most gorgeous hunk of man I've seen in ages. Think Josh Hartnett mixed with a healthy dose of a young Tom Cruise. Except Adam's six feet tall." She sighed. "I'd like a piece of that action."

Adam? Selene's attention sharpened, even though she felt as if every person in the place suddenly knew she was eavesdropping.

"Maybe—until he opens his mouth," her friend said. "I won't argue with the hunk definition, but the man is a dead bore. I went out with him once, years ago, and I am tellin' you, my eyes positively glazed over after the first twenty minutes."

The first woman shrugged. "I don't need them to be real bright," she said with a sly laugh.

"That might be the problem." The brunette who'd gone out with the man in question dug her wallet out of her purse. "He's *too* smart. Once he gets rollin' on the ghosts and legends stuff, you might as well order another drink and get out your earplugs. Every time you think he's windin' down he heads off in a new direction."

Selene could barely contain her amusement. The pair *had* to be talking about her Adam.

No! Not your Adam!

Adam Danforth. She supposed that to many women, his fascination with history and local legends might be a trifle boring, but to someone who'd actually enjoyed her university years studying dead languages and ancient literature, he couldn't have been more interesting.

She threaded her way past the other waiting customers toward the door. It was a good thing she hadn't seen him. This had been a stupid move and she would have regretted it had they met again.

Of course she would have.

She had to wait for a large party to enter just as she reached the door, and while she did so, her attention was caught by the spacious bulletin board on the nearest wall. One message read: "SWF seeks SWM to share frangelica cappuccino and opera. Must love small, yappy dogs." There was a phone number beneath. Another was a boldly drawn heart: "Elena, will you marry me?" She smiled and kept reading, even though the entryway had cleared. Apparently this message board had become something of a dating service!

She read another couple of messages, including one extended exchange that the couple involved apparently added to each day. And then she saw it.

To S., my flower garden ghost: I'm wilting without you. Call me. A.

Her breath caught, her heart stuttered. Flower garden ghost? Who else could have written that? And who else could it have been intended for?

Adam. Adam had written that. For her, Selene. Only him. Only her.

Her hands were shaking as she pulled a pen and a notepad from her purse. Without giving herself time to think of the wisdom of what she was doing, she unpinned the small piece of paper and placed it in her pocket. Then she wrote on the notepad.

To A. from your flower garden ghost: The lovely flowers you sent have wilted, too. My thoughts of you haven't. Shall we meet? S.

Quickly, she pinned up her response, then fled the coffeehouse before common sense could prevail. She was halfway down the block before she realized her cell phone was ringing.

Digging it from her pocketbook, she flipped it open. "Hello?"

"Selene!" The voice was rich, husky and deeply accented by the speaker's native French tongue. "How are you, *ma petite*? I am very angry that you have not called to ask me all about the wedding plans."

"Guillemette!" Joy rushed through her. Her boarding school roommate and dearest friend in the world was the daughter of a French family of noble lineage. Willi had recently become engaged to a distant cousin of the queen of England. "How are you?"

"Glowing, dear girl. I want to hear about *you*."

Selene realized she was shrugging. "There's nothing to tell. Life in the States is staid and dull. My father's campaign is chugging along, but I'm staying well out of it. I have no desire to become fodder for the American press."

"What? No handsome men? Shame on them all."

Selene hesitated as Adam's lean features leaped instantly into her head.

"Selene! There *is* a man, isn't there? You can't fool me! I'm the closest thing you have to a sister, and I can read you like a spread book, darling. Now spill."

"That's *open book*, Willi. Get your similes straight." Ahead of her, there was an empty bench in a small park just off the street. Heading for it, she spoke again. "It's not exactly a relationship."

"Start from the beginning," her friend demanded. "I want to hear everything."

She thought for a moment. "The beginning? Well, that was actually back in July, about five days after I arrived in Savannah. Do you remember I came home at Father's request…?"

"Try to look more cheerful, Selene. If you go to this fund-raiser looking like that, people are going to notice you, I can guarantee it." John Van Gelder's voice was filled with censure.

"I don't want to go, Father. It would be one thing to attend a function to support your senate campaign, but this is nothing more than spying on Abraham Danforth. I'm terrible at things like this. Someone is going to find out." Selene concentrated on shaking out the folds of her white silk evening gown, avoiding his eyes. Maybe he'd relent.

But her father brushed aside her concern. As he'd brushed her aside her entire life. "No one will find out if you don't call attention to yourself. And how would they know you? You've been out of the country for years. I don't even know when the last public photo of you was taken."

She did. She'd been nine, home for a visit with her father in America. Overwhelmed and missing the familiar environs of the exclusive Swiss school where she lived, largely ignored by her surviving parent, she'd been crying when the picture was snapped.

Her father's voice cut through the memory. "And it's not spying. All I want you to do is keep your ears open for anything I should know about the Danforth campaign. Danforth can't possibly be as squeaky clean as he appears."

"He isn't," she pointed out. "But he's honest about his mistakes—"

"Right." Her father sneered. "Everyone knows he was forced to welcome that illegitimate Vietnamese daughter into the family, but he managed to turn it into political gold. And before you came home there was an enormous brouhaha when his nanny's kid's body was found right there on his estate. That one almost sank him, but the authorities swear he had nothing to do with it." He snorted. "I wish I had his spin doctors."

Selene sighed. Her arguments fell on deaf ears and in moments she found herself bundled into a car, headed for the Danforth political fund-raiser. Fine, *she thought rebelliously.* You can make me attend, Father, but you can't make me spy for you.

The dinner-dance was held at the historic Twin Oaks Hotel in downtown Savannah. Selene entered just behind a group of other guests and quickly took stock of the room. Lovely French doors opened onto extensive gardens at the rear of the hotel, while dancers created graceful patterns on the polished wooden dance floor. Other guests mingled around the tables throughout the room.

She quietly headed toward the doors at the back of the room. It would be hot outside, but that was good. No one else was crazy enough to come out in the humid evening air; she could stay ten minutes and then leave.

So there, Father. I've attended the fund-raiser, and gee, so sorry, I didn't hear anything.

As she moved around the edge of the room, she passed the ladies' room and decided to freshen up. When she entered the lounge area, she found a young teenage girl crying there. Selene and another young woman each attempted to comfort her. The child appeared to be having parent troubles, and her distress tore at Selene's all-too-sympathetic heart. Selene knew, however, that she couldn't afford to get involved in the young stranger's problems. After all, she wasn't even on the guest list and she doubted anyone would be thrilled to find a Van Gelder at a Danforth fund-raiser. After a few moments, she slipped out of the restroom and made for the gardens.

She had just taken a seat on a stone bench out of sight of the ballroom doors when a deep, masculine voice said, "You're not a ghost, are you?"

She turned with a startled laugh. "You sound disappointed."

A man materialized from the darkness. He was elegant in a dark tux with an equally dark collarless shirt, and the moonlight glanced off his dark hair. Her first thought was that he wore the clothing awfully well for an American. She immediately scoffed at herself. Just because she'd gotten used to Continental men, many of whom were pickier than women about their wardrobes and their facelifts, didn't mean she should be an equal snob. Still, this man had been born to wear a tux.

He said, "I am disappointed. I saw you flitting about the garden a few minutes ago in your white dress and I was sure you were the Twin Oaks ghost."

"Sorry." She shrugged, smiling. "I'm ordinary old flesh and blood."

"I wouldn't, by any stretch, call you ordinary," the man said.

His tone was warm and admiring and she was glad for the darkness because she felt herself blushing. She'd never been good at flirting, or the small talk men and women shared. Her deportment instructors had despaired of her socially. Her only saving grace was that she could dance like an angel.

She cleared her throat. "Were you making that up about the ghost?" She'd said it to divert him, but she really was interested.

"Absolutely not. May I join you?"

When she nodded, he straddled the bench on which she sat, facing her with an easy air. "Well over a hundred years ago, a young woman was kidnapped from her family's suite and ravished by a blackguard on the third floor of the hotel. She threw herself from the window and was killed. Legend has it that on a clear night, you can see her walking through the gardens, crying for her lost virtue."

Selene was fascinated. "And is there any truth to substantiate the legend?"

He nodded. "The hotel's records give her name and the date of her death, which has been confirmed with U.S. census records of the time. She's buried in a local cemetery."

"Do you know anyone who's ever seen her?" She cast a quick look around, not out of fear but curiosity.

"My paternal great-grandfather supposedly did. He was at a ball here in the nineteen-forties and he came out to the garden to wait for a girl who'd agreed to meet him there. He heard a woman's voice behind him but when he turned, he clearly saw what he described as "the shade of a young girl.""

"'Shade' is a dated word for ghost," Selene mused.

"Exactly." Her storyteller nodded, his deep voice animated. "He wrote down the whole account, with a great many more details and it's still in our family today. It's only one of about a dozen alleged sightings of the young lady."

"No wonder you were disappointed," she said.

Perfect white teeth flashed as he smiled. "Could I possibly retract those words? I'm not usually so gauche."

She was charmed. "Consider them erased."

He pantomimed relief. Then he tipped his head to one side, studying her. "You don't seem the least bit unnerved by that story."

"You said she's sad, not dangerous," she pointed out. "I'm sensible that way. Now if you were to take me to Bavaria, there's a certain castle you couldn't pay me to enter. The spirit who haunts the place was killed defending his family from a neighboring kingdom's warriors, and he's chased any number of visitors through the halls. One woman fell down the stairs and broke an ankle, and she swears she was pushed."

He was nodding at her story. "Vindictive ghosts are fairly common. Your accent isn't German," he said *thoughtfully, "but I'm willing to bet you've spent quite a bit of time in Europe?"*

She smiled. "You'd win the pot. I lived in Switzerland most of my youth before attending university in the U.K."

"So you're British."

"Oh, no, I'm American," she said. "Although I've only been home for five days."

His smile was wide and direct, his eyes too dark to name their color in the moonlight, but filled with an interest she couldn't miss. "And will you be staying for a while?"

"Yes." She returned the smile. If she'd ever met a man with such charisma before, she couldn't recall it.

There was a brief moment of silence while he held her gaze. She was aware of the singing insects around them, the sweet strains of orchestral music filtering from the ballroom.

"My flower garden ghost," he said in a husky tone. He rose and offered her a hand. "Would you like to dance?"

In response, Selene put her hand in his, feeling the strength in his fingers as he lifted her to her feet, the hard muscles of his arms as they went around her, the warm promise of his big body so close to hers. Clouds of butterflies rose in her stomach, making her hand tremble in his.

"Are you cold?" His voice was a rumble in his chest, his breath stirred the silky tendrils of hair near her temple. She realized that all she had to do was turn her head and lift her chin and his lips would be on hers.

It took all the willpower she had to prevent herself from doing exactly that.

* * *

"It was heavenly," she told Guillemette. "We danced for nearly an hour. We talked. He loves folklore, ghosts and local legends and such. He was just fascinating. And handsome, and so sweet…"

"So who is he? And what's happened since then?" Guillemette prodded her. "You said that was two months ago."

Suddenly, the pleasure drained from the day. "It was. And nothing's happened since."

"What? Why?" Her friend began to sputter in French, and if she hadn't been so upset, Selene would have laughed.

"Willi," she said, "don't you want to know what his name is?"

"Oui." Her friend's voice grew wary.

"Adam Danforth."

"Who's Adam Danforth?" Guillemette's response reflected her lack of comprehension.

"His father is running against mine for the senate," Selene told her. "My father would be furious if I got involved with his rival's son."

"Why?" Guillemette seemed to take it in stride.

"Because…" She floundered, unprepared for the question. "Because Father's very competitive. His political career means everything to him. He's constantly looking for scandal that he can leak about the Danforth family. He isn't—isn't always very nice." That was difficult for her to admit.

Guillemette's silence spoke volumes. Finally, she said, "Does this Adam know who you are?"

"Oh, yes. He sent me flowers the next day." The memory made her smile. "A beautiful arrangement with a note thanking me for the evening."

"And you…?"

"Sent him a thank-you note, of course," she said. "But you must see why I shouldn't see him again."

"I see nothing of the sort," her friend said, more than a little heat in her voice. "Selene, there is no rational reason why your father should mind you going out with this man. This is the twenty-first century, not the Middle Ages!"

"They don't exactly have a friendly rivalry," she said in a defensive voice as she recalled some of the more offensive tactics her father had resorted to recently. "It just wouldn't be that easy, Willi."

"Nothing good in life comes easy," Guillemette said firmly. "Look at me. I had to be vetted by the *queen*."

Selene laughed. "So tell me all about it. I'm dying for details. Did you curtsey correctly? What did her crown look like? Did you have to kiss the glove?"

Lea was going to kill him if he was late for lunch again. The thought of his petite half sister's eyes sparkling with ire made him grin as Adam Danforth breezed into D&D's with the weekly payroll envelopes. He handed them off to the manager of the coffeehouse, checked the mail and his messages, and rushed back out again.

He checked his watch. He might just make it. He'd made a habit of getting together with his newfound sibling once a week or so as she adjusted to being a part of the large and loud Danforth clan—

It was gone! He stopped inside the entryway, his cursory scan of the bulletin board halted. For weeks after he'd first posted the note, he'd checked that board several times a day. But as the days passed and he never heard another word from Selene Van Gelder, anticipation and hope had shriveled and died.

He'd given up on finding a woman who liked him for what he was—a dorky guy who liked to talk about history and ghost stories. He'd had women chasing him for years but none of them really wanted *him*. They wanted his family's prestige, they wanted his money, some of them even wanted his body, to which he honestly couldn't say he objected—but not one of them appealed to him on an intellectual level.

And then he'd found Selene.

He'd been amused by his mistake that night at the fund-raiser, and initially assumed she would find him quaint and rather boring just like every other woman. He'd launched into the ghost tale more to get rid of her than because he thought she would really be interested.

It was a technique he'd perfected over the years since he'd overheard Angela DuFrayne laughing at him. He'd actually dreamed of marrying Angela until he'd realized he was nothing more than a cash cow to her. And a boring one at that. He should probably thank her one day, he thought bitterly. She'd taught him what women really thought of him. These days, he got a perverse pleasure from seeing a woman's eyes glaze over after she thought she'd snagged herself a conquest. He supposed he had a really sick sense of humor.

But Selene had been different. He'd never seen her in the light so he wasn't sure, but he imagined her eyes were a deep, dark blue. She was pretty in an old-fashioned kind of way, with a demure presence and a surprising, delightful sense of humor. Her nose was small and straight, her lips full and bowed like a doll's and there was an irresistibly cute little cleft right in the center of her chin. Her heart-shaped face had been emphasized by her upswept hair, which left wisps of curl dancing along her cheeks and forehead. Those great big eyes had fastened on his face attentively, and within moments he'd forgotten he was boring old Adam, the dull Danforth brother.

They'd talked, and then he'd asked her to dance, feeling he had to get his arms around her or die trying. She'd fit into them as if she'd been made to rest there, with her head on his shoulder and her face turned into his neck, and he'd felt the small gusts of her breath warm on his throat. He'd wanted to kiss her, wanted it badly, but he'd sensed that she was as skittish as the high-strung mare he'd ridden while visiting his cousin Toby in Wyoming a year ago, so he'd restrained himself. The last thing he'd wanted to do was scare her away.

And then he'd asked her name.

"Van Gelder? Related to John?" He didn't have the acting ability to hide his shock. This beautiful young woman was related to that—that slimy piece of work?

Her little chin lifted defensively and the glittering earrings and necklace she wore sparkled in the moonlight. "His daughter."

He couldn't help it; he laughed. Of all the ridiculous coincidences...!

Her chin hitched even higher. "Care to share the joke?"

He stopped laughing. "I'm Adam Danforth."

She recoiled. There was no other word for it. "Danforth." It was so faint he barely heard her. "Oh, God."

She looked even more appalled than he'd felt a moment ago, and it irritated him. "Look," he said, "there's no reason our last names have to matter, right?"

She didn't answer.

"I want to see you again, Selene." He savored the unusual name. It suited her.

"No." Her voice trembled. "That wouldn't be wise."

"It can't be that big a deal," he said, feeling stupidly panicked. God, he'd just met the woman. "You're acting like we're the Hatfields and McCoys."

"More like the Montagues and the Capulets," she said, and he realized she wasn't kidding.

"Selene—"

"I have to go now." She took a step back, and her hand lifted. He felt small, cool fingers cup his jaw and rest along his cheek. "Thank you for a lovely evening, Adam. I'm sorry I can't see you again."

It wasn't until later that he'd wondered what she was doing at his father's fund-raiser, and then it was too late to ask.

Adam shook himself out of reminiscence, realizing he was still glued to the spot in front of the bulletin board. He'd tried to call her twice the day after the fund-raiser, but she hadn't been in either time, and he hadn't wanted to leave a message and get her in trouble with her father. He'd sent her flowers that same day, and then he'd left a note at the coffeehouse a few days after he'd received her very correct little thank-you note for the flowers. Her card had been so dry, so devoid of anything other than the barest social nicety, that he had finally realized that she truly didn't intend to contact him again.

He wasn't a stalker, and if she didn't want to see him, he had to respect that. But perhaps one day she'd read the message on the bulletin board and change her mind. Couldn't she see how perfect they were for each other?

Cautiously, he reached out and traced the writing on the small sheet of paper that had replaced his note. *The lovely flowers you sent have wilted, too. My thoughts of you haven't. Shall we meet?*

Shall we meet? Had he just died and gone to Heaven? It was signed "S." Could it really be her?

His heart was actually hammering with excitement. Slowly, he detached the little note, a million fragmented thoughts bombarding him. Should he call her? He whipped out his little cell phone, then realized he could hardly call her father's house and identify himself. Not after the way that jerk had treated his father, doing his damnedest to ruin Abe Danforth's good name. And that reminded him of how difficult her decision to leave the note for him must have been.

After a long moment, he decided not to rush her. It had taken her two months to make contact with him; the last thing he wanted to do was frighten her away again.

He took one of his business cards from his pocket and turned it to the blank side, reaching for the pen inside his suit coat.

So what if he was a few minutes late to lunch? The girl of his dreams had given him the high sign and his response had to be just right.

Two

Three days went by and every time her cell phone rang, she crossed her fingers, hoping she would hear Adam Danforth's deep tones through the connection. She didn't always keep her cell phone on since she got so few calls but since she'd pinned that message and her hopes up on that bulletin board, she'd been carefully charging it and keeping it with her.

But the call she was waiting for never came.

Maybe Adam hadn't gotten the new message, Selene thought. *Maybe it was a sign that this was a bad idea.*

And yet she couldn't convince herself to forget about him. Maybe it was simply that he didn't want to call her father's home. He had no way of knowing the number she'd left was for her personal cell phone.

She'd just take one little trip by the coffeehouse, she

decided, to make sure her note hadn't fallen off the bulletin board, or gotten hidden beneath others. And while she was there, she could add a line that the number she'd left was her cell phone number. That way, he would be able to reach her without concern.

But when she stopped in front of the bulletin board at D&D's, her note was gone. And in its place was a business-size card.

Her heart began to pound and her mouth went dry. Slowly, hardly daring to believe she might get to see him again, she reached up and plucked the little card from the bulletin board. Turning it over, she saw it was indeed Adam's business card, inscribed with the elegant D&D logo in gold.

Here was proof. It hadn't been just a dream, or a message meant for someone else that she had misunderstood. Adam wanted to see her again. Even after she'd dismissed him when he'd sent those lovely flowers, he still wanted to see her again. Her fingers shook, making the little card tremble as she read the note on the back.

To my flower garden ghost: Meet me in front of the statue in Oglethorpe Square on Monday at 3:00 p.m.

Monday? *Today* was Monday! And it was half-past one already. But...which Monday did he mean? Well, she supposed it didn't matter. Today or next Monday, she'd be there waiting both times. She was going to meet Adam.

She reread the message. Oglethorpe Square. Where in the world was Oglethorpe Square? She had to get a map of Savannah right away!

An hour later, she not only had discovered that Oglethorpe Square was only about five blocks from the Cotton Exchange, where the coffeehouse was located, but that Savannah's historic district was a fascinating place. The proximity of the square left her plenty of time to browse through some of the shops in the area.

Although it was September, Savannah was still hot during the day and everyone wore summer clothes. Thankfully, she'd worn a lightweight day dress of mossy-green today. It wrapped over her breasts and buttoned at the waist and she'd worn a chic pair of Italian sandals with a matching purse. Of course, she thought ruefully, very few tourists walked around dressed as she did. American style was so much more casual than she was used to! She imagined people passing her assumed she worked in one of the many businesses in the area.

She walked leisurely through the pretty old streets. Before reaching Oglethorpe Square, she came to another of the unique landmarks that dotted the historic district's grid of streets at regular intervals. This one was…Reynolds Square, she noted, consulting her map. It was extraordinarily lovely, with live oaks covered in moss shading the thick grass.

And surprise, there was yet another statue right in the center of the little square. Savannah could probably win a contest for the most historic statues in a given area. This statue depicted a man named John Wesley, and as she read the plaque, she saw that Mr. Wesley had been the founder of the Methodist Church. Goodness, she certainly had a lot to learn about Savannah's history. She felt guilty that her own mother's family had lived here for generations and yet she, Selene, knew virtually nothing about her native city.

As she continued through Reynolds Square, she saw a gorgeous theatre on her left. The Lucas Theater. Idly, she wondered if the building's inside was as stunning as its exterior. Walking on down Abercorn Street, she could see the next square two blocks away. And if her guide book was correct, that would be Oglethorpe Square.

The butterflies in her stomach intensified. She was afraid he wouldn't be there, afraid he *would*. She glanced at her watch as she approached. Only two-forty-five. Fifteen minutes to get her nerves under control.

As she approached the square, her gaze found the statue mentioned in Adam's note and she paused to read about it. Ah, James Oglethorpe landed along the river in 1733 and promptly proclaimed the area the thirteenth colony in the name of King George II. No wonder he got his own little park.

She looked around. Tourists strolled the pretty little green square and what traffic there was on the adjacent streets moved sedately. An old-fashioned carriage with large back wheels and a roof that folded down idled at the curb. A driver in period dress and a top hat controlled the two beautiful white horses that pulled the vehicle.

Then she saw a man climb down from the carriage. He spoke to the driver before he turned and began walking her way.

Her heart stopped. She couldn't breathe. *Adam.*

She didn't move, couldn't move as he approached, could only drink in the wonderful sight of his tall, broad-shouldered form in a dark Italian-cut suit and white cotton shirt open at the throat. He was smiling and the autumn sun turned his dark hair to gleaming ebony. Then he stopped in front of her.

"Selene." His voice was deep and warm, matching the expression on his face as he surveyed her. "I'm so glad you came."

"I—" She had to stop and clear her throat. "I just got your note today."

His dark eyebrows rose. "I was hoping you'd find it. I was prepared to come by here for several Mondays if I had to." His eyes had been leached of color in the moon-silvered garden. Now she saw they were an unusual hazel, shining almost amber in the sunlight. He offered her his arm. "Would you care for a carriage ride?"

She made a small sound of surprise. "That would be lovely." She took his arm and let him lead her to the carriage. Beneath the lightweight fabric of his suit jacket, his arm felt solid and muscular. When they reached the carriage, she turned to take his hand so she could step up on the box to get in, but instead Adam set his hands at her waist. Before she could more than suck in a startled breath, he had lifted her into the carriage.

Her hands grasped his biceps to steady herself. She looked at him from beneath her lashes, feeling ridiculously shy. "Thank you."

"It was my pleasure." His voice and accompanying smile told her he meant it. Then he swung himself up inside the little carriage.

With the roof up, the carriage was a small, intimate cave. Adam wasn't a huge man, probably no more than six feet, but since she was barely over five feet, he seemed enormous. "Would you like the roof down?" he asked her.

She hesitated. The sunshine might feel nice...but it was so hot it easily could be too warm. And then there was her deep-seated fear of being discovered... "No thank you. It's very pleasant this way."

He smiled and nodded and she realized he'd been hoping she wouldn't want him to fold back the top. He leaned forward. "Okay, driver."

"Would you like a tour as you ride, sir?"

Adam glanced at Selene questioningly.

She shook her head. "I think I'd rather just talk with you, if that's all right."

He smiled. "That's terrific." Turning to the driver, he called, "No tour, thanks. Just a leisurely drive." As the driver picked up the reins and clucked to the horses, the carriage lurched into a steady rhythm. Adam looked at her again. "Would you like a snack?" He lifted a small cooler he'd stashed beneath the seat. "Grapes, cheese and chilled shrimp with cocktail sauce. And sweet tea and fresh juices." He grinned. "I would have preferred wine, but I didn't think you'd appreciate it if we got arrested."

She nodded, making a rueful face. "Wouldn't that be awful?" First the carriage ride, then the snacks... "This is wonderful. You're so thoughtful."

He was smiling at her, but the smile faded as she spoke and he seemed to be searching her face. "All I've been able to think of is you," he said. "I was afraid you might never come to D&D's, and you'd never see my message."

"I was hoping that I might run into you if I went there," she confessed.

"I wanted to call but I know how you feel about…"

"I appreciate that," she said. "You can call and leave a message on that line from now on. It's my cell phone."

His eyes lit up. "All right."

He flipped up a special little tray table feature atop the cooler and spread out the food, and as they nibbled, they chatted. She learned that he had been privately educated and that he had a degree in marketing and management. She told him about studying the classics and Greek literature at Oxford. "I graduated last year and haven't decided what I want to do with my degree yet," she said.

"The night we met, you said you'd be staying in Savannah," he said.

"Yes, at least until Father's campaign is over."

There was a momentary lull in the conversation and they both concentrated on their food. There was bound to be some awkwardness, she reminded herself, given the topics that were certainly off-limits.

"Have you always lived in Savannah?" She made an effort to get past the moment.

"Yes. Our family home was built in the late-nineteenth century. It's east of the city, actually, not far from Tybee Island." He smiled wryly. "We have a few ties to the area."

"I do, too," she said, "although I know very little about it. My mother was from one of Savannah's oldest families."

"She's not living, is she?" he asked gently.

"No. I never knew her. She died when I was born. She was the last of her family." He probably already knew that, just as she knew he'd lost his mother in an automobile accident when he'd been a young child. The media gave political candidates very little privacy these days. She might have learned even more about him if she'd cared to, but she'd deliberately refrained from investigating Adam's life in more than a cursory manner. It felt too sneaky, somehow.

"My mother died when I was small, too," he said.

"I'm sorry." She was well acquainted with being motherless. Growing up with a father who had barely been able to stand the sight of her had made for a lonely childhood. "Do you remember her at all?"

"I have a few vague memories of her, but that's it. My oldest brother remembers her better than any of the rest of us."

"Goodness," she said. "Exactly how many of you are there?" She'd read a number of different Danforth names connected with the campaign over the past few months and had wondered how they were related to Adam. Adam, about whom she'd never stopped thinking.

"I've got three brothers and a sister. And a half sister, too. Although we just met last month. She didn't grow up with the rest of the tribe."

Her eyes widened. "I bet your household was lively."

A little of the warm light went out of his eyes. "Not really. We all were sent to boarding school at a young age."

"I attended boarding schools in Switzerland," she said. "Actually, school felt more like my home than this does."

"You didn't come home often?"

"No." She swallowed, remembering those years when she'd waited in vain for a holiday invitation from her father. "I was only in Savannah twice in twelve years."

"Our father never came to see us at school," Adam said, clearly assuming her parent had.

"Oh, mine didn't, either. He was so busy that he said it would be better if I just stayed in Europe. It would have been a long trip for very brief visits."

Adam looked sincerely shocked. "You saw your father twice in twelve years?"

She nodded, aware of how very odd that sounded. "But I loved school. I made some wonderful friends and I usually spent the holidays with one of them. I didn't miss home."

"I did." Adam's cheery manner sobered a bit more. "I hated being away from my family and being separated from my brothers. We also have three cousins we're very close to, and I missed them and my aunt and uncle like crazy. We always spent school holidays and vacations with them."

"What a big family!" She didn't like seeing him sad and she sought to distract him from the unpleasant turn the conversation had taken. "Where do you fit?"

He smiled again. "Smack-dab in the middle. I have two older brothers, Ian and Reid, one younger brother Marcus, my half sister Lea and my other sister Kimberly, who's the baby of the family. My cousin Jake is older, his brother Tobias is my age and Imogene is younger." A shadow crossed his face.

She was so tuned in to him that she sensed his mood

had suddenly changed. "What are you thinking? You look so sad."

"I am," he admitted. "I have another cousin, the youngest of all of us, who disappeared five years ago."

"Disappeared? Was she kidnapped?" It sounded like something off Court TV, something she'd discovered she loved watching since she'd come to the States.

"If she was, we've never been contacted with a ransom demand." Adam sighed. "She went to a rock concert with a friend. There was a miniriot and when everything was sorted out, her best friend was located in the hospital but Victoria, my cousin, was missing."

"What did the friend say? Surely she could tell you where your cousin went."

"She suffered some injuries." He shook his head. "Tanya never recovered any memory of what happened that night."

"Not ever? Sometimes things come back as people grow older."

He shrugged. "She's not still in the area, I don't believe. But if she'd remembered anything helpful, she would have contacted us. I hope. She wasn't exactly the most reliable person."

She was aghast. "But…people don't just *vanish*."

"That's what we thought, too." Adam seemed to shake himself. "Life goes on and we all want to believe there's still hope she'll turn up eventually, but some days it's harder than others to stay hopeful."

"I imagine it is," she said softly. Without thinking, she laid a comforting hand on Adam's arm. He immediately placed his free hand over hers and squeezed her fingers.

"I don't think about it every minute anymore," he said. "Sometimes I feel guilty for that, but another part of me realizes that the rest of us have to continue to live as normally as we can."

"Do you see your brothers and sisters and cousins often?"

He smiled again and she felt a sense of relief that her question had lightened his heart a little. "I see most of them at least once a week," he said. "And that's excluding all this campaigning that we're doing for Dad."

"I always thought it would be so much fun to have brothers and sisters," she said. "Do any of them live close?"

"They all do. And most of my cousins do, as well. I think I told you my cousin Jake and I co-own the D&D chain, so we work together every day. And then there's Jake's best bud Wes, who's sort of been unofficially adopted by the Danforth clan—"

"Gracious! How do you keep them all straight?"

He grinned. "When you grow up with it, I guess it's ingrained." Then he pointed to another of the lovely little squares they were passing. "See that big boulder? It marks the grave of a local Indian chief. This is Wright Square. It's named for James Wright, who was the last man to govern the colony of Georgia before the States became independent."

"I wish I knew a tenth of what you know about Savannah," she said.

"I could give you a moonlit walking tour of the haunted spots around the historic district some evening." He hesitated and she was surprised by the flash of vulnerability that she caught in his eyes. "If you think that would be interesting."

The conversation she'd overheard at the coffeehouse on her first visit rose to the surface of her memory, and she knew a surprising anger at the shallow women who had hurt this intelligent, interesting man. "It sounds fascinating," she assured him.

"How about tonight?"

Her face fell. "I can't. Daddy needs me to attend a fund-raiser at a place called the...the Crab Shack?" She smiled. "He told me to dress down. I have visions of a small one-room cabin with a latrine in the back."

Adam laughed. "The Crab Shack at Chimney Creek. It's informal but not *that* bad."

"You've dined there?"

"The food is excellent and it's very picturesque." He took her hand from where it still rested on his arm and linked her fingers with his. "How about tomorrow night, then?"

"Tomorrow evening would be fine," she said. "Where would you like me to meet you?"

"I could—" he began, but he stopped as she shook her head. "No," he said, "I guess picking you up is out of the question." He snapped the fingers of his free hand. "Could you meet me at about 6:45 at the ferry dock? There's a dinner cruise that begins at seven," he said. "It's two hours long and afterward we could walk for a while."

"That sounds lovely," she said. "Where is the ferry dock?"

He smiled. "I'm going to have to remember this city

is new to you." He squeezed her fingers. "That will give me an excuse to spend lots of time showing you around."

She was beautiful, Adam thought the following evening. He watched as she smiled and thanked the captain for the cruise. The man was at least two decades older than she was, but he sucked in his stomach and actually bowed over her hand with the silliest smile on his face that Adam had ever seen.

Adam figured he probably looked just as dazed when she smiled at him.

She'd been beautiful that evening in the garden, her white gown had seemed to glow in the moonlight, but it had been a dreamlike beauty, in gentle shades of shadow. At first he'd thought she was a ghost but in truth she'd looked more like an angel.

But yesterday, in vibrant Technicolor, she had come alive, her eyes not the blue he'd imagined but a deep, mossy, unforgettable green. Porcelain skin, roses blooming just beneath the velvety surface of her cheeks, her nose a pert little slope upon which he could barely resist dropping a kiss. Yesterday her hair had been down, floating around her shoulders, but tonight, like that first night, she'd worn her shining chestnut hair in a pretty twist in deference to the river breezes. She'd donned a nautical-themed skirt and top and she looked…perfect.

He gave up trying to find adequate words to describe her. As she turned and took his arm, she smiled at him and his heart gave a funny little leap. She seemed too good to be true. Beautiful, intelligent, great sense of humor, she even seemed to genuinely enjoy his penchant for spouting historical trivia and ghost stories. She was poised and confident enough to deal with the pressures of being a Danforth— *Whoa!* he cautioned himself. *Slow down. You haven't met a woman yet who likes the real you.* But in his heart, he didn't feel he was moving nearly fast enough.

"Thank you so much," she said. "No one should ever visit Savannah without taking a cruise on the river."

"And you didn't even get seasick," he said, smiling at her enthusiasm.

She smiled back, rather smugly. "I took motion sickness medication. Experience has taught me well."

"Aha," he said. "So you do have a flaw!"

Her eyebrows rose. "Plenty of them." She started to laugh, leaning her head against his arm, "But I don't plan to share them with you. Now where are we going on this walk?"

"We'll start with the pirate's house," he told her. "For years, rumor had it that a tunnel led from the rum cellar out to the river, and unsuspecting patrons of the tavern were sometimes drugged and carried aboard ships that needed a full complement of sailors. One Savannah policeman who stopped in for a drink woke up on a China-bound schooner. It supposedly took him two years to get home. Some people dismissed it until the tunnel was found during renovations."

"Can you imagine being one of those poor men conscripted in such a way?" she said. "And isn't this the building that Robert Louis Stevenson is said to have described in *Treasure Island*?"

"Yes!" He knew he sounded as astonished as he felt. And he felt the last of his doubts sliding away. "You're the first woman I've ever met who knew—or even cared about—a detail like that."

"Maybe you just haven't met the right women," she said, slanting him a shy smile.

"Until now." He gently removed her hand from his arm and then placed his arm around her, hugging her close to his side. "That's better."

"Yes," she said, letting her own arm slide around his waist. "It is, isn't it?"

They walked for nearly an hour as he regaled her with stories of Savannah's history and a few ghostly sightings as well. As they passed the birthplace of Juliette Gordon Low, the founder of the Girl Scouts and a building said to be haunted by the ghosts of two of Low's ancestors, she asked, "Have you ever seen one of these ghosts?"

"No," he said slowly. His family home immediately sprang to mind and he wondered if she'd think he was crazy if he told her. "I've never seen a ghost."

She hesitated and he realized she must be more tuned in to him than he expected when she said, "But you know someone who has?"

"My family's home is haunted," he said baldly. She might as well hear it all.

"By whom?" To his surprise, she didn't sound skeptical, but was very matter-of-fact.

"We don't know," he said. "Let me amend that. We

think it's the spirit of a governess named Miss Carlisle. She was hired by one of my ancestors in the early 1890s but on the night of her arrival, her carriage overturned on the road up to the house and she was killed. She was buried on the estate beneath a young oak tree."

"Poor girl." Selene sounded upset, as if they were speaking of someone they'd known. "Where was she from? Did her family ever learn her fate?"

"I don't know," he said. "I'm not sure anyone knew very much about her."

There was a short silence while they contemplated the fate of a young girl from an earlier age.

Finally, Selene said, "Who has seen her? And why do you believe it's her? This Miss Carlisle?"

"There were no sightings, no rumors of ghostly goings-on at Crofthaven until after her death. She was seen quite a few times during the twentieth century," he told her. "Every sighting was near the tree where she's buried. It's still there," he added belatedly. "One of my ancestor's guests described her dress in great detail and a historian confirmed that her apparel reflects turn-of-the-century clothing."

"How long has it been since anyone's seen her?" They had stopped walking altogether and she turned to face him, the smooth oval of her face tilted up attentively.

"That's the strange part," he said. "In the past nine months, she's been seen three times."

"Oh!" Selene rubbed her hands up and down her arms. "I've got goose bumps. Tell me all about them."

"Okay." He led her to a stone bench along the edge of a square they were passing and indicated that she should take a seat. As she did, he sank down beside her. "In February, Kimberly's fiancé saw her along the road. She tried to speak to him, but Zack couldn't figure out what she was saying. The way he tells it, she got ticked off just like any woman with a guy who doesn't get it, and left."

Selene smiled, and he could see the flash of her teeth in the dark that had fallen over the city. "I wonder what she was trying to tell him?"

"We don't know. She was seen again in May. This time, it was a houseguest—my sister-in-law's brother—and Dennis actually thought she was another guest who walked into the wrong bedroom. He didn't even realize who he'd seen until the next day."

"Goodness! Had she been seen in the house before?"

"No," he said. "That one was a shock to all of us. She came around again in July, and Lea's fiancé saw her this time. He swears she kept saying something that sounded like 'farther' or 'father.'"

Selene was shaking her head. "Poor thing. I hope someone can help her find whatever it is she's looking for one of these days."

"So do I," he said. "She does no harm wandering around, except for startling a few people. But I think there must be something specific she wants, or wants to communicate or find."

"I wonder if there's any significance to the fact that recently she's been seen only by houseguests or people who aren't related by blood to the Danforths," she said.

Adam stared at her. "I missed that completely," he said slowly. "You're right. I may have to go back through some of the older accounts to see if the folks who had a sighting were family."

"Blood relatives," she clarified. "Not people who married into the family."

"Blood relatives," he echoed. He took her hand. "Thank you. I guess it seems silly but it's been bugging me, the thought that she's so unhappy."

"It doesn't seem silly at all," Selene said gently. "It seems thoughtful. And caring."

Was that what she really thought? Warmth spread through his chest and he leaned forward, taking both her hands in his. "I'm so glad you agreed to see me again."

Her eyelids lowered. "I shouldn't have, I know. If my father finds out…"

"Why don't you take me to meet him?" Adam said. "Then we won't have to sneak around and you won't have to worry. The election is only two months away. As long as we keep it low-key until then, surely he won't mind."

"Adam, you don't understand." Her fingers had tensed in his. "My father doesn't—he wouldn't understand. If he finds out I'm seeing you, he'll forbid it."

He tried to smile, although the certainty in her tone had his stomach curling into a knot. "Surely it isn't that bad. I could—"

"No!" she said. "You can't do anything. Or I won't see you again." She tugged her hands from his and rose, clearly agitated.

Adam sat very still, looking at her rigid spine. He didn't know what to say. He hated feeling as if they had to watch over their shoulders every moment.

Then she turned, and he could see the track of a single tear shining in the moonlight as it streaked down her cheek. "I don't want you to be unhappy with me," she whispered. "I just know that until this election ends and Daddy settles down, he's not going to be able to deal with me dating a Danforth."

"All right." He rose and went to her, taking her into his arms. She felt small and soft against him, and when she wrapped her arms around his neck and let her body rest trustingly along his, he thought his heart might just burst right out of his chest. "We'll do it your way. Just promise me you won't let your father stop you from seeing me."

"Of course not." She drew back and looked up at him. "You're the best thing that's ever happened in my life, Adam."

He drank in her stunning features, the appeal in her wide eyes, and he was lost. "As you are in mine." And then he bent his head and found her mouth with his.

Three

She was lost the moment his lips touched hers. Adam's mouth was warm and gentle as he kissed her, cajoling her to return the kiss. His arms were hard and muscular and yet he held her as though she were made of crystal.

With a murmured sound of pleasure, she ran her palms up his arms to his shoulders and gave herself to the sweetness of the moment.

After a moment, he drew away. "When can I see you again?"

"Soon," she said dreamily, feathering her fingers through the soft hair at the back of his head.

He kissed her again. "Tomorrow."

Immediately, she felt a return of the dread that hovered in the back of her mind, the fear that her father might find out. She was usually home much of the time. He might get suspicious if she suddenly was busy every moment.

"The day after tomorrow," she said. "Tomorrow's a little crowded." It was a lie, but she wasn't going to take any chances.

"All right," he agreed. "Lunch? Meet me in Oglethorpe Square where we met the other day."

She smiled, relieved at his easy acceptance. "All right. Could we go somewhere outside the city to eat, though? I'd like a change of scenery." And then there would be no chance of running into anyone either of them knew.

She didn't get home until nearly eleven, and she let herself in quietly, hoping her father was asleep already. But as she tiptoed toward the grand staircase that led to her suite of rooms on the second floor, he appeared in the doorway of his study.

"Selene! I was beginning to wonder where you'd gotten to." He switched on the large chandelier that hung in the entrance and she blinked in the sudden bright light.

John Van Gelder looked tired. And…old, she thought. Older than a man of sixty-three should look. Even the silver that had replaced his blond hair in places seemed tarnished and dull. His dress shirt ballooned over the waistband of his creased linen slacks, poorly concealing his girth. She'd been a little shocked to see how much weight her father had put on compared to her memory of him.

"Hello, Father."

"Out on the town, I suppose? You do realize that your actions will attract the attention of every reporter, don't you?" His pale gray eyes were as sharp as his tone.

"Yes, Father. I took a tour of the historical district." That wasn't a lie. Exactly. Not like what she'd said to Adam about being busy tomorrow.

"At night?"

"It focused on ghosts and legends. Did you know that there really was a girl who stood where the statue of the Waving Girl is? She waved a cloth over her head just like the statue is depicted to signal boats on the river, and some people swear they've seen the stone cloth of that statue ripple as well."

John snorted. "There's a ghost associated with practically every old building in Savannah. You're nobody if your home isn't haunted in this city." He chuckled at his own wit. Then he sobered abruptly. "Did you catch the interview with Abe Danforth tonight?"

Silently, she shook her head. *Danforth.* She felt as if the name were written in black marker on her forehead.

He smiled grimly. "Cable news. They had him scrambling to explain why his kids spend more time with their aunt and uncle than they do with him. Rumor has it his own kids can't even stand him. And I wonder how they feel about a bastard half sister?"

Appalled at her father's coarseness and lack of empathy, Selene shook her head. "I imagine it's a difficult time for them."

"I hope so," her father said with relish.

Not for the first time, she wondered what her mother had been like. Why she had married John Van Gelder.

Had he been kinder, gentler, more *human* once? He'd been handsome as a younger man, though time and temperament had taken away most of his good looks and left him looking calculating and less than pleasant. "Father," she said suddenly, "how did you and my mother meet? What was it about her that you fell in love with first?"

Her father went still. Every muscle in his body froze. "Why would you bring that up?" he asked, a fleeting expression of anguish twisting his features before he wiped it away.

"I know nothing about her, nothing about her family," she said. "I just wondered…"

"Well, don't wonder," he said abruptly. "There's no sense in talking about the past." He swallowed, then, almost reluctantly, he added, "You look like her, you know. Damn near a dead ringer."

"I do?" She was thrilled. "Do you have any pictures of her?"

To her surprise, her father didn't answer. In fact, he didn't even appear to hear her. As she'd been speaking, he had turned and disappeared into his study again, his shoulders slumped, his eyes unfocused.

Slowly, she turned and made her way up the stairs, treading lightly on the lovely runner that echoed the soft colors in the upstairs hall. Unless she was very much mistaken, her father was still grieving for her mother. Still! After twenty-three years, he could hardly bear to speak of her.

And another realization swept over her as his words echoed in her ears. *You look like her, you know. Damn near a dead ringer.* She, Selene, reminded him of what he'd lost.

As she entered her suite, decorated in subtle shades of lavender and spring-green with dainty, feminine touches provided by an interior designer, her eyes began to sting and a true feeling of hopelessness crept into her soul.

All these years she'd told herself her father was merely busy, a single man with a political career who probably thought boarding school was the best option for his only child. But now she had to face the truth. Her father had sent her away deliberately. Because he couldn't stand to have her around, reminding him of what he'd lost.

A sob hitched her breathing and she bit down hard on her lower lip to contain others. Her father didn't love her. Didn't want her. The only reason he'd brought her home, she saw, was because her presence was good for his image in this campaign.

Another sob threatened and she swallowed it, nearly choking on the lump in her throat. She would *not* cry, she told herself fiercely. She didn't need her father. He'd never allowed that.

But now…now she had Adam. The ache in her chest lessened a little and she focused on thoughts of him, of the warmth in his striking amber eyes when he smiled at her. Unless she was completely reading him wrong, he was feeling the same things she was. Attraction, both physical and intellectual. He made her laugh. Made her think. Made her wonder at the strength of the desire that had swamped her when he'd kissed her tonight.

She wanted him to kiss her again. Soon. Wanted more

of the magical sensations he sent racing through her system. She hugged thoughts of him to her and carefully avoided thinking of her father, of the hurt he'd inflicted on her over the years. In two days, she would see Adam again.

The two days took forever to pass. Every minute seemed to have hours built into it.

But finally, *finally,* she stepped out of the taxi and walked into Oglethorpe Square, and there he was.

He was dressed in a finely woven patterned sport shirt and khaki pants and his eyes lit up when he saw her walking toward him. No, they didn't light up so much as they caught fire, she amended, her heart skipping madly at the heat that blazed a trail over her short, flirty sundress and finally landed on her mouth.

He opened his arms as she reached him, and when he drew her to him for a kiss, she couldn't have objected if she'd tried. All she could do was wrap her arms around his wide shoulders and kiss him back, delighting in his obvious pleasure.

When a passing tourist whistled at them, Adam chuckled and loosened his arms. "I can think of better places to be doing this," he said, smiling. "Good afternoon."

"Good afternoon," she repeated, unable to prevent a silly smile from curving up her own lips. How could he make her so happy with one little kiss?

He took her hand and led her to a sporty little American car. "I thought we could drive over to Hilton Head for lunch," he said. "It's less than an hour away, and it's a pretty drive."

He could have taken her to the moon for all she cared,

as long as she could be with him. On the drive out, he regaled her with stories of the area through which they were passing. They lunched at a charming little restaurant by one of the Savannah River's last fingers before it reached the sea. Their waiter showed them to a table on a shaded deck and brought them steaming plates of lobster with dishes of butter. There were white aprons to protect their clothes and Adam teased her about setting a new fashion when the apron extended below the hem of her dress, making it look as if she wore nothing beneath the apron. They cracked lobster claws, drank a bottle of white wine, and once again she realized how comfortable she was with him.

"Tell me about growing up in Europe," he said after he'd finished telling her about Hilton Head Island's evolution into a golf mecca. "You must be getting tired of hearing me talk."

"Not at all," she assured him.

"Well, *I'm* getting tired of hearing myself," he said, grinning. "Your turn. Where was your school?"

"There were two, actually," she said. "I began in Zurich and was there for seven years. My best friend was French, and when her family decided to transfer her to a school in Geneva for secondary school, I begged Daddy to do the same. After I finished, I attended Oxford. What else do you want to know?"

"Which country did you like better?"

"Switzerland," she said promptly. "It's far too dreary in England to suit me."

"What did you study at Oxford?"

"Classical languages and Greek literature."

"So you speak other languages?"

Her eyebrows rose. "Well, I spent a lot of time with my friend Willi's family on holiday, so I learned French quite young. I'm also fluent in German—it's hard not to be when it's one of the national languages the Swiss speak. Other than that, I've studied Latin. But that's a dead language, of course."

Adam laughed. "I've always thought that sounded so morbid. Wouldn't it be better to say, 'languages that have passed away,' or, 'deceased languages'?"

Now it was her turn to laugh.

While she was still chuckling, he said, "When I met you I thought you had an interesting accent. Now I know why."

"I don't have an accent," she said indignantly. "Not like y'all do." The sentence was a perfect imitation of a slow Savannah drawl.

"There you go," said Adam. "Now you sound normal."

She was about to answer him when she caught sight of a familiar face. She froze.

Two tables away, one of her father's chief campaign workers was being seated at a table with three other men. She couldn't see the faces of the others, so she had no way of knowing whether or not she might recognize them also.

Immediately, she shifted sideways so that Adam's body was blocking her from view. "Adam," she said in a low voice. "Don't turn around, but there's a man behind you who knows me. He's working on my father's re-election and I've spoken to him several times at events."

Adam's eyebrows rose. He had rinsed his fingers

with lemon and he laid aside the napkin with which he was drying them. "And you're sure that telling your father about us is such a terrible thing?" His voice was very neutral, very careful and she realized she had hurt him with her insistence on hiding their meetings.

She leaned across the table, searching for words to explain. "My father has spent his whole life in politics. This race is terribly important to him.... If he—I don't know what will happen if he doesn't win. I don't think he's ever even imagined what life without politics would be like."

"There are a lot of other ways to contribute to the democratic process than by being an elected official." For the first time since they'd met, his eyes were cool and distant, and she couldn't tell what he was thinking.

"You don't know my father," she said in a small voice.

There was a brief, tense silence at the table.

"Well," he said at last. "If you're so eager to get out of here, we may as well go."

He rose and came around the table to pull out her chair. She noticed that he stayed between her and the man she had recognized as much as he could, and she used the opportunity to duck her head and put on the huge dark sunglasses she had with her.

Shortly afterward, he handed her back into the car and they set off for Savannah again. She'd expected it to be a long and painfully quiet drive, but Adam began to tell her stories of some of the scrapes he, his siblings and his cousins had gotten into when they were all younger. She was fascinated and her imagination ran wild trying to picture being part of such a tribe of children. She told him of school escapades, though they generally were much milder than some of the tales Adam had to tell. She enjoyed it so much that she forgot the change in his behavior over lunch, forgot the disagreement, if that's what it even had been, that they'd had.

But when they'd parked, Adam turned to her and said, "Are you going to see me again?" and his face was so sober that the constraint between them earlier immediately returned in a rush.

"I—I'd like to," she said. "I'd really like to. If you want."

"Of course I want to see you," he said. He picked up her hand and lightly rubbed his thumb over the knuckles, then raised it to his mouth and pressed a kiss to the back of her hand. "I wish we didn't have to sneak around behind your father's back, but I respect your concerns. But after the election, no more stalling. No matter what the outcome of the election, we tell him. Agreed?"

She nodded, huge butterflies taking wing in her stomach and making her feel oddly breathless. "Agreed." Happiness rose in a steep, giddy rush. The election was still weeks and weeks away.

Weeks and weeks in which Adam clearly assumed they would still want to be together. She couldn't think of anything that would make her happier.

He drove out to Crofthaven after dropping Selene off at the edge of the historic district where she said she intended to take a cab. Ian had called earlier in the morning and asked him to meet him at the Danforth family mansion at four.

He parked in front of the palatial estate a short time later, barely noticing the grandeur of his family home. He thought about the ghost sightings every time he drove onto the property lately. And since his father's campaign had begun, he'd driven out here a whole lot more than he normally did.

"What do you want?" he murmured. "Can I do anything to help you?" Was it significant that she'd been seen inside the house, as Selene had wondered? Even when he was a child, he'd been enthralled by the stories of ghostly visitations in his home. Oddly enough, he'd never been afraid. He could remember waiting at windows, sneaking out after dark on the rare occasions he'd spent time at home, hoping for a glimpse of the ghost. But he'd never caught so much as a flicker of another presence.

"Hey, my partner!" His cousin Jake stood on the front steps waving at him, suitcoat slung carelessly over one shoulder.

Adam felt a rush of affection. Jake. Slightly taller, seriously broader through the shoulders, the two men still resembled each other enough that people often assumed they were brothers rather than cousins. Only a year apart, they had been buddies since childhood, often uniting against the older or the younger kids when squabbles arose. It had seemed natural for them to go into business together. Jake had approached him about it even before he'd graduated from college, and they'd begun planning immediately. Then Adam's older brother Ian wanted a piece of the action, although he hadn't wanted in on the operation. He'd offered to go in as a silent partner, and the combined investment of the three of them had paid off handsomely, thanks to Jake's and Adam's hard work. He was proud of D&D's, proud of what they'd accomplished.

"What's up?" he responded rhetorically to the greeting. He'd just seen Jake in a meeting yesterday before they'd gone their separate ways to check on various arms of their corporation.

"Don't know," Jake said as Adam reached him and they climbed the steps together. "Ian called and asked me to come out."

"Me, too." Adam puzzled over it for a moment. "Guess we'll find out in a minute. How's my man Peter doing?" he asked. Peter was Jake's four-year-old son, a son of whom he'd just become aware earlier in the year when Jake's old college friend Larissa had been forced to reveal their son's existence to Jake before a reporter did. A reporter who'd gone on the trail of Danforth dirt the moment the campaign was announced.

"He's good," Jake said and the warmth and pride in his tone dissolved Adam's moment of annoyance. "The asthma seems to be under control for the moment, and he's been bugging me to take him fishing again."

Adam chuckled. "So you're adapting well to fatherhood."

Jake grinned in response as he pushed open one of the massive doors. "Well enough that we're considering giving Peter a sibling one of these days."

They stopped inside the massive foyer, letting their eyes become accustomed to the lower light. It was cool and comfortable, but as always, Adam felt like a stranger there.

Not unwelcome, exactly. More…unnoticed. Just as he had when he was a child and his father had been too busy for any of his offspring.

Then a head peered out from around the door of the library, several yards down the main corridor. "You coming in here anytime soon?"

"Hello to you, too, Ian," said Adam with mock sarcasm. "Awfully good to see you."

His oldest brother grinned and Adam and Jake approached. "And even better to see the two of you, you money-making machines."

Jake made a rude noise. "Takes one to know one."

"You got that right." Ian held the door wide and beckoned them in. "Anybody want a drink?"

Adam shook his head. "No, thanks."

Jake eyed Ian speculatively. "Am I going to need one?"

Ian shrugged as the three men took seats in the club chairs in one corner. "Maybe."

"Why are we meeting *here?*" Adam said, making a gesture that encompassed their surroundings.

"Because this is one of the few places I'm certain is private and hasn't been bugged." Ian took a deep breath. "I've got a bad feeling about this Colombian corporation."

Adam sat forward. "The same one that tried to intimidate you into buying our coffee beans from their recommended sources by blowing up your offices?"

"And the same one we think was behind Marcus getting questioned by the police in June," added Jake. Marcus was Ian and Adam's younger brother, a lawyer for the family firm run by Ian.

"The same," Ian confirmed. "They're still trying to dictate to me. They've hinted that there will be more trouble for Marc if I don't cooperate."

"Hell." Jake stood and stalked to the window. "What are you going to do?"

Ian shrugged. "I don't think there's a lot I *can* do. But I can't give in. I'm positive the legal side of that business—the coffee bean business—is just a front for drug and money-laundering activities."

"So what do you want us to do?" If there was anything Adam could do to protect his younger brother, he'd do it.

"I don't know." Ian sighed. "I just want you to be aware that something could happen. Be on the lookout for anything weird or unusual."

Jake turned from the window and rolled his broad shoulders beneath the white dress shirt he wore. "Have you told Marc?"

Ian nodded. "We talked this morning. He's still pretty shaken by those questions about racketeering that got thrown at him in June."

"I bet." Adam stood, too. "I don't know about you, Jake, but I've changed my mind about the drink."

The men talked for another quarter hour, tossing around information and ideas, but no great strategies came to mind.

"We have to handle this carefully," Adam reminded

them. "Ian can't be implicated in anything illegal. It would blow Dad's campaign right out of the water."

"Yeah, but if Marcus gets in trouble, the end result is the same," Jake reminded them.

"God, I wish I knew how to resolve this," Ian said. "I can't go to the authorities. It would leak, and can't you just see the headlines?"

"Yeah," Adam said, bitterness rising as he thought of his own experience being the target of a media manhunt a decade earlier. "You're guilty until you're proven innocent."

"Danforth Son Allegedly Involved In Drug Deal," said Jake. "Drug Cartel Controlling Danforth Family? They skate right on the edge of libelous language without going far enough to get nailed."

"Exactly," said Ian.

The brothers and their cousin talked for a few minutes longer, then Ian said, "I wish I had something more specific to go on, but there's nothing I can pin down." He rose and Adam rose as well.

"We'll keep our eyes open," Jake promised, moving away from the window.

As they walked into the foyer, the front door opened and a shaft of sunlight fell across the marble floor. Abraham Danforth stepped into the room and stopped short when he saw the three younger men.

"Well," he said, "this is a surprise. Ah, welcome."

"Hello, Dad." Ian's voice was cool. "We borrowed your library for a meeting. We're just leaving."

"It's your home, Ian," Abe said. "You can use the library any time you like."

"Thank you."

There was an awkward silence. Abe said, "Hello, Adam."

"Hello, Dad." It was an echo of Ian's greeting.

"Hi, Uncle Abe." Jake cleared his throat. "I've got to get going. I promised Larissa I'd cook tonight."

"We've all got to go," said Adam. "Tell Nicola to call if you need us at any campaign functions in the next few weeks."

"All right. Thanks."

Adam thought his father's voice sounded wistful but he wasn't about to stick around and find out. He and his old man had never had a single conversation of any consequence that Adam could recall. It was hard to have *any* conversation with a father who was either traveling all the time or too busy for his kids. Why start now?

As the front door closed with a heavy thud behind them and they started down the steps, Ian shot a look at Jake. "You're *cooking?*"

"I'm a good cook," Jake said defensively. "Besides, if I want to get out of the house to play soccer on Saturday, I have to help out during the week."

Adam chuckled. "Aha. The truth comes out."

Ian was grinning, too. "Sounds like Katie's been giving Larissa pointers on how to manage a husband." Both Ian and Jake had only been married a few months.

"Give Katie a kiss for me and tell her hello," Adam said to Ian.

"With pleasure." Ian's eyes lit up with warmth at the mention of his wife and Adam stared at his older brother for a moment. Would he ever be that transparently in love with anyone?

Selene. Her face was in his head even before the thought had passed. *Whoa,* he thought. *There's no point in even thinking long-term until this stupid election is over.* He thought of her expression when she mentioned her father. He might not particularly enjoy his, but he certainly didn't have those conflicted emotions that she so clearly did. What had the man done to her to make her resent him and yet feel compelled to obey him?

"...and give this to Peter," Ian was saying to Jake as Adam tuned back in to the conversation. His older brother withdrew a small package of candy from his pocket and handed it to their cousin.

Jake laughed. "Larissa will kill me—and you."

"Then you'd better not let her catch you," Adam said.

Four

The tennis match was vicious. Adam was dripping with sweat as he walked to the net and shook hands with his opponent, a player from the country club with whom he had a match every other week from April through October. Then he turned and walked to the door leading off the tennis courts, a warm feeling of anticipation burgeoning within him.

Selene stood just outside the fence. She had arrived in time to watch the final set of the match and Adam knew a sense of satisfaction that he had beaten his buddy six-love that time.

"Hi," he said, taking her hand. He wanted to kiss her, wanted it badly, but he was conscious of his less-than-enticing appearance. "I'm glad you could make it. Do you mind waiting while I grab a quick shower? I stink."

She smiled. "I don't mind at all."

"I'll hurry." He squeezed her hand, wishing he didn't have to let go. "Did you have any place special in mind for lunch?"

She shook her head. "Wherever you like."

"Okay. You can sit on that bench while you wait. I'll be right back." He'd called her yesterday on her cell phone and invited her to have a picnic lunch with him after his match. It pleased him that she'd come a little early and watched him play.

With a final wave, he entered the building where the locker rooms were located. Stowing his equipment, he rushed through a shower and dressed, then headed back outside.

He smiled as he saw her still seated on the bench where he'd left her. She was so lovely—

"Adam! Hey, what's happening?"

He turned automatically as he recognized Jake's voice. From the corner of his eye, he saw Selene get to her feet.

"Hey, Jake." His expression warmed as he saw his cousin's best friend, Wes Brooks, as well. Wes had lived with Uncle Harold's family when they were teens and was practically another cousin. "Wes. How's married life treating you?"

"Excellent," Wes answered, gripping the hand Adam extended. His dark skin gleamed with chestnut highlights and his teeth were a white slash in his dark face. "You're soon going to be outnumbered by us happily married folks."

Selene's face flashed through Adam's mind. "You never know," he said. He wanted to turn and beckon to her to join them, wanted to introduce her to his family so badly he could almost taste it. But he knew how upset she would be, so he forced himself not to even glance her way.

"What's that supposed to mean?" Jake demanded, alert to Adam's cryptic comment.

"He's got a lady," Wes proclaimed. "Adam has found himself a woman, my friend."

"Okay, spill." Jake punched him lightly in the shoulder. "You can't keep a secret like that from us."

"Wanna bet?" Adam grinned. Then a couple walking toward the clubhouse caught his attention and the smile faded. "Oh, hell, there's Dad."

Jake and Wes both turned.

"He's got Nicola with him," Jake observed. "Maybe you can sneak away—"

"Adam!" For the second time in a few minutes, his name was called.

Slowly, he turned fully to face his father, wishing he had, indeed, been able to sneak away. "Hi, Dad. Hello, Nicola."

"Hey, Uncle Abe, Ms. Granville. You remember Wesley Brooks?"

"Of course." Nicola smiled as she shook Wes's hand, although Adam thought she looked distracted. "Good to see you."

"Are you two having lunch?" Jake asked and Adam silently blessed his cousin for initiating the small talk. He never knew what to say to his father. Consequently, there were a lot of awkward silences when they met.

"Yes," said Abe.

"No," said Nicola at the same instant.

The couple looked at each other and immediately looked away again. Adam was astonished to see a faint rise of red color climbing his father's neck, while Abe's normally unflappable campaign manager was looking everywhere but at her candidate.

"Ooo-kay." Adam gestured toward the court, simply for the sake of having something to say. "I just finished a match."

"And we just arrived to begin one." Jake made a show of checking his watch. "Wes, we're going to miss our time if we don't hurry."

Wes nodded. "We'd better go." He extended a hand first to Abe, then to Nicola. "Good luck with the campaign."

Jake followed his lead, giving his uncle and Nicola a hasty handshake. It was clear to Adam that the two men had picked up on the odd tension between the pair and didn't want anything to do with it. He couldn't blame them.

There was a brief, uneasy silence in the wake of their departure. Adam searched for something to say. But what was there to say to a man who'd been around so rarely during your childhood that you barely knew him?

"Adam," said Nicola, "I have a list here of some upcoming events we'd like you to attend." She balanced her briefcase in one arm and set her hand on the latches, but when Abe's hand came down over hers, she froze, still looking down at the satchel.

"We can get those to you later," said his father.

"That's fine." He tried to ignore the way Nicola stepped a pace away from Abe, but he wondered just what in hell was going on. "Just stick 'em in the mail or fax them to my office. I'll show up at whatever you want."

"I really appreciate your help," his father said. "Would you like to join us for lunch?"

"We're *not* having lunch," Nicola said, her face darkening as she looked up at Abe. "I told you I won't be staying."

"Ah, thanks, but I already have plans," Adam demurred. Jeez, *what* was going on with these two? "In fact, I'm running a little late myself."

"We won't keep you then," his father said. He opened his mouth as if to say something else, but then closed it again without speaking. "It was good seeing you, son."

A similar response was in order. But as his father hesitated and the silence grew again, he couldn't bring himself to echo the words. "I, ah, I'll be at those events you mentioned." He directed the words to Nicola.

"Thank you." She nodded once at him and moved on.

Abe looked after her, then back at Adam. "I'd better go." And he strode off after her.

Adam stood where he was. Okay, that had been weird. Really, really weird. Was he imagining it, or was his father personally involved with his campaign manager? Or maybe he wanted to be?

He shook his head as the two disappeared inside the clubhouse, then turned toward Selene. He was more than ready to get out of here and find a quiet spot to picnic with her.

The bench where she'd been sitting was empty.

His heart sank. Glancing around, he realized that she

hadn't simply moved farther away. She was nowhere to be seen. Frustration rose. Was she going to cancel on him?

He wanted to see her, dammit!

Whipping out his cell phone, he punched the button that would automatically dial her cell number. He'd programmed it in the very day she'd told him it was her personal number. The line rang once, then twice. And then someone answered.

"Hello?" Selene's voice sounded slightly breathless.

"Why did you run off?"

"I saw your father. And Nicola Granville. I was afraid one of them might recognize me."

"And that would have been the end of the world?" he demanded. The moment he said it, he was sorry. The last thing he wanted to do was upset her.

She didn't say anything.

He sighed, not caring if she could hear him. "My family isn't full of ogres. Okay, my father's a little clueless when it comes to how to be a father, but he's not—"

"It's not *your* family, Adam." Her voice sounded thick, as though she was on the verge of tears.

"If you won't even let your father meet me, how can you predict what he's going to do?" he demanded. "Selene, I—"

Love you. He caught the words just in time, as shocked as she undoubtedly would be if he'd said them aloud.

Holy hell. He was falling in love with her. Despite the awkwardness of their family situations, she was the woman whose face sprang to mind when someone talked about marriage. Marriage! Good God, he barely knew her.

But as he thought of the discussions they'd had, the interest she'd shown in the things that he enjoyed sharing with her, the gentle smile that lit her face when she first caught sight of him, he realized that deep inside, where it counted, his heart recognized its other half.

Years ago, he'd thought he was in love with Angela. But he'd created an ideal image in his mind that had been nothing like the self-centered, shallow reality. Selene, he knew, was the real thing.

"Adam?" Her voice was tentative. "I'm sorry. I didn't mean to hurt you. It's just that…we have to wait until the election is over. I don't want to do anything that might affect my father's campaign."

He couldn't see how the two of them being together would have any impact one way or the other on either of the candidates, but she sounded so desperate that he couldn't disagree. "All right," he said soothingly. "I promised you we'd wait, so we'll wait. But the day after this damned election is over, we're visiting both your father and mine and announcing our—our relationship."

"Okay. Thank you." Again, she sounded as if she might be crying.

"Where are you?" he asked. "I promised you a picnic and I never break my promises."

She laughed, a small, precious sound that lodged squarely in his heart. "I'm waiting in the little garden near the parking lot.

He couldn't see the parking lot from where he was standing. "Don't move. I'm on my way."

* * *

The next day was Sunday. When they'd finally had their picnic yesterday in one of the city's pretty squares, Adam had asked her to go out to Tybee Island with him.

She went to church with her father, then headed straight for her room to pack a bag. Her bathing suit went underneath her clothing. She grabbed a beach towel, sunscreen, her small bag of toiletries so she could shower off if she needed to afterward and went down to see if the cab she'd called had arrived.

"Where are you going?" Her father came down the hallway from the kitchen. "Lunch will be served soon."

"I told them not to set a place for me," she answered, turning to look at herself in the large gilded mirror over the marble-topped table in the foyer. "I'm going to the beach."

"You were gone all afternoon yesterday."

She turned, exasperation rising. She'd come home to help with his campaign. He'd never cared before where she was unless he needed her; in fact, he'd made it plain he didn't want her underfoot constantly. Maybe that was it. "What did you need me for?" she asked politely. "You could have called and left a message on my phone."

"I just wondered where you were," he said in a quarrelsome tone.

"I had lunch downtown and then I went shopping," she said, summoning her most reasonable tone. That was true enough. She *had* gone shopping after the luncheon picnic. "Do you need me for something today?"

Her father eyed her from beneath brows drawn together in a fierce line. "No," he said shortly. "Not today."

A horn beeping out front saved her from further interrogation.

"All right," she said. "Then I'm off to the ocean for the day. I don't know when I'll be back."

As the cab carried her to the little restaurant where she'd arranged to meet Adam, she wondered what her father would do if he found out who she was involved with. It almost seemed sometimes as if he hated Abe Danforth, but she couldn't imagine why. Adam's father seemed to be a middle-of-the-road candidate whose military service would make him look attractive to the voters. He'd never done anything heinous or illegal, and although there was one irrefutable instance of an extramarital affair, it was hardly shocking enough to ruin him. According to recent media reports, Abe had been surprised to learn that he'd left a daughter behind after his service in Vietnam and was intent on helping her fit into his family here. What would it be like to find out you had a sister you'd never known existed?

Adam was waiting by his parked car when she stepped out of the cab. She wanted to run to him and throw herself into his arms, but she contented herself with a warm smile as he touched her elbow. "Hello."

"Hi." He saw her into the car, then came around to his side. "Are you ready to head for Tybee Island?"

"More than ready. I adore the beach."

He shot her a surprised look. "Have you vacationed at the ocean regularly?"

"Not with my father," she said, understanding his confusion. "My best friend from school is French. Her family frequented the Riviera and since she was always dragging me home on holiday with her, I went along."

"The Riviera." Adam's eyebrows rose. "The Atlantic coast is beautiful but I'm not sure it can compete with that."

"Is there sand? Surf? Sun?" She grinned at him, her spirits soaring. "It will do just fine if it has those things."

"This is a good time of year to visit," he told her. "The summer is over and most kids are back in school so there are a lot fewer tourists around."

He was right, she saw when they arrived.

The beach was wide and white, and medium-sized breakers rolled gently to shore in a mesmerizing rhythm. They found a spot away from the few family groups and Adam spread out a blanket, set down the cooler and opened a small folding chair for each of them.

"You've thought of it all," she said, smiling.

"I even ordered good weather." He tilted his face back to the sky and she watched for a moment as he soaked up the warm rays of the sun that beat down on them. Then he shrugged out of his shirt. She couldn't keep her gaze from lingering on his hard, flat chest and stomach and the surprising bulge of muscle in his arms. A line of dark hair spread across his breastbone and then headed south, swirling around his navel and disappearing beneath the waistband of the royal-blue swim trunks he wore.

When she met his eyes, he was smiling, a slow, warm smile that unfurled a ribbon of heat from her head to her toes. "Your turn," he said softly.

Her breath caught in her throat. Slowly, she unbuttoned the oversize shirt she'd paired with casual shorts.

She stepped out of the shorts without looking at him, then slipped the shirt off and laid it across the back of the chair he'd set up.

Adam made a sound deep in his throat. "You're beautiful," he said hoarsely.

"Thank you." Flustered, she turned to conventional courtesies to hide her pleasure at his words. Sinking down into the low chair he'd set up, she patted the second one he'd dropped on the sand beside it. "Come and sit."

She rummaged in her bag for her dark sunglasses, very conscious of the proximity of his nearly naked body. She'd never felt self-conscious in a bathing suit before, but today she had to stifle the urge to reach back for her shirt.

"Tell me about your new sister," she said, trying to distract herself.

"Lea?" He sounded startled. He dropped into the chair beside her. "What do you know about her?"

"Only what the press has printed." She smiled wryly. "And I imagine the real story is probably very different."

He nodded, his mouth set in a grim line. "Yeah, the media likes nothing better than to take an innocent situation and make up a good, juicy story to go along with it. Who cares if it's true or not? Who cares who it hurts?"

"You sound like that's a personal statement." And indeed, there had been some note in his voice that told her there was more to the story.

"It is."

"If you'd like to talk about it, I'm a good listener," she offered.

He sighed. "It was years ago. I had a study session

planned with a friend who was in one of my college classes. I stopped by her house to pick her up, but when she started to walk out of the house, she fainted. It turned out she had the flu."

"And?"

"I caught her before she hit the ground. Her family is very wealthy and often is a media target. That day there happened to be a photographer who got a juicy shot of me holding Karis. Unfortunately, her fiancé wasn't the most trusting man in the world and it very nearly ruined their relationship. Not a real big deal, but it still leaves a bad taste in my mouth. Making up stories about people without knowing any of the facts should be illegal."

"Have there been stories made up about your new sister?"

He nodded.

"I imagine her sudden appearance has been difficult for your family," she said carefully.

He shrugged. "Not difficult, exactly." He sighed, reaching across the small space between their chairs and twining his fingers with hers. "We were surprised, for sure. Dad had no idea Lea existed."

"I imagine it was a bit of a shock finding out that your father had feet of clay," she said, trying to empathize.

"We knew that before." His voice was matter-of-fact. "He wasn't much of a dad when we were growing up. His military career came first. After my mother died, he didn't have a clue about how to deal with five rowdy kids."

"I suppose I meant that it must have been a shock to find out he'd had an affair," she said.

"It was a bad set of circumstances." He shrugged. "It wasn't as if he set out to cheat on my mother. He suffered a head injury in Vietnam and lost his memory. A group of villagers took care of him and he got involved with Lea's mother but he was rescued without knowing she was pregnant. Then, before he could get back to her, her village was torched and he was told there were no survivors."

"Oh, how awful."

He nodded. "The Viet Cong didn't take kindly to anyone helping Americans. And," he added, "it wouldn't have been much easier if he *had* found out about the child. After all, he was married with several legitimate children already."

She winced. "I imagine that would have been difficult to explain to his wife."

He made a sound of agreement. "From everything I hear, my mother's position in Savannah society was very important to her. It wouldn't have gone over well, I can guarantee."

They were silent for a moment, then he spoke again.

"I'm glad, though, that we've found Lea. Found out about her."

"So you like her?"

He nodded. "Very much. She's really beginning to feel like a sister."

"That's how I feel about my friend Willi," she said.

"Willi." He repeated the name. "Please tell me that's short for something."

She laughed. "Guillemette. I think I told you before that she's French. She's an only daughter, nine years younger than any of her brothers, and she says we're sisters of the heart." She sobered. "Most of my best memories are of times I spent with Willi and her family."

"Most of mine are from times at my uncle Harold's house. After my mother died, my brothers and sister and I spent most of our school holidays there instead of at Crofthaven."

She felt a surge of empathy. Even though he'd grown up in the midst of a large family, it sounded very much as though Adam had missed the same basic sense of belonging she had.

"My children," she said, "are going to know they're loved. No, they're going to be *smothered* in love." Abruptly, she realized how passionate she sounded, and embarrassment flooded her. Scrambling out of her seat, she flung down her sunglasses and headed for the ocean. "I'm hot. I think I'll get wet."

"Wait for me." Adam was beside her in a minute. He caught her hand as they walked toward the water. "In case I haven't mentioned it," he said, "you look terrific in that bathing suit."

She smiled, relaxing a little as she recalled his earlier words. "I got the impression you liked it," she said. "So do I. I just bought it when I moved here. Most of my old ones aren't legal in the United States."

"Wait," he said as she began to wade into the gently foaming breakers that rolled in to shore, "you mean you went topless?" He sounded mildly shocked.

"Well, yes. Everyone did."

"Yes, but I can't imagine you being comfortable—"

"When you're one relatively small set of breasts on

a vast beach of European women sporting implants, comfort level increases dramatically," she said, grinning. "No one was looking at me."

A wave larger than the rest surged past them and they both had to jump to avoid going under. Adam turned and did a lazy sidestroke around her. "I can't imagine you went unnoticed." He stopped and moved closer, catching her around the waist and tugging her gently toward him. "I'd notice you anywhere."

She put her hands on his shoulders, enjoying the flirtation. "You may be prejudiced." The drag of the water pushed her firmly against him and their legs tangled.

He drew her even closer. "Come here and let me kiss you and I'll show you just how prejudiced I am."

She laughed until his mouth covered hers. And then she gave herself to the sweet invasion, kissing him back, enjoying the slick feel of his skin sliding against hers beneath the water.

His leg slid between hers and she breathed out a moan as secret shocks of pleasure raced through her. Adam held her loosely, letting the water press her against him, then take her inches away again. He kissed her again and again as their bodies touched, parted and touched again, as she slid up and down his strong, muscled thigh and the hard press of his arousal flirted with the softness of her belly.

Finally, he set her away from him with a smile. "We'd better stop before we attract the wrong kind of attention," he said, touching her lips with a dripping finger. "This feels private out here but it's not. There's a whole beach full of people who think they know what we're doing right now.

Her eyes widened with shock at his blunt pronouncement. "Then we'd definitely better stop. Getting arrested wouldn't make either of our families very happy."

"It wouldn't make me happy, either, considering we weren't even doing what we'd be getting arrested for."

They grinned at each other for a moment, then she burst out laughing. "You," she said, propelling herself backward and swatting a sheet of water at him, "are a bad, bad man."

"Not half as bad as I'd like to be with you." The words were teasing but the look in his eyes was hot with promise. Then he tossed water back at her with one big hand and the sensual moment was over.

They played and swam for perhaps half an hour before Adam pointed toward the shore. "Time to go in. You need more sunscreen."

She pressed a finger to her forearm, looking for signs of sunburn. "Thanks for reminding me."

They waded out of the surf and dried off, then forsook the chairs to lie side by side on their stomachs on the big blanket he'd spread on the sand. She got them each a can of soda from the cooler and they let the warm September sun and the pleasant breeze take the excess moisture from their bodies.

Adam was quiet for so long that she thought he'd gone to sleep, but when she glanced over at him, she saw that his amber eyes held a faraway look.

"You're deep in thought." She smoothed a hand over his brow. "What are you thinking?"

To her surprise, his gaze shifted away from her. "Just…kicking around an idea."

This was important. She didn't know why, but she felt sure that whatever was going on in Adam's head right now was a key to understanding him. She propped her chin on her forearms and angled her head so she could see him better. "Sometimes it helps to talk an idea through."

Abruptly, his eyes focused on her again. He hesitated and she wondered what he was searching for as he gazed at her intently, almost as if he were trying to read her mind. "You can't laugh," he said.

She gave a small, unladylike snort that would have annoyed her father. "When have I ever laughed at you?"

He nodded once. Short and sharp. "I'm thinking about writing a book."

She was instantly intrigued. "A book about what?"

"A serious study of the ghosts and legends of the Savannah area."

"Sounds like an exciting project." She made no attempt to hide her interest. "What do you mean by 'a serious study'?"

A warm flare of gratitude and pleasure lit his eyes and the tension left his shoulders as he smiled at her. He propped himself on one elbow. "There are a number of books out there already about Savannah's ghosts," he said, warming to his theme as he apparently realized she was serious about her interest. "But most of them are simply a recounting of the more popular stories, with a little embellishment to titillate the tourists. I want to do more." He gestured with his free hand. "Which ones are simply legends and tall tales? Which ones might be exaggerations of something that occurred? Which ones are unexplained and persistent enough to be considered some kind of real psychic phenomena?"

"You've really given this some thought," she observed. "I think you should do it."

"Just like that?"

"Just like that." She nodded decisively. "I'd be happy to help with the research if you'd like a silent partner."

He was grinning, an exuberant, uncomplicated expression that made her smile in return. "You're amazing, do you know that? Most women run the other way when I start talking about Savannah history or ghosts." Then his smile faded as he looked into her eyes, and a deeper, warmer emotion lit the amber depths of his gaze. "Selene...we haven't known each other very long. But I've never met a woman like you. I've never seriously considered marriage and forever and kids before. I am now."

"Oh, Adam." She dropped her head against his shoulder, rolling on her side to hold him close for one dangerously hot, sweet moment. "You make me think about things like that, too. But until this election ends, I can't—we can't—"

"I know." He pressed a kiss to her temple. "I don't want to pressure you or make you uncomfortable. But I thought it was important to tell you how I feel."

"It's very important," she said. "*You're* very important."

Five

By unspoken agreement, they spent the rest of the afternoon on safer, less personal topics. The sun was warm and gulls wheeled and called overhead. In the background, the low, rhythmic roar of the waves was a soporific counterpoint to their conversation, and eventually, they dozed.

The stretch of beach emptied as the vacationers headed for their hotels to clean up for dinner and evening activities. Finally, they decided to pack up their things as well.

Folding the beach blanket he'd brought, Adam watched as Selene walked to the water's edge to rinse off the sand from her hands. She was long and lean, slender and yet definitely all woman, and the sight of her in the brief bikini she'd worn had kept his system at a low boil all afternoon. He felt like pinching himself as he recalled the feelings shining in her emerald eyes. Was it possible she could care for him as much as he was growing to care for her? He was almost afraid to consider that perhaps he'd found a woman with whom he could share his life. Sad as it was to admit, he'd almost given up on finding love.

Or maybe he hadn't really thought love existed. He couldn't even remember anymore why he'd thought he was in love with Angela. She'd been beautiful and attentive and he'd been young and dazzled. But he was positive he'd never seen the look in her eyes that he saw when Selene looked at him. And she'd certainly never tried to pretend more than cursory interest in anything he pursued. God, he could still practically taste the humiliation he'd felt when he'd overheard her with her best friend, laughing over his nonstop talk about the history of Savannah.

Honey, I just tune him out when he starts with that old-time stuff.

But, Ang, her girlfriend had said, *how can you stand it?*

The Danforths are loaded with a capital L. Believe me, I can stand a lot more than being married to a bore for that kind of money.

Selene started back toward him and he forgot all about the past, mesmerized by the gentle sway of her breasts and the play of muscle in her long, slim thighs. She hadn't known who he was when she'd met him. And while John Van Gelder might not fall into the same category of wealth that Adam's own family did, he certainly had more financial resources than the average

American. So even if he was concerned that she was after his money, which he hadn't considered at all after the first night, she would have no reason to need him in that way.

No, the soft smile she was aiming at him had nothing to do with money and everything to do with happiness. The same simple happiness he'd felt when he first caught sight of her. The kind that made his heart feel as if it were going to burst right out of his chest.

He wasn't ready for the day to end. And as she stopped at his side, he dropped the blanket and reached for her.

"Want to have dinner with me?" He had to stifle a groan of pleasure as her scantily clad body pressed flush against his.

"I'd love to." She stretched up to kiss his jaw. "I don't have anything on my schedule for this evening."

Regretfully, he set her away from him. Much as he'd like to continue holding her, a guy in swim trunks on a public beach had to exercise a little self-control. And his was fading in inverse proportion to the fit of his trunks. "All right. If you don't mind casual dining, the hotel right up there has an oceanside bar where we can order off the menu."

"That's fine." She tied a short skirt that matched her bikini around her hips. "Is this too casual? I can dress again if you like."

"No." He couldn't keep himself from grinning. "I think what you're wearing right now will do nicely."

She shook a finger at him. "You're so transparent."

He made a production of looking down at his trunks and acting scandalized. "I sure hope not.

That startled a genuine laugh out of her, and they gathered up their things and took them to the car.

"She's gone for hours at a time," John Van Gelder said to the burly man standing in front of his desk. "I want to know where my daughter goes and who she meets."

The man nodded. "Not a problem."

"She usually takes a taxi," the politician said, "and comes home in one as well."

"I can pick her up no matter what kind of ride she's got. You want pictures?" One beefy hand patted the camera hanging from a strap around the private investigator's neck.

"No! No pictures." Van Gelder studied the man. He wasn't altogether comfortable with this person, but the P.I. had been recommended by one of his constituents, so he probably was worrying for nothing. Just as he hoped he was worrying about Selene for nothing.

She'd been so quiet when she'd first come home. So compliant. But lately she'd been flitting out of the house for long periods with no real explanation and she seemed...distant. She'd always been eager to please as a child and he hadn't expected that to change. It worried him. What if she'd met some unscrupulous fellow who knew she was an heiress, if a modest one? What if she'd been seduced by some disreputable mongrel? There were a thousand unpleasant possibilities and he worried about every single one of them.

Selene was all he had, and although he suspected she thought he was as rotten a father as he believed he had been, he did care about his daughter. He closed his eyes briefly as an image of Elisabetta came to mind. Grief struck, sharp as it had been the day his beloved wife had died. Had it really been more than two decades since he'd last held her in his arms? Not a minute of his life had been worth living after she'd died. He had poured himself into work, into politics and campaigning, simply because it occupied his mind, kept him from thinking.

Until he saw Selene. His beautiful daughter so resembled the wife he'd lost that sometimes he barely could bring himself to look at her. It was an ignoble sentiment for a father, but there it was. Over the years, his life had been much easier to get through when Selene wasn't around to remind him of what he'd lost.

The recent months had been rough, but he needed her. And he was getting used to seeing that too-familiar face, almost looked forward to their usual breakfasts together. She'd grown into an astute, intelligent young woman. In any case, he needed Selene by his side, to counter that damned Danforth and his huge, seemingly perfect family that made for such great press. No matter what occurred with the Danforth tribe, Abe Danforth's campaign managed to spin it into pure gold. He wished he'd thought of hiring Nicola Granville before Abe had gotten to her—

"Mr. Van Gelder?" The gravelly voice brought him back to the present. "Anything else you want?"

"No," he said curtly, tossing an envelope containing the P.I.'s retainer across his desk toward the man. "Just go do your job. And get back to me as soon as you have information."

* * *

Adam knew he should take her home after dinner. Or to a busy corner where she could catch a cab, since he knew Selene would never consent to him driving her home. But he didn't want the day to end.

"Would you like to see where I live?" he asked as they drove back toward the city after a leisurely meal.

She hesitated for a moment. "I really shouldn't. I've been gone a long time."

"You didn't have any plans for this evening, did you?"

"No," she admitted. "My father was having a campaign strategy meeting over dinner, so he didn't need me. I imagine that will drag on for hours. They usually do."

"Then you have plenty of time for a visit," he said, ignoring the hesitancy in her tone. Every time the campaign came up between them, she seemed to withdraw from him. He reached across the seat and laid his hand over hers, squeezing gently. "I'm not ready to let you go yet."

"All right." She turned her hand up and he felt the tension drain from her as she let him link their fingers. "I'd like to see your home. But I can't stay long."

Euphoria rose within him and he had to tamp down the urge to yell, "Yes!" Raising her hand to his lips, he kissed the back of her fingers lightly. "Terrific."

When he pulled into a parking space in front of his home on West Gordon Street, Selene laughed aloud. "I suppose it would be very silly of me to imagine you living anywhere but here in the heart of the history of Savannah."

He felt a little sheepish. "I like the area," he said. "And it's not far from my main office, which is pretty handy."

"This is a lovely building," she said as he came around and opened her door. She swung her legs out of the car and stood, still wearing the bikini top and little skirt she'd had on at dinner, and he took her hand.

"I don't live in the whole thing, although I own all of it," he said. "It was a single-family home at one time, but in the late 1960s it was divided into two apartments. I have the main floor and there's a tenant upstairs."

"How long have you lived here?"

"Since I graduated from college and went into business with my cousin." He led her through the wrought-iron gate. "A couple of blocks that way," he said, gesturing, "is Mercer House. A best-selling book was set there and they made a movie from it. A lot of the scenes from the movie were actually filmed there."

"There are so many beautiful homes here," she said, glancing up and down the street. "Have many of them been broken up like yours?"

"A lot," he said. "There are some beautifully restored old town houses two blocks over on Jones Street. There also are a lot of bed-and-breakfasts and inns. These old properties are astronomically expensive to maintain and there just aren't that many people willing to pour a fortune into them."

"What a shame," she said softly. "I understand, of course, and I think it's wonderful that even in an altered state they still retain the historical ambience. But what a shame that things couldn't simply stay the way they were. It's much the same in Europe. Most of the old castles and historic buildings are either museums or tourist accommodations because the families simply can't afford the upkeep."

He nodded as he escorted her up the steps to the wide front door. "That's exactly what happened with this house, only it has an even more interesting tale. It was designed and built in 1819 by a famous Savannah architect named William Jay. Fortunately, it was located far enough south to survive the fire of 1820, which destroyed over four hundred homes closer to the waterfront. The original owner died in a yellow fever epidemic the following year and it was sold, but the family lost it after the Civil War when Sherman—" Suddenly, he realized he'd assumed a lecturing tone. "I'm sorry," he said ruefully.

"For what?" She tore her gaze away from the beautiful rose brick and white columns of the stately architecture and looked blankly at him.

"For, ah, boring you," he said. "I forget—"

"You forget that this could never bore me," she said firmly. "Tell me the rest."

He was silent for a moment. "I owe you an apology. I keep comparing you with other woman I've known."

"You must know a lot of the wrong type of woman." She smiled and laid her hand on his arm. "There are just as many who appreciate the history and cultural heritage of an area. Now please, finish telling me about your home."

"There was another fire in 1889," he said, "and that one came within a block of the house, but the owners and their servants stood outside with wet rags and beat out the sparks. They even got up on the roof and kept the embers from starting a fire. That family had the house the longest. In 1918, their only son was killed in World War I and the house was eventually left to a great-nephew, who lost it in the Crash of '29. It's been sold and resold several more times since then. The man who owned it before me is the one who split it up."

"How hard would it be to restore it?"

"I don't think it would be too difficult. He didn't change anything significant except add a few nonload-bearing walls that could be knocked down again."

"It would be an extraordinary project to restore the place, wouldn't it?" She made a sound of pure pleasure as he showed her into the grand entrance hall, comfortably cooled by the central air conditioning he'd installed. "Oh, Adam, this is lovely."

"The paint color is an original Savannah shade called 'Peach Leather Tint,'" he told her. "If I ever do restore it, I want to combine period furnishings and fabric designs with modern conveniences so that it reflects both the past and the present."

She laughed. "You're amazing," she said. "You should do it."

He shrugged. "I never had anyone to share my interest before."

"And now?"

"Now," he said, "I am constantly amazed that I haven't bored you to tears babbling on about Savannah history."

"You could never bore me," she said softly. She turned and smiled at him with the same warm glow in her eyes that he saw every time they shared an intimate moment. His body responded to the look, reminding him forcefully that he was alone in his house with a very desirable woman wearing very few clothes. Selene lifted a hand to his cheek and touched him gently with a single finger, and his blood heated. And then he saw her shiver.

"I'm sorry," he said. "I'm not being much of a host. Would you like to clean up and put on some dry clothes? I have a guest suite you can use."

He took her down the hallway to the guest room he'd restored. It had a private bath and he laid out towels and one of his bathrobes for her before forcing himself to walk toward the door. "I'm going to catch a quick shower, too," he said. "Just come out to the living room when you're finished."

He was in and out of the shower in ten minutes, and he caught himself pacing the living room after five more. He glanced at his watch. He estimated he had three-quarters of an hour or so before she showed up—

"You have a lot of books," Selene said as she appeared in the doorway.

He spun around. "Wow," he said at last. "I've never known a woman who could shower that fast."

She pretended to glare at him. "That's an extremely sexist remark."

"It also was a compliment," he said, grinning. He eyed her appreciatively.

She wore his bathrobe belted around her slim figure; the sleeves draped well past the ends of her fingers. Her hair was wrapped in a large white towel, and still she looked hauntingly lovely. "I glanced into your library," she said, apparently unaware of his thoughts. "Do you have a favorite genre?"

He shrugged. It was hard to concentrate on what she was saying when he was all too aware that with one tug on the belt of that robe, he could have it open, have her soft, lovely flesh in his hands, put his mouth on the warm slope of her breast—

"Tell me about your reading habits." She smiled when his gaze met hers and there was no flirtation in the look. But as their eye contact held, he saw the moment when she became aware of his interest. Her eyes grew heavy-lidded and a small, secret smile curved her lips.

He cleared his throat, determined to stop ogling her like a horny adolescent. "I'll do better than that. I'll show you. Would you like a drink first?"

He opened a bottle of wine and they carried it to the library, where they discussed his book collection. He showed her the extensive trove of volumes on local history and was amused when she took the towel out of her hair, and sat right down on the carpet with one of his favorites, a compilation of Savannah's history that included some of the earliest and most stunning photographs ever taken of the city.

"You can borrow that," he offered, sitting down beside her when she showed signs of forgetting his presence altogether.

"Oh! Forgive me." She laughed, slamming the book shut. "Willi used to get so mad when she tried to talk to me while I was reading. She says I'm hopeless."

Her face was lit with laughter, her striking eyes glowing emerald in the setting rays of sun slanting through the window. She was seated with her long legs tucked to the side and she lifted a hand, tucking her hair behind one ear as she chuckled.

Adam felt something tighten in his chest, a warm fist of need and desire that shocked him with its intensity. He leaned forward and set his lips against her laughing mouth.

Selene's hands came up to grip his shoulders as she made a small, sexy sound that inflamed his desire even further. He leaned forward and slid an arm about her waist, pulling her into his lap. He parted her lips easily and invaded the sweet recesses of her mouth, and her body relaxed against him.

The promise implicit in her surrender sent a bolt of heat boiling through his blood. "Selene," he muttered. He gathered her closer, deepening the kiss as his hand slid up the length of her leg where the robe had fallen open. He skimmed lightly up her torso and burrowed beneath the terry cloth, flattening his hand against the warm, satiny skin below her throat, then sliding his hand down, seeking softer, richer treasures.

Heedless of the bra she wore, he cupped her breast in his palm, seeing in his mind's eye the firm flesh of her body in the scanty bikini she'd worn. Lightly, he let his thumb graze her nipple. She moaned and arched her back, pushing herself against his hand, and he repeated the motion again and again until she was twisting and writhing in his lap.

Her movements pressed her hip against him, and he rolled to one side, laying her on the carpet and leaning over her as he kissed her, his hand still at her breast. He threw one leg over hers, bringing the throbbing length of his arousal directly against her hip, and the breath whooshed out of his lungs when she turned and arched against him, pressing her soft belly directly against the hard ridge behind his shorts.

He groaned, a harsh sound that echoed in the room as he yanked the fabric of the robe out of his way, baring her lacy bra to his avid gaze. "I want you," he said hoarsely.

Her cheeks were pink and her long lashes swept down to hide her eyes from his gaze, but she didn't tell him no. He could see that her bra clasped in the front, and he lifted his hand, twisting his big fingers until it popped open with a snap. Almost reverently, he lifted the lacy covering away, revealing her breasts, and she was so pretty, so perfect, that he almost stopped breathing. Her breasts were round and generous, the flesh paler where her bathing suit shielded her from the sun. They were crested by tight little points of rosy pink, and when he bent and took one taut peak into his mouth, she gave a strangled cry as her hand came up to press his head even closer to her.

He suckled her lightly, then paused to flick his tongue back and forth, blowing on her until her fingers tightened in his hair, pulling him back for a deeper taste again. He was only too happy to oblige, drawing her into his mouth with a strong suction and lightly scraping his teeth over the little pebbled point as her hips wriggled and pushed against him, shortening his breath with every motion.

He tugged impatiently at the belt of the robe until he'd pulled the garment completely apart and her soft belly was bared to him. Then his hand went to the fastening of his own pants. He felt frantic, wild for her, his body begging for direct contact. He couldn't open his zipper without fumbling, couldn't free himself fast enough. And at last, when he finally shoved his briefs out of the way and brought his rigid, straining length against the soft warmth of her belly, the sensation was so exquisite he heaved a sigh of relief that was almost a groan.

For a long moment, he simply held her there, clamped tightly to him with his erection firmly sandwiched between them.

She squirmed against him a little and his breath caught on a rush of ecstasy. "You feel so good," he said hoarsely.

"So do you." Her voice was little more than a whisper. He felt her hand slide down his side and palm his buttock.

"Touch me," he said, drawing back a little. He tugged at her wrist until she let him draw her hand between their bodies. "Feel what you do to me." She was still for a long moment, her hand unmoving in his. Then, slowly, her fingers uncurled and he shuddered as he felt her reaching out. As she touched him, his breath literally stopped.

And then she was exploring him with a light, tentative touch that brought the blood rushing to his head and tripled his heart rate as he fought to control his response. He let her explore, let her brush the length of him and forced himself to stillness even when her hand drifted lower to cup the sensitive flesh there. Finally, he couldn't take it anymore. He reached down and wrapped his fingers around hers, guiding her into a grip and rhythm that pleased him, groaning aloud when she eagerly picked up the motions on her own. An electric sizzle shivered down his spine and abruptly he grabbed her wrist before he came apart right there in her hand.

"Sweetheart," he said, even as his hips involuntarily arched forward, thrusting against her hip, "you have to stop that."

She withdrew her hand immediately and as he looked at her lowered eyelids, he realized she was embarrassed. "I didn't mean you're doing anything wrong," he elaborated. "But I want you so badly that I don't trust myself to be able to hang on to my control." He lifted a hand and tipped her chin up with one finger until she looked at him. "I want this to be perfect for you, too," he said.

"Oh." Her voice was faint. She cleared her throat. "That's not very likely, actually. I haven't, ah, haven't done this before."

It took a moment for the meaning of her prim words to register. "You haven't...?"

She shook her head. "No."

He was stunned. He blurted out the first thing that crossed his mind. "We can't do this." Agitated beyond measure, he haphazardly pulled his robe around her before rolling away and rising, keeping his back to her as he tugged his briefs over his aching flesh and fastening his pants with difficulty.

"Adam?" Her voice sounded hesitant, unsure.

"Get up," he said. He knew his voice sounded harsh

but he was waging an internal battle that demanded all his willpower. Half of him, the noble, courteous half, told him he couldn't take her virginity, especially in a rushed act on the floor of his library. The other half was wildly aroused by the thought that she was willing to give herself to him, that she thought he was special enough to share such a gift—and that part wasn't easily dissuaded from finishing what they'd started.

He heard a rustle as she got to her feet unassisted and remorse shot through him. Relief, too. If she was upright, his nobler instincts were much more likely to triumph than if she'd continued to lie there waiting for him.

Then he heard another sound. A sniff. "I'd better go," she said in a subdued tone. Alarm shot through him and he whipped around.

"Wait!" he said, rushing across the room. She was nearly at the door and he grabbed her arm, swinging her to face him. She wouldn't meet his eyes but a tear escaped even as he watched, trickling down over the smooth peach of her complexion. "Oh, baby," he said, "don't. I didn't mean to hurt your feelings."

"It's all right," she said, drawing in a deep breath that made her chest rise and fall and nearly shot his good intentions to hell. "I understand."

"No," he said firmly. "You do not." He drew her to him, ignoring the resistance that stiffened her limbs, and slid his arms around her. "Virginity is a very special thing," he told her bent head. "I'm honored that you want me to be the man you share this moment with, but it isn't something that should be rushed, or made light of."

Her head came up and she eyed him cautiously. "I thought…I thought you didn't want me anymore," she whispered.

An incredulous laugh exploded from him. "Selene," he said, drawing her flush against him until she couldn't possibly miss the proof of his desire for her, "does this feel like a man who doesn't want you?"

She sniffed and smiled, shaking her head. "No," she said. Her gaze grew mischievous and she slowly rubbed herself back and forth over him until he closed his eyes and groaned softly in frustration.

"You're making me crazy," he said. He put a hand beneath her thigh and lifted one leg until she caught on and wrapped it around his hip. The position opened her intimately to him, and he tugged the robe out of the way until all that separated them were a few layers of fabric. Her panties were small and satiny and already wet when he slipped an exploratory thumb over the sensitive flesh between her legs.

Selene shuddered and her head fell back as if it were too heavy for the fragile stalk of her slender neck. "I thought you didn't want to do this."

"Now," he clarified, dropping his head and nuzzling the side of her neck as he reluctantly withdrew his hand. "We're not doing this *now*. I never said I don't want you. But if I'm going to make love to you for the first time in your life, I'm going to do it with plenty of time to get it right."

Before he could make a liar of himself, he forced his

hands away from the temptations of her body and set her from him, fisting his hands in the lapels of the robe and holding it closed. "Go get dressed. I'm taking you home before I change my mind and keep you here all night."

Selene lifted her hands and placed them over his, and when she raised her eyes to his he read indecision, need and more in their emerald depths. "You have no idea how badly I wish that were possible," she said softly. Then she lifted herself on tiptoe and kissed his cheek.

As she turned and left the room, he let the fabric of the robe slide slowly through his fingers until she was gone and he stood alone. There weren't even two months left until this election, he told himself. Then they could be together as much as they wanted.

You could marry her, said a little voice in his head. He bent and picked up the book he had told her she could borrow, but his mind wasn't on what he was doing.

"I just might," he said aloud, slowly. "I just might do that."

Six

Adam left a message on her voice mail the next morning, telling her he'd like to have dinner with her that evening. Selene called him back on his office line the moment her father left the house for a brunch appointment. When his smooth, deep voice answered "Hello?", she swallowed through a throat suddenly so dry she wouldn't have been able to spit if she'd needed to.

"A-Adam?"

"Selene." His voice dropped to an even lower register, growing husky and intimate. "I miss you."

"I miss you, too," she said honestly.

"Can you make dinner tonight? We need to talk."

"We talked all day yesterday," she said automatically.

"Not *all* day," he said, and she could hear the humor in his tone.

She blushed, even though he couldn't see her. Thank God. "I'm not sure I can get away tonight," she said regretfully. "Father might get suspicious. I've hardly been home lately." Not that he would miss her presence at the dinner table. On the rare occasions that they ate at home together, he usually had the television on and his eyes glued to the news.

"All right," he said. "I didn't want to do this over the phone, but…I've been thinking about what you told me last night."

She knew, from the tone of his voice, he meant about her lack of experience. "Yes?" she managed. "Thinking what?"

"Your first time," he said, "should be special. Do you trust me to make it special for you?"

"Of course." She didn't even have to think about it. "I would trust you with anything."

She could hear the smile in his voice when he said. "Good. Can you find a way to get away for the night on Friday evening?"

"You mean…all night?"

"All night," he confirmed. "We're going to take our time, not rush anything." He paused. "I want to wake up with you in a bed in the morning."

Her body tightened with anticipation even as her heart melted. "I'd like that," she whispered.

"So can you get away?"

She thought about it. "I don't see why not. But I can't go far."

"I'm going to take you further than you've ever been before," he promised her, and once again she felt a hot blush wash over her from head to toe. He chuckled. "Nothing to say?"

She cleared her throat. "Not on the phone."

He laughed even harder. But his voice dropped to a rough whisper when he spoke. "I can't wait to get you in my arms again."

"I can't wait to be in your arms again," she told him. "Where shall we meet?"

He gave her the address of a restaurant in the Historic District. "I'll meet you outside and we'll stow your bag in the car before dinner. I'm going to make reservations at a restored inn close by and we'll go there after dinner."

"We're not going to your house?" she asked, startled.

"No. This is going to be special. I'm hoping my home will be your home one day and that wouldn't exactly make it memorable, would it?"

Silence fell.

Had he really said what she thought he'd said? Meant what she thought he'd meant? "Adam—"

"Selene—"

They both spoke at the same moment.

"You first," she said promptly.

"All right." He spoke slowly, as if he were thinking about what to say. "I apologize for rushing you. I know you don't want to have lengthy discussions about the future until the campaign ends."

"I may have changed my mind," she said faintly. Was he thinking of *marriage?*

He chuckled again, and the intensity of the moment lightened. "If you mean that, we'll talk on Friday night. Among other things."

The sensual intent was back in his tone and her pulse hammered with excitement. "Friday night," she said. "Is that a promise?"

"I promise," he said. "We're both going to remember Friday evening for a long, long time."

Adam fumbled the phone back onto the cradle absently, imagining the blush that he was sure had crept into Selene's cheeks. Did she blush like that all over? *Soon,* he told himself. *Soon you'll know.* It was amazing that just the sound of her voice could make him feel so stupidly happy.

A knock on his office door interrupted his reverie. "Come in."

"Hey." His brother Ian stepped into the room, closing the door behind him. He stopped halfway across the room, eyeing Adam speculatively. "What's that sappy expression mean?" His hazel eyes sharpened. "You've met someone!"

Adam shot him a wry look. "Is it that obvious?"

Ian laughed. "To those of us who've been there, yes." He settled into one of the chairs opposite Adam's desk, crossing one leg over the other. "Spill it."

Adam shrugged. "Yes, I've met someone." He hesitated. "I think I love her."

Ian's eyebrows rose. "Whoa. This is fast."

"How long did you know Katie before you realized she was the one?"

His brother grinned. "Good point." He studied Adam speculatively. "You trust her?"

Ian knew how badly Adam had been hurt by Angela's callous attitude all those years ago. "I do." He sought for words to explain. "She's different. She's interested in the things I am. She likes talking about history and ghosts. She likes my home. She doesn't need to be escorted to the most exclusive party in town every night."

"Do I know this lady who's captured your affections?"

Adam hesitated. God, he wanted so badly to talk about Selene, to share the perfect woman he'd met with everyone he knew! "You know her family," he hedged.

Ian's brows drew together. "Why do I think there's a problem in that statement somewhere?"

"Because there is." Adam couldn't contain himself anymore. "Her name is Selene Van Gelder."

Ian's eyes snapped wide. "*John's* daughter? The one who just came back from Europe a couple of months ago?" When Adam nodded, he whistled. "Man, do you know how to find trouble."

Adam's lips curved ruefully. "It could be easier."

"But you think she's 'the one'?"

"I *know* she's the one," Adam corrected. "I've known it since the night we met."

"Which was when? And where? I wouldn't have thought it likely that you two would be running in the same social circles. Her old man thinks running for office is a blood sport."

"She was at the Twin Oaks fund-raiser near the end of July."

Ian's brow wrinkled. "At a Danforth campaign fund-raiser? That's weird."

Adam nodded. For the first time since the night they'd

met, he wondered what she had been doing at a fundraiser for her father's opponent. Everyone knew John Van Gelder despised Abe Danforth way out of proportion to the elected office they both were hoping to win. "Yeah," he said, "but she didn't stay long. And it wasn't until a few weeks ago that she'd consider going out with me."

"So all this has happened in a matter of weeks."

"You didn't know Katie any longer than that." Adam felt unaccountably defensive.

"No, I didn't," Ian admitted. "But her last name wasn't Van Gelder, either." He hesitated. "So you're pretty serious about Selene?"

Adam nodded. "I was thinking of asking her to marry me." At the look on Ian's face, he quickly added, "Oh, she won't even introduce me to her father until after this campaign is over, so if she says yes, it'll be just between us for a while."

"I don't know whether to wish you luck or tell you you're insane," Ian said wryly. "But good luck, anyway."

Adam's office assistant buzzed him, and he held up a hand to his brother. "Excuse me for a sec."

"Jake's on line two," the young man said. "He says there's a management problem at D&D's in Atlanta."

Ian stood. "I'll get out of your hair." He turned, then looked back over his shoulder. "Good luck with your girl."

"Wait," Adam said. "What did you come in here for?"

Ian waved a hand dismissively. "Nothing major. I'll catch you later."

Adam picked up the phone, but his attention was still on his eldest sibling as the door closed. He couldn't shake the feeling that Ian had been going to tell him something important, and he wished he'd been more attentive. He knew Ian was still having trouble with their coffee bean suppliers—was there something more he hadn't told Adam?

By the time the taxi arrived to take her to the restaurant where she was meeting Adam on Friday evening, Selene was a nervous wreck. While her father had been preoccupied with the headlines yesterday morning, she had casually mentioned that she would be going away. As she'd anticipated, he'd barely acknowledged her. Surprisingly, his coolness didn't wound her as it once had.

Maybe that was because of Adam, she thought. Now that she had him, her father's approval didn't seem so important anymore. Had she simply been looking for love all these years?

Love. Oh, she had to admit it. She loved Adam Danforth. As unsuitable as his name would make him to her father, it was too late to turn back, to stop the feelings from growing into an entire body-filling feeling that made her so happy she almost thought her skin wasn't strong enough to contain it. She loved him. But she couldn't tell him yet. It wouldn't be fair until after the election.

As she was heading out the door with her overnight bag, a voice behind her demanded, "Where are you going?"

Selene jumped and turned around. "I told you, Father," she said in the calmest voice she could manage. "I was invited to spend the night with a friend." She couldn't quite meet her father's eyes, and her chest felt as if there was a hundred-pound weight resting directly on it. Had he somehow guessed what she was doing? She stifled an urge to laugh hysterically as she realized that if he knew *who* she planned to do it with, he'd be locking her in her room this very minute.

"Hunh." Her father made a dismissive gesture with one hand. "I forgot. Have a good time."

"I will." *Understatement of the decade!* She turned and slipped through the door before he could say anything else to her, before he could read the guilt on her face.

John Van Gelder watched his daughter climb into the taxi to meet her girlfriend, his face taut with displeasure as he realized he'd forgotten to ask her about her schedule for next week. He hadn't even gotten the friend's name, so he couldn't call her. And she probably had her cell phone with her, but without her planner, which was probably on her desk, he doubted she'd be able to answer him definitely. Besides, he knew from experience that she didn't have the phone turned on much of the time, anyway.

Oh, well, no matter. He could ask her tomorrow. Still, it irritated him that now he wouldn't be able to confirm his plans to have her attend several campaign events until she returned. Perhaps he should take a look at her calendar. Leave her a note asking her to reserve the dates he had in mind. Turning, he headed for the wide staircase.

A few moments later, he entered the small sitting room attached to his daughter's bedroom. Her delicate writing desk stood before one light-flooded window, computer and planner in plain view. He crossed the room and sank into the chair before the desk, but before he could check the dates in question, a beautiful coffee table book laid to one side caught his eye.

He drew the tome to him, idly flipping through the pages of extraordinary photographs of Savannah history. Very nice. He wondered where she'd gotten it. He wasn't big on history and was sure he had nothing like this. Selene always had been an odd child. For all he knew, she could be collecting things like this book now.

But as he closed the book, something written on the flyleaf inside the front cover caught his eye. Opening the book again, he read the handwritten signature and a muscle began to twitch in his jaw.

Adam Danforth.

Adam Danforth! What in hell was his daughter doing with a book that belonged to one of Abe Danforth's sons? As far as he knew, she had never even met them. He scoured his memory, but couldn't come up with a single time when Selene would have been introduced to any of the Danforth family. Even when he'd sent her to that ball at Twin Oaks a couple of months ago, she'd come home early saying she hadn't seen or heard anything interesting.

Maybe it was an accident that she'd acquired a book that had belonged to Adam Danforth. A coincidence. But still…he hadn't gotten to this point in his career by being careless.

Wheeling, he stalked into his office and rapidly punched in a number. When the line was picked up on the other end, he said, "I have a new assignment for you.

Adam Danforth. Find out everything about him and get back to me as soon as you can."

Adam was waiting for the taxi in front of the restaurant, and he helped her out, then leaned forward and gave her a brief but possessive kiss that nearly melted the shoes right off her feet. Then he tipped the cabbie and lifted her small bag. "Just let me put this in my car, then we'll go inside."

"Adam?" She clutched at his hand as he began to lead her toward the car parked nearby. "Do we…" She gathered her courage and began again. "We don't have to eat."

He stopped in his tracks. His eyes searched her face slowly. "You haven't had dinner."

"I'm not hungry," she said. *Except for you.* "We could eat…after."

Something moved deep in his eyes, something that sent a flash of heat through her body. "Are you sure?"

She nodded, smiling tremulously. "Oh, yes."

He smiled then, too. "All right," he said. He led her around to the passenger side of the car and helped her in. Once he was behind the wheel, it seemed a very short drive, only a couple of blocks, really, until he pulled into a parking space in front of a lovely old building that a discreet sign proclaimed was an historic inn.

He retrieved her bag and led her inside, holding her hand in his, and she wondered if he could feel her fingers trembling. She was trembling all over, or at least it felt like it, with anticipation, excitement and probably more than a few nerves as well.

Apparently he had registered before she arrived and

he took her straight to the lift that led to a room on the second floor. The hallway was hushed and cool and there was a stateliness about the old house that made her feel as if she should speak in whispers.

When he fit the key into the lock and ushered her into the room they would share tonight, she was charmed by the beautiful four-poster bed with its pineapple motif. The ceilings were high and there was a fireplace along the far wall. Two floor-to-ceiling windows were covered by lavish fabric and opposite the bed French doors led out onto a small, elegant balcony that overlooked a private garden. Tall trees at its far end gave the illusion of total privacy, since all view of other buildings was blocked by the canopy of branches.

"This is lovely," she said, taking in the small table on which stood a silver compote piled high with fresh fruit.

"Yes," he said, "it is."

But when their eyes met, he was looking at her rather than the room. He smiled and held out his hand. "Come here."

She went to him, lifting her arms around his neck as he drew her close. He was big and hard and warm and she felt fragile, feminine in his arms. A sudden pang of apprehension shot through her at the thought of what was to come, and he must have seen it.

"Are you certain this is what you want?" His eyes were golden in the late-day light slanting across the floor.

She saw from the tension in his face what it cost him to ask the question. "Positive," she said quietly, forcing her silly female fears to the back of her mind. Adam had never been anything but gentle with her, she reminded herself. He would make it as easy as he possibly could. That thought led to another, which she voiced. "I want you to be my first." *My only.* She slipped a hand from his shoulder up to his strong jaw, tracing the firm line of his lips with a single finger. "Make love to me, Adam."

His eyes caught fire. "With pleasure," he murmured.

He drew her finger into his mouth and sucked lightly on the single digit, his tongue swirling a warm pattern around and around, and she felt herself breathing faster, a heavy ball of arousal settling deep in her abdomen. She smiled, her eyes closing in pleasure as she swayed toward him.

He released her finger. Slipping one large hand beneath her chin, he tilted her face up to his and took her mouth, giving her deep, drugging kisses to which she could only respond helplessly. Her hands gripped his broad shoulders. Her head fell back and she gasped for air as Adam slid his mouth down her throat.

Cradling her in one arm, she felt his free hand between them, stripping off his tie and working down the placket of his shirt. "We've got on too many clothes," he said softly against her skin.

Willingly, she lifted her hands to the buttons as he released her. He shucked out of his suitcoat and tossed it at a nearby chair, then pulled his shirt free of his trousers. As she opened the last button, he unfastened the cuffs and tossed it at the chair, then took hold of his V-necked undershirt and peeled that off, as well.

She'd seen him just two days before in bathing trunks, but here, he suddenly seemed much larger and much…barer than he had on the beach. Was barer even a word? His chest was a solid wall of muscle, lightly dusted with dark hair that eased down to a thin line and disappeared beneath the waistband of his pants. His flat male nipples were small copper circles studded with tiny points.

Adam caught one of her hands and lifted it to his chest, lightly brushing her fingertips over one tight tip. His eyes closed and he made an approving sound deep in his throat when she whisked her fingers over him again. "That feels good," he said in a husky whisper. Then he lifted his hands to the line of buttons that marched down the front of her strappy sundress. "Will it feel good to you, too?"

She couldn't speak, could only stand on trembling legs before him as he unfastened her dress until it hung loosely, exposing a thin strip of flesh down just past her waist. She hadn't worn a bra because the dress had built-in cups, and when his fingers hooked beneath the straps and tugged them off her shoulders, the fabric separated abruptly, baring her breasts to his eyes.

"Sweet," he said hoarsely. He brushed the straps down until the dress caught at her hips, then gave it one last push so that it dropped around her ankles.

Selene felt herself blushing as she stood before him in nothing but a high-cut pair of lacy panties and the high-heeled sandals she still wore. Adam was breathing heavily, his gaze riveted to her breasts. "You're so beautiful," he whispered. He palmed her breasts almost reverently and her embarrassment faded as he cradled them, tenderly brushing his thumbs back and forth over the taut peaks he'd uncovered. The caresses shot streamers of fire licking through her system, zinging down to light a blaze between her legs where she felt herself soften for him. She shifted restlessly and saw him smile. "Yes," he said. "Do you want me?"

"Adam," she said, hearing the plea in the single word, and his smile widened as he bent his head and closed his lips over the tender tip of her breast. He suckled strongly, wringing a cry of pleasure from her as her knees went weak and she clutched at his smooth, bare shoulders. His arms came around her, pulling her hips firmly against him, and she gasped as she recognized the solid weight of his aroused flesh pressing hard into her soft belly. He still wore both his belt and his pants and the fabric of his trousers against her bare flesh was an erotic stimulant. The fire inside her was raging now, stoked by the incessant tugging of his mouth on her sensitive flesh, and she writhed against him, moving herself helplessly over his firm length.

Adam groaned. He released her and fumbled with his belt, tearing it open and unzipping his pants in the same motion. "Help me," he said, and his voice was little more than a growl, his eyes blazing with heat and need. Obediently, she put her hands in the waistband of his trousers and pushed them down. As they fell around his feet, she couldn't resist looking down at the white briefs he wore, stretched taut by the pressure of the very male flesh caught behind the elastic and fabric of the briefs.

Adam hooked a finger in the briefs and pulled them away and down and she swallowed at her first full sight of him completely unclothed, jutting forward proudly from the thicket of dark curls at his groin. She helped him tug the briefs over his hard buttocks, and then all his clothes were gone. Breathing as harshly as if he'd just run a mile, Adam set his hands at her waist and lifted her, stepping forward to free them both from the tangle of clothing on the floor, and as he drew her against him, she gloried in the satiny feel of his rock-hard flesh prodding at her soft belly. She curled her arms around his neck and her bare breasts were crushed against the hard planes of his chest, the springy hair teasing her nipples. He thrust his hips forward and she practically purred with pleasure. This was what she had been born for, this moment, this man. Slowly, she moved her hips against his, her breasts sliding over his chest.

He took her mouth again and she felt his hand on her thigh, urging one leg up and holding it wrapped around his waist as she had the other night. The position left her vulnerable, balanced on one slender high heel, and when he pulled her into firm contact with him, they both groaned. She still wore the small panties, and as she felt him rubbing himself steadily against the satiny fabric that barely covered her, she was astonished by the waves of pleasure lifting her higher and higher. Moaning, she angled herself against him to increase the wonderful sensation.

He swept her into his arms and carried her to the bed, setting her on her feet so that he could sweep the covers back. Then he placed her on the mattress and came down beside her, propping himself on one elbow as he looked down at her.

She looked up at him, eyes wide. She'd felt exposed when he'd first removed her clothing, but now, lying down, she felt much more vulnerable. Against her hip, she could feel the hard proof of his desire for her, twitching and moving occasionally.

Slowly, he lifted his hand and laid it flat on her belly and she sucked in a startled breath at the heat that leaped between them. "I want you," he said, "more than I have ever wanted anything in my life." He let his gaze slide down from her face over the rest of her body, and a slight smile touched his lips.

"Adam," she whispered, overwhelmed by the intensity of his tone, "kiss me."

The smile widened. "Gladly."

Leaning over her, he touched his lips to hers, lightly at first. Then, with more and more amorous intent, his mouth grew firmer. He touched the line of her lips with his tongue and when she opened to him, he immediately swept in to claim the sweet recess as his own. His free hand slipped up over her torso and found a breast, and he firmly rotated his palm over it as the temporarily banked fires he'd lit within her flared to life again. Her body arched and he chuckled. His hand left her breast and began to slowly journey down her body. At the same time, he slid his mouth from her lips along the line of her jaw until she felt his hot breath in her ear. She jumped as he drew her earlobe into his mouth and began to suckle, and her hips lifted involuntarily at the shocking sensations his mouth produced. Who would have thought an ear could be so erotic?

But the thought barely cleared her consciousness before it scattered again as his hand slowly traced firm circles down past her naval, each time slipping a little farther, making her shiver with anticipation.

Finally, he slipped a finger beneath the elastic edge of her panties. "These have to go," he said, making short work of them.

As he tossed them over his shoulder, she realized she was still wearing her shoes, and she said, "Let me take off—"

"No." He grinned, lifting one long slender leg and looking down the bare length of it. "I kind of like this look." Then his gaze traced a path back up over her body until he came to the newly exposed nest of soft curls that covered her. He combed his fingers through the curls, watching his hand as his fingers slipped down, curving between her legs. "And this look," he said hoarsely. "I *really* like this look."

He moved his fingers a little, and she jumped, squeaking as spears of pleasure shot through her body.

"Relax," he whispered, pressing against her inner thigh with the heel of one hand until she let him open her.

"I can't," she whispered back. "It feels…too good."

His eyebrows arched and she felt the fingers rubbing tiny circles, spreading the moisture that he'd found between her legs over his hand and her flesh, making the contact even more pleasurable. "You're so wet," he murmured. "Wet for me."

"Adam!" She clutched at his shoulders, uncaring that she was pleading. "Stop! I can't—I can't—"

"Yes, you can." There was a smile in his voice, but the tone was strained. "Let go, sweetheart. Just let go." He was crooning to her, low syllables of praise and encouragement, but she barely heard him. Her body was gathering tight, a taut fist of trembling need in her abdomen, her heels digging into the bed as she pushed herself against his hand, unable to resist the seduction of those knowing fingers.

He rose over her, still touching her as he lowered his head and took her breast into his mouth, and she cried aloud as sharp arrows of pleasure assaulted her. She couldn't stand it, and her needy, aching body rose again and again to the sweet lure of his magic fingers, drawing her tighter and tighter...

Until the delicious tension snapped and she screamed, arching against his hand. Waves of incredible pleasure swamped her, breaking over her head and she felt his hand between her legs, fingers plunging deep as she thrust herself against him over and over.

"Adam!" she cried out through the storm of sensual fulfillment.

"I'm right here." He bent and pressed a kiss to her forehead.

She was panting and winded, lethargy rushing through her to replace the wild excitement of moments ago. But the feel of his hard strength still pushing at her hip was a seduction all its own. She reached down and circled him, softly stroking the hot, smooth length of him, and incredibly, she felt a lingering echo of the intense pleasure she'd just known. "I want you right *here*," she said, spreading her legs wide and urging him to her.

He rolled atop her and she gasped with pleasure as he settled intimately against her. "Here?"

"Oh, yes. Please," she breathed. She moved a little, and he closed his eyes.

"Wait," he said. "We need protection."

He reared up on his knees and reached to the table at the side of the bed, and as he efficiently tore open the small package he must have placed there earlier, she was warmed by his care. As he rolled the condom into place, she reached out to help him, and with a groan, he thrust himself into her hands, letting her stroke and explore.

Finally, he came down onto her again. She wrapped her legs around his hips and held tightly to his shoulders as she felt him begin to sink into her. Closing her eyes, she waited for the pain.

Adam was slow and careful. She felt him hesitate when her body resisted—and then a single stroke pushed him deep inside her. Amazingly, there was almost no pain. The small pinching discomfort quickly faded and she opened her eyes to see his worried face above her. "Okay?" he asked.

She loved him even more for that. His arms were quivering and his whole body trembled with his need, and yet he was still concerned for her. "Perfect," she answered. She lifted and lowered her hips experimentally, enjoying the sensation of smooth full pressure that brought a return of the wild pleasure she'd already known.

And then Adam began to move. Long, powerful strokes that moved her body on the bed. Deep thrusts that ground her sensitive woman's flesh against his hard male length as their bodies came together again and again, wet flesh rubbing and slapping in erotic rhythms. He was breathing loudly in the quiet room and she suddenly realized that the small whimpering sounds of pleasure were coming from her own throat. In mere moments, the thrilling sensations hurled them over the edge into intense fulfillment simultaneously.

She dozed in the circle of Adam's arms but when he shifted, she blinked sleepily. "Sex must be like a drug," she said. "I'm exhausted and I didn't even do anything."

"That," he said, "is entirely a personal point of view." He grinned as she blushed, then glanced at the wristwatch he still wore. "It's almost nine o'clock. Are you hungry? We missed dinner, remember?"

"I remember." She considered the question as she lifted a hand and lightly traced a pattern across his breastbone. "No, I don't think I'm hungry. A piece of that fruit on the table would be fine for me."

"Good," he said with deep satisfaction, and she felt him stirring against her inner thigh where she'd laid one leg across him. His hand slipped down to her breast and she drew in a gasp of delight at the way her body immediately responded. "I can think of a lot of things I'd rather do than eat."

Seven

Adam woke slowly, filled with a deep happiness. The first thing he was aware of was that he wasn't alone. The second conscious thought was that Selene lay beside him, snuggled into a little ball while he curved possessively around her.

He opened his eyes and took in the warm light of day seeping around the edges of the curtains he'd closed last night. Glancing at the clock on the bedside table, he saw that it was just past seven. In a few short hours they would have to part.

Dissatisfaction rushed through him and he tightened his arms, drawing her closer. He didn't want to let her go. Not today, not ever.

The thought crystallized immediately. No, he didn't want to ever let her go. He loved her. He wanted to marry her. He wanted to wake up every morning with her in his arms, he wanted to see her belly swollen with his child. He wanted it all.

"Ummm." Selene stretched as she came awake, pushing her bottom back against him, and he forgot every thought in his head as he responded to the press of her soft flesh against his hips.

He slipped a hand up to her breast, idly flicking his thumb back and forth until he felt the tight little nubbin. "Good morning," he said into her ear as he kissed the side of her neck.

"Good morning." She reached behind her, wrapping one delicate hand around him and slowly sliding it up and down. "It feels like a *very* good morning." There was a smile in her voice.

"It surely does," he agreed. He could barely get the words out through the passion that clouded his brain as her fingers teased him.

He put one big hand on her thigh, lifting her upper leg and hooking it back over his, shoving himself forward into the warm, moist little nest between her legs but not entering her. "Are you sore?"

She turned her head so he could see her face, and she was smiling. "No."

"Good." He reached for protection and rolled it into place, then angled his hips and pulled her leg higher, opening her as he pushed deep into her. She was soft and wet and so warm he had to stop moving and grit his teeth in order to keep from ending their pleasure too soon.

And the next time he looked at the clock, nearly an

hour had passed. He was lying on his back this time, and Selene lay on his chest, her head against his heart.

"Are you awake?" he whispered.

"Mmm-hmm." She turned her head and kissed his chest.

"I think—" he said reflectively. "No, that's not right. I *know* that I love you."

Her head shot up and she propped herself on his chest, her mouth forming an *O* as shock widened her eyes. "Don't tell me that!"

To say that he was taken aback was an understatement. "Why not? It's true."

"It's too soon," she said, pushing herself upright. "Don't you think it's too soon, Adam? You barely know me."

He raised his eyebrows and slowly smiled. "I know you."

"I didn't mean *that*!"

"I know. It was just the perfect opportunity and I couldn't resist."

She shook her head, smiling now herself.

"And I think you're falling in love with me, too."

Her eyes softened. "Maybe I am," she said. "But we can't talk about this again until after the election."

Hurt began to create a dull ache around his heart. "You're willing to sleep with me, but I can't tell you I love you?"

"I'm willing to make love with you," she corrected, and he saw the now-predictable blush beginning to spread up her cheeks.

"Selene, you're not making a lot of sense." He tried

to keep smiling, though it was an effort. "I promised you that we wouldn't say anything to anyone about our relationship until after the election. But I am not going to promise not to say what I'm thinking."

"I'm afraid we'll jinx it," she said, still blushing. "Us, together—we're so wonderful, Adam, so perfect and amazing. Do you know what I mean? I guess I'm afraid that something will go wrong if we aren't careful."

"Sweetheart." He gathered her into his arms again, pulling her against the long, hard length of his body as the hurt receded. "Nothing is going to go wrong. We just have to be careful for a few more weeks, and then we can announce it to the world."

She sighed, angling her head to rest against his shoulder. "You don't know my father. It isn't going to matter if it's a day or a year after the election, and it isn't going to matter who won and who lost. All he'll see is that I'm crossing enemy lines."

"Crossing enemy lines," he repeated. It sounded ridiculous, but he'd seen some of Van Gelder's rabid attacks on his father, so maybe it wasn't so far-fetched.

"Thank you for last night," she said into the hollow of his throat. "It couldn't have been more special if I'd planned it all out."

"You're welcome." He gently ran his palms up and down her back, not feeling the need to say more.

"I do care for you," she said quietly. "More than I've ever cared for anyone. And once this campaign ends, I promise you we'll make plans. No matter what my father says."

"Good. I'll hold you to that." His voice was warm with satisfaction. "And we'll announce it to the media *before* they leak it, for once."

He let her have the shower first, sensing that she needed some private time. He had breakfast brought up while she finished in the bathroom, and after he'd taken a quick shower and dressed, they sat down to eat.

Afterward, they prepared to leave.

Adam glanced at her as he prepared to heft their bags, then abruptly reached for her, shocked to see tears filling her beautiful eyes. "Don't cry, baby," he said roughly. "It won't be long until we can be together as much as we like, remember? Just seven weeks."

"Just seven weeks," she repeated shakily.

"I promise," he said. "You know in your heart we have something special here. Something lasting."

She looked up at him then and smiled, though her lips trembled. "Yes," she said. "Something lasting."

He wiped the tears from her cheeks with his thumbs and kissed her forehead tenderly. Then slowly he stepped back and released her. "Are you ready to go home?"

She nodded.

Adam picked up her small bag and held the door open, and she preceded him into the hallway and down to the lobby. He glanced at her as he held the lobby door open. She was smiling rather sheepishly, her tears gone.

"What?" he said.

Her smile widened. "I feel like a wicked woman," she whispered. "Everyone's staring at us. I'm sure they know we never left our room once after we arrived."

Adam chuckled. "I think you're giving people credit

for being a lot less self-absorbed than most of them really are. I doubt anyone even could describe us." He steered her through the front door and began to lead her around to where he had parked.

"Wait," she said. "I'll take a cab."

"It's all right." He opened his trunk and set her bag inside. "I don't have anything big going on this morning. I have plenty of time to run you home."

She glared at him as he walked her around to the passenger side and opened her door. "It would be better for me to take a cab."

"No, it wouldn't," he said, calmly ignoring the fact that he *knew* she didn't want him to take her home.

She narrowed her eyes, but he was impervious. "All right," she said. "But only because it's the middle of the morning and I know my father won't be home."

He grinned, victorious.

And when they arrived in the big circle in front of her family home, he wouldn't let her out of the car until they'd made arrangements to have dinner again the following evening and she'd given him a very satisfactory farewell kiss.

"Why do you have a book that belongs to Adam Danforth?"

She was barely in the front door when her father popped out of his study and came toward her.

She froze, shocked that he was still at home in the middle of a weekday morning. Even more shocked at the chance she'd just taken. Had he seen Adam? She didn't think so or he wouldn't be half as calm as he was.

She focused on his question, schooling her face and voice to reveal nothing. There had been so few reasons in her life to practice lying that it never even occurred to her to try.

"I met him at that fund-raiser you made me attend," she said simply. Not a lie at all.

"I thought you said you didn't find out anything important there."

"I didn't. He isn't any more interested in campaigning than I am."

"But you did speak with him."

"He's a font of knowledge about Savannah history." Well, that was no lie, either. She took a deep breath. *You're a consenting adult,* she reminded herself. *You don't need his permission to do anything and he can't keep you from seeing Adam.* To her surprise, she couldn't prevent a slight sharpness from creeping into her tone when she spoke again. "This city is where my mother's family lived for generations, and yet I know next to nothing about it."

Her father looked completely taken aback. "Uh, I suppose we can fix that."

"I've already taken care of it myself," she said coolly. "And what were you doing snooping around in my suite?" She knew exactly where she'd left Adam's book. Not in a million years had she imagined her father would think to enter her rooms.

"I, uh, I wanted to check your schedule," he said, still staring at her as if he wasn't sure who she was. "I just wanted to leave you a note asking you to be available for some campaign activities this week and next."

"All right," she said. "I doubt I have any conflicts. I'll let you know." She swept past him and moved toward the stairs, out of patience with her father's odd behavior. "And good morning to you, too, Father." She colored her tone with the sarcasm he so often employed.

"Selene?" Behind her, his voice was strangely diffident.

She stopped with one hand on the newel post and turned to look back at him, eyebrows raised in inquiry.

"I...thank you for coming home," he finally said, gazing down at the thick rug on which he stood. "It means a lot to me."

"I understand that it's important to you to win this election," she said.

"No, that's not it." Her father lifted his gaze to hers and shock slapped at her. He looked as if...as if he were *fond* of her. "I'm just glad you're here. And I promise as soon as this election is over I will spend some time showing you the things your mother loved about this city."

Tears stung the backs of her eyes and she bit her lip. If he'd ever mentioned her mother before, she had no memory of it. "I'd like that," she said quietly. "I'd like that a lot." But as she turned and began to mount the stairs, she cautioned herself not to count on anything. If he won the election, he was going to be far too busy to bother with her. As usual.

And if he lost...she shook her head silently. If he lost, she couldn't imagine how he was going to react.

As she climbed the stairs to her room, her cell phone rang. Her heart gave a little leap of excitement and she realized she automatically assumed it was Adam, since very few other people had the number.

"Hello?"

"Hello, dearest!" It was Willi.

"Hi, Willi." Even though it wasn't Adam, it was the second-best thing. "How are you?"

"Utterly wonderful. But I want to hear about you! Last time we spoke, there was a lilt in your voice I've never heard before. Are you still seeing your Danvers fellow?"

"Danforth," Selene said in a near-whisper. She slipped into her suite, closed the door and crossed to her bedroom. Only when that door, too, was solidly closed behind her did she resume a normal tone. "His name is Adam Danforth."

"So you *are* still seeing him!" Guillemette's voice was triumphant.

"Yes."

"Selene! You sound as if things are going well."

"Things are going very well." She knew she sounded dreamy but she couldn't help it. "Adam says he loves me."

"Ohhh." Willi's sigh was nearly a coo. "Darling girl, that's wonderful. Are you making any plans I should know about?"

"Not yet." Selene sighed, the bubble of happiness leaking a little. "We don't want to do anything until after the election."

"The election that either his father or yours will lose?"

"Exactly."

Willi was silent for a moment. "How do you think it's going to go?"

"I have no idea. But if my father loses, telling him my boyfriend's last name is Danforth is going to send him through the roof. You'll probably see the fireworks in the sky from your side of the Atlantic."

Willi chuckled. "Surely not that bad. What's the very worst that could happen?"

"He could disown me, I suppose. Never speak to me again."

There was a loaded silence. Finally, Guillemette said, "Well, darling, I hate to point out the obvious but the man has ignored your existence for most of your life." There was a bite in her tone. Willi's family had strong opinions about the lonely little girl Willi had begun dragging home for boarding school holidays all those years ago. "I mean," she added, "you've lived without him quite well, and I daresay you could do so again."

"You're right." Selene sighed. "But you know, Willi, I feel sorry for him. He can barely mention my mother's name. Still, after all these years, he's grieving."

"And you know this because…?" Willi wasn't so quick to forgive the years of emotional neglect.

"He's been speaking of her a little bit. He says I look a lot like her."

Willi made a noise that possibly could be construed as sympathetic. "I can see how that would be difficult for him." She hesitated. "But, Selene, you aren't going to allow him to dictate whom you love, are you?"

"No." She had resolved that concern, and it showed in her voice. "Adam and I aren't going to let anything get in the way our relationship."

"Wonderful! I am going to have to start planning a trip to the States to meet this man. Or," she added slyly, "you could always bring him along to my wedding, get married while you're here and take a long honeymoon trip on the Continent."

Selene just smiled. "Perhaps."

"Has he asked you to marry him?" Selene had to hold the phone away from her ear.

"No," she admitted. "He knows I couldn't accept right now. And we haven't known each other very long—"

"Pah. Time means nothing when two people fall in love."

From Willi's perspective, that probably was true. She'd accepted a proposal after just four dates with her husband-to-be. The fact that it had sent royalty across half of Europe scrambling to be sure it was an acceptable match had been of no consequence to either of them. Selene felt cowardly and small by comparison. Adam had met her more than halfway. Maybe he was right. And so was Willi. If she wanted him, she needed to show him that she didn't care about what the world thought. Especially her father.

"Well, I can't tell you how to live your life." Willi sighed dramatically. "Much as I want to."

Selene chuckled. "I appreciate your concern. You know that. Now tell me why you *really* called. Have you made a decision on the color of my maid of honor gown yet?"

Two days was a ridiculously long time to be separated from Selene, Adam decided the following day. Why did her father dislike his family so much? And why, given that he was pretty sure the man hadn't figured prominently in Selene's childhood, was she so determined not to upset him?

John Van Gelder might be a complete loser as a father, but he was all Selene had, Adam reminded himself. Selene hadn't had the love and support of other family members throughout the years of her father's neglect as he had. In her mind, even a loser was better than nothing. He could understand that.

His own father hadn't been around a lot when he was a kid. And while he saw his father's actions from a different perspective as an adult, there was still a little kid inside him who would never understand or forgive the benign neglect to which he'd been subjected. Thank God for Uncle Harold and Aunt Miranda. The "other" Danforth home had been filled with laughter and love and warmth and caring, and Abe's children had been as welcome there as Harold's own.

He was returning to the office from having lunch with Lea, when he stopped at the desk of his administrative assistant, Geoffrey.

"There's a lady to see you," the young man said. He grinned. "A fine-looking lady."

Adam lifted his head, alerted by something in the tone. "Did she leave her name?"

Geoffrey shook his head.

"Where is she?"

"I let her wait in your office. She has a book that belongs to you. When she showed me your signature on the flyleaf, I figured she was okay."

A book…Selene! He was shocked by the surge of pleasure that rushed through him. He practically bolted for his office door.

"Hey," he said as he entered the room and closed the

door firmly behind him. "What are you doing here?" He couldn't believe she'd been bold enough to come here. He knew how she worried about her father finding out about them.

"I wanted to return your book." She rose from the seat she'd taken at the small arrangement of chairs around an antique coffee table he'd found several years ago. His book lay on the table before her. "And maybe," she said, smiling, "I thought I could get a kiss or two to keep me going until tomorrow night."

He grinned, delighted at her unexpected appearance. "I think that could be arranged." He met her halfway across the room and put his hands at her waist, pulling her to him. "Hello," he murmured as he set his mouth on hers. But even as he sank into the embrace, his mind wouldn't shut off. "What about your father?" he murmured. "You're taking a huge risk coming down here."

She shrugged, framing his face with her small fingers. "You're worth a few risks." Her eyes were very green and determined, and he wondered what had occurred that had emboldened her so. She certainly couldn't be described as timid, but she worked hard to avoid controversy. If she had been recognized coming in here, things could get tense between her father and her in a hurry.

"Tomorrow night is too long to wait to see you," he said, cuddling her against his chest. "Let's get together tonight. We'll go out for dinner and then head back to my place."

"I can't," she said regretfully. "I need to stay at home this evening."

"Why?" He kissed her tenderly. "I don't want to wait until tomorrow evening, Selene."

"It's only a day," she teased him. Then her smile faded. "But I feel the same way. I shouldn't have stopped in here today but I wanted to see you." She paused, letting her hands slide up into his hair and he shivered as her fingers lightly traveled over his scalp. "I *needed* to see you."

"I'm glad." The tenderness faded from his expression, replaced by hungry desire. "I've been missing you, too."

He bent his head and found her mouth, kissing her deeply, sweeping his hands over her slender frame as his body sprang to full alert. She was like wildfire in his arms, twisting against him, igniting passion with every touch, every brush of her soft curves against him. He arched her backward, kissing her neck and sucking her earlobe into his mouth as he swirled his tongue over her satiny flesh. She shivered and clutched at his shoulders. As she lifted her arms, the short sweater she wore rode up her midriff and his seeking fingers encountered bare, creamy skin stretched over the delicate bones of her rib cage. He slid one hand up beneath the sweater, seeking her breast—

—And the door opened.

The sound was like the shock of cold water being thrown over his head. His head jerked up and he straightened, although he didn't let go of Selene, palming the back of her head and pushing her face into his shoulder to hide her identity.

His brother Marcus stood frozen just inside the door, his face a picture of amused surprise. "Well, hey. Guess there was a reason Geoffrey was trying so hard to head me off."

Adam's flustered assistant appeared in the doorway behind Marcus. He was practically wringing his hands. "I tried," he said to Adam, shaking his head in annoyance as he eyed Marcus. "I really did."

"It's all right, Geoff," Adam said. To his brother, he said, "Hello, Marc. I imagine there's a good reason for you to barge into my office."

His younger brother's grin was a rare sight. Marcus had always been driven, but after he'd caught his fiancée in bed with his best friend a year ago, his smiles had all but disappeared. "It can wait. Introduce me."

Adam heaved a sigh. "All right, but you have to promise not to tell anyone you met her until after the election."

Marc's brow furrowed. "After the election?"

"Selene, this is my idiot brother, Marcus Danforth. Marc, Selene Van Gelder." Gently, he set Selene away from him as she lifted her face from his shoulder and turned to greet his brother.

Instant comprehension lit Marcus's dark eyes. "Whoa." He offered Selene his hand. "Your father doesn't have much use for anyone named Danforth, I understand."

Selene shook her head ruefully as she took his hand. "No, I'm afraid not." She glanced up at Adam and smiled when he met her gaze. "But that isn't going to matter. We're only waiting until the election is over so that we don't distract either of our parents."

Marcus gave a short snort of unamused laughter. "You'd have to do a lot more than hang out with Adam to distract our father." He released her hand and backed toward the door. "I apologize for barging in."

"Wait," Adam said. "What did you want?"

But Marcus only shook his head. "Not important." Another of the rare smiles lit his sober features. "Carry on. Nice meeting you, Selene. I'll see you again when you two come out of hiding, I hope."

She smiled. "Most definitely. It was nice to meet you, Marcus."

As the door closed behind him, she turned to Adam, still smiling. "Now where were we?"

Eight

Adam didn't smile in return. It was as if his delight in her visit had vanished with his brother. "It's only September," he said. "Are we really going to have to hide our relationship for another month and a half until this damned election's over?"

She stilled at the grim note of frustration in his tone. "It would be best."

"Best for whom?" he demanded.

She'd never seen this side of him, this restless impatience, and it made her feel small and selfish. "Best for us," she said quietly, trying not to give way to her distress.

"It's not best for me." His tone was distinctly grumpy. "My father doesn't give one flying damn what any of his offspring do or who we date. Your father is the only one with the problem."

"I know." She was near tears. "But he's the only living relative I have, Adam, and I don't want to alienate him needlessly. All I'm asking for is seven weeks. Is that really so much?"

His expression softened, and to her relief he reached for her again, gathering her close. "No. Not compared to the rest of our lives."

The promise implicit in his words thrilled her. So he really was thinking of marriage!

He sighed. "It's just that I want to be with you all the time. I want to take you out to dinner or to a party and not have to worry about someone seeing us and tattling to some gossip columnist." His voice had risen again. There was a moment of tense silence and then she felt his taut muscles relax. "I want to introduce you to my family," he said in a more moderate tone. "I want the world to see us together."

"No more than I do," she told him softly, reaching up to cradle the strong line of his jaw. She understood now why it was so important to him; he'd been crucified in the media once and wasn't about to let it happen again. "I know seven weeks seems like a long time, but it will go quickly. I promise."

"Not quickly enough for me," he grumbled. But he bent his head and kissed her again and she realized the moment of discord had passed.

"Tomorrow night," she promised when he finally lifted his head. "I'll see you then."

"I don't guess you'd let me pick you up," he said, though it was clear he already knew the answer.

She shook her head. "Why don't I take a taxi to your place and we can go from there?"

He was watching from a window when Selene's taxi pulled up outside his gate the following evening. He opened the door and stood waiting as she came up the walk, marveling at the good fortune that had brought her his way. She walked with the fluid grace of a dancer, and he recalled how gracefully she'd matched his steps that first night in the garden, how perfectly her body had fit against his.

She came up the steps smiling quizzically. "Good evening. You look as if you're a million miles away."

He smiled, murmuring, "Not so very far." He stepped aside, holding the door wide for her, enjoying the slight brush of her body against his as she entered his home.

She stopped on the patterned rug in the foyer and laid her purse on the hall table beneath the wall-mounted mirror. For a moment, her back was to him, and the perfect curves of her heart-shaped bottom were beautifully outlined beneath the little skirt she wore. The pleasant arousal that had been simmering inside him since he'd first glimpsed her long legs uncoiling from the cab ratcheted up a notch and he stepped in close behind her. Setting his hands at her waist, he drew her back against him. He used his mouth to brush aside the hair at her neck and set his lips against the gently beating pulse he found there, kissing her lightly beneath her earlobe until she shivered and pressed herself back against him.

Adam groaned as he was sandwiched between their bodies, nestled between the sweet globes of her bottom.

He slipped his hands beneath the short sweater she wore and boldly palmed her breasts through the lacy bra she wore.

Selene made a small sound deep in her throat as he flicked his thumbs across the sensitive peaks until they were pebbled and hard, standing out even through the bra. Her small hands slid back to clutch his buttocks and pull him harder against her, and she gently rotated her hips, rubbing her bottom against him.

The world around him receded to one simple, overwhelming fact: he wanted her. Now.

Quickly, he slid his hands down her hips to the hem of the skirt and he tugged it up to her waist. To his delight, she wore a lacy black thong beneath it. Tracing his fingers gently along the scrap of fabric, he followed it down between her thighs. When he applied gentle pressure, she willingly widened her stance. He looked down her long slender legs and realized she still wore the small strappy heels in which she'd minced up his steps, and suddenly, he couldn't breathe, couldn't think, couldn't wait.

He slipped his fingers beneath the edges of the thong, feathering through the tight little curls to the soft, moist flesh beneath. She was slick and hot, and as her readiness registered, he drew back just far enough to unzip his pants and push them out of the way in a few deft moves, sighing in relief as his throbbing flesh pressed into the satiny bare skin before him.

He reached down and moved himself into position, nudging her legs wider, and she automatically leaned forward, bracing her arms on the small table before which she still stood. Slowly, deliberately, he pressed forward, groaning in relief, delight, ecstasy, as her tight channel admitted him. Forward and forward again, until there was no telling where he left off and she began, until he was snugly embedded within her.

She wriggled a little, searching for a comfortable fit, and he was reminded of how new she was to this. Tenderness swept him, and he slid his palm around to her abdomen, flattening it there and extending a seeking finger down over the soft rise of her mons until he found the pouting bud between her legs.

She cried out when he gently pressed it, and he smiled as he initiated a circling pattern of magic that quickly had her moving and shifting in his arms.

He paused for a moment, and she said, "Adam!" in a threatening tone. And then she rolled her hips once, twice, and he was lost. Beginning a slow steady rhythm, he clung grimly to control, but she wouldn't let him wait, and as her body writhed and shifted on him, he felt the control slipping away, vanishing in the mist of passion, and he began to move faster and faster, bare flesh slapping against bare flesh. He anchored her to him with his hand on her abdomen, and their movements pressed his finger hard against her, making her cry out again and again until, with a near-scream of incoherent pleasure, she began to convulse in his arms. Her body shook and surged, tightened around him in a sensual grip he was powerless to resist. Faster and higher the tight coil of tension within him flew until he felt shivers of completion rushing along his spine, surging down to empty him into her in final great thrusts that arched his back and left him spent and gasping, curved over her back as she lay across the table.

For long moments, neither of them spoke. Finally, he stepped back, reluctantly disengaging their bodies. Selene still didn't move, and he took a second to fasten his pants before moving to her side and drawing her to him. She circled his arms with her neck, then squeaked in surprise as he bent and scooped her into his arms.

He bent his head and kissed her, lingering over the sweetness of the moment. "Sorry," he said when he lifted his head. "I think we got a few things out of order."

She smiled up at him, laying her head against his shoulder as he began to carry her up the stairs. "And we forgot something, too."

Adam stopped dead, shock ripping through him. What the hell had he been thinking? He'd completely forgotten about birth control! "Oh, hell," he said. "I never gave it a thought."

"It's all right." She stroked his face with her fingers, appearing amazingly calm and unaffected under the circumstances.

"How is it all right?" he demanded. "If you get pregnant—"

"We'll deal with it together," she said, still nonchalant. "It would make all this worrying about keeping it from my father until after the election seem a lot less of a problem, wouldn't it?" There was actually a note of humor in her voice.

"It isn't funny!" he said.

"It is," she said, openly laughing now. "*You're* funny. I've never seen you so panicked."

"With good reason." But he was relaxing again as he started on up the stairs, and a smile tugged at his lips.

He set her on her feet in his bathroom, keeping one arm around her as he reached in to turn on the shower. Then he turned to her, tugging the sweater over her head and tossing it onto the wide counter.

Her eyes widened as he unhooked her bra. "We're going to shower together?"

He grinned. "Yeah." And with that, he stripped off the rest of their clothes and tugged her into the shower. "And this time we're using protection. Much as I like the idea of you having my baby, the timing would really be lousy."

She softened, curling into his arms and pulling his head down for a kiss. "Make love to me again. With or without protection."

Afterward, they toweled each other dry and he led her into his bedroom. "I've wanted you here," he confessed, "in my bed."

"I can't stay," she said. But she let him pull back the sheets and lay her down.

He gathered her into his arms and tugged the sheets over them, creating a cozy cocoon. "Just for a few minutes." He stroked her back. "I love you, Selene."

She stilled in his arms. For a long moment she didn't speak, and resignation seeped through him. She was determined not to let him tie any strings between them until after this damned election.

Then she said, "I love you, too." She tilted her head back and kissed his chin. "If I'm pregnant—which I doubt—I promise I'll tell you right away."

"And we'll get married right away."

She smiled. "You know, I should be worried. You're just sneaky enough to get me pregnant and force the issue."

He grinned. "Much as I'd like to plan something like that, I'll only insist if it turns out we have a baby on the way. If not, we'll wait until after the election."

She hesitated, her pretty face growing serious. "I'm sorry I've been so difficult about our relationship. I don't want you to be unhappy."

"It's okay," he murmured. And it was. She loved him. She loved him enough to actually hold a discussion about marriage and children. About their future together. Knowing that, he could wait seven weeks to share her with the world.

Two hours later the telephone trilled, jarring him out of a daze. As he reluctantly released Selene and reached for the handset, he glanced at the clock. Twelve-thirty. Who in hell would be calling him after midnight? Dread coalesced in his belly, the dread that inevitably accompanied such a late call. Something must have happened to someone in his family.

He sat up in the bed. "Hello?"

"Adam. Thank God you're home." It was his father.

"What's wrong?" he demanded.

"It's Marcus," his father said in a voice filled with more fear and concern than Adam had ever heard him use before. "He's been arrested."

"Arrested?"

"Yes. For racketeering."

"Rack—? That's ridiculous and they know it. I thought this was settled the last time they questioned him."

"Apparently we were wrong." His father's voice was worried. "Ian is sure it's a frame-up."

"The cartel." He knew immediately. "They haven't been able to pressure Ian into switching to their coffee bean exporters any other way." He was already scrambling out of bed. "Call a lawyer. I'm on my way."

"Marc already has. He called some friend from the bar association who will do for the bail hearing, but he's going to need more than that. Ian's calling Jake and the rest of the family. I'll meet you at the police station. I'm going to push to get him released tonight. We can straighten the charges out tomorrow."

"All right. I'll be there."

Adam and his father disconnected simultaneously. He tossed the phone in the general direction of the bedside table as he grabbed fresh suit pants from his closet.

"What's wrong?" Selene was sitting in the middle of the bed, apprehension etched on her pretty face.

"My brother's been arrested. Marc—the one you met. They're saying he's involved in racketeering. I've got to get down to the police station." He thrust his arms into the sleeves of a dress shirt and frantically buttoned it, before stuffing the shirttails into his pants.

Selene jumped out of bed and tossed on his robe, hanging on the back of the bathroom door. "Is there anything I can do?"

"No." His mind was caroming in a dozen different directions as he belted the pants and knotted a tie around his neck, then slipped into his suit jacket. "Yes. Get yourself home. Take your time, just lock the door on your way out." He picked up his wallet, keys and cell phone and grabbed the briefcase that contained his laptop. He strode to the door where she waited, pausing briefly.

She wore his robe but she hadn't tied it, and as frantic as he was, he couldn't resist sliding one hand inside and pulling her to him, fondling the smooth, bare curves as he lingered over a final kiss. "I love you. I'll call when I can."

"I love you, too." She stepped back and nodded her head at the door. "Go. Hurry."

That night, back in her own bed after leaving Adam's silent, lonely home, she didn't sleep well at all. His words kept ringing in her ears. *My brother's been arrested.*

Of course it must have been a mistake. Adam hadn't believed it for a minute, she reminded herself.

But if she'd heard Adam correctly, it wasn't a mistake, but a deliberate act by persons in a cartel. Which implied drugs.

At six-thirty she rose and dressed, then went down to the breakfast room. Normally she didn't eat this early but she knew the morning papers arrived before seven and she was anxious to see if anything about Marcus Danforth had gotten into the early editions. Although she'd spoken encouragingly to Adam last night, she had known from the grim expression on his face that his brother's arrest was cause for real concern.

As she entered the room, her father was just taking his seat at the table. "Good morning, Father," she said.

"Good morning, Selene. You're up early."

It wasn't a question so she didn't volunteer a response, merely smiled and nodded as she made a beeline for the table. The papers lay in a neatly stacked pile beside her father's place, and she glanced at them longingly. She couldn't pounce on them and scan the front page without making him suspicious.

Slowly, she took a seat across from him. The housekeeper bustled in with coffee.

"So." Her father shook open his newspaper without looking at it as he glanced measuringly over the top of it at her. "You were out late last night."

"You must have gotten home earlier than usual," she countered, "because I wasn't really late at all. I'm usually in bed by the time you stagger in."

Her father's eyebrows rose. "It was after midnight."

"In Europe, parties are just getting started at midnight. I tend to forget how provincial the States can be." She smiled. "It will be wonderful to be in France again when my friend Willi gets married."

"Just for a visit, right?" Her father lowered his paper an inch.

She shrugged, reaching for the silver coffee carafe. "Who knows?" Her father, above all else, craved control. This inquisition into her personal life wasn't really *personal*, she reminded herself. He wasn't really interested in her; it was simply an exercise in ownership. And she knew the only way to make him back down was the implied threat that if he continued to probe, she would leave.

"Well," he finally said, rustling his papers. "I had hoped after the election that we could spend more time together."

She sent him a bland smile and stirred her coffee. "As had I."

Stalemate.

As her father finally turned his attention to the paper, Selene held out a hand as if she weren't particularly interested. "Would you hand me one of those, please?"

"What section?"

"I don't care. Front page, I suppose. I really should keep up with the campaign developments."

Her father reached absently for another newspaper, but as his gaze fell on the above-the-fold headline, she saw him freeze in midmotion.

"Whoo-*hoo!*"

She jumped a foot in the air, her hand going automatically to her throat as her father continued to hoot and cackle. "What on earth is the matter?" she asked, raising her voice to be heard over his jubilant celebration. She watched him warily, half expecting him to leap to his feet for a victory dance.

He turned the paper so she could see the headline. "One of those damned Danforths has been arrested!"

She snatched the paper from his hand and rapidly skimmed the article. Over her father's noise, she saw that the article told her little more than Adam had the night before. Marcus Danforth, fourth son of prominent politician and senatorial candidate Abraham Danforth, had been arrested, charged with racketeering by the FBI.

"This will sink Danforth's campaign," her father sneered. "He's managed to wriggle out of the last couple of sticky spots the press has caught him in, but there's no way to whitewash this."

"Unless it's a mistake," she said quietly. "He hasn't been found guilty yet."

"It won't matter," her father predicted. "There are fewer than two months left now until the election. Danforth's not going to be able to bounce back that fast." He rubbed his hands together. "This couldn't have come at a better time."

"I'm sure Marcus Danforth doesn't share your sentiments." She shook her head sadly. "I don't care how it affects the campaign. I refuse to wish ill luck on anyone just for the sake of winning."

"That's not what I meant," her father said impatiently.

"Oh?" She reached for a slice of toast and began to spread butter over the top. "Then what did you mean? It sounded like you were pleased that this poor man has been arrested because the resulting bad publicity would further your political goals."

"Well, perhaps, but—"

"What are you going to do if you don't win?" she asked.

Her father stopped talking. Stopped smiling. "What?"

She repeated the question.

"What kind of a thing is that to ask me?" he demanded. "Don't you have any faith in your own father?"

She ignored the aggressive tone. "Of course I do, but there can only be one winner. I honestly want to know what you plan to do if you aren't the one the voters elect."

John Van Gelder looked at his daughter with a blank expression. "It's never occurred to me that I wouldn't win," he said simply.

She realized he was telling her the exact truth—he had never even considered losing.

"But what if you do?" she persisted.

He frowned at her again. "I don't know. I suppose I'd...get involved in a business again." But he didn't sound certain.

Pain pierced her heart. *Don't be silly,* she lectured herself. *Surely you weren't expecting him to say something about spending more time with you?* "Well," she said crisply, "maybe you'd better think about it a little bit. In the unlikely event that you lose—" she worked hard to keep any hint of sarcasm out of her voice "—you might want to have some future plan to share with the press. Otherwise, you're liable to look ridiculously foolish, or conceited, or both."

She turned her attention back to the paper she held, aware that her father was gaping at her. No wonder. She'd never spoken to him like that before in their entire, albeit limited, history.

At the bottom of the article about Adam's brother was a small, italicized sentence: *See related story, p. 4C.*

Page 4C? That was the society section. The gossip corner. As always, during a hotly contested election, the media scavenged for any juicy tidbits they could find. As she flipped to the fourth page of the section, she idly wondered what they'd found now. Given the number of people in Adam's extended family, it was a sure bet there were plenty of skeletons hidden in closets. And probably a number of perfectly innocent mistakes that could be made to look far worse than they ever had been, as well.

But as she caught sight of the article, her brain stopped functioning and shut down altogether.

It was a photo of Adam and her. Together. Coming out of the hotel where they'd spent their first glorious night.

So shocked she couldn't even react, she simply sat and stared at the damaging photo.

They had just come through the front door of the small hotel; its sign was clearly visible just to their left. Adam had one arm around her. In the other, he carried her small overnight case. He was smiling down into her upturned face, an unmistakably tender expression that she might have been pleased to see under different circumstances. A large caption with bold type below the photo read: *Danforth-Van Gelder Campaign Takes Intimate Turn.*

There was an accompanying article. She scanned it automatically, a sick, lurching feeling growing inside her.

> *Abe Danforth's youngest son might be under siege, but his third son has reportedly made friends with the enemy. Adam Danforth was seen escorting heiress Selene Van Gelder, daughter of his father's chief rival for the senate seat, from a well-known historic hotel recently. This Danforth son, while still a bachelor, has been seen in the company of heiresses before, most notably with the former Karis Dougherty...*

The rest of the article was even more scurrilous. There was a picture of Adam—clearly a much younger Adam—carrying a woman in his arms, standing on the stoop of what looked to be a private home. The article explained that Karis Dougherty had been engaged at the time the picture had been taken, that Adam insisted that it had been nothing more than a study date for which he'd offered to give her a ride. It ended with arch insinuations that made her heart ache for Adam and infuriated her. No wonder he'd been so determined that they share the news with the press at their own pace. This made something so special seem...cheap and ugly.

She had barely absorbed the article when her father said, "What in hell is this?" It was a roar of anger and she knew he'd found either the same or a similar article in the edition he was reading. "Selene, there'd better be a damn good reason for you to be in a photo looking intimate with Adam Danforth. This could ruin the campaign!"

She tore her gaze away from the paper. "How could it possibly hurt your campaign?" she asked wearily. She'd feared that if her father found out about her relationship with Adam, he'd go ballistic. It was disheartening to be right.

"Are you telling me you're...seeing this boy?" Her father stood, papers sliding sideways to the floor. His face was red with rage. "He's a *Danforth!*"

"I know that, Father. I have yet to discover what's so objectionable about the family, other than the fact that you're running against one of them for office." Her own voice was louder.

"Abe Danforth," John gritted, "is a philandering wastrel. He had designs on your mother's fortune years ago, until her family got wise to him."

There was a stunned silence in the room. She could see in her father's eyes that he hadn't intended to blurt that out. And of all the things she'd expected him to say, that hadn't even been among the possibilities. "He...what?"

"He was one of your mother's suitors many years ago," her father said stiffly.

"Before you?"

He nodded once.

"Did you know her then?"

He nodded again, his eyes softening. "She was the most beautiful of the debutantes that year. I loved her the moment I saw her." His gaze was distant. "Every man in the room did. But none of them could get near her after Abe Danforth set eyes on her."

Suddenly, the reasons for her father's antipathy toward Abraham Danforth made sense. Not good sense, given that the events must have occurred nearly forty years ago, but at least she understood the connection at last. "But she married you," she prompted.

"Yes, after her father put a stop to an unsuitable alliance with the Danforths."

"Why was it unsuitable? The Danforth fortune puts ours in the shade, so he can't really have been after her money. I don't understand. Were they related?"

John Van Gelder shook his graying head. "No, nothing like that. Abe's father had gotten the better of your grandfather in business on a number of occasions. There was bad blood between them."

Bad blood between them. And her father appeared to have carried on the grudge.

So her mother had been forbidden to see Abraham Danforth. Her father's antipathy became even clearer—he hadn't been her first choice and he knew it. Had she loved Abe? Had she simply accepted the first man who came along after the relationship was forcibly ended? Selene doubted she would ever know, but she felt a surprising pang of pity for her father. He'd clearly adored her mother...and probably had never known if she cared for him in the same way.

"We intended to talk to you after the election was over," she said. "I didn't want to upset you while you had so much going on with the campaign."

"We?" Her father's face darkened again. "Selene, I forbid you to see Adam Danforth again."

She stared at him. Was he serious? Didn't he understand that words like those were what tore families apart? "You'd better be careful about what you say," she warned him. "I never would have met Adam if it weren't for you—"

"Me? How?"

"That stupid fund-raiser at Twin Oaks," she reminded him. "You insisted I attend. I met Adam there, remember?" She lowered her head and glared at her father. "And I have no intention of allowing you to dictate whom I see." She glanced back at the paper. "I can't imagine how they got this photo. Surely there aren't media hounds following all the members of the Danforth family around. There must be dozens of them!"

It was only chance that led her to glance back at her father.

He had an odd expression on his face. Almost a guilty one, if she wasn't mistaken. A little alarm bell began ringing hectically in her mind. "You didn't," she said slowly, "have anything to do with this, did you?"

"Er, no." Her father wasn't a good liar.

"You did!" She rose, facing him across the table. "Tell me you didn't set me up for this photo op."

"Of course not!" This time, truth rang in his tone. Then, as she watched, he seemed to deflate like a slowly leaking balloon. "Not on purpose, anyway." He sighed. "I hired a private investigator to follow you and report back to me. I was concerned when you began spending so much time away from home."

She was beyond appalled. "You hired someone to take pictures of me and Adam just because you have an imaginary grudge against Abraham Danforth? Are you *crazy?*" She never shouted. But she was shouting now.

Her father seemed to shrink in upon himself even further. "I didn't know who you were seeing when I hired him."

With each new revelation her shock and fury swelled. "That shouldn't have mattered! You hired someone to snoop on your own daughter instead of simply asking me who I was going out with?" She laughed wildly, bitterly. "You got more than you bargained for, didn't you?" She regarded him as if he were a very small and very repellent bug on her breakfast plate. "I will never forgive you for this." She spoke very slowly and very distinctly, each word quivering with the rage she couldn't repress. "I have spent most of my life wondering what was wrong with me to make you dislike me so. I got used to being ignored. I suffered through this damned campaign because you needed a family prop to make you look good. I even went to your opponent's fund-raiser because you insisted—and guess what? I met Adam Danforth there. I fell in love with someone you hate just because of his last name."

"Selene, I—"

"And here's another newsflash for you, Father. I do not intend to stop seeing Adam. Ever. He wants to marry me." She shook her head. "My own father spying on me."

"I asked him specifically not to take pictures," John said quietly. "The man must have recognized your— Adam—and decided he could make more money with those than he could working for me." Then her words sank in and his eyes widened. "You're going to *marry* him?"

"I am." She started for the door of the breakfast room, then turned and regarded her father again. "And do not assume you'll be invited to the wedding." She stomped out, slamming the door behind her. She'd never lost her temper like that in her life, as far as she could remember. Her hands were shaking and her insides were quivering. She felt like she was going to cry. Or throw up. Or both.

And dear heaven, she needed to call Adam right away. What on earth would he think when he saw that? She knew how he felt about publicity. The jelly in her stomach congealed into a hard ball as she ran to find her phone.

Nine

Adam had been asleep less than two hours when someone knocked on his door. He rolled over and peered at the alarm clock, but when he saw the clunky old clock of his boyhood rather than the more modern one that graced his bedside table at his own home, memory flooded back.

He was at Crofthaven, in his boyhood room. His father hadn't really done much with the house in the more than fifteen years since Adam had left home. While the more public areas that visitors saw were periodically refurbished, the bedrooms that belonged to the kids hadn't been changed much.

A second rap sounded on the door. More forceful. Impatient, maybe.

"Come in," he called. He sat up, scrubbing his hands over his face. When he saw the familiar features of his younger brother Marcus, relief joined the parade of memories from the night before. It had been several hours until they'd been allowed to take Marcus home from the police station. Anxious hours during which the lawyer Marc had retained had refused to let Marcus or any of them speak to the FBI, hours during which they hadn't been permitted to so much as see him. It had taken all the Danforth influence as well as a ridiculously sizable bail to get him out. "How are you?" he asked.

Marc's handsome face was sober. But he'd clearly showered and looked a lot better than he'd looked hours earlier when Adam had brought him home. He tossed the morning paper onto the edge of Adam's bed. "How would you be if you were arrested for something you didn't do?" he asked.

Adam grimaced. "Point taken." He eyed his brother. "Family support is one thing, bro, but you'd better be in here for a damned good reason. I didn't get to sleep until after five. And it's barely seven now. What's up? Have you heard something?"

Marc shook his head. "No." He hesitated. "There's something in the paper you need to see."

His brother's manner stirred Adam's nerve endings to alert. "Such as?" He pushed himself up straighter.

Marcus silently reached for the paper and handed it to him. Adam noted that the front page had been folded back to a section inside. His brother pointed to an article and photos near the top of the page.

At the first glimpse of the photo, Adam couldn't believe what he was seeing. He remembered the morning well, the feel of Selene's slim shoulder as he hugged her against his side, the way she'd laughed up into his face. He even remembered consciously restraining himself from leaning down and kissing her because they were in public...and the whole time, someone had been skulking in the shadows with a camera.

Selene's father was going to flip out. He forced himself to read the article, his features hardening in disgust. Of course they had to drag that old story up. Poor Karis. Her husband George was going to be livid, too. When the story had broken a decade ago, he'd nearly called off the engagement. But Adam and Karis had finally been able to explain the misunderstanding, and Karis's wedding had gone forward as planned. The couple still lived in the Savannah area and George wasn't going to be happy at this latest smearing of his wife's character.

Character smearing. His father's campaign was going to take a hit from this mess with Marcus, and to have Adam falsely broadcast across the media as a playboy wasn't going to help. John Van Gelder must be dancing a jig this morning if he'd seen this article, even if he was furious that Selene was involved with Adam.

If he was furious...how far would Selene go to earn her only parent's love? Although he despised himself for it, he couldn't banish the stirrings of suspicion that curled around the edges of his mind.

Adam thought of the pain in her eyes, the longing that lingered in her tone when she spoke of her father despite the flashes of resentment he'd also seen. It was obvious she'd never felt loved. What, he wondered, would she do to gain his attention, his approval?

And then the cold, unwanted thought he'd been fruitlessly trying to evade exploded in his brain. Could she possibly have planned all this?

He remembered his shock when he'd learned her last name. He'd been too caught up in the romance of the moment to ask what a Van Gelder had been doing at his father's campaign event, but he'd wondered about it off and on ever since. He'd intended to ask Selene but he'd forgotten. Several times.

His mouth tightened into a grim line as he recalled why he'd forgotten, the explosive passion they'd shared, their last happy discussion of a future complete with children. Had it all been an act?

Another knock on the half-open door interrupted his anguished thoughts, and he and Marcus both turned as their father strode in. He carried another copy of the paper, folded back to the same page at which Adam had been staring.

"Are you all right?" Abe's voice was gentle.

Adam swallowed. He shook his head. "I don't know. God, Dad, I'm sorry. This can't be good for the campaign."

Abe shrugged. "There are things in life a lot more important than the campaign." He held up the paper. "I didn't even know you knew her."

There was a long moment of silence in the room.

Finally, Adam admitted the hard truth. "Apparently, I didn't."

Marc stirred. "How, exactly, did you two meet?"

Adam swallowed. "She was at the Twin Oaks fundraiser in July."

Both his father's and his brother's eyes went wide with disbelief.

"What was she doing there?" Marc demanded.

"I don't know. I didn't think to ask her at the time, and since then, I keep forgetting when I'm with her." It sounded unbelievably naive and feeble when he said it aloud. "I'm sorry, Dad."

There was a silence in the room.

Then his father chuckled. "Women have a way of making you forget any common sense you have. I knew Selene's mother. If the daughter is half as beautiful, no wonder you forgot."

"Oh, she's beautiful," Marc growled. "On the outside, at least."

Adam felt too sick to speak.

Abe laid a hand on Adam's shoulder and squeezed briefly. "Don't worry about it. If people are so easily swayed by ridiculous tabloid stories that they choose not to vote for me, then so be it."

He swallowed. "But I don't want to cost you votes," he said, "and I may have been stupid enough to—"

"Adam," said his father, "is—was she important to you?"

Was oxygen important to breathing?

Before he could answer, Marc nodded his head. "Yeah," he said quietly. "She was."

His father and brother left the room again, but Adam barely realized they'd left. Numbly, he picked up the offensive newspaper again, looking at Selene's smiling face. Sharp claws of pain ripped at his heart. He'd thought she really cared for him. He'd thought he'd finally found a woman who didn't want anything from him, didn't need anything except his love.

He'd been wrong. Again.

Selene was growing more frantic as the day wore on. Since she'd walked away from the breakfast table that morning she'd been trying to get hold of Adam without success. She'd called his home repeatedly, had left several messages there as well as on his cell phone. There was no answer at his office and the machine merely said that the D&D offices were closed temporarily, that someone would be in the office tomorrow.

Four times, her father had knocked on the locked door of her bedroom suite, but she'd ignored him. If she never saw him again, her life would be perfectly fine. He'd treated her like secondhand goods for her entire life, fobbing her off on others and ignoring her as much as possible. And she'd learned to survive it. But he'd gone too far this time.

How could he have hired someone to report on her movements? The very fact that he didn't appear to understand how bizarre such an action was showed her just how out of touch her father was with the whole concept of being a parent. It had never occurred to him to simply *ask* her where she was going. No, he *paid* someone to report on her. And according to her father, it was simply an unfortunate mistake that the man he'd hired had been unethical and taken photos even though he hadn't been instructed to.

Pain squeezed her heart. If he'd loved her, he never would have let this happen. She shunted aside the pain and concentrated on the hard core of anger settling in her heart. She would never forgive him for this. He'd done something which could harm Adam's family and through them, him.

Adam, she thought on a wave of longing. She couldn't believe he hadn't called her. Was it possible he hadn't seen the picture and accompanying article? She doubted it. More likely, he was holed up somewhere avoiding the media.

God knew, she couldn't blame him if he couldn't contact her right now. Answering the phone had been a nightmare. But she was afraid she might miss a call from Adam if she didn't answer it, and many of the calls couldn't be identified with the caller I.D. screening system. She'd said, "No comment" so many times today that she'd lost track. So she'd suffered through the nosy questions in stony silence each time and simply hung up, hoping that the next time she lifted the handset, she'd hear Adam's voice.

If only she could go to him. But she couldn't leave because there were at least five members of the media camped outside her father's house. And even if she could, where would she go? He wasn't home, he wasn't at his office.

And then it struck her. Crofthaven. He'd gone to his family home. Or possibly to his uncle's. But she'd bet he'd wanted to speak to his father when the news broke, and perhaps he still was there. And she'd completely forgotten his brother's troubles. If Marc was at the family estate, Adam would want to be with him.

New hope flared within her heart. He probably

hadn't called for fear her father would answer. Not because Adam feared her father, but because he would be worried that his call might make things more difficult for her.

Fingers trembling, she found a phone book and looked up the home number for Abraham Danforth.

It rang three times before the connection opened.

An unfamiliar male voice said, "Danforth residence, Whittaker speaking. May I help you?"

"Yes," she said. She had to stop and take a deep breath. "I'd like to speak to Adam, please."

"Who is calling?"

"Selene Van Gelder."

There was a long pause. "Selene Van Gelder?" There was a distinct emphasis on her last name.

"That's correct." Even to her ears, it sounded defiant and she winced. She didn't want anyone in Adam's family to think badly of her.

"Just a moment."

She waited and waited. And waited some more. He must have put her on hold because she heard none of the ordinary noises of a household, no approach of footsteps, nothing. Finally, there was a click and she heard a new voice. "Adam Danforth."

"Adam! I'm so glad I found you. I've left you dozens of messages at your home and on your cell. Are you all right?"

Silence.

Uncertainty assailed her. "Adam?"

"Selene." His voice was oddly flat. "What do you want?"

She was taken aback. "I want to know if you're all right. You had to rush off last night to help Marc and then this morning that odious article—"

"About which you knew nothing, of course." There was a distinct note of sarcasm in his voice now.

"No, I—" She stopped as the tone and the meaning penetrated. "You think I...? Oh, no, Adam, it was my father. He—"

"You, your father, what's the difference?"

Now it was her turn to be silent. He'd never spoken to her like that, faintly accusatory and without a shred of the warmth and intimacy with which his tone usually was imbued. "What," she finally said, very careful to keep her voice neutral, "do you mean, what's the difference between my father and me?"

"Never mind," Adam said. "What were you doing at my father's fund-raiser in July? The one where we so conveniently met?"

He thought she'd set him up. The pain was so sharp and sudden she nearly dropped the telephone. "My father made me go," she said truthfully, knowing it would only nail shut the coffin of his former good opinion of her.

"I see."

No, he didn't see at all. And though a part of her already recognized that it was futile, she loved him so much she had to try to explain. "I didn't want to go," she said, "and I refused to spy on your family, but I said I would attend just to shut him up."

"What a sacrifice," he said. "I suppose you went out with me just to shut him up, too."

"No! You know better than that."

"Do I?"

There was another silence.

"I knew I shouldn't get involved with you," she said. "I knew my father wasn't rational in his dislike of your family. But when I saw your note, I couldn't stop thinking about how perfect that night had been..."

"Perfect, all right. It was the perfect opportunity to do something that would get you into your father's good graces."

"No!" She was growing frantic. "I only wanted to be with you."

"You wanted," he said deliberately, "to do anything that would make your father notice you."

That was when she realized how hopeless it was. His voice was cold and hard, completely unlike the man she'd grown to love.

"What happens now?" She pressed the back of her hand against her mouth to hold back the sobs that made her throat ache.

"Nothing," he said. "Nothing at all." And the receiver on his end went dead.

Selene clung to the receiver, pressing it against her ear. Her last link to Adam. Finally, feeling as if she would break if she wasn't very, very cautious, she pressed the button and killed the buzzing of the disconnect sound that was all he'd left her. Slowly she set the handset down. Then, very carefully, she lay down across her bed and laid her head on her crossed arms as the tears began to flow.

Adam thought she'd betrayed him. On purpose. Funny, but to her the concept of betrayal had always had some sort of medieval overtone. She'd grown up in Europe, where generations had fought over lands since ancient times, and where betrayal of family and fealty featured prominently in many of the old tales. Now, however, it had become very modern and very real.

Her father had betrayed her trust and the unconditional love she'd offered. And in doing so, he'd ruined her chance at a future with the man she loved.

Adam thought she'd betrayed the love and trust he'd offered her. Did he really believe she wanted her father's approval so desperately?

Apparently, he did. How had it all gone so wrong?

She cried for a long time, until her duvet was tear-soaked and her emotions were dulled. Until pain had given way to numbness and blank despair. She sat up finally and reached for a tissue, feeling stiff and far older than her years. Sliding off the bed, she looked at her swollen eyes in the mirror. Bleak shadows of loss met her when she gazed into her own eyes.

What was she going to do? She had no reason to stay in Savannah, and yet she had no reason to go, either. There was no one who would miss her, no one to welcome her.

And then she thought of Willi. Of Paris. An ocean away from the memories that would haunt her forever if she stayed here. Picking up the phone, she dialed the airlines. The earliest flight out was tomorrow just after eleven.

She took it.

He didn't go home that night.

For one thing, there were reporters everywhere, according to Ian and Jake. Marc had decided to brave the hordes and had escaped earlier in the company of his female bodyguard. Emphasis on *body,* Adam thought with perhaps the one real flash of humor he'd felt all day. His brother had seemed more alert and alive in the short hours since he'd met his attractive new bodyguard—more as if he gave a damn whether he lived or died—than he had in a year.

The house was stifling him. He wished he could leave like Marc had, but the sad truth was that he really had nowhere to go. If he went home, he'd just be hounded by the press. And he'd already screwed things up enough for the old man without courting more trouble.

Courting…he stepped through the French doors onto the terrace, closing them gently behind him. When he was a child and the house had become too oppressive, he'd escaped in this very same manner. He walked across the perfect lush green of the lawn, prettier now in early autumn than it had been during the heat of the summer, and headed past the gardens, past the peach orchard into the grove of trees at the far edge of the property.

As a child, he'd spent hours beneath the cool, dark canopy of leafy branches festooned with Spanish moss. Even then, he'd been convinced he'd see the ghost that had haunted the property since the time of his great-grandfather Hiram.

Today, for the first time he could remember, he didn't even bother looking around as he stomped his way along the path. The trees gave way to massive bayberry and other shrubs as he neared the cliff above the property's private beach, but he didn't intend to go that far. He liked the solemn anonymity of the forested land.

All he could think of was Selene, which was the height of stupidity after what she'd done. How could he have been so wrong about her? The night they'd met, he'd felt an astonishing sense of rightness with her that he'd never felt with any other woman. Certainly he'd never felt it with Angela—that had been nothing more than a crush. He was even more grateful to have escaped *that* mistake now that he knew what a real, loving relationship should entail.

But you don't, he reminded himself brutally. *You don't have any idea what a real relationship would be like. You've been living a lie with a woman who was using you.*

But his anger had begun to fade, replaced by a sweeping sadness that pervaded his thoughts and sapped his energy. Had it really all been a lie? He'd been so sure of her love.

And she'd sounded so miserable on the phone. If she'd truly intended to string him along for the sake of making him look like a philandering fool in the media, why had she been so upset? For that matter, why had she called him at all? She had to know he'd figure it out, realize that she'd only been with him in an effort to dredge up gossip and tarnish his father's campaign.

He snorted. She'd gone awfully far. What would she have done if the media hadn't picked up this story? Accused him of rape?

The pain he'd buried returned with a vengeance and he sank down onto a fallen tree trunk along the side of the path, putting his head in his hands.

"Adam." It was a mere whisper of sound but it scared the hell out of him. He'd thought he was alone. He leaped to his feet, realizing even as he did so that at the far side of the clearing was something he'd never seen before in his life. Goose bumps rose along his arms, prickled up the back of his neck and along his scalp.

A young woman stood on the far side of the small clearing where he'd stopped to sit. But she was no ordinary young woman. She was barely visible, a mere cloud shimmering in the afternoon light and he swallowed as he realized he could see right through her to the shrubby undergrowth behind her.

She wore a traveling cloak from decades past over a floor-length gown. What little he could see of the dress was modest and unassuming, and she carried a small ladies' bag and a bonnet over one arm. Her hair appeared to be dark and was parted down the middle and tightly pulled back from her face, woven into a braided twist that was anchored at the back of her head. Strangely, despite the fragile appearance of the…the vision, or whatever she was, her pretty features were plainly visible. She was young. Very young, probably not even twenty, he'd guess, if one could apply age to a…a ghost.

His mouth was dry as a dust. His heart was thumping as if it would jump right out of his chest. For all the times he'd longed to see a ghost, it had never occurred to him that such an encounter would scare the pants off him. "Who are you?" he managed.

"Priscilla Carlisle."

He was caught by her eyes, gazing straight at him

with an expression of ineffable sadness. "Miss Carlisle." He realized, even as he said it, who she was. "The governess."

She nodded somberly. "You know of me."

"Only a little. You were hired by Hiram Danforth. But as your coach arrived, a fierce storm hit. Your carriage overturned and you—you died." He nearly pinched himself, just to make sure he wasn't dreaming. He was *talking to a ghost*!

She nodded again, and he had the sense that she was pleased. "There is more."

"More?" He was confused. "But that's all I know." He hesitated. "We know you were buried here."

She turned and looked back over her shoulder. "He planted a tree for me."

"Who planted a tree for you?"

She looked back at him and her eyes were deep wells of sorrow. "My father."

"Your...?" He didn't understand. "Who was your father?" Had she been the child of one of Hiram's servants? He'd had several, although to their knowledge, he'd never owned slaves but had paid for the labor he needed. "Were you from a local family?"

"My father," she said, "was Hiram Danforth."

"Hiram Danforth? But he was my grandfather. He was married."

She very nearly smiled and he sensed her amusement. "Yes," she said, "he was. But not to *my* mother."

"Ah. I see."

"I was coming here to live at his request," she continued. "My mother was a maid in his family home in

Boston when he was a young man. A match between them was out of the question. She was an Irish indentured servant; he was the only son of a wealthy industrialist."

"Did they care for each other?" Adam dared to ask.

"I don't know," she said. "I like to think so. My mother died in an influenza epidemic, but Hiram made sure I was kept with the household. He even saw to it that I received an education. Of course, he eventually married and came south. When his children were of school age, he asked me to come and live with him as a governess. It was a good opportunity," she said, "for an orphan with no protection and no prospects. And it was a chance to be near my father."

Adam considered her story. Very practical, he imagined. In the 1890s there was little tolerance for marriage outside one's social class. Then something occurred to him. "Hiram never told anyone you were his daughter, did he?"

She shook her head and he felt another wave of sadness permeate the air around him. "He couldn't," she said simply.

He was astonished at the wave of emotion he felt. "So all these years," he said, "more than a century, you've just wanted…"

"To be part of the family." She nodded.

"You've tried to speak to so many people. Why me?"

"You're the first one who *wanted* to speak to me," she said, a slight smile lightening her features. "I have waited for you for a very long time."

Somehow, he knew what to do. He stood, made a formal bow that amazingly didn't feel silly at all. "Priscilla

Carlisle," he said, "welcome to the Danforth family. Our home is your home."

The diaphanous figure in front of him literally brightened before his eyes, and he had to squint at the radiance that shone from her. "Thank you, Adam," she said. And as he watched, the ghostly form began to fade from sight, until the small clearing in which he sat looked no more remarkable than any other forested glade on any other afternoon.

The pervasive sadness was gone, and a peaceful quality had taken its place. With a sense of certainty he didn't even question, he knew the ghost of Crofthaven had been seen for the last time.

Ten

That night after dark, Adam returned to his own home. Most of the media frenzy surrounding Marc's arrest and his own splash as a subject of gossip had died down and the few reporters still on the story were easy to ignore.

Harder to ignore were the questions rolling around inside his head. How could she have done that to him? Had she ever really loved him or had it all been an act?

After his unbelievable encounter that afternoon, he'd rushed back along the path the way he'd come. His mind had been racing, eager to get back to the house and write it down. He'd had a moment's wild thought: *Imagine what Selene will say when—*

And then it had come back to him again. He wouldn't be telling Selene.

The extraordinary encounter had erased his troubles

from his mind for a few brief moments. But as the memory of the photo from the paper came rushing back, he tasted bitter disillusionment again.

Something was bothering him, though. Something even more than missing her as if she were a limb he'd had amputated. More than the betrayal that still stung every time he cautiously nudged around the edges of the memory.

I love you, too, she'd told him. She was either one of the best actresses on the planet or she'd meant the words. He couldn't have been mistaken about that. God, she'd been a virgin! Why had she ever let things go so far between them if all he'd been to her was a means to an end?

The only answer was that it meant more than that to her, too. But if that were true, then why in hell had she gone along with her father's scheming?

The only way he would ever know, he decided, was to ask her. He glanced at his watch, noting that it was nearly ten, but it didn't matter now that he'd determined he needed to find out what was going on in her head.

Steeling himself for the encounter, he picked up the phone and called the Van Gelder home. He called the house rather than her cell phone, which he'd often seen her turn off when she wasn't expecting any calls. This was going to be difficult enough without the problematic reception cell phones sometimes encountered, anyway.

"Van Gelder residence." The voice was rough and aggressive and Adam felt his hackles rise. He'd bet his life he was speaking to John Van Gelder himself.

"This is Adam Danforth," he said. "May I please—?"

"Danforth!" The word was explosive. "Where's my daughter?"

Adam was completely dumbfounded. "Isn't she at home? I called to speak with her."

There was a heavy silence on the other end of the telephone. "She's not with you?" the man asked suspiciously.

"I haven't seen her since before my brother was arrested. Since before I read the news," Adam said evenly. "Are you telling me you don't know where she is?"

"That's correct." The words sounded as if they were being pulled from Van Gelder's throat. "We had an argument after she saw the paper this morning and she spent the day in her room. Wouldn't talk to me," he admitted. "I tried again at dinnertime but she was gone. The maid said she took a bag with her and got in a cab but Selene didn't tell anyone here where she was going."

"And you haven't called in your private investigator to track her down?" The moment the words were out he regretted them, but the anger was too close to the surface to be completely controlled.

Surprisingly, Selene's father didn't slam down the phone or take offense as he expected. Instead, the man sighed. "I deserve that. And I can assure you the last thing I would do is call a private investigator to report on my daughter's movements again."

Again. A chill rippled down Adam's spine as the words registered. "What?"

"I said I would never—"

"I heard you. Selene didn't know you'd gotten someone to take pictures of her?"

"I didn't," John said testily. "In fact, I specifically told him no pictures. I just wanted to know where she was going. I guess the S.O.B. thought he'd make a quick buck on the side when he realized who she was with."

"Selene didn't know about the P.I.?"

"No. Wha—oh, hell." Her father sounded truly distressed. "Did you think—?"

"Yeah." Adam leaned his forehead against the wall and closed his eyes. God. She'd tried to tell him, but he wouldn't listen. A sick feeling blossomed in his stomach and spread through his system as he realized what he'd done.

"Look," he said to her father. "Can you think of any friends, anyone she might have called? The only friend she's ever spoken of to me is Guillemette, her school roommate who lives in Paris."

"Yes, Willi. She's the only one I know, as well," John said. "Do you think…?"

"I'll check the flights to Paris. If she didn't leave the house until late afternoon, she probably didn't catch a flight out today. She may be spending the night in a hotel, planning to leave in the morning." Adam paused. "Can you call Guillemette?"

"All right, but what do you have in mind?"

Adam took a deep breath. He decided he might as well ask for the moon. The worst the man could do was refuse to help. "Mr. Van Gelder, I love your daughter. I want to marry her. I don't know exactly what your relationship has been in the past but I know Selene wants—needs—you in her life."

"And I want her in mine!" Van Gelder sounded desperate. "Selene means a lot to me. More than I've let myself realize until recently. I lost her mother when she was a baby and it...kept me from letting Selene become too important, I guess. I've spent most of her life shuffling her off to one side, and it was wrong of me. I barely know my own child." He cleared his throat. "I want another chance, if she'll give me one."

"As do I," Adam said quietly.

There was a short silence. Then Van Gelder said, "Maybe a Danforth wouldn't have been my first choice for my daughter, but she says she loves you. If she'll marry you, you have my blessing."

"Good." Adam wished he felt more confident. He was afraid he'd hurt her too badly to deserve forgiveness. He thought again of Priscilla Carlisle—his ancestor, he realized suddenly. She had spent many lonely decades seeking the one thing she'd desired above all else. He would be a complete idiot if he spent the rest of his life—or more—alone and unhappy because he'd been afraid to try to fix the damage he'd done, to try to reclaim the happy life he so wanted with Selene. "What would you do to get her to come back?" he asked.

To his credit, John didn't hesitate. "Anything. I'll even drop out of the senate race if that's what it takes."

"I don't think it will come to that." Adam smiled despite himself. "Here's what I think we should do," he said to the father of the woman he loved.

"Ms. Van Gelder?"

Selene looked up from the magazine that she'd been

staring at for the past half an hour. She sat in a lounge at the Savannah airport, waiting for a flight which would take her first to La Guardia in New York, and then across the Atlantic to Paris. She'd come to the airport hours earlier than she needed to, simply because she'd had no other plans and her mind was too numb to make decisions. She'd barely had enough energy to pack her things and check out of the local hotel into which she'd moved late yesterday when she'd been unable to stand being beneath the same roof as John Van Gelder for one more minute.

Now, right in front of her, an airport employee stood. "Ms. Van Gelder?" the woman said again.

"Yes, I'm Selene Van Gelder." She set aside the magazine and looked up, sighing mentally. Security these days, extremely tight for very good reasons, could still be an amazing pain. What was wrong now?

"Ms. Van Gelder, would you come with me to the VIP lounge, please?"

Selene gathered her purse and carry-on bag. "What's this about?"

"We've been asked to show you something," the woman replied. She turned and began to move away, clearly expecting Selene to follow.

As she walked after the woman, her brow wrinkled at the odd statement. What could they possibly want to show her? Wasn't it usually the other way around?

She followed the airport employee around a corner and down a long corridor into an empty lounge. The woman indicated the comfortable seats scattered around and the coffeemaker along one wall. "Please sit down and make yourself comfortable." Then she pointed to the television on the wall. "This will be coming on in just a moment." And she left Selene alone.

Thoroughly puzzled now, Selene dutifully sat, fidgeting with the strap of her handbag. Then she sat up straighter as the television crackled to life.

The channel flipped to a local morning talk show that she'd often watched. The smiling coanchor was speaking to the television audience as the sound came up.

"...don't know who said the path of true love never runs smoothly, but today we have living proof of that old adage. With me this morning are two gentlemen whom the Savannah audience has probably never expected to see in the same room, much less on the same side of an issue. But this morning, they are united in a common cause. Help me welcome senatorial candidate John Van Gelder and Adam Danforth, the son of Abe Danforth, Van Gelder's chief rival in this race."

The audience dutifully applauded as two men very familiar to her eyes entered the studio and took the guests' seats. They were smiling at the host and looked amazingly comfortable together.

Selene didn't move. She couldn't. Her gaze was riveted to the television. What was going on?

"So," the woman conducting the interview began. "Why don't you tell us, John, what brings you here today."

Her father smiled. He was older and heavier than

he'd been when she was small, but he still had some of that same charisma, and he used it to good effect. "Well, Adam did, literally," he said wryly. After an appreciative laugh from the audience, he went on. "Adam and my daughter Selene have been dating. I only learned about it recently." He sighed. "I'm sure Selene thought I wouldn't be rational about her getting close to any of the Danforth clan and—" his eyebrows rose in self-mockery "—I'm sad to say her instincts probably were right."

"So you didn't want her seeing Adam?" the host inquired.

"I didn't even know she was," John repeated. "But I was concerned because she suddenly began spending a lot of time away from home."

"So what did you do?" The interviewer was relentless.

For the first time, her father looked uncomfortable. "I hired a private investigator to let me know where she was going."

"You *hired* a private investigator?" The woman professed shock. "Isn't that a bit strange? Most fathers would have just asked their daughters, wouldn't they?"

"I'm not most fathers." It was a confession. He almost squirmed in his seat. "Selene's mother passed away when Selene was an infant and I—I had a hard time getting past my grief enough to deal with a child. Selene spent most of her youth at European boarding schools." He shook his head but it didn't look like a rehearsed move. "That was a poor choice, and I've come to regret it."

"Mr. Van Gelder," the interviewer said. "What do

you hope to gain by coming here today with Adam Danforth?"

John spread his hands helplessly. "I want another chance. I'd like Selene to know how sorry I am for the mistakes I've made, and to assure her that I'd like to get to know her."

"How do you know Selene is even listening to this?" the woman asked.

"We don't," said Adam. "We think we may have alerted her to watch, but we're not sure." His broad shoulders seemed to sag a little.

"Short of hiring another investigator," added John, "we have no way of knowing where she is unless she chooses to contact us. And neither one of us is willing to do that, right?" He looked at Adam, and she was stunned anew to see the unspoken moment of understanding that passed between them.

"It has to be her choice," added Adam.

"Is there anything you can say that might induce her to get in touch with you?" The studio host was working every dramatic moment, but Adam and her father didn't seem to notice.

Her father looked down at his hands. Adam nodded.

"Selene, I love you. We both do." He took a deep breath. "Your father and I have made unforgivable mistakes but we're asking you to forgive us, anyway."

Beside him, John fumbled in his pocket. Finally he withdrew something small and handed it to Adam.

It was a small box, she saw as Adam held it up. "This," he said, flipping open the lid, "was Selene's mother's wedding ring. John graciously offered it to me when I asked him for Selene's hand. Selene, will you marry me?"

In the lounge, she gasped as the tears streamed down her face. *Her mother's wedding ring!* How difficult, she wondered, had it been for her father to make that gesture?

In the television studio, Adam smiled straight into the camera. "Meet me in our garden, Selene, and let me put this ring on your finger." His smile wavered just a fraction and his anxiety showed in his eyes. She figured with that tiny lapse, he'd just won the heart of every woman watching. He'd certainly taken hers by storm. "Please?"

The camera narrowed in to focus tightly on his face, then pulled back to reveal John's worried expression. "Well," said the coanchor, "that was certainly one of the more unique proposals I've ever seen. Thank you, gentlemen, for sharing this moment with us and be sure to let us know the lady's response."

As a commercial replaced the faces of the men she loved, Selene leaped to her feet and headed for the door.

Adam paced in the lovely garden behind Twin Oaks. He thought of the night they'd met. It had been dark and mysterious, Selene's eyes sparkling in the shadows. She'd been so beautiful and ethereal in her white gown that even after he'd been assured she was real he still was afraid she was going to vanish.

Had she indeed vanished from his life now, through his own mistrust and stupidity? He wasn't sure what he was going to do if she left for Paris—

And then she was there. Coming down the flagstone

steps from the terrace in a flowing floral-print dress that made her look as exotic as the gardens around them. She stopped in front of him, a few feet away, enormous emerald eyes fixed on his face.

She wasn't smiling. His heart sank, and he steeled himself for the blow of rejection.

There were reporters up on the terrace with cameras. He'd negotiated for space to speak privately in exchange for a full view of the meeting, if it occurred. Either way, they'd have a great story.

For a moment, he was tongue-tied, not knowing what to say. And then the simple truth emerged. "I'm sorry. I wronged you when I failed to trust you."

She nodded. "That hurt."

To his horror, he felt his eyes filling with tears as the pain he'd caused fully registered. "I think, deep down, I believed that I wasn't really interesting enough to hold you, that maybe there did have to be some other reason why you were with me."

She started to speak, but he held up a hand.

"Better let me finish before I can't." His voice was shaking now but he didn't care. "I love you. Can you find it in your heart to forgive me?"

"Of course I forgive you, Adam." But her voice, her expression, was still serious and reserved.

For the first time it occurred to him that her forgiveness and her love might not come hand in hand, and his heart felt like a lead weight in his chest.

"Thank you," she said, "for whatever you said to my father to bring him to his senses."

He shook his head, forcing himself to concentrate on her words. "I didn't. He loves you. He just didn't know how to show it, and honestly, I think he was afraid of caring too much for you. Losing your mother almost destroyed him. He couldn't take a chance on going through that again."

"But life is full of chances," she said.

"He knows that now," he told her, "and he's anxious to start fresh with you."

Silence fell.

"The press is on the terrace," he said. "I had to promise them that in exchange for the television time."

Her eyebrows rose. "What would you have done if I hadn't come?"

He shrugged. "They could have run some great footage of me looking like a total fool."

She smiled faintly. "Lucky for you I showed."

He searched her face. "Is it? You haven't answered me yet."

"What was the question?"

Understanding dawned, and with it the first glimmer of light returned to his world. He reached into his pocket and withdrew a small box. "Since you apparently saw the interview, you know what's in here." He dropped to one knee. "Selene Van Gelder, may I have your hand in marriage?"

She stood stock-still, closed her eyes for a moment, and when she opened them again, she was the one with tears in her eyes. "Yes," she whispered. "Oh, Adam, yes!"

Relief, heady and sweet, poured through him. He stood

and opened his arms, and she came into them without hesitation. Her body was warm and soft and familiar and he pressed her close, seeking her mouth. "I thought I'd ruined things forever," he confessed when he lifted his mouth.

A shout from the terrace distracted them. "Put the ring on her finger, Danforth!"

Adam grinned, turning his head to acknowledge the intrusion. Then he looked down at her, nestled securely in his arms where she belonged. "Shall I?"

"I'd like to wear your ring," she said.

He stepped back a pace and opened the little box. "You did see the whole interview, right? So you know where I got this?"

She smiled tremulously. "Yes. To say I was stunned would be a gross understatement."

"Your father loves you," Adam said. "He knows he needs to work on how to show it." He removed the lovely diamond with its smaller matching stones on each side, and gently worked it onto her ring finger. "This is a symbol of our love, but it's also a symbol of family. Yours, mine and the one I hope we create together."

"Soon," she added, as they admired the ring together.

"As soon as you like." He drew her to him again. "Let's get out of here," he murmured against her mouth. "I don't want an audience for what I want to do with you next."

Selene laughed. "Why do I think I'm going to like it?" She feathered her fingers over the back of his neck and smiled as her hips brushed his.

He shivered as need rushed through him, and drew

away to take her hand. "You'll never believe what happened to me yesterday," he said as he led her out of the garden toward the rest of their lives together.

* * * * *

From governess to mother and wife!

Two brand-new heartwarming historical romances featuring:

More Than a Governess by Sarah Mallory
The Angel and the Outlaw by Kathryn Albright

**The special gift of a mother's love.
Perfect reading for Mother's Day!**

Available 6th March 2009

www.millsandboon.co.uk

On sale 20th March 2009

3 NOVELS ONLY £5.49

The Chisholm Brothers: Friends, Lovers...Husbands?

by Janis Reams Hudson

Featuring

The Daddy Survey
The Other Brother
The Cowboy on Her Trail

Available at WHSmith, Tesco, ASDA, and all good bookshops
www.millsandboon.co.uk

MILLS & BOON
Spotlight

A Secret Child...
An Irresistible Attraction...
A Passionate Proposition!

Three brand-new stories featuring:

The Billionaire's Baby Surprise by Barbara Hannay
Expecting His Child by Meredith Webber
Claiming the Ashbrooke Heir by Mary Nichols

Perfect for Mother's Day!

Available 20th February 2009

www.millsandboon.co.uk

Passion. Power. Suspense.
It's time to fall under the spell of Nora Roberts.

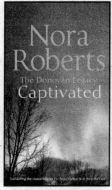

2nd January 2009

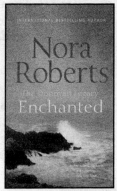

6th February 2009

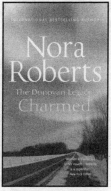

6th March 2009

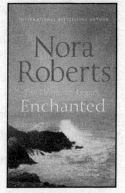

3rd April 2009

The Donovan Legacy
Four cousins. Four stories. One terrifying secret.

He's her boss in the boardroom – and in the bedroom!

Her Mediterranean Boss
Three fiery Latin bosses
Three perfect assistants
Available 20th February 2009

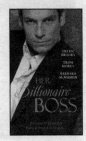

Her Billionaire Boss
Three ruthless billionaire bosses
Three perfect assistants
Available 20th March 2009

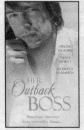

Her Outback Boss
Three sexy Australian bosses
Three perfect assistants
Available 17th April 2009

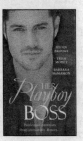

Her Playboy Boss
Three gorgeous playboy bosses
Three perfect assistants
Available 15th May 2009

Collect all four!

www.millsandboon.co.uk